ADVANCE PRAISE FOR
The Infinite

"Nick Mainieri is the real deal, and *The Infinite* is stunning. A compelling, brilliantly told debut, written with power and clarity."

—Philipp Meyer, *New York Times* bestselling author of *The Son*

"With a sharp eye for detail and careful, generous prose, Mainieri conjures whole worlds with a few words, taking the reader on a thrilling, heartbreaking journey. *The Infinite* is a sparkling debut, a novel that seems to guarantee you'll be hearing Mainieri's name mentioned in the same breath as contemporary masters like Denis Johnson and Cormac McCarthy."

—Ron Currie, Jr., author of *Flimsy Little Plastic Miracles* and *Everything Matters!*

"*The Infinite* is a surprising novel of border crossings and desperate violence, of young love and hardship, of adventure and identity, of bravery and the lack thereof. It also introduces us to one of the more complicated and capable heroines I've come across in a long time; the beautifully scrappy and haunted Luz Hidalgo, who you do not want to back into a corner. I flew through this book, half hopeful and half terrified of what was coming next. This is a powerful and propulsive read. Highly recommended."

—M. O. Walsh, *New York Times* bestselling author of *My Sunshine Away*

"*The Infinite* is that rare, beautiful first novel, so contemporary and yet as timeless as first love itself. And Nick Mainieri does what great novelists do with their first great works. He creates unforgettable characters in young lovers Jonah and Luz who, both together and alone, navigate the rushing river of the borderlands that mark our two Americas. *The Infinite* is a heart song, and Nicholas Mainieri is one of our next great storytellers."

—Joseph Boyden, Scotiabank Giller Prize–winning author of *Three Day Road, Through Black,* and *The Orenda*

"Spanning northern Mexico and the Gulf South, *The Infinite* is an entirely modern western, with a visceral sense of place and an ear for the small anxieties that shape our most courageous actions. In this tale of borders—national, familial, psychological—Luz and Jonah are more than just teenagers in love; haunted by their pasts and grasping for an uncertain future, they guide us through swampland, desert scrub, high school hallways, and a sicario's hideout. This is a thriller with heart, a romance on the run, and a manifesto for our increasingly tenuous landscape."

—Katy Simpson Smith, author of
The Story of Land and Sea and *Free Men*

"Nicholas Mainieri has written a profound and sensitive novel about the ways in which disasters, both natural and unnatural, can all too often make us who we are. The star-crossed love story at its heart makes *The Infinite* an unforgettable debut that also happens to be impossible to put down. It has all the makings of an American classic."

—Andrew Ervin, author of
Burning Down George Orwell's House

"*The Infinite* is a novel that defies easy description. A gripping, edge-of-your-seat thriller following two star-crossed young lovers set adrift—but also a lyrical, beautifully written, and affecting meditation on many of the big questions. Nick Mainieri has crafted a page-turner, yes, but these sentences, and these characters, will linger for a long, long time. A remarkable achievement."

—Skip Horack, author of
The Other Joseph, *The Eden Hunter*, and *The Southern Cross*

"The title of Nick Mainieri's wonderful debut novel is perfectly apt. *The Infinite* takes the reader on a heart-pounding, heart-rending adventure through the infinite complexities of being alive in the world today. Part *City of Refuge*, part *Breaking Bad*, this novel takes you by the hand and won't let go. I couldn't put it down, and I can't stop thinking about it since finishing. The writing is smart, beautiful, and unafraid to ask the big questions. This is fiction that stays with you and heralds the beginning of a wonderful career."

—Andrew Malan Milward, author of
I Was a Revolutionary

THE
INFINITE

A Novel

Nicholas Mainieri

HARPER ● PERENNIAL

NEW YORK ● LONDON ● TORONTO ● SYDNEY ● NEW DELHI ● AUCKLAND

HARPER ● PERENNIAL

HarperCollins books may be purchased for educational, business, or sales promotional use. For information please e-mail the Special Markets Department at SPsales@harpercollins.com.

FIRST EDITION

Designed by Jamie Lynn Kerner
Title and part title page photograph by Jose Gil / Shutterstock

Library of Congress Cataloging-in-Publication Data has been applied for.

ISBN 978-0-06-246556-6

16 17 18 19 20   OV/RRD   10 9 8 7 6 5 4 3 2 1

For Kate and for Jonathan

Es transparente el infinito.
—OCTAVIO PAZ

THE INFINITE

I

I need you to remember this.

1

THE RIVER WAS THERE, BROAD AND BROWN. CALM, IT SEEMED. Clouds swept low, fled with the current. Luz sat with Jonah on the levee between river and sky, a nowhere place. He took her hand and the river did seem calm, but she heard the water at its turbulent depth, beating against a floor carved through millions of years.

"We used to come up here a lot," Jonah said. "My family."

"No more?" Luz asked. Over his shoulder, a gull shrieked and banked toward picnickers along the riverwalk.

"Nah," he said. "My brother moved away."

"Your mother?"

"My mom died when I was little," Jonah said. "A car wreck." Luz tried to apologize, but he interrupted to say, "It's all right. It feels like a long time ago."

A tug drove a column of barges in the middle of the river. A beat emerged from the wind—a kid playing drums on overturned buckets for the dog walkers and the joggers and the tourists arm in arm. Upriver, a cruise ship squatted heavily in the water against the bridge, near the hotels and the casino.

"My mamá," Luz said, "she passed away, too. Almost six years now. Sometimes, yes, it feels like a long time ago. But only sometimes."

Jonah's grip on her hand grew firmer.

"After that I came to the United States. To be with my papá."

"Wow," he said. "I'm sorry."

"She was sick," Luz said, a small smile. "We didn't know."

The wake of the tugboat and the barges finally reached the bank, cresting against the rocks of the levee. It was spring, and the river was high.

Jonah wanted to know if he could ask something.

"Okay," Luz said.

"Did people tell you to talk to your mom? Like, talk to her in your head because she'd hear you and all?"

And she was there, at home in Las Monarcas, in her grandmother's apartment. The old woman held her hands and peered at her through her glasses. An uncle lingered in the doorway, waiting to ferry the little girl to El Norte and her father, and her grandmother said good-bye and told her to pray to her mother, always, for her mother would be watching and listening. "My abuela told me to pray."

"I got that a lot, too. The priests at school. Everybody." He was looking at their hands—hers was small and bronze; his was large and fair, some freckles. "Does she ever answer you?"

Luz closed her eyes and reached for her mother. The clouds broke and the sun was on her face. "No," she answered. "Not so that I can hear her." The gull screeched. A jogger passed, brief and mild hip-hop pumping from his headphones. "I believe she hears me, though."

He nodded, watched her. His eyes were green, almost gray, and steady like the river seemed to be. But Luz sensed the pull beneath Jonah's eyes, and it made her ache.

2

Jonah and Luz grew closer as the summer passed and edged into fall. He had been living alone in the camelback shotgun house in Central City, New Orleans, where his family, the McBees, had lived for three generations. Flaking lavender paint, a sagging porch, a dirt back-yard shadowed by an ancient live oak. Jonah's older brother Dex owned the home, but he lived like a recluse down the bayou. On only a few occasions had he come back to the city—the last time being for their father's funeral, after the old man's heart attack. Dex had stayed until Jonah turned eighteen—that is, until Dex's legal guardianship had ceased—and then returned to the swamp and the old family fishing camp, where he made his living as a hunter.

"Me and Dex, we hardly talk," Jonah told Luz. "He sends some money every now and then to help with bills."

Jonah's brother was his last living relation. The absolute nature of Jo-nah's loneliness had staggered Luz, but it was of course familiar, and part of what drew her to him was this residue of his experience. It suggested he might be able to understand her in a way that nobody else—not her track teammates, not her father—was able.

During afternoons when there was neither work nor track practice, they took to reclining on the couch in his living room and talking, learning each other's histories. Jonah had pictures all over the walls of his home, photographs of his family. He had explained to Luz that while he was growing up his father never wanted to see the images, wanted to leave them buried. They reminded him of too much. "At the camp, here at the house, bare walls," Jonah had said. But once Jonah was alone, he put them up. He was much younger than his brothers, nine years junior to Dex and ten to Bill. Jonah had been six when a drunk driver blew through a stop sign and broadsided his mother's car less than a mile from their home. He needed the pictures, markers to trace out his own beginning.

Luz got up from the couch and circuited the living room, looking at the framed shots while Jonah commented on each.

There was a photograph of his father in which the old man stares through the grass of the duck blind, hair rumpled and face confused—as if wondering why this moment called for a permanent likeness at all—as droplets of mist freeze in the flash against the predawn dark.

There was a photograph of Jonah's mother, a blond bob and green eyes, and she stands on the riverwalk, slightly turned from the camera, her hands resting atop her belly.

"Maybe she's pregnant with me in that one," Jonah said.

Luz watched the wide river roll behind his mother, the steeple of a church on the far bank. The view was not far from where Luz had first sat with Jonah on the levee.

"I remember small things," Jonah told her. "Just flashes. Mom walking me to church while my brothers watched football with Pop. Tracing symbols on my back after she tucked me in."

Luz smiled and returned to the photograph. Jonah's eyes were like his mother's. Luz imagined his father taking this picture, pride swelling. A wish rose for her own possible future with Jonah.

Luz prayed, quick: Please, señora McBee, help us.

Jonah did not pray to his relatives, so Luz had begun to speak to his mother. It was a small thing she could do for him. Luz imagined Jonah's loss as an anchor obscured by dark water. Jonah neither saw it nor understood how it restricted the range of his drifting. If you would only reach for her, Luz had tried to tell him.

Luz paced the living room and stopped opposite the couch, where in the center of the wall there waited a photograph of Jonah's eldest brother, Bill, with a crew cut and in dress blues. The American flag the government sent, cotton folded in a triangular frame, hung next to it. Jonah told her that a land mine had killed his brother. Something old, something the Soviets left in Afghanistan more than twenty years before Bill showed up. "How fucked up is that," Jonah whispered.

Alongside the jamb of the kitchen doorway Jonah had hung the only photograph he had of him with both brothers. Little Jonah stands in front of them. Bill and Dex are in high school. Bill is eighteen, just before he graduated and enlisted. "He's my age now in that picture," Jonah said. Bill was sandy haired and green eyed like Jonah, but he was stocky where Jonah had become tall. In the photo Dex is darker, rangier, wearing a sour look. All three stand on the dock at the camp, the cypress and the early pale sky behind them.

"Think I'll ever get to meet Dex?" Luz asked.

Jonah shrugged from the couch.

Luz again sensed the implacable sadness roiling within Jonah and tried to find something to say. She glanced over the photographs and told him that he looked like his mother. "You and Bill both," she said.

Jonah grinned and picked at a thread in the couch cushion. "You must look like your mom, too, huh?" He had seen her father once or twice, though he'd not yet spoken with the man. Her father was lanky and his skin was cooked like a baseball glove and his eyes were blue, which had surprised Jonah.

"I do look like my mamá," Luz told him. She explained how her mother used to tell her that they were descended from Guachichil warriors, who had lived five hundred years ago and fought the Spaniards. The Guachichiles were the fiercest of the Chichimec people. As Luz grew older, she began to understand that her mother couldn't know for certain whether they had Guachichil ancestry as opposed to anything else—all that history was lost—but it didn't matter. It was more, Luz recognized, a matter of what they wanted to believe and what that belief could do for them. Her father couldn't care less, practical as he was. But her mother liked the stories, appreciated their power: This history makes you strong, my Luz. And Luz saw it, watching herself age in mirrors. Sometimes, now, she looked at herself before track meets, narrowed her eyes like a hawk, and imagined herself to be a warrior.

"What do you mean, you don't know for sure?" Jonah asked.

"I don't know," Luz said. "It doesn't matter."

But this troubled Jonah, how something could be unknown and known at the same time. Something so essential. He could know, for instance, that the McBees had lived in the Scottish Highlands a long time ago. Then they left those for New World highlands. Sometime later they showed up in New Orleans, and here he was. It made sense.

"Look," he said, getting up and directing her attention to another frame on the wall. Within it a sheet of parchment depicted the McBee family crest—a disembodied hand running a sword through a green dragon. "I don't care that much about it all," he said, "but it's something I can know, at least. Doesn't it bother you at all, that you can't know for sure?"

Luz, though, was thinking about all the countless things that had happened on different parts of the planet in different eras in order for her and Jonah to be together now in New Orleans. It was a strangely sobering thought. An image popped into her head: she saw them as an impossible couple, five centuries before. Jonah wore a plaid skirt and swung a sword, and straw-colored dreadlocks fell over his bare shoulders. She clutched a spear and wore the head of a wolf for a hat and painted her face red and munched peyote before battle. She began to laugh.

"What?" Jonah said, breaking up before he even knew the joke. "What's funny?"

Luz shoved him so that he fell backward over the arm of the couch. She leaped after him and, in the breath before she kissed him, she said, "You are, Jonás. You."

ALL THE GUILT THAT HAD BEEN THERE AFTER THEIR FIRST TIME AND the times after—it eventually passed when the retribution Luz had been taught to expect never arrived. It amazed her, how quickly they learned each other. She figured him out without a word, and once the guilt ebbed, giving in felt good, and with it came a new and special understanding of the world. After a while she imagined that God might consider them a special case. And if not, she might convince Him otherwise. Maybe they had been given a unique opportunity.

And likewise, Jonah learned to treat the geography of her body with diligence, with the terrifying knowledge that the moment would end. She was small, she was strong. The first time she threw her leg over him, he was surprised by the hardness of her muscle, the solidity and weight of her leg, and he could summon that moment any time he wished and

it would excite him. They discovered their own rhythm, created it between themselves, called on it together in his bedroom. Sometimes
Spanish words left her lips when she forgot herself, and this was a fact no
other man but Jonah possessed. Sometimes she called him Jonás. It was a
thing with which he came to define himself.

3

JONAH DROVE TOWARD LUZ'S APARTMENT IN THE TREME AND parked down the block from the double shotgun house. He heard the music, buoyant guitar. The sun was going down behind the overpass, bleeding orange down the street and backlighting the small crowd gathered in front of the building. Luz's father—his name was Moses Hidalgo—sat on the steps, a beer at his side and his guitar balanced on his knee. The man wore canvas pants and a paint-splattered work shirt, but he had taken off his boots. His bare toes gripped the edge of the step. His eyes were closed while he fingerpicked the nickel strings. Luz stood behind him, elbows on the railing, singing some old Spanish tune. She had told Jonah she sometimes sang, but he hadn't heard her until now. He could feel the melody sinking between his ribs. The dilapidated shotgun homes around him, the crooked telephone poles and their buzzing nests of electric cables, the palmettos with their decaying fronds—it all seemed to diminish. Luz sang with a full, warm tone. She neither tarried nor rushed. She sounded at home. Each note centered and lingered beneath Jonah's breastbone. He felt his feet moving freely and safely toward her, as if her voice had conjured on this street corner a refuge unencumbered by the prosaic dangers of the city.

Jonah joined the handful of neighborhood folk. Together they were suspended, as if they'd all been en route to someplace else when they heard the music. There was a black kid holding a skateboard; a white twentysomething with a beard and thick-rimmed glasses; a Latino neighbor from the other half of the shotgun with a beer in his hand, bobbing his head to the music. Small evening insects stirred, rising and falling above the length of the broken pavement, catching the sunlight and sparking. The air was hot and damp, but they were all there together. Jonah smiled and listened and felt his heart swell in its cage. But when Luz noticed him and stumbled over the words, her father cracked an eye at Jonah and ended the song in an awkward, atonal swipe. He stood and turned and grabbed his daughter by the arm. He pulled her inside, the screen door clacking shut behind them, staccato and harsh.

"The fuck happened?" asked the kid with the skateboard.

Jonah kept quiet. The skateboard's wheels rumbled low on the pavement and faded away. The neighbor's door hinges squeaked. Jonah was alone, and his embarrassment burned in his face. Another feeling had arisen by the time he climbed back into his truck, however, and he nearly snapped the key off in the ignition.

4

JONAH STOOD WITH HIS FRIEND COLBY IN THE WARM HALLWAY. Jonah was laughing at him.

"You don't know shit about style, Mickey-Bee," Colby retorted, jacking his sneaker against the lockers and running his fingertips along the fin of his new haircut, a short Mohawk. Sweat glistened in a fine glaze where his head was shaved above his ears. "I could give you my barber's number if you interested in learning, though."

First bell had rung some time ago, but the hallway was as crowded as ever. "My head ain't as shiny as yours," Jonah said. "Wouldn't look right."

Colby smiled and hooked his thumbs on the straps of his backpack. "I don't think he knows how to cut white people's hair anyways."

The school, downtown on Carondelet Street, was big and old. Cracked marble, an air of former grandeur. It was in the Recovery School District, which had been a mess since Hurricane Katrina and the flooding of New Orleans, more than four years ago. The city was going to close the school come the end of the semester, no secret, and reopen it again as a charter school. New administration, new students, new money. All the kids who had been able—most underclassmen, good athletes, and decent students—transferred to other public schools on the fringe of the city's attention. Most of the faculty members spent their days fretting over their careers. The leftovers were those without any other recourse, waiting for the end. Jonah was here because he'd been expelled from two previous schools.

"They won't let you keep that hairdo, you know." Jonah meant the army. Colby was planning to enlist upon graduation, and Jonah had said he'd do it with him. Jonah didn't actually want to enlist, but he went along with Colby's talk, with his jokes, for his friend's sake. This was easier than focusing on the absence of other options. Jonah thought of Bill and knew where they sent guys like himself and Colby, kids who came from nothing—the same place they sent his brother, the same war.

"Course they won't let me keep the 'hawk," Colby answered. "Why I'm rockin' it now." His eyes never stopped moving, never stopped scanning. He muttered to a passing kid, "Got good weed," but the kid ignored him. To Jonah, "I been researching. Lots of cash in bonuses if we sign up right. Like, if we sign up now saying we're in when we graduate, that diploma gets you a bonus. What you think about that?"

Bounce music played down the hall, a high-capacity rat-a-tat thumping through the crowd. Jonah was watching another kid rip up the black strip of electrical tape that had been stuck down the center of the corridor only the day before. The tape had been the brainchild of the principal— stay on the right side of the tape when you walk down the hallway. It was a measure to curb the fights between bells, during class time, whenever; fewer and fewer teachers felt compelled to make students sit in their classrooms.

"I'm telling you, Mickey-Bee," Colby went on, grinning sidelong. "You make a lot of money up front, and you could take care of that little chickadee."

"Uh-huh," Jonah said. The kid in the center of the hall was winding the tape around his fist, making his arm into a tangled nest of black.

"Need weed?" Colby muttered to a passerby. The kid stutterstepped, marched on.

Jonah waited. "How's the army gonna feel about your bonus when you get busted for selling drugs?"

"It's a better living than whatever else you got right now, Mickey-Bee," Colby said, spreading his arms to encompass the chaotic stretch of hall, "and this is a good market." He turned and slapped Jonah's arm. "Don't worry, this time next year we'll be arguing about who shot the most Talibans."

Jonah feigned a laugh. The kid with the electric tape was backpedaling as he ripped it up, and soon enough he bumped into another guy. Jonah saw it coming. Fights struck like lightning, often only because you brushed against somebody who didn't want to get clowned in front of his boys. The kid with the tape turned, a stupid smile on his face. The other guy shoved him, heels of his palms to collarbones, and then they were grappling each other to the floor. Handfuls of shirt, electrical tape flaring and snaking around them. The hallway collapsed, kids crying out, cheering, calling for blood. Cell phones blinked to life, documenting this occurrence forever. It happened multiple times every day. Colby's potential business was gone for the moment.

Teachers made their way in, tried to pry the combatants apart. The police liaison dashed down the hallway, swimming past students. He elbowed gawkers aside and put the tape kid in a bear hug. A graying teacher clutched the other. Only then did the crowd begin to disperse. Once the thrill was over, it was over.

Students here had learned to enjoy what they could while they could. Enough of them had friends or classmates or family members involved in the drug trade or other rackets. Murdered or jailed or simply disappeared. Often enough, students ferried blood feuds and drug drama from their neighborhoods into the hallways. Not many here envisioned old age. Jonah hadn't grown up looking at the world this way, but he could understand it, for he was in similar circumstances, even if he didn't deal drugs. For somebody like Colby, deciding that the army was the best choice he could make ensured something, even if—Jonah was thinking of old, unknown land mines—that something was another roll of the dice.

Jonah felt a thrilling lurch when he spied Luz navigating the crowd and coming toward them. She clutched her books to her chest and she was as beautiful as she was serious. She had told Jonah that this had been the only school that would enroll her. But she seemed to make the best of it, crafting what opportunities she could. Jonah had witnessed her in nearly empty classrooms, standing at the teacher's desk and asking earnest questions about something or other in the textbook. She also ran on the ragtag track team, and she was pretty fast, one of their better runners. She was the lone Latina in the school, and she seemed to have a knack for steering clear of much of the fighting, even the basic macho posturing. Sometimes, she had told Jonah, I am invisible.

"Señorita," Colby said to her, tipping an imaginary hat.

Luz winked at him. "I like your new haircut, Colby."

Jonah gathered Luz in his arms. She asked if he had work later—he was a part-time mechanic at the Walmart auto shop on Tchoupitoulas Street. "No," he said. "Free."

"Me, too," Luz answered. She pulled away, saying she was going to class. "Adiós, Colby." And with a sly grin: "Adiós, Jonás."

Once she had disappeared, Colby mimicked: "Jonás, Jonás. Sound like she saying 'ya own ass.'"

Jonah started to laugh.

"Adiós, ya own ass, adiós. She was saying good-bye to your ass, Mickey-Bee." Colby, grinning, ran his fingers over his hair. "Likes my 'hawk, though, ya heard?"

5

THAT AFTERNOON THEY LAY IN HIS BED, LUZ'S HEAD AGAINST his chest, and she told him about San Antonio, Texas, and the time she had spent there. Sharing a bit more of the history that had been only hers, that she would have him keep now, too. They have a cathedral there called San Fernando—she whispered it to him. She told him how people had gone there for hundreds of years. Wars were fought, the city's flag turned over. They were Spanish and Mexican and Texan and finally American. And all the Latino families would gather at the cathedral for the parade on the feast of Guadalupe. There were other children who were her friends. Not like a Mardi Gras parade, she explained. They gathered and marched from the cathedral with a portrait of la Virgen. Flowers and music and dancing in the street. "It is a beautiful place," Luz said, "and I miss it."

The weight of her head on his chest was something Jonah could not lose. He asked if she loved San Antonio more than she loved New Orleans with him.

She sighed, laughed. "That's not what I mean."

Luz had known her father only sparingly through her childhood. There were brief telephone calls and postcards written in his poor print, and his few journeys home to Coahuila, during which she was expected to pretend she loved him and missed him terribly—which she did, in a way, because her mother instructed that she must. Luz was eleven when she crossed with an uncle, who delivered her to her father in San Antonio. She was a little girl who had lost her mother and made a terrifying journey. She did come to love her father very much during their time in Texas.

Then Katrina came, and the flood followed. Her father was one of the thousands who came for work. The apartment they currently lived in was one half of a double, and they shared it with a friend of her father's, a former stonemason from Matamoros named Rodrigo. A revolving group of Hondurans lived in the other half of the house. Luz and her father had stayed in this apartment for a while now—housing was in demand as the city continued to fill—but in those early days they had moved around a lot.

"I was only thirteen," she told Jonah. "I was scared." She had discovered, upon moving to New Orleans, that not many of the other men like her father had their children with them. Things had been different in San Antonio, where there were families and friends. But post-flood New Orleans was a place for young men or grizzled veterans only. Workers who shared decaying apartments and wired meager amounts of money home. Those first few months, the nights were impossibly dark, impossibly quiet. Soldiers in the streets, window-rattling Humvees. There were few people in the neighborhoods. More grim-faced workers arriving each day. "It was different," Luz said. "That's what I mean."

"Damn," Jonah said. "Pop and me, we couldn't come back for months. We evacuated to Houston. Didn't know it would take so long for them to open the neighborhood back up, so we went to the camp. Pop and Dex, they were at each other's throats the whole time. It sucked." Jonah inhaled the scent of Luz's hair. Then he said, "You wanna go for a ride with me?"

"Hmm?"

"There's something I want to show you."

Jonah drove an old Ford F-100 that had belonged to his brothers before him and their father before that. He had kept the thing running when it should have died years ago. He drove with the windows down, glancing at Luz and feeling good when she tucked her thrashing hair behind her ears and smiled. The steering wheel was smooth in his grip. The suspension groaned and creaked against the buckled roads. He hung his arm out the window and enjoyed being on the move.

He pulled over across from a one-story cinder-block building half swallowed by creeping vines. Boarded windows. Tangles of graffiti snarled across the battered garage doors, above which the fading sign was just legible: McBee Auto. The spray-painted X alongside the door—a code left by security forces after the flood, once they'd booted in the door and looked for bodies—still remained. Red paint bleached to faint orange. There were numbers and abbreviations scrawled in each of the

X's quadrants. The building had been Pop's business. Both of Jonah's brothers had worked here, too, when they were growing up.

"Is this where you learned to fix cars?" Luz asked. She had come to look forward to the motor-oily scent hanging about him when he'd meet her after her own work shift at an upscale restaurant on St. Charles Avenue, where she washed dishes to help her father and Rodrigo pay the rent.

"The storm took the shop," Jonah explained, meaning that he was too young to work when it was open. But there were memories, he said, of standing in the grease-stained pit with Pop or with his eldest brother, Bill—once or twice with Dex, even—beneath the lift while they reached with blackened hands into the undercarriages of cars and explained their movements. But those times felt distant, when his family liked to share things with one another. "Pop never even tried to reopen. There was some insurance money, but I think he drank most of that up."

The business had already been falling apart, truthfully, before the storm. Jonah's father lost interest, lost energy—well, he lost too many things. "After Mom died," Jonah said, "Pop kept on drinking. After Bill enlisted shit just got crazier around the house, Dad and Dex fighting and all. Once Bill died, well, Dex just got the hell out of town. Went to hide down the bayou."

Jonah felt Luz reach across the bench seat and take his hand, and he knew that she understood: one tragedy begets another. The humidity pulsed, and the neighborhood seemed apprehended between breaths. The squat, ugly auto shop was a ruined monument to a world that made more sense than the one Jonah presently occupied. But now he had Luz. Fortunes were changing. He felt drawn to her out of a great and hopeless dark.

Luz jutted her chin at the shop. "Do you ever think about reopening it?"

Jonah looked at his lap. "Not really. Sometimes. But it's like a fantasy, you know? It would take a lot of money." He raised his head. She was looking at him, her dark eyes waiting. There was a sheen of perspiration on her face, and he felt himself sweating, too. "The world's getting on fine without McBee Auto." He squeezed her hand and smiled. "I'm getting on fine."

6

THE LIGHT WAS FADING AND LUZ NEEDED TO BE HOME BY DIN-
nertime. Jonah drove while the orange streetlamps came on. Luz
was thinking about the empty auto shop and the X painted next to the
door. You still saw them on a lot of buildings. The abandoned buildings,
certainly. Some folks left them on renovated homes as points of pride.
The first thing she'd looked for on the front of the empty auto shop was
the number in the bottom quadrant of the X. Thankfully, she had seen
a zero.

Her father had learned what the codes meant so he knew what to
expect in a house he'd been hired to gut. He'd explained it all to Luz one
evening back then: Sometimes you see boys going into a house, no mask
or anything. God knows what they get in their lungs.

The top and left quadrants formed by the X indicated the inspection
date and the specific security force that conducted the inspection. The
right quadrant explained hazards: rats, black mold, chemical spill. The
bottom quadrant was always a number, and what you wanted was a zero
because this meant that no corpses had been found inside. In homes
such as these, some of the bodies would have lain there for a month or
more while the waters receded. Papá had indeed been hired to remove
rotten floorboards and drywall from structures that had crooked numbers painted next to their doors.

One time he told Luz, in an unusual fit of confession, that he had
worked in a home with the number four beneath the X. How could that
not have been a family? he whispered. Young Luz was sitting with him
after a long day, his guitar cast aside. He didn't feel like playing, and
that was all right because Luz didn't feel like singing, either. Papá's eyes
were seeing other things. I wondered, he said, where they had lain. He
pointed, seeing once-fine cypress floorboards. Maybe there, he said. Or
maybe there. And the smells, too. Which one is death? And what is that
stain, that one? You wonder if a person's soul leaves a mark, like a burn.

Papá had shaken his head, had said to himself, Basta, Moses. Then he'd said, I'm sorry, my Luz.

Luz came out of memory with the bouncing and pitching of Jonah's truck. Some streets deep in forgotten neighborhoods were broken to the point of being unnavigable. Asphalt pinched into steep crests or fell away into sinkholes. The streets had sat underwater for too long and everything beneath them had shifted too much. Nothing was where it used to be.

"They're never going to fix 'em all," Jonah said.

"What?" Luz asked.

"The streets. I don't see how they'll ever get to them all."

"No." After a moment she added, "Thank you for showing me the shop."

Jonah shrugged. "Sure," he said. "I wanted to."

"I don't have anything like that to show you. Not here."

Jonah glanced at her, his brow quizzical.

"I mean," she said, "I don't have any landmarks to show you. To say, I did this, or this was where something happened. Nothing to tell you, Here is where I lived my life. I am a recién llegada." She translated: "It means, like, I'm new here."

"Shit," Jonah answered. "You've been here for almost five years. Half the city wouldn't exist anymore if guys like your pop hadn't rebuilt it."

"People like me and my papá, we're always newcomers. That's what I have learned. We are always just arriving. Where is home when that is how people see you? Any places I would like to show you, those things are all in another city."

"Las Monarcas," Jonah said, glancing at her. "Maybe you can show it to me one day. We can take a trip."

"Sure." Luz smiled, but she didn't say anything else.

A purple light had descended by the time he pulled to a stop in front of her apartment. Down the street, silhouettes danced in front of the corner bar. Taillights streaked red across the overpass where it cut the neighborhood in half. Luz looked to make sure her father wasn't outside or peering through the window, then leaned over and kissed

Jonah good-night. "I'll see you at school tomorrow," she told him, and got out.

She waited for the old truck to whistle away before she went inside.

Rodrigo sat on the futon, eating a sandwich. The small television was dark, but the radio was tuned to the local Spanish station. Rodrigo had kind, hazel eyes and chubby cheeks. His wiry hair tufted at his sideburns and winged at the nape of his neck. "Buenas noches," he whispered, and Luz grinned, taking the meaning of his tone—her father was angry with her, and Rodrigo didn't wish to be the one to announce her arrival.

In the shotgun apartment, one passed from the front room directly into the kitchen, and there was her father, pacing with his hands on his hips. He wasn't tall but he was thin and wiry, with big strong hands. Stubble dotted his cheeks and there was gray in his hair. He was darkly sunburned, perpetually. Luz, like her mother, never needed the sun to get so tan. A deep red blossomed and flushed through his face when he saw her. Luz aimed to walk around him and keep the conversation as short as possible.

"¿Dónde estabas?" he demanded.

"I was with Jonah, Papá." Luz answered in English in hopes of sparing Rodrigo the argument, but she heard the screen door creak as her father's friend made a quiet exit.

"What are you supposed to do if you are going to be home late?"

"I'm sorry, I forgot. I'll call next time, I promise."

"Luz. This boy. He keeps you out late. I don't know where you are. He makes you forget things."

"I didn't forget anything, Papá. I had him bring me home."

"I want you to come straight home after school tomorrow."

Luz sighed. She turned and left the kitchen, passing into her father's bedroom. Her father called after her: "I'm serious, Luz. Straight home."

"I have practice," she called back. "Jonah is a nice boy, Papá."

There was a loft over her father's bedroom that contained Luz's mattress. She climbed the ladder and plopped down. She could hear her father talking to himself, now in Spanish, either scolding himself or rehearsing a future scolding of her.

Luz knew that her father was worn down by stress. As time passed, work became scarcer. There used to be days when her father and Rodrigo waited outside the home improvement center with the other workers and had their pick of jobs—the whole city needed repair. The further they got from the hurricane, though, the less need there was for the labor they provided. Storm or no storm, it had happened to her father before, in other American cities; when the work grew too scant, it would be time to move on again. There were days now when her father came home empty-handed, days when he baked in the parking lot all day, standing with Rodrigo and watching trucks pull into the lot, waiting for a window to roll down, for someone to say they needed folks who knew roofing or drywall or brickwork. If today had been a bad day, well, that would help explain her father's mood. But Luz wouldn't let her father begrudge her Jonah, not after the lonely years she'd spent in New Orleans. What other friends did she have? When else had she done anything but study or work?

Her first year in New Orleans, Luz had sometimes awakened frightened. It had been the dark and the ominous thumping of a helicopter, or the shaking when a military truck passed by in the street, or it had been simply the dead and utter silence and its own catalog of monsters. The city was desolate. But this was a different fear than a year or so later, when folks returned to New Orleans in droves, when the drug gangs came back and reignited old hostilities and fought to redraw territory in a place where the traditional borders had been washed away. The early days, they were a different fear—Luz waking in the dark and Papá turning on the lamp and saying, Come here, come here, my Luz.

Papá would scoot to make room, and Luz—whichever apartment they were in—would lie down. Did I ever tell you about how I met your mamá? Papá asked.

No, Luz answered, even though he had.

I was in Piedras Negras, Papá continued, for work. And some friends dragged me to a dance. I'm not much of a dancer, me, but I knew there would be beer. The dance was in a courtyard. There were lights strung from the walls—I had seen fireflies once in my life and they were like this. The dancers were kicking up dust. I could feel it in my throat. I needed a drink, but there was a woman dancing. She was wearing a white dress and swishing it around, and it was like the dust parted around her. I forgot my thirst. I was standing in front of her. I don't know how I got there. It must have been God, nudging me. She stopped dancing and looked at me like I was a crazy person. I said, What is your name? And she said, Esperanza. Then she grabbed my hand and made me dance. She could dance, your mother. Yes, Esperanza danced.

And now Luz lay in the loft, listening to her father rattle a pot in the kitchen as he angrily prepared dinner. She reflected on the reality that she hadn't heard any stories from him in a long time.

7

THE CITY STIRRED TO LIFE AS JONAH DROVE HOME. THE STREET-car on St. Charles tunneled through the dark, following its lone headlight. Jonah's F-100 tooled alongside. He glanced at the folks packed into its illuminated interior. People were also bunched on the sidewalks, sifting in and out of bars, waiting outside restaurants. He turned into his neighborhood, and the streets grew dimmer, quieter. A group of kids sitting on the steps of a raised home stared at his truck as he passed by.

We are always just arriving.

Luz's words looped in Jonah's mind. That means—Jonah thought—you're always leaving somewhere, too.

Jonah turned around and drove again to the auto shop. They still owned the structure and the land—well, Dex did. The titles had transferred to him after Pop's heart attack. There were other shut-tered businesses alongside—a barbershop, a grocery, a laundry—gray plywood sutured across windows and tagged with graffiti. Jonah's headlights cut across a figure in a black hoodie spraying paint onto the auto shop's facade. The kid didn't startle, didn't move. Jonah sat in his truck and looked at the place. It occurred to him that of all the graffiti plastered across the auto shop and the other buildings, too, nobody had painted over the X codes left from Katrina. The spray paint skirted around the markings. Jonah imagined an unspoken bit of etiquette between faceless taggers who knew one another only by their symbols and their brashness. I might paint over your shit, but we'll leave that there alone.

The truck idled and Jonah breathed. Luz had asked if he ever thought about reopening the shop. He hadn't really, not in earnest, not any more than a quick, fanciful daydream. But now he envisioned a future in which he cleaned the place up, got it running, made a good living. He did it for Luz in this vision. He could take care of her. They would be married, live in the house, raise a family together. It was clear. He was alone now, but he wouldn't be. He might build a family with Luz one day, and the business would allow him to do that. There was so much Jonah had believed was forever lost to him. He shifted into gear and drove home on a wave of hope.

8

NIGHTS LATER THEY WERE OUT, AND SHE MADE HIM CHASE HER through the French Market, at the edge of the Quarter. She squeezed between the stalls and ducked behind stands of hats, of bags, of kitschy paintings. Glimpses of her through the crowd, teeth shining as she smiled. She passed a stall selling Louisiana-themed trinkets to tourists and disappeared into the crowd. He came even with the stall, adorned with embalmed gator heads and chicken feet and straw voodoo dolls. He stood on his toes to search over the heads of the shoppers. As he stepped forward, she leaped out and shouted and scared him. He grabbed her and kissed her. She laughed into his mouth. She pulled away to look at him.

"We will be responsible for each other."

He tilted his head.

"I need you to remember this."

He looped his arms around her waist and lifted her. He kissed her again and made the promise in his heart. He held her amid all those others who were not her and were not like her because she was his and they were there together, so near the river.

9

THEY GOT SOMETHING SMALL TO EAT FROM A VENDOR, AND they watched night fall on the levee. Then it was time to go home. They walked together away from the river through the lower Quarter. As they passed from the market and then crossed Decatur, the blocks became calmer, more residential. Something itched in the back of Luz's mind. Responsible for each other? She felt like she had been repeating something—the thought had risen and verbalized so naturally—but once the words left her lips, she wasn't sure where they had come from. She was a little embarrassed by the sentiment, but Jonah didn't seem to mind, didn't seem to think what she said had been weird at all.

It was a cool night. The street was wet, and while they walked moonlight flashed like sallow fish bellies in the black water puddled on the asphalt. Ahead, a car blipped through the intersection. All at once, Luz was aware of movement like a gathering of shadow, and she felt Jonah tense beside her. Two figures slid out from a darkened doorway and blocked their path. They wore navy hoodies. One was taller than the other, eyes wide and glaring out. They both held pistols.

The taller of the two said something quick, a demand, but Luz couldn't latch onto the words, though she understood and pulled from her pocket five dollars, all she had, and the boy's fingers shot forward and snatched the cash, and Jonah's wallet was out and gone, and Luz noticed now the shorter of the two. He was holding his pistol with two shaking hands. The barrel wobbled, and Luz saw his finger on the trigger and prayed—please no, please no! The face swaddled in the hood was a child's face, a scared little boy. "Let's go," said the taller of the two, and they spun, and they ran, sneakers smacking against the wet sidewalk. They turned the corner, and the sound of Jonah's ragged breathing filled the quiet street.

"Motherfuckers," Jonah wheezed, voice higher than usual. He took Luz's hand in his. "You all right?"

"I'm fine," Luz said, soft. And she was. Her pulse raced, but she felt calm otherwise. Almost suspended, detached. Jonah was holding on to her, but the sensation—his cold, damp hand—didn't seem to touch her, as if she had become a distant observer.

Muggings were a common occurrence, particularly in this part of the Quarter, where tourists might wander away from the busier corridors, and Luz found herself unsurprised by the experience. What had scared her was the little boy, his shaking hands on the gun. Nevertheless, it had been quick. A transaction. She and Jonah played their roles without hesitation.

"I shoulda done something," Jonah said.

"They had guns," Luz heard herself say.

"I shoulda done something." His voice took on an edge.

"Don't worry about it, Jonah." Luz shivered, felt herself coming back to the earth. Adrenaline began to burn in her limbs. She tried Spanish, which Jonah didn't understand but sometimes thought was cute: "No te preocupes, Jonás."

"I feel like a pussy." He let go of her hand and stalked a few steps in the direction the boys had gone.

"It was just a few dollars."

"It's not about the fucking money," he snapped, turning toward her. He softened after a moment: "I'm sorry. Come on. My phone's in the truck. We'll call the cops."

"No," Luz said.

"Huh?"

"No police, Jonah."

He cocked his head. A question formed on his lips even as he was figuring it out.

Luz spoke first: "I can't call the police."

"But—"

"All we need is for one of them to be an asshole," she told him. "To ask me where I'm from because I have an accent."

Jonah pursed his lips, lowered his eyes. Luz's own father had been robbed twice, just so. Rodrigo once, that she knew of. Others they knew—they'd all been mugged. It hadn't taken long for the city's thieves to figure out that the workers made easy targets. They got paid in cash and wouldn't go to the police, concerned that some enterprising cop might notify la migra.

The last time her father had been robbed he fumed, just like Jonah. Luz tried to reason with him—You couldn't do anything, Papá, it's okay—but he'd gotten angrier. What a way for a city to thank the people who had rebuilt it.

"All right," Jonah said to Luz. "No cops."

"I'm sorry," Luz said.

Jonah squeezed her hand to say he understood.

When they got into the truck, Jonah sat there for a few breaths without turning the ignition. He ran his hands over the steering wheel, worn smooth by his brothers' and his father's hands before him. He moved quickly and punched the wheel once, hard.

Luz jumped. Jonah closed his eyes and hung his head. Luz watched and waited. He finally spoke. He sounded worn out.

"It's not about the money," he said. "I hate feeling helpless. I hate that I couldn't do anything about it. The world taking what it wants. Like, Fuck you, Jonah."

And that's it, Luz thought. Every loss had the touch of Jonah's greatest loss.

She watched him drive—the streetlight like water over his face, hardened with frustration—and she loved him.

10

THE TEAM USED ONE OF THE PUBLIC TRACKS IN CITY PARK FOR practice because there were no sports facilities at the school. Jonah dropped Luz off and parked under the live oaks to wait and give her a ride to the restaurant afterward. There were other people about, walking strollers in the lanes, throwing footballs in the infield. Folks wore sweaters in the cool air. Luz's teammates jawed while they sat on the rubber surface and stretched.

Luz had her own routine. Their coach was a math teacher who had been pressed into service. He didn't try to tell the girls much of anything, except for organizing the list of events and having them sign up for what they each wanted. Two girls came to blows over the relay anchor, so Luz waited and took what was left: the 400 and the 800.

The track team was not very good; the girls weren't very athletic. But Luz discovered she had a talent for the sport herself, and took her practice seriously. There was something she liked, something she couldn't quite define, about the craft of getting somewhere new as quickly as possible. And when she felt particularly good about herself, this ability played into the fantasies she allowed—a future with Jonah, college, a life she could build on her own with him.

She took herself through her warm-ups and form drills, exercises she'd found on the Internet at Jonah's one day. The other girls gibed, and if Luz retorted at all she'd make a sweet face and say something in Spanish, which made them laugh.

She ran a few lazy laps and then readied for a full-speed 400. When she ran, she imagined a ghost runner chasing her. A cold presence at her hip. It was never truly the other girls she competed with but rather this figure—she always imagined it as a he—who was compiled out of whatever lay at hand. The ghost runner came from the thin, limbo feeling she lived with as the only Latina daughter in the neighborhood—even if there were boys she knew, other recién llegados, who were close to her own age. The ghost runner came from the Spanish she spoke at home and the English she spoke at school. The ghost runner came from the frequent despair, those feelings that flared when she thought of the future and the deep truth that none of her fantasies was reality. It came from when she thought of her past, and the country where she'd left her mother buried. That nowhere place she'd crossed, thirsty, with her uncle, whom she'd not seen since he left her at her father's door in Texas. When she thought of her father's own despair, when the work started to thin. Times her father and Rodrigo had been robbed. Her ghost runner derived from all these feelings, and as she broke into her sprint he sprang to her side, cold, shouldering against her. She often had nightmares in which she couldn't outrun him because her legs wouldn't work well enough, but in real life she reached with her strides and outpaced him, and when she outpaced him she always won.

Today, though, her legs felt numb, as in the nightmares. Muscles that normally fired more quickly than she was aware were sluggish. A glacial stride, and slowing. Her breasts ached, bouncing in her sports bra, and she finished her circumference of the track more breathless than usual. She straightened with her hands on her hips and sucked at the cool, lung-searing air.

11

SHE WAS TWO WEEKS LATE BY MARDI GRAS DAY, BUT SHE HADN'T said anything to Jonah yet.

She had promised to meet Jonah and Colby in Central City for the Zulu parade. It was cold out, but Luz felt like she was burning up. The parade was already rolling when she arrived, floats packed tight with riders in black-and-white face paint. They wore vibrant frills and robes and skirts made of straw. They chucked beads and toy spears into the throngs of people bunched against the curb. Sometimes a rider held aloft a rare, prized coconut, painted gold or silver or decorated with rhinestones. This was the evolution of a century-old tradition. The crowd lost themselves at the sight, held arms high, strained their fingers, and the rider picked his favorite and tossed the throw. The bouncing cadence of the bands between the floats punctuated all of it.

The boys were already drunk by the time Luz found them. Colby had a bottle of whiskey stashed in his backpack. They offered Luz a swig. She put on a good face and abstained, and they kept offering, having forgotten they'd already tried. There had been good moments earlier in Carnival season—dancing with the boys to marching bands, competing for the best throws from the floats, celebrating the Saints' victory in the Super Bowl—but today, the ability to be present eluded Luz.

A sharp smack near her ear made her snap to.

Colby was standing there, shaking out his hand. He bent and picked up the coconut, a beautiful thing painted a solid and gleaming silver. He grinned. His drunken eyes bloodshot. He tapped his temple. "Thing was gonna hit you right there," he said.

Relief blossomed in Luz's belly and she leaned and kissed Colby on the cheek. An overwhelming release, like she might float away. Certainly she could have been injured and Colby had saved her from that, but the feeling struck her as incommensurate with simple personal gratitude. Luz backed out of the crowd.

Toward the end of the day they found themselves in the Marigny, downriver from the French Quarter. Luz followed as the boys listed through the costumed people on Frenchmen Street, and in the darkening day they stumbled upon some otherworldly drum corps on the corner. Men and women wearing costumes of horns and chains and red flashing lights. They had snares and bass drums, and some had triangles they dinged or cymbals they crashed, and one man wearing a skeleton mask shouted dancing orders into a megaphone as the revelers passed. Jonah and Colby fell in with the gathering group. Luz did her best to laugh as Jonah pulled her into the fold, but everybody reeked of liquor and sweat. The stench clawed up her nostrils and thrust itself down her throat, and her stomach clenched against it. Wet bodies slid against her. She was jostled about, vulnerable, exposed.

A panic rose like acid and she ran. The boys found her halfway down the block, but she couldn't explain what the matter was. She didn't want to.

And this was why such relief had flooded her when Colby blocked the coconut. Conscious thought drew even with her biology.

The world went wobbly, and Jonah caught her, and he laughed, thinking she was drunk like him.

II

I'm not afraid.

1

NOW CAME A MONTH OF SMOLDERING, INEXPLICABLE DREAD. Something sliding between them, Jonah didn't know what. It did not feel to him like the natural sclerosis of attraction, the blunted edge of a love running its course. He had held his vision for the future close, guarding it from public consideration. He still imagined his triumph over loss—McBee Auto reopened, happy and fulfilling years to come with Luz, a family of their own—but the vision had begun to blur at the edges, bleached of color. He didn't know what was happening between him and Luz, and he sensed possibilities slipping away. In one respect, he wasn't surprised—this was what he knew of life. In another, he was angry and perplexed.

He stood with Colby in the hall. Colby was saying something about Georgia.

"Huh?"

"Where the army sends you first, Fort Something, I can't remember."

A ruckus erupted, traveled down the hall. Shouting. People whooping, calling out. A teacher was dragging a student by the collar and hollering for the police liaison.

"Check this young man's pockets!" the teacher cried. He was a short and stubby white man, balding. "He's got it in his pockets!"

"Aw, fuck," Colby muttered. Jonah also recognized the kid, a dude named Davonte. Colby was friendly with him. Cell phones flickered around the scene. Photos snapped, text messages punched. The police liaison appeared, swimming through the crowd, and he glared at the teacher. The teacher, however, was glowing and oblivious, proud he'd caught a kid slinging.

"Stupid ass," Colby said, and Jonah knew he wasn't referring to Davonte.

The liaison wrested Davonte away from the teacher and hurried him down the hallway. The teacher pivoted on the balls of his loafers and marched. There had been too many smartphones out and the teacher had been too loud. Somebody surely made a call, spreading the word: Davonte got caught, got his product confiscated.

"Hey." It was Luz. She had sidled up to Jonah sometime during the fracas.

Jonah pulled her in and embraced her. She didn't smile and she didn't say anything else. Jonah felt sick to his stomach but didn't know what to say.

"I've got to go to class," she said, off before he could say good-bye.

Jonah glanced at Colby. Colby shrugged and looked away.

Davonte didn't come to school the next day. Nor the next. Kept his head down. A whisper of reckoning in the halls—what would happen to Davonte, who would get him?

And this, they knew, was the way things went.

2

A TINY BLUE CROSS PULSED WITHIN THE SCREEN AND SET THE world to trembling. Luz stared at the cross for a moment and then left the stall. She looked like herself in the mirror, but beneath her feet the earth labored, lurching onto a new axis. She looked again at the test in her fist. She'd been afraid of the confirmation, had kept running from it. But here was the truth, inescapable as her ghost runner. She squeezed the plastic stick and closed her eyes, and then she moved, chucking the test into the trash and leaving the ladies' room.

Saturday morning found the private school quiet. She padded barefoot down the dim hall. Her running spikes hung from her fist. There were glass cases full of trophies, medals. Photographs of merit scholars, smiling white girls in plaid skirts. Outside, she looked across the lawn and the lot to the track. Someone shouted in the distance. A ringing cowbell in the grandstand. She laced up her spikes and jogged over.

Luz's hair was drawn tightly into a bun. The sun soaked into her neck, and sweat slid beneath the mesh of her jersey. At the starting blocks she normally had a stretching routine, but she forgot it just now and crouched, readied. Four hundred meters was a distance to think through, to plan for. But today, she wondered whether she could run hard enough to bleed. To alter this reality before she must share it with anyone else.

Guilt wormed through her with the thought. She apologized quickly, to God and also to her mother, and she saved a word for Jonah's mother as well. Once you tell yourself that they are there, watching . . . well, her acts were subject to their judgment, and she remembered this.

And there came the sound of the gun.

Luz accelerated low into her sprint, gaining ground with long strides. Normally, there was a point early in this kind of lengthy race where she would settle into a tempo that reserved something for the final stretch. Not today.

Her ghost runner hugged her hip—she must outrun him now more than ever. Get somewhere new. The claustrophobic white borders of her lane. Run. Breathe. Through the first turn, into the straightaway, her legs already dragging. She couldn't keep this pace up, but she already knew that. For now, she outpaced her ghost runner.

The girls on the team teased her, saying she was fast because she had an ass like theirs. Luz usually laughed and let it go. Her body was her mother's. Luz remembered her strong, brown legs. Mamá's back glimpsed when she spun out of her towel to dress, muscles sculpted in graveyard nights at the laundry where she worked, hunching and lifting and scrubbing. Mamá's hands, rough when placed along Luz's cheek.

Luz leaned through the bottom of the track. Her bronchi burned and her breath tasted like copper. Luz had always been a runner, of a kind. She ran from Las Monarcas. She ran to America, to San Antonio. She ran to New Orleans.

Into the homestretch, secondhand spikes gripping the fine rubber track, each footfall bringing her somewhere—somewhere, she had to believe it. Her quadriceps were going wooden. Mouthfuls of oxygen caught in her trachea like cotton. The other girls began to pass her. Their ragged breathing. Blond ponytails bouncing, track shoes gleaming. All the while, Luz's ghost runner gained. Cold, sliding past. Her body wanted to quit, a little begging voice. Yes, that's right. Quit. Quit. She must run hard enough to undo it. She craned her neck, pulled at the air, threw her feet forward.

Luz was the last to cross, arms and legs wobbling out of form. She came to a jerky halt and hunched and retched dryly. Four hundred meters. Nothing had changed, of course: the finish line was the starting line.

She stood, hands locked atop her head, and this was when she spied her father—Papá, who had never seen her race—down at the belly of the turn. He stood outside the track, gripping the chain-link. He wore jeans and work boots and a T-shirt, plastered to him with sweat. He held on to the fence, watching her. He turned away, toward some Uptown mansion, perhaps, where today he would undersell his carpentry skills to hang drywall. The boughs of the live oaks swung low over the street. Plastic beads were still wound about the limbs, put there during the Carnival parades last month. Her father looked alone, shrinking as he went.

Luz slipped through the crowd. She saw Jonah across the lot. Tall and sandy haired, she couldn't miss him. He was with Colby. She thought briefly of Jonah's arms and the freckles she traced with her fingertips, but when he scanned in her direction she ducked out of view. She was afraid to speak with him. What would she say? How would he react? She made for the street, where it shaped itself to the river, bending in both directions. Another kind of track, another kind of loop.

The streetcar lumbered to a stop in the neutral ground between lanes. She boarded and closed her eyes. The whirring against the rails, the buzz of the stop cord.

She went up the concrete steps of their place, and inside, Rodrigo lay on the futon, head propped on his fist. A baseball game played on the television, splotchy through the antenna, broadcast muted. Luz was surprised to find him home while her father worked.

"¿No estás trabajando con Papá?"

Rodrigo's eyes flicked toward her. "El hombre sólo quería uno."

Luz passed through the rooms of the shotgun, one after the other. Her father's guitar rested against the wall in his bedroom. When Luz sang with him, she used words her mother had taught her. She climbed the ladder to the loft and her mattress and reclined, but the more she tried to quiet her mind the more suffocated she felt. A drumbeat swelled behind her eyes, like the one from the drum corps they'd stumbled on during Mardi Gras. She woke, her heart pounding and her body still stinking from the track meet. Rodrigo was calling up to her to see if she'd like some lunch. "No, gracias," she told him, adding that she had work.

When she left, Rodrigo was again sprawled on the futon. The local news flickered soundlessly on the screen.

She paused in the doorway. She said, "I'm pregnant."

The words were real, heard aloud. They took shape and had weight to them. They forced acknowledgment. Everything seethed. Inside, she seethed. Her skin was nothing more than a thin veneer. Hold yourself together. Rodrigo only looked at her in the way he did when she forgot to speak to him in Spanish. It was a patient look. Luz's stomach twitched—she felt she might be sick. But she held on to her calm appearance and told Rodrigo, "Nada," and he sat there uncomprehending as she exited, steadied herself against the railing, and marched down the steps, thinking of Jonah.

JONAH AND COLBY STOOD IN THE GRIDDED SHADE BEHIND THE grandstand. The starting gun popped again and some parent in the bleachers began to shake her cowbell. Families and students and other runners in their uniforms milled about. Across the lot reared the Uptown private academy. The sun balanced, swollen, on the rampart.

"You see Luz anywhere?"

Colby shook his head. "She don't usually run that shitty, do she?"

"No," Jonah said. He loved watching her go. Strong legs, reaching and recycling with natural grace. Watching her reminded him that some things in the world did indeed work as they should. Until today, though, he had never seen her finish last. She wasn't always first, but she was never last. "She should be out here by now."

"Don't see her." A kid with long hair passed and Colby said, "Get high, player?" but the kid only glanced at him with a slightly frightened expression. Colby grunted. "Thought Luz would run better for me, Mickey-Bee."

Jonah looked for the shimmering black length of her hair. There wasn't another remotely like her in the crowd. Anxiety coiled in his gut. She had known he would be here. He had hoped to spend the afternoon with her.

Heat rose from the fissures in the asphalt. The big school loomed. Jonah's first high school had been a private academy much like this one. His experience there had ended fairly quickly, however.

Colby had moved into the shade beneath the bleachers, where he exchanged something with a lanky, pimpled kid and then sauntered back.

"You know," Jonah said, "this is a Catholic school here and shit."

"I'm good, Mickey-Bee."

"Think they'll look the other way if you get caught?"

"I ain't worried about no teachers."

Jonah thought about Davonte, who had skipped school since he'd been caught slinging and still hadn't surfaced. It wasn't the authorities he was hiding from. It was your employer, not the law, that made getting caught a dangerous thing. "I could get you on down at the Walmart, man. Show you how to do a few things, get you started." And one day, Jonah thought, I could hire you at McBee Auto. When it's up and running again. If Luz isn't through with me.

"Don't start that shit again. I'll stop when I have to."

Jonah knew what had propelled his brother Bill toward the Marines: a lack of purpose. Bill was looking for something. After Mom died, there were no answers to be had. Nothing made sense. Bill enlisted as soon as he'd been able. Jonah had imagined the causality over time, the need for something that would offer definition, parcel out the world and say: Look, this is how it works and why. Contentment might come with the promise of a collective purpose. Just give yourself over and pare away the personally threatening or existentially burdensome questions—those things just wouldn't matter anymore. Jonah saw this same need in Colby. Even if Colby's reasons were different, the need was the same. But Jonah knew how false the promise actually was. All he had to do was look at his brother's picture on the wall, the flag hung beside it. Jonah's chance at purpose now resided with Luz. He saw it in their future together. And he saw their future becoming more and more unlikely.

Jonah dropped Colby off in front of his house just as Colby's mother came out. She wore black slacks and a teal polo, the casino logo embroidered over the breast pocket. "Why don't you stay and eat something, Jonah? Left some lunch in the fridge." She beckoned with red fingernails. She had told him that the better her nails looked, the better she slung the cards.

"No," Jonah said, "but thanks. Got some things to do."

"All right, then." She collared Colby and kissed him. "You need anything, Jonah, you holler."

"Yes, ma'am."

When Jonah pulled up to Luz's house, her father's friend—whose name he never remembered—looked at him from the front steps. Jonah got out and waved. The man barely nodded. Jonah knew he didn't speak English. "Luz?"

The man shook his head, grumpy look unchanged. Jonah got back into the truck and laid into the horn, two bursts. The man on the steps jolted, glared at him. Jonah waited. She wasn't home.

People were on their stoops with beers. A group of children shooting hoops in the street halted to let his truck pass. He drove to the Quarter and parked near the wharf. He hiked through the gravel around the streetcar tracks and climbed to the levee and the riverwalk. A man on a bench was playing the saxophone for tips. A steel container ship stood in the water downriver. Jonah sat on a bench, watching the seabirds. The tourist steamboat swung out, wheel churning. The saxophone submerged into the wind and surfaced again. The Hidalgos owned a cell phone, but her father usually had it. Jonah thought about that first trip to the river with Luz, last spring.

When the McBees used to come to the river, it was all because of his mother. They sat on a blanket on the grassy stretch of park. Here was a rare memory. Bill and Dex played catch, and sometimes Bill would hand the ball to Jonah so he could heave it, bouncing, back to Dex. Jonah couldn't have been more than five or six. The remembrance was flimsy, like Jonah might wake up tomorrow and it wouldn't be there at all, scrubbed away like so much detritus in his sleep. And if the memory left him, who could tell him that a family trip to the river had ever taken place? Luz, maybe. He told her about those times. Is that the point, then—to remind each other of who we are as we move on? And so Jonah sat on the river, sheltering himself from the unknowns of both future and past by thinking of the bars of light that fell through his window and lay across Luz's brown back. Her fingertips, rough from washing dishes at the restaurant, tracing out the patterns only she saw in his skin. Her hair in his fist, her sigh into his mouth. Her heartbeat mere inches from his own. Tell yourself there is no border between them. Believe it because you must.

He needed everything to be all right.

3

HIP-HOP PUMPED IN THE CHROME KITCHEN. LUZ SPRAYED BÉAR-naise sauce from a plate and then dunked the plate into a basin, the scalding water up to her wrist, and set the plate into a perforated rack to dry. How often she imagined her mother in that laundry in Las Monarcas. The late nights when Luz would lie awake in bed, waiting to hear the squealing of the building's gate that meant that her mother was home. The hands Mamá flexed in the morning, grinning to hide the pain of her stiffening knuckles, before being able to lift her coffee to her lips.

Mamá, Luz prayed.

But Luz didn't know what to say, what to request. Forgiveness, perhaps, first. The retribution Luz had been taught to expect had only arrived after she lost faith in it. She had been told, as a young girl, that this would happen, and worse. Abuela told her. Mamá, too, in her own way. Papá told her no such thing, but when could he have? Once Luz joined him in America, this was never a thing they discussed. From time to time he ordered her to stop seeing Jonah, but that was as far as it ever went. Nevertheless. She had been warned throughout her life, and in the end she ignored the warnings. There were things she had imagined that might have been possible. Lives she had allowed herself to dream. But now she couldn't even imagine tomorrow. She rinsed and dunked another plate.

At the end of the night the chef and owner, a large man with earrings and a goatee, paid her and two of the cooks in cash. The rest of the staff would have their paychecks deposited. She folded the money and put it in the pocket of her jeans. The two cooks were also Mexican, she thought. Or Honduran, perhaps, but she'd never really spoken with them. That was the way her nights went.

When she went out through the service entrance Jonah was there, leaning against the brick of the opposing structure. She didn't know what to say, but he pushed from the wall and she pressed into him, folding her arms between their bodies. Her hands throbbed, a raw feeling. She wished all of her could feel this way.

The streetcar jingled past before they could get there, so they sat to wait at the stop. The globe of the trolley's taillight bobbed and receded through the dark like some kind of spirit. Jonah mentioned that he had been at the track meet.

"I had a bad day," she answered. He wanted more than that, though, of course.

"You were in first for a while."

"I know."

"Colby thought you'd win for him, because he came to see you."

The humor didn't occur to her. "I ran too hard too early."

They sat there. Luz knew she was not being herself, and she knew Jonah didn't understand. One of the American cooks sat at the other end of the bench, palming his smartphone, a cigarette clamped in his lips. When the smoke wafted her way, an immediate nausea swept from belly to throat. She got to her feet. "Let's go to your house."

"You sure?" Jonah asked, opening his own phone to check the time.

"Come on."

They crossed the avenue into his neighborhood. A corner saloon, iron bars across its windows. A food truck, the smell of barbecue, a gathering of men. They passed the whitewashed brick of the cemetery where Jonah's parents and brother were buried. Palms arched out over the street, dead fronds underfoot.

Señora McBee, Luz prayed. Help me find the right words, help him listen. Please.

His bedroom was dark and cool. Luz closed her eyes. How to start? He kissed her, and she realized that she had been wrong in everything. There was no unique opportunity. There was no special consideration. What she had, in totality, was this singular moment, this lone moment with Jonah in which they could ascend together. Tomorrow, her being would shift. Tomorrow, everything changed.

Forget it, she told herself. Forget it, for just a while.

They lay afterward in the quiet, and Jonah was saying something. Luz's mind swung wildly between a numb stasis and a jittering frenzy. Focus, she thought, listen.

"I haven't wanted to say this out loud," Jonah said. "I was worried how it would sound or I'd jinx it or something. But I keep thinking about the future and the old auto shop and how perfect it would be if I could get it open again. If I could make some money and, you know, we'll be together. We'll make a life together. That's what I want."

His words had come out quickly and now there was nothing. Luz realized she wasn't breathing. His vision was the kind of thing she had wished for, too. The kind of good thing she had believed Jonah could fashion into reality. She heard him withering with doubt, and he started up again, fast, nervous.

"I mean, I know it seems impossible, but I'm gonna try to talk to Dex and see what he knows about loans and—"

Luz spoke into the dark: "I'm pregnant."

A moment of absolute silence. She heard him swallow. He rolled toward her. She could hear him blinking. "Pregnant."

"Yes."

He began to stammer with questions. What? When? How? She told him she'd suspected it for weeks. She told him of the test that morning that confirmed it.

"Wow," he said.

She had imagined him panicking, rattling off options in an attempt to fix it all at once. But to be quiet, to take it in—this was his way, and she loved him for it. She let him hold her. She told him she was staying the night. "What about your pops?" he asked.

"I'm not afraid."

"Does he know yet?"

"I'm not afraid of telling him, either."

"It's going to be okay," Jonah tried. She didn't reply. He said, "I promise." Then he said, "The auto shop stuff, that can wait. Colby and me, we were talking about the bonuses you get for enlisting in the army.

Well, you know, he's been talking about it. Thousands of dollars. I mean, I'll do that with him. We're gonna need something quick. We'll be all right. We'll be okay. I'll help take care of everything."

Luz listened to him dismantle his dream for them in a moment, and saltwater burned in her eyes, and she whispered, "Not tonight." She wouldn't let him hear her cry. She pressed into him. "Not tonight."

4

THEY WOKE, SUNDAY MORNING. THEY WALKED TO THE CHURCH on St. Charles at her request. The same one his mother used to bring him to. A cavern of a church, rafter beams in shadow. It had been a long time for Jonah. They sat in a pew near the back.

An ancient priest read at the lectern: "Where two are gathered in My name, I am there . . ." And another rare memory surfaced—he had been here with his mother and heard these same words, and they made him imagine some large and invisible being crouching among the rafters. It felt very silly now, sitting here with Luz, watching her pray. She clasped her hands, shut her eyes. He remembered his mother praying, just so. What did they ask for, and of whom did they ask it? Jonah wished to understand.

But he couldn't. He couldn't know that Luz knelt and spoke to their mothers, asking them to look kindly on her. She asked for something solid and definable to emerge from the murk of tomorrow. She asked them for strength.

5

HER FATHER WAS RED-FACED AND FUMING WHEN SHE FINALLY got home. She walked past him and Rodrigo to the back of the house so that her father would have to follow. She sat on the edge of his mattress. No longer was she the frightened little girl, and no longer was he the father who comforted her in the night with stories of her mother.

Her father was bellowing in English, demanding to know where she had been, and so Luz said she'd spent the night at Jonah's and stayed there with him all day. Her father's cheeks bulged and the vein in his forehead stood out and his skin darkened. He was shouting in Spanish now, and Luz bowed her head and let it wash over her.

She said it quietly, in English: "I'm pregnant."

Her father shouted for another moment, and then he stopped when he finally heard her. Luz looked at him and repeated herself.

He blinked and his mouth worked. He turned and seemed bewildered. He grasped at the air in front of him like he was blind, and then he pivoted and collapsed to sit on a lower rung of the loft ladder. His shoulders sagged and his arms hung limply. He wasn't looking at her. "Please tell me this is not the truth."

"It is true, Papá."

"Luz." It was a whisper. He covered his face with his hands. "Luz. Luz." He asked her how long.

"Six or seven weeks." The words were like misshapen objects in her mouth.

He shook his head. "And you tell me now."

"I didn't know. I didn't know how to tell you."

He sighed, said her name again, but wouldn't look at her.

"It is going to be okay, Papá. It is." She paused. She didn't know if she believed this, but she said it to her father again anyway. Her own reckoning was yet to come. Her own reckoning and the reimagining of everything that lay ahead, everything she might hope for. Her father didn't speak. She went on: "Jonah is nice, Papá. He cares for me. I think, I think one day he will want to m—"

"¡Basta!" her father shouted, standing and raising his hands. He called her irresponsible. Foolish. And how many times had he ordered her to stay away from that boy? "Who have you become, my daughter?" He was screaming. He swiveled and kicked the ladder and it fell, slow like a tree, and Luz watched it falling, and it slammed against the ancient cypress floorboards with a boom she felt in her heels. She pulled her feet off the floor and drew her knees to her chest. Her father stood, back turned, hands on hips, head hanging. When he spoke, his voice was quiet, hoarse. He spoke with resignation: "You will have to go back to Las Monarcas." He turned and threw his hands up. "You will have to be with your grandmother."

Luz was on her feet but she didn't remember getting up. "Papá—"

"Luz," he said. He didn't raise his voice but he punctuated with a hand chopped through the air. He turned the hand over and ticked items off with a finger against his palm, beginning with the fact that they were not American citizens. "We have no money. How can we pay for doctors? Raise a child? Look at me."

Her vision warped, melted, bled away. Woozy on her feet.

"What do I know about taking care of you? How am I to do this? The work is going away from here, this city." He grunted with disgust. "Do you know how I worry for you, every night you walk home from the streetcar? After the things that have happened to me, to Rodrigo, to the rest of us? And now I must worry about you and your child? No. No. It cannot work. Your grandmother—"

"Papá, no—"

"Yes, Luz. Your grandmother will take care of you. She will help you through this. I will still send her my money after you are back. I will be able to send more."

"I won't go."

"Yes. You will."

Luz crossed her arms, willed her world to steady. "I am staying in New Orleans."

He massaged his brow. He pointed to the door. "I am going for a walk." He said that she would indeed return to Mexico. They would talk more once he was calmer.

"I won't go!" she cried after him, but he didn't reply.

She sat again on the mattress. The front door opened, clacked shut. The world dimly trembled. She heard Rodrigo get up and nervously shift his weight before settling down again. Her father was gone a while. Nothing would hold in her mind—words she sought skittered away like pebbles thrown against pavement.

6

"No school," Papá said the next morning. "There is no need."

"I'm staying in New Orleans," she said. "I'm not going back to Las Monarcas."

He said, "You will do as I say."

He hadn't raised his voice, and so she was the one to scream. He endured it with a blank face. Winded, she turned from him and stomped to the back door but stopped; he had forbidden her from leaving the apartment.

He stayed home all day to make sure she did as well. Work for him wasn't assured, anyway, he reasoned, and Rodrigo might have luck on his own. Regardless, in a few days' time there'd be one less mouth to feed on their American dollars. Luz vacated whichever end of the house her father decided to occupy. A charged silence gridlocked them. When Rodrigo returned at the end of the day he didn't speak, shuffling around the apartment and averting his eyes.

Her father stayed home with her again on Tuesday. Luz sat alone on the stoop, blind to the hot, crawling day. Inside, her father planned her departure. The street blurred, and Luz contemplated what it would take to truly defy her father—to defy him in an active way. If Jonah drove past, could she run from the stoop and get into the truck and never turn around? Let her father go to the cops then, she thought. Let him wager that the police would care to find a single undocumented Mexican girl more than they'd care to call la migra on his behalf. This was the only way: get up and go. Run, as fast as she was able. But the prospect put cold fear in her belly, and so she sat and waited, and Jonah didn't come by, and there was nothing she could do to get in touch with him.

The day darkened, and Luz remained on the porch steps. Rodrigo mumbled greetings when he returned and climbed around her. When the screen squealed open again, it was her father on his way out. He looked down at Luz. "Walk with me—?" her father began, but Luz got up, stepped around him, and went inside. "Luz, please," he called after her. "Come talk with me."

But Luz didn't answer, striding wordlessly past Rodrigo on the futon toward the rear of the house. When she finally glanced back, her father had disappeared.

Luz paced the shadowed recess of the back bedroom. She began to stretch, her instinctual prerace routine. Hamstrings, then quads. She sat on the floor and did hurdlers. She twisted her trunk, loosened her back. She looked at the back door.

If you're going to go, go right now. The soles of her feet prickled. Start running.

7

ACROSS HIS KITCHEN TABLE HE'D STREWN PAMPHLETS GATHERED at the recruiting office with Colby, as well as Internet documents he'd printed at the library. It had been two days since he took Luz home. She hadn't shown up in school, she hadn't called. His stomach throbbed like some dull-toothed creature had been gnawing it.

But his fear and anxiety did not derive from the idea of fatherhood. There was something vertiginous about the surprise and acceleration of it, sure, but the reality was still a thing he had imagined for himself and Luz. And it wasn't even the disintegrating of his fanciful vision concerning McBee Auto and some kind of idyllic American future that frightened him, either. Maybe that kind of life just wasn't meant to be available to them—and that could be okay, as long as their life was vested with purpose. The new responsibility, once it came to be, would shove any questions about the reason for his own being to the periphery. He looked at his brother Bill's photo on the wall. Jonah, now, would go into the military for his family with the force of necessity—this was a different thing. He wouldn't be combing the indifferent world for something to fill the void. No, Jonah would construct his own meaning. Do it himself, create it and name it and know it. This was a gift, and with it came great relief.

What did frighten him, however, was Luz's father. Why hadn't Luz called? Where had she been? How could he get in touch with her if her father was keeping her locked away?

Jonah was pacing when there came a knocking on the door.

It was Luz, panting, weeping. Jonah had never actually seen her cry before.

"Luz!" Jonah said, letting her inside. "Jesus! Did you run all the way here?" Then, "Should you be running like that?"

She was shaking her head, composing herself. "I ran to and from the streetcar. Jonás—" She leaned into him.

He got her a glass of water. Jonah waited for her to say something. Then, "Are you okay?"

She seemed to be wrestling with the words. "Papá, he . . ."

"Listen," Jonah said, "no matter how angry he is, we'll get through it. I've got a plan. I've—"

"He wants to send me back to Mexico."

"What?" Jonah said.

Luz wiped her eyes. "He says I need to go back to Las Monarcas. Abuela can take care of me. We can't afford to keep me here . . ."

"No, no," Jonah said. "That can't happen. No. Look, here—"

He started gesturing at the documents on the kitchen table.

"I told him no," Luz said. "I told him I won't go. But he won't let me out of the house. He's going to make me go back."

"No, Luz," Jonah tried to interrupt. She was going on, frantic. "No!" Jonah said. "I've got a plan. I've been doing research." He started lifting brochures and printouts from the table. "You've got to tell him about my plan. I'm going to enlist, I'll be able to take care of you and—and the baby. I'm going to."

"Jonah," Luz said, her voice falling to a whisper. "Jonah."

He rifled through the papers. "Right here. I found out that families get extra money for housing. So if we have to go somewhere or whatever. I mean, we'll have to go wherever they send me, but—"

"Jonah. This isn't what you want."

"Yes," he said. He set the papers down. He reached for her hands. They were hot against his fingers, freezing with nerves. His heart hammered. "We would have to get married."

Her features jolted.

"To really make the army thing work, I mean. But—but that's what I want, too."

Light caught in the water around the rim of her eyes.

"Can you tell your pops that? Tell him I want to marry you and take care of you. He doesn't have to send you back. You can stay right here."

8

JONAH DROVE HER HOME. SHE TOLD HIM TO GO QUICKLY, BECAUSE the apartment's front door was open and the light inside was on and she knew that her father must have come home from his walk furious. She wanted to be able to go in and speak to him without having to contend with his anger at seeing Jonah's truck.

She kissed Jonah and told him she'd call as soon as she could.

The truck whistled off and she waited a moment on the sidewalk. She breathed. Closed her eyes. Felt the night heave around her. "Okay," she told herself.

She climbed the steps and went inside and halted. She had prepared to be screamed at as soon as she entered. Her mind failed, at first, to interpret the scene. Papá sprawled on the futon. Rodrigo paced.

Rodrigo looked at Luz and started to speak. "Moses fue a buscar—"

For me, Luz thought. He was looking for me.

Blood covered Papá's face. His shirt was wet. He held an ice pack to his forehead and blinked, lids slick and red, as Luz came and fell to her knees beside him. "Papá, Papá," she was saying, and he reached for her hands with his free hand, and Luz thought, I made you go looking for me, even as she imagined what must have happened—Papá walking, distraught over his daughter. He spares the apartment a last glance and passes beneath the watery globe of a streetlamp, a seething cloud of insects. He loses himself in thought—Oh, my Luz—as the dark clings to him and he marches himself breathless. Is it my fault, bringing her to this place? Of course he wonders this. Can he trace his daughter's mistake to the choice he made, long ago, to leave home for El Norte? His Luz, his daughter, who has she become to allow this to happen? And this is when, his senses shrouded by thought and the heavy night air, somebody behind him grunts: Hey. Papá turns and glimpses a figure and a flash of movement. Dread ices through him in the helpless instant before the pistol barrel whips out of the dark, and everything—inside and out—

bursts bright and soundless. He is on his back, the world reassembling in a dim throb, as the figure turns out his pockets and disappears. Warm blood floods into one eye, and Papá thanks God for the small grace that most of his cash remains back at the apartment. Nothing hurts yet but it will soon, and he thanks God.

"This is my fault," Luz told him, while he lay bleeding on the futon. "I'm sorry, Papá," she said.

Her father's eyes sought her. Guilt thickened like sludge in her belly.

"Okay," Luz said. "Okay, Papá. I will go."

9

TWO DAYS. TWO DAYS OF FRAYED NERVES AND A TIRED, FEEBLE feeling. Two days of waiting, minute by minute, for his phone to ring, and nothing. He finally mustered the courage to call the Hidalgos' cell phone, but when her father answered he hung up. Luz didn't appear at school and Jonah didn't know what to do, save go to their front door and make demands. He visualized steady hands and a steadier voice, a confidence that would eliminate questions before their inception. Jonah hesitated, and, worse, he knew he hesitated because he was afraid.

By the end of Jonah's afternoon work shift on Thursday he had resolved to go there himself, to rap on the door, to speak with her father, and to make himself clear.

When he entered their street, however, Luz was sitting on the front steps with her elbows on her knees. Jonah's throat went scratchy. She saw his truck and stood. She looked as if she had been waiting for him. Jonah parked across the street, and she ran to meet him as he exited. Locusts thrummed. The sound was growing and something was wrong.

"Jonás," she said as she crashed into him.

"What happened? Did you tell him?"

"I couldn't," Luz said, "I couldn't, not with him bleeding like that."

"What are you talking about? What happened?"

"He's already bought the plane ticket, Jonah. I'm leaving tomorrow." Her voice broke.

"What, Luz, no. No."

"It was my fault. He was almost killed because of me. I couldn't tell him no, Jonah. I—" She reached into her pocket, withdrew a scrap of paper, and pressed it into his hand, saying it contained her grandmother's address. "I have to."

"No," Jonah said. "No. I can make it work."

And she rose onto her toes and kissed him. Taste of salt on her face.

"I'll call you when I'm home." She was crying.

Her father appeared at the door, his face purple and swollen around an eye.

"Ven aquí, Luz."

As Luz pulled away from Jonah, she was speaking Spanish. Hushed and hysterical. Weeping as she did, and speaking too fast.

"Vuelve conmigo, por favor. Jonás. Ven conmigo."

"Wait—Luz!—I don't understand!"

She turned and ran and went up the steps.

For a beat her father glared at him.

"Wait! Luz!"

Her father yanked the door shut.

But she was already gone. She was running home.

III

Old Mexico way, huh?

1

THE CLAMOR OF A GARBAGE CREW IN THE STREET, THE DRONING of the engine and the shouting of the men. The squalling as the maw of the truck's ass end opened, and the slamming of the trash bins against the street. Jonah blinked to life, vision quaking, whiskey burn lingering in his throat. He sat up on the couch under the eyes of the photographs and began frantically searching for his phone. He had gone to sleep with it in his hand, hoping Luz would call. He found the phone between the cushions. Today was Monday. Luz had gotten onto a plane Friday. Her father had kept her away from him after the tearful good-bye in the street, and then she was gone. Jonah scrolled through his messages, his e-mails. Nothing from Luz. Three days, and not a single word. He was sick with worry, and when he set out for school he realized he was still a little drunk from the night before.

There was a gap in the chain-link fence behind the school where Jonah could go through the back door and not wait in line for the metal detector. If the liaison officer knew about the entrance, he couldn't do anything about it. Through the door, Jonah turned the corner into a ruckus. A fight was being broken up. A teacher, a big man named Mr. Sise, was pinning Colby against the wall with a forearm across his throat and straight-arming another student away, grasping a handful of T-shirt. A mug lay in shards, coffee streaking over the tile. Mr. Sise had been a college basketball player, and they had once watched him demolish the school's best player in a game of one-on-one out on the courtyard's concrete half-court after the kid wouldn't stop harassing him. There was only a finite number of ways to earn respect.

Colby was screaming fuck-you's at the other kid.

"Are you talking to me?" Mr. Sise's voice had heft.

"No, sir!" Colby said, even as the other guy screamed that he would kill Colby.

Mr. Sise swung the kid around and slammed him into the wall next to Colby. He brought his face in close: "You walk away right now, you hear me?"

The kid nodded, enthusiastic.

"You ever spill my coffee again," Mr. Sise threatened, and shoved him away. The crowd fell apart, in search of the next entertaining thing.

Jonah's previous school, his second private school, had expelled him after he got into a particularly nasty fight, but they didn't kick you out for that kind of thing here. Sometimes they joked: you end up in jail or the cemetery, or you graduate.

Mr. Sise let Colby free, slapped him on the back. Jonah overheard: "I'm glad you stuck up for yourself, but you gotta be careful." The teacher nodded to Jonah and marched away through the hall.

Colby's lips were dry and he rubbed his face with a trembling hand. "I dunno. Kid runs into me and next thing I know we bump into Mr. Sise. He's strong."

"I'm sorry I wasn't here," Jonah said. "I woulda stepped in." Jonah's head ached, and he needed an outlet. "I coulda used it."

2

THE GUY WHO MONITORED THE COMPUTER LAB HAD VANISHED. A couple of boys and a girl with a heavily pregnant belly sat in the back row, laughing at something on a computer screen. Jonah went up and down the aisles, punching power buttons until one of the machines wheezed to life.

At Jonah's first school he had worn a tie every day and kept his hair short. He was able to attend the private academy on a scholarship, based on his good junior-high grades. He intended to try out for the baseball team. Early on in his freshman year, he'd sat in computer class thinking about Bill, trying to imagine what life had been like for his brother in Afghanistan. Jonah thought a lot about that Soviet land mine, left over from the eighties. He wanted to understand the mechanism that had killed Bill because there was so little he could know about his brother at all anymore. So Jonah searched for Afghan minefields. From page to page he went—land mines, Dragunov rifles left behind, newer IEDs. Weapons of all kinds. Did another young man, brother to someone else, bury that bomb, pat the dirt firm atop it? Did he have any notion that it would wait more than twenty years to erupt and call Jonah's brother from reality? But Jonah couldn't know anything. That was what he learned. And later, during a free period, the computer teacher went through the browsing history of the machines as he was required to do, and he reported Jonah for looking up how to build bombs. The private academy had a zero-tolerance policy, and like that, there was no more scholarship money.

Jonah waited for his e-mail to load. Behind him, the group watching the video groaned. The girl said, "Nasty."

Jonah scanned the subject lines of his e-mail. Advertisements, potential viruses. Nothing yet from Luz.

3

THE FLOODLIGHTS GLARED ON THE COURT. THE STUDENTS SAT and bickered and laughed. Some watched the game, but most did not. They had cigarettes or sweet cigarillos tucked behind ears and plastic flasks tucked into pockets, and some concealed pistols tucked into waistbands. Metal cradled warmly to skin. Some students feared for themselves because of lingering arguments or past drama. Many stoked anger in their hearts. Anger that he or she folded into rage for something larger and impossible to name, harbored in deep, secret places. And here they all were, hot and irritable and packed together on the gym bleachers, but where else could they be? The fans caged high in the walls spun, drawing the heat from the court and expelling it out into the night, but the temperature never seemed to drop. From where he sat, Jonah watched the fan blades spin and thought that something was always being lost but nothing ever changed.

Jonah lowered his eyes to the game just as an opposing player stripped the ball from Colby, took it coast to coast, and tomahawk jammed it. This was the final game of the season and they were down by thirty points in the third quarter. It was typical.

Jonah took his cell from his pocket. No missed calls, no new text messages. He tapped his foot nervously, and the game played on before him without registering. He thought of her crying, saying something in Spanish to him that he couldn't understand. He needed to hear her voice.

He was sitting dumbly when the students around him began to shout, to grapple, to climb over one another. There was a lot of noise. Jonah reacted like a man coming out of sleep. He turned his head and a knee caught him across the jaw, clacked his teeth, woke him up. He recognized the gunfire now. He stood and joined the flood, tumbling, clawing down the bleachers. Two more reports cracked and crackled back. The mob pushed, crushing, sweeping the players away and the game with them. Rubber soles shrieked against the court. Jonah was lifted and moved, pressed between bodies.

He couldn't breathe. The mob swelled toward the doors.

He caught a glimpse of the corner, where the police liaisons were pinning someone to the court. Another kid was on his side, walking himself around his shoulder, smearing a pinwheel of blood through the glare of the floodlights. Jonah raked at someone's collar to stay on his feet and lost sight of the wounded kid. Then he was bundled through the gym doors into a night that felt suddenly much cooler.

NOPD cars, lights bursting in blue pulses, soon tore into view and barricaded the lot. People yelled, shoving one another. Others embraced, weeping. It took Jonah a long while to find Colby.

His friend wore a T-shirt pulled over his basketball jersey. The flashing lights beat in the sweat on Colby's face, making him look cold.

"Fuck was that?" Jonah asked.

Colby was shaking his head.

"What?"

"That was Davonte, man. Dude came in to get Davonte."

Jonah looked at the gym doors, as if there might be more to see. He imagined Davonte restless, needing to get out of the house. This was the first time anyone would have seen him in two weeks. Maybe someone had sent a text saying, Davonte's here at the game. Jesus. Jonah put his arm around Colby.

They were held in the lot until the ambulance left. Whispers through the crowd that Davonte wasn't dead, shot through the arm. Nobody else caught a bullet. Lucky.

"You know," Colby whispered to Jonah, "Davonte and me, we sell for the same crew."

Jonah looked at him. "What?"

"Same crew, same dude." Colby glanced around the lot, seeming suddenly fearful. He mopped his face with his shirt. "Let's get outta here, Mickey-Bee."

4

COLBY NAVIGATED THEM TO A NEARBY BAR THAT HE CLAIMED they could get into. A residential block. Shrubs with leaves like green elephant ears flourished in the gaps between the shotguns. The power lines bellied, tangled, out of the sky, cables buzzing. A jukebox pumped from within the corner bar, a narrow structure of sand-colored brick and blue stucco. As Jonah and Colby rounded the corner, though, a security cop in a black uniform regarded them from a folding chair next to the entrance. He nudged his glasses higher onto his nose and thrust his chin at their school's logo on Colby's shorts.

"Kidding me, right?"

"How long they had you for?" Colby asked.

"Few months."

"How come?"

"Somebody get stabbed inside, somebody gonna take note." He removed his glasses, breathed on the lenses, and buffed them. "Well, sometime they do."

"We could slide by?"

The man put his glasses back on, smiled, shook his head.

Jonah grabbed Colby by the arm and pulled him away. "Y'all be good," the cop called.

Back in the truck, the starter clicked. Nothing. Dead battery.

Colby went, "This piece of shit."

"Let me know when you get a car, all right?"

There had been a day when they'd gone cruising, no plan. They ended up in the East, lifting over the industrial canal on the high rise, driving toward the abandoned Six Flags. They parked in the desolate lot and sat a while on the hood, watching the roller coaster rails where they arched from the tall grasses like vertebrae. Colby suddenly turned to Jonah and asked if he could teach him to drive. And so they made circles around that big empty lot, Colby starting and stopping, whooping and laughing, and eventually he did get it, driving smoothly, tires bouncing over the bubbled tarmac. When he braked and levered the truck into park, he turned to Jonah, smiling and out of breath as if he'd run instead of driven. There was no one else around in that desolate place. They felt the absence of stricture and perception. They were two friends, and that was all that mattered.

But now the truck wouldn't start and so they walked out to the grass bank of the bayou where it split the neighborhood in a gentle curve. Jonah paused when they came even with a bright corner store. The air smelled like fried chicken and spilled gasoline.

"Come on," Jonah said. "Gonna cheer you up."

He instructed Colby to walk around where the cashier could see him. They went in, and the tall aisles obstructed Jonah from view while he removed a couple of tall boys from the drink coolers in the back and stuck them inside his shirt. Then he walked back down the aisle and out the door. He crossed the street and waited by the water, and when Colby joined him he tossed him a beer.

They sat on a set of crumbling steps that led down to a swamped canoe. A breeze stirred and died, the faint odor of rotten sea life. A fish the color of the moon leaped and splashed, leaped and splashed. Mullet, Jonah thought. He took out his cell phone and stared into the darkened window.

"You worried, huh?"

Jonah didn't need to answer.

"Phones don't work in Mexico," Colby said.

Jonah scoffed. "If phones work in this broke-ass city, they work in Mexico."

"Shit," Colby agreed, drinking to it.

"Told you her pops got pistol-whipped?"

"Say what?"

"That's why she went. They were arguing and he went for a walk and came back all bloody. Mugged. She couldn't say no anymore."

"Mexicans get paid cash, yo. People know it." Colby hawked and spit into the bayou. "He okay?"

Jonah shrugged. "I don't think it's the first time it's happened."

"Something I don't get," Colby said. "If the kid is born in America, it would be an American, right?"

"It?"

Colby waved his hand. "She."

"She." The word hung in the air over the water.

"Boy, then."

"A son."

"Whatever, man. You see what I'm saying, though? American grandbaby ought to appeal to her pops."

Jonah flicked the tab on his beer can with a thumbnail. "They can barely afford to stay here together, how could they afford a kid, too?"

"That's where you come in, Mickey-Bee."

"Well. That ain't how her old man sees it."

Colby belched and crushed the empty and tossed it into the canoe.

"Here." Jonah held out his untouched beer.

"Yeah?"

"Yeah."

A dark shape scurried along the cement embankment on the bayou's far side. The nutria stopped and sniffed and moved on, dragging its long ratlike tail.

Jonah elbowed Colby. "Check it out."

"Sick."

"They all right."

"Big-ass water rats. That's all." Colby set his beer down and raised an imaginary rifle. He bumped his eyebrows at Jonah. "My turn, right?"

Jonah slipped into their practiced charade, hefting his own rifle. It was easy, this pretending for his friend. "What you smoking? You got the last one."

"You must be crazy. You shot the last three Talibans in a row."

Jonah stayed Colby's rifle with a hand. "Man, I thought we was a team. How's that if you the one shooting everybody?"

Across the way, the nutria flopped into the bayou waters.

"There you go," Colby said, beginning to chuckle. "Another one got away." He sipped his beer and sighed. "This time next year you'll have enough money to bring her and y'all's baby back." He paused. "And I gotta tell you, it'll be good to have Luz back. I miss that sweet ass."

Jonah laughed.

"An ass that could launch a thousand ships."

"Where'd you get that one?"

"I don't know."

5

ON THEIR WAY HOME AN OLD MAN SPOKE TO THEM WITH A damaged voice. He sat on his step with his elbows on his knees, offering a metal thermos. "Hey, kid, you wanna pop?"

Colby replied, "What you got?"

"The good shit."

"Don't," Jonah said.

But Colby grabbed the thermos and swigged from it. He coughed, spitting out what he could. "Fuck is that?"

The old man swiped the thermos back. "Finest mouthwash money can buy." He took a long pull and cried, "Yessir!"

The old man's laughter chased them down the street. "Stupid ass," Jonah said.

"I mean, mouthwash."

"I told you."

A car roared through the intersection, stereo pumping. The sound like quick jabs to the breastbone. Colby tensed next to Jonah, but the car was already gone, bass beat dissolving to nothing.

"You okay?"

"Yeah," Colby said. "Thinking about Davonte."

Jonah gripped Colby's shoulder. "Come on." Sirens blipped and faded out there. Colby wasn't speaking, so Jonah decided to broach it. "Dude don't play."

"Huh?"

"Dude you sell for."

"Oh. No. He don't."

They passed through the Central Business District and into their neighborhood, walking again along the cemetery wall. A tugboat's whistle soaked through the air, mournful. The street ran through several stoplights to end at the river levee a mile farther, and the lights of a gigantic cruise ship slid past the neighborhood's canopy like a mobile, fantastic city.

"It was my brother got me into it," Colby said. "I ever tell you that?"

"No."

"Yeah. Jamal."

"Your brother made you start selling?"

"No, that ain't what I mean. Jamal, see, he got sent away after the storm. He's got some years left still. He older than me. Anyway, it's the crew he worked for. They came around after that. Wanted to help out, take care of me. A lot of history there, ya heard? Has something to do with why I can't take you up on all your mechanic offers and shit. I mean, the money is there, too, but, you know. Complicated, like I said."

Jonah didn't know what to say. All the inaccessible world, it enraged him. But at this moment an opportunity unfolded. It was clear: "We should visit Luz."

"Ha," Colby coughed. "We should."

"I'm serious. I mean, let's just go."

Colby glanced at him. "You saying this just because she ain't called you yet."

"No. Maybe. But I mean it. We could drive and be in Mexico in no time, man."

Colby waved his hand. "We gonna fix this, Mickey-Bee. Need to be patient."

"I know, I know," Jonah said. "We'll be fucking saluting people before you know it. But life is about to pick up and move on, you know what I mean?"

Colby scratched his chin. "An adventure before the adventure, huh."

"Yeah." Jonah bobbed his shoulders. "And it'll be good to get you away from all this bullshit for a while, right? Just get out of town."

Jonah liked the idea that he could do something about what had happened to him, that someone had been taken away but for once was not lost. He promised himself, right then, that once he got the first US Army bonus check he'd bring Luz and the baby back to America. But first he could visit—he could prove something to himself and to her. He could show her that coming back to be with him was the right and best thing to do. Here was promise. Here was purpose.

Colby looked like he was thinking it over. It would be good for him, too, Jonah thought. For Colby to get out of New Orleans and away from the daily grind in which he took part. They'd come back soon enough, and school wouldn't have missed them. They would still graduate and enlist.

"Shit," Colby said. He laughed with something like relief. "Let's do it."

When Jonah got home and passed through the ghosts of the house, he felt buoyed by the decision. As if he had already begun to alter the shape of his own reality. He found some old road maps in a drawer, hunched beneath the lamp in the kitchen, and traced their route with a marker after he searched it out on the Internet. He saw a link to an article or two about drug-related violence in Mexico, but he hadn't seen it much in the news before and didn't linger on it. After all, whatever was happening in Mexico couldn't be any worse than what they saw every day. No one was surprised by a shooting at a basketball game, for God's sake. He had Luz's grandmother's address in Las Monarcas. He'd need a new map of Mexico. He felt good. He looked at the border. Others had made this journey, many others. But this would be for his reasons, his purpose, and that would make his crossing different. He believed it. And in making the crossing himself, he might learn something about Luz, something that might bring them closer. He could understand her in a new and essential way.

6

THEY HASHED OUT A FEW MORE DETAILS AT SCHOOL THE NEXT day, but before anything else could happen Jonah needed to retrieve his truck with the dead battery from Mid-City. He rode the streetcar out in the afternoon and gave the ignition a few futile tries before an older man with skin the color of pecans appeared in the window and asked him if he needed a jump.

"That'd be great."

The man removed his tattered baseball cap and gestured at the corner bar Colby had wanted to visit the night before. "Time for a beer first?"

"I dunno, I'm kind of in a hurr—"

"Quick beer," the man said, already turning and beckoning. He smiled, revealing a gap between his front teeth. "Everybody got time for that."

The man's name was Gil, and his hand was large and rough when they shook. A rooster stalked along the serrated top of a wooden gate next to the bar. It hopped to the ground and strutted, pecked at something in the grit.

"Lookit that thing," Gil said. "You know, the feral chickens go around screwing the pigeons."

"Yeah?"

"Yeah," Gil answered, busting up into laughter. "Making a bunch of chigeons."

Gil rang the bell at the door and the bartender, a pretty blonde, buzzed them in. Small candles flickered on the bar top and on the tables arranged against the wall, and the lamps suspended from the ceiling were the same color as the candle flames. Paintings of vintage nudes hung on the walls. Cigarette smoke slithered, and the video poker machines in the back of the room jingled in the lull between jukebox tracks.

They sat at the bar and Gil asked Jonah if he was picky. Jonah shook his head. The bartender brought them beers in cold cans, and Gil said, "Couple roll-a-days, too. The young man feels lucky to me."

The bartender retrieved a plastic cup, rattling the dice inside it. "Who's first?"

To Gil, Jonah said, "Show me how it's done."

"What's the pot up to?"

The bartender scanned a page in a lined notebook. "Twenty-one hundred."

Gil whistled. "Five of a kind wins the pot. Easy as pie."

He lifted the cup and slammed it, opening side down, as if no outcome would surprise him. He lifted the cup again, and the dice gave him a mix of numbers. "That's that."

The bartender slid the cup to Jonah, wrote his name in the ledger, and winked.

Jonah allowed himself a quick, silent wish before slamming the cup down.

I could visit her again, at the very least. Maybe stay for a little while longer.

He lifted the cup. Four threes and a one.

"Roll again!" the bartender said. "Four of a kind gets you another."

Gil slapped Jonah on the back. "Think good thoughts, young man."

Jonah gathered the dice, shook the cup, and flipped it over.

"Hey!" Gil cried. Jonah had again rolled four of a kind. "Hey, now!"

The jukebox switched tracks and Jonah could hear his heart in his temples. Something was happening. He flipped the cup.

Two pair and a solo.

The bartender swept the dice away. "Sorry, babe," she offered.

"Still," Gil said. "Damn lucky. Should take you to the track with me. Drink up."

Gil paid for the beers and the dice rolls. Jonah thanked him, and then Gil said, "Woulda been enough for a new car battery and then some, eh?"

Jonah shrugged. He'd steal a new battery from work. "What would you do with the money, Mr. Gil?"

Gil looked at him sidelong. "Well. Let's see." He lit a cigarette and exhaled smoke. "Suppose I'd like to put it toward a bike. Had my eye on a '69 Triumph some cat down the road's selling. But . . ." He paused and laughed, a rich sound. "Probably I'd tell my wife we won some money and we'd take a vacation. Then we'd come home and I still wouldn't have that bike."

"I'd use it. I'm taking a trip."

"Where to?"

"Mexico."

"Old Mexico way, huh?"

"Well. I got a girl."

"So you know what I mean, then." Smoke trailed from his smile.

"She lives in Mexico."

"I see."

"Yeah."

Gil nodded thoughtfully. He exhaled. "Since forever, men been doing stupid things for the women they love." He sipped his beer and set the bottle down on the bar, and then he placed his palms flat on the bar top and stared at his hands. "But if there be a worthier cause for foolish action, I don't know it." He lifted his beer again and drained it. "Come on. Get you jumped."

Dark had fallen. The rooster regarded them from his fence. They got Jonah's Ford started and shook hands.

"Ride that good luck of yours a while yet," Gil offered. "Take care, young man."

7

JONAH LEFT THE TRUCK RUNNING AT THE CURB AND WENT UP THE couple of steps to the Hidalgos' front door. He knocked and waited. Knocked again.

"You."

There was her father returning home, swaying down the sidewalk with his friend. They were leaning on each other. Mr. Hidalgo's face was drawn, leathery. Gray flecked his hair. His hands had always seemed huge. He had a black eye. Jonah thought of the way he'd once looked at him, when he'd stopped playing the guitar and dragged Luz inside.

"You," he said again.

"Can I talk to you, Mr. Hidalgo?"

The men staggered forward, one at a time grasping the railing and climbing the steps. They listed around Jonah.

"Please," Jonah said. "I just want to know she got home okay."

"Is all your fault," her father said, and he unlocked the door and went in, followed by his friend.

Jonah glimpsed the futon and small television with rabbit ears. Jonah got the toe of his boot in the door before it shut, and the friend turned, face reddening, saying something in Spanish.

"Please," Jonah called.

Her father returned, pushed his friend aside, and caught himself with a hand on either side of the doorframe. "This is no place for her." Sweat slid down his face, and now Jonah spotted the purpled cut running through her father's eyebrow, where he'd been pistol-whipped. Jonah could smell the booze, too, just like he'd been able to smell it with his own father.

"Mr. Hidalgo—"

"This is no place for a baby." He slapped his chest. "For my grand-child."

"You mean my kid."

The man stared for a breath, then he grunted and lunged. Jonah sidestepped, and her father stumbled against the railing, reeled around, and lost his balance. He fell down the few steps and landed on the concrete. The friend was shouting at Jonah, and Jonah jumped down to try to help her father up, but the man slapped Jonah's arm away and sat. He waved a hand to shut up his friend and braced himself, palms on concrete.

"I haven't heard from her," Jonah said. "Tell me, please."

Her father sighed and labored to his feet. "I don't want to talk to you about Luz."

"I wanted to keep her here," Jonah went on, his voice cracking. "I woulda took care of her."

"You cannot do this," he said, as he climbed the steps. "You do not understand."

"Yeah. But you coulda helped me to."

Jonah pivoted and got into his truck, and he floored it away. Through his anger, the question glared. Why hadn't Luz called him?

He called Colby from his cell: "I'm leaving tomorrow. You in?"

IV

I'm not from anywhere.

1

THE AIRPLANE TOUCHED DOWN IN MONTERREY, A CITY LUZ had never visited. She disembarked onto the tarmac and followed the crowd toward the terminal. Heat danced over the runway. Already the air tasted different.

Her father had called his mother in Las Monarcas, and Luz had spoken with her. Her grandmother would expect her home this evening. We will take care of everything, her grandmother said. But all Luz could think of was the last time she had seen her abuela, the night Luz's uncle took her away, bound for El Norte. She ended up crossing the river in the dark, early hours. There was a group of them—they'd waited in the willows for the coyote, and her uncle put her on an inner tube in the water and held on, trudging and then swimming alongside her and guiding her as the water pulled at them. Today was the first time she'd ever been on an airplane, and she had boarded, relieved that she'd been passed through security. She'd flown with her forehead pressed to the porthole glass, watching the earth turn far below. She sought the border, but from her vantage tens of thousands of feet above the ground she couldn't even locate the river.

Her father had reserved a taxi service for her online. In the loop she found the apple-red sedan with the company name stenciled across its doors. The driver was a young man with a toothpick in his mouth and an oxford shirt open at the throat. He loaded her bag into the trunk and hustled her into the car. An old woman was already sitting in the backseat. A man with white hair sat up front, wringing his hands. The elders would be dropped off in Monclova en route to Las Monarcas, the driver explained.

He drove fast, shouting into a cell phone. The cab rocked and pitched, and it was hot inside, in the roiling stink of the driver's cologne. Luz was queasy. To the south, the mountains cut the haze like colossal incisors. The old woman grinned at Luz, eyes sunk in her creased face. Luz dozed and dreamed of her mother, her eyes that changed in a flash when she scowled. The look reminded Luz of warrior ancestors.

2

SHE WOKE TO THE WOMAN DRUBBING HER SHOULDER WITH A clawed hand. The woman's wrinkles deepened. Her Spanish was slow, careful: "You are very beautiful."

Luz was sweating and her heart pounded. The highway carved through a fin of rock. Lime-colored lechuguilla bristled on the shoulder. Luz needed a moment to gather her bearings, to remember where she was. Her father's bloody face, his eyes blinking at her, the lids slick and red. The guilt surging. The cab banked and leveled out along the scorched scrubland, and Luz breathed deeply to settle her stomach. Power lines swooped in and out of view, strung along wooden telephone poles. A green ridge arched on the horizon. Luz did not know how long she'd slept. Was she almost home? Home. The word tolled in her skull. The place she had left behind forever.

The old man labored to pivot and peer at Luz over the headrest. Toothless, his gullet bounced as though he was gumming something. "Yes," he said, "you are beautiful."

He was old, but still something hungry glimmered in his eyes. Early on, boys at the school in New Orleans had looked at Luz and suggested nasty things, well within earshot; she was a new body to them. And even after she faded again into near invisibility, from time to time she'd catch a boy leering at her in the hallway. Men had looked at her this way for a long time, and she had noticed it even before she was able to explicitly define what that look meant. She had noticed it when she was crossing into America. After the river they were walking, and her uncle gave her a plastic jug of water to bear. This is your water. Yours alone. And she sat on the ground during a midnight break, cradling the water in her lap and watching the heavens, stars as distant as her own destination, as different. Word came back that it was time to walk again, and they trudged forward, the dry land winnowing individuals away. There were the men all around her, watching her. She carried the jug of water and the men watched, and Luz saw that it was not simply thirst glowering in their eyes.

3

THE TAXI ENTERED A SMALL TOWN AS DARK CAME ON. Streetlamps spilled in a pallor across gas stations and boxy truck-stop restaurants. The driver paused his cell phone conversation and said they were not far from Monclova now. Las Monarcas next.

They rounded a bend, slowed with the mild traffic, and then came to a stop. Behind them a large truck with a covered bed honked. Luz jumped, took a deep breath, and placed a hand on her stomach. Her belly was as flat as ever.

The old man still watched her over the headrest, gullet bouncing. Luz turned her eyes to the row of businesses and noticed a red graffito like a fresh cut alongside the open-air entrance of a café. The painted symbol consisted of a large letter *C* with a slash through it, resembling the sign for American cents. Faces in the dimly lit café lifted from their coffees. Pale and sad-faced phantoms. A shiver passed through Luz.

The woman nudged her, and Luz realized that the old woman had been speaking. "Excuse me?"

"I said"—the woman dropped her eyes to Luz's hand, still pressed to her belly—"you have received good news. You have, yes?"

A lance of cold shock. The old man's mouth sagged as he looked at the woman and then at Luz and then at the woman again.

"I am a midwife my whole life," the woman continued. "I sense these things."

Luz's mouth went dry. Would others sense her pregnancy now, too? She cared little for what others might think, but would her grandmother care? The vantage into her future constricted to a keyhole. Options peeled away like wood shavings, and she imagined not leaving her grandmother's apartment for months. She put herself back in Jonah's bed that night she'd told him. His quiet acceptance, his promise for their future together. Would he still mean it? Would she still want it? Right now she did. Right now she needed to be out of this cab. To be back there with him. She needed to hear his voice, to hear his promise.

The woman watched her, eyes glittering, waiting for some response. The cab started and stopped. The truck behind them honked again. The woman waved her hand and opened her mouth to speak, but it was as if this was some kind of signal: an angry buzz skewered the taxi, and with it Luz's eardrums depressed and the air inside the cab ballooned. Her cheeks pulled out from her face while pressure jabbed her sternum. The woman's skull snapped backward and unzipped itself onto the head-rest, and the rear windshield shattered. The old woman's corpse slumped against the safety belt.

The driver dropped his phone and clamped a hand to his throat. Blood spurted from between his fingers, spraying across the windshield and the spiderweb-like bullet holes in the glass. The old man opened his toothless mouth and screamed. The engine revved and the taxi leaped from its standstill, tearing through the back corner of the car ahead. Luz was a pair of eyes atop something formless, bolted into the seat. A white-hot silence filled her. No thought or feeling or sound.

A car speeding in the other direction clipped them. The world yawed, and the cab slammed into an aluminum billboard. The windows atomized. The cab came through the billboard and the ground fell away and night sky swung around the vehicle. Luz's stomach bottomed out, and then the cab crashed sidelong into the roadside ditch. The seatbelt punched the wind from her lungs. Sound surged back, the complex weaving of it—gunfire, sporadic reports linking into an automatic rip.

Luz hung suspended in the higher side of the car. The air tasted like motor oil. The old woman lay dead in drainage water and window glass, and the old man had disappeared entirely. The cab's engine continued to climb. The wheels droned, chewed up sludge. The driver seemed to be reaching for something, but he jerked and died and his foot fell from the gas pedal and the revving ceased. The air and all the rest shimmered. Luz wondered if she was dying, too. But now everything cleared again. Sharp. Her bruised sternum ached. And for the first time in such a way Luz thought of the future growing inside her. She thought: We are alive.

4

THE STREET HAD EMPTIED OF BYSTANDERS. TIRES SQUEALED.
Someone was wailing. A man strolled out from a doorway into the
yellow glow of the streetlight. He held a large silver blade at his side.
People watched from where they huddled in the café. They recognized
him and would spread the word. The big truck with the covered bed
had run itself into a wooden telephone pole. Car alarms bleated. One
of his men, with an AK-47—el cuerno de chivo—slung across his back,
pulled the deceased passengers from the truck. A pickup sped into view
and braked, and men got out. They carried an assortment of weapons.
One of them slashed the tie-downs over the big truck's flatbed, and the
men began loading the plastic-wrapped parcels into the pickup. They did
not rush, but they did not lag, either. The municipal police would wait
until the scene cleared, and the federales were occupied elsewhere. The
man with the silver blade squatted over one of the dead men, pinched the
corpse's lips together, and sliced a diagonal through them. This was the
moment Luz came upon as she crawled out of the ditch.

The mud had soaked through her jeans, plastered itself to her forearms and hands. It was cold, but the sensation seemed to exist at a great
distance from her. The yellow globes of streetlight were haloed, as seen
through water, and she looked at her mud-slathered hands and felt un-
troubled. She glanced at the cab behind and beneath her, thought of her
bag in the trunk, her things. The old woman dead in the backseat. Luz
shut her eyes against a ringing that came from deep within her own head.
When she opened them again she saw a man hunched over a body in the
street. He did something to the corpse's face and then he noticed Luz.

In a flash he pulled a pistol from his belt. He glared at her for a
moment and Luz's hands rose. The man cocked his head and lowered his
arm, and he began to walk toward her. A little urgent voice was babbling
at the bottom of her mind, but her legs were too heavy to move. In the
man's other hand he held the large knife, a red blade.

His skin was the color of the mud and his black hair was smooth, combed against his skull. He might have been handsome but for the scar that began at the corner of his eye and slanted around his nose and through his lips to his jawline. He grinned, and the pale cicatrix stood out like an ineffective suture. He gestured, and two of the men working on unloading the parcels from the truck stopped and came toward her.

They wrenched her arms around her back. When she felt the coarse twine brush against her wrists, hot adrenaline finally bolted through her limbs.

As with the sound of the starting gun, she broke low into her sprint. She made three strides—not even enough time for her ghost runner to spring to life—before something hard clipped her across the space above her ear. She fell. Stars hailed. A spasm of thought—This is what it felt like, Papá?—crushed into the void growing in the center of her skull.

They held her down as they bound her wrists at the small of her back, yanking hard so that the bones bit into one another, and then they hauled her to her feet. The man with the scar was still grinning, shaking his head. Luz tried to speak. Words wouldn't come, and with the misfire, pain sparked in her head. The man with the scar had an olive-green bandanna around his throat. He sheathed his knife, shoved his pistol into his waistband, and untied the bandanna. He tossed it to one of the others, who whipped it into a blindfold and dropped it over Luz's eyes. It was damp and rank.

They dragged her, blind and stumbling, and someone lifted her and deposited her onto a solid, ridged surface. She scrunched like an inchworm to her knees, and her cheek slammed back to the surface, a boot in her back. An engine started, vibrating in her teeth, and she slid a little as the truck kicked into gear. They held her down against the bed, and every bounce of the truck knocked through her vertebrae.

5

BY THE TIME THE TRUCK PARKED SHE WAS EXHAUSTED, BATtered like a sheet of aluminum. The blindfold ripped free when they dragged her from the truck, her cheek scraping along the bed. There was an adobe house and a dirt yard, cast in a weak orange glow from a solitary lamp on the corner of the building. Outside that, the dark pressed in. This was all she could see before they deposited her onto the tile floor of a small shed.

Walls of corrugated tin spotted with rust. The men unloaded the rectangular packages from the truck and stacked them against the walls around her. She was lying on her back, her own bound fists punching into her tailbone. The ligaments across the front of her shoulders howled.

A man entered and shut the door behind him. Near-total darkness. He smelled of sweat and liquor in the tight space. He sighed, then hunched and clamped his hand to her thigh, fingers digging into her quadriceps. Luz writhed and rolled and kicked. The man let go and backed off, laughing quietly. "Calm down, girl." A voice like water dripping in a cave.

Luz lay there, crushing her own fists, heaving with breath. Her heart jumped against the floor. The fingers squeezing into her muscle had revealed her absolute exposure. She had nowhere to go, nowhere to run. She watched his shadow and anticipated his falling to her. She tried to time her kick. Tried to ignore the feeling of defeat that already clamored. The finish line approached, her ghost runner led.

The man squatted on his heels, exhaled. "I don't want what you think I want, but there are others here who would take it, and take it at my order. Behave yourself, okay?"

"Who are you?"

"Listen to me. Be calm. You won't be here more than a few days."

Hot water ran from her eyes. "Why are you doing this?"

"Oh." He reached out and brushed her cheek. She jerked her head away. "You might consider yourself lucky. When I saw you with your wet clothes shaped to you, I appreciated your form and thought you might fetch a good price. Otherwise I would have put a bullet through your eye."

He stood and stepped to the door and opened it. "Sleep well," he said. "I will see you in the morning." Then he went out. A chain rattled and clanked against the outside.

6

Luz was of course no stranger to despair, that incurable sickness cultivated in the lonely years before Jonah. It was despair from which her ghost runner sprang, but at this moment she encountered despair distilled to its essence: she was alone in the dark and there was no way out and there would be no way out. She coughed, choking on phlegm, and turned her head against the grit-strewn tile to breathe. What light leaked into the shed was hardly noticeable. It must have been very late. A wind rose, sand clinked against the tin. She missed Jonah. Even if she now bore a part of him within her, he himself was a world away. Still she fought her despair in the way she had learned to, remembering the sound of his heartbeat while they lay there, her body pressed to his. And if I can only match the beating of my heart to your own, we might become something different, something perfectly tuned, like Papá's guitar. We can be safe, if only for a little while.

She remembered, too, another one of those frequent evenings when her father took down the guitar and sat on the steps and played. His thick fingers drew forth the notes, and in the street a cat slunk through a cone of streetlight, and water burbled from around a manhole cover and flooded a corner of the asphalt. Luz sat next to him on the stoop, and the music thrummed through the neighborhood. A Honduran neighbor came out, bobbed his head. Luz sang the folk songs her mother had taught her and wondered, as she often did, whether her mother had once sat with her father, too, singing while he played. When they were young and in love, before Luz was born, maybe, and certainly before her father departed for El Norte. People passed and glanced, but when Luz sang they stopped to listen. There was something in her voice, and they stopped in a half-moon on the sidewalk, swaddling themselves in her voice. People of different ages and colors. A shirtless little boy stepped forward and danced, sneakers scuffing against the concrete. He danced until the streetlight gleamed on his skin. The others clapped. The boy took a bow.

Luz woke from the remembrance into searing pain. She could not feel her arms from the shoulders down, lying as she was, and the sharp stretching from her shoulders to her clavicles was acute, burning brightly in the dark. An ache spread from where her numb fists still punched into her tailbone, and she needed to pee. It was enough to make her cry out in the hot, stale air.

She arched her back into a bridge, heels and shoulders on the tile, slid her bound hands beyond her tailbone, and then pulled her ass down through the loop of her arms. The bones of her wrists ground together, a flicker from within her dead limbs. She pushed her arms and pulled her waist down and managed to get her wrists—sliding against her sweat-soaked clothes—to the crooks of her knees. She lay flat again, pulled her knees to her chest, slipped her arms around her sneakers, and rested her hands on her stomach.

She sat up, sensation prickling back. Pain jigged over her ear. She touched the raised cut where they'd hit her. Her skull throbbed and the room spun. Once the nausea passed she got to her feet and unbuttoned her jeans. She squatted in the corner, leaning against the stacked packages, and urinated on the floor. There was nothing else to do. She pulled up her pants and sat in the adjacent corner. She worked on the twine around her wrists with her teeth for a while but made no progress. She tasted her own blood where the bindings had rubbed her raw.

Somebody could have seen them take her, sure. Somebody in the street, or one of those ghostly faces in the café. But would they be on their way to rescue her? No. No, they probably wouldn't, Luz figured. She was alone. She rested her forehead on her knees and sighed. The tears in her eyes stung.

"Mamá," she prayed, "señora McBee."

7

LIGHT ROSE IN THE GAP BENEATH THE DOOR. HER EYELIDS WERE swollen. She hadn't slept. A rooster crowed outside. When they moved to New Orleans after the storm, she'd drifted with her father and Rodrigo from apartment to apartment, following the cheap rent, and in most neighborhoods someone had kept chickens. Roosters gone feral could be found everywhere. It was funny to see them strutting down the street.

She heard a door open and clack shut, and someone was whistling. Soon enough the chain rang against the far side of the door. The door squealed open. The flood of light was blinding, a rush of hot dry air. The man who ducked into the room was the one with the scar slashing across his face. He smiled, scar taut. The large knife hung from his belt in a leather sheath. He looked at the spot where she'd pissed but he didn't say anything. Neither did he mention Luz's hands, no longer behind her back.

He dropped to a knee in front of her and set down a plate and a tin cup, toast and water. She didn't move. He crossed his arms over his knee and watched her. His eyes were dark and darting. From time to time he tongued the furrow through his lips.

"I need you to eat."

Luz looked at the twine around her wrists, brown with blood, and didn't answer. It was the same voice, the man who had hovered over her and grabbed her thigh.

"You will eat or I will take it away. Here." He lifted the cup toward her. "Drink. It will be very hot in here today."

She was indeed thirsty and the cup was cold in her hands, and she drank the water in several gulps, throat aching. The man said, "Good."

"What's your name?" Luz asked. He cocked his head and Luz realized she'd spoken in English. She asked him again in Spanish.

"I am called Cicatriz," he said, tracing a finger along his scar. "That is all you need to know." His grin was curious, and he tried some clunky English: "Where you from?"

Luz shrugged. Cicatriz nudged the plate with the toast toward her. It made an unpleasant sound against the tiles. He tried again: "You are American?"

The question felt somehow absurd. "I'm not from anywhere."

The corner of his mouth twitched, and he returned to Spanish: "But you lived in America."

"Yes."

"And where were you going when we found you?"

"Home. Las Monarcas."

"Does your father have money?"

A bitter taste leaked into her mouth. She understood. "He is a laborer."

Cicatriz clucked with regret. He gestured toward some far-off place: "My father worked on a horse ranch. He did not own the ranch." He said it as if they should understand each other. A black and viscous loathing whipped in Luz's gut. She imagined she could kill him in that instant, if she were able, but then he drew his knife.

It was a silver-hilted thing with a leather grip. Symbols were etched into the blade, Chichimec designs perhaps, similar to the pictograms her grandmother branded into leather wares for resale at the Las Monarcas market. The symbols meant nothing more to her grandmother than business, and Luz didn't know their individual significance, either, but she had always associated them with her mother's stories.

"Do you like this?" Cicatriz asked, meaning the knife. "It is pretty, no? I got it when I worked for them—" With the knifepoint he tapped one of the plastic-wrapped packages. "When I was a sicario. Do you know that word?"

Luz shook her head.

"A," he said, trying in English, "hit man. That is how I mean?"

"They are a cartel?" She meant the people he'd stolen from.

Cicatriz hummed, returned to Spanish. "A group affiliated, more or less, with the Cártel del Golfo." He sat back and rested the knife across his lap. "I lived in Monterrey." He told her that as a sicario he had lived alone in a nice place they bought for him and he would wait for cell phone calls telling him whom he needed to kill, and then he and his team would kill them and get paid. He had killed many. "I cannot remember them all," he went on. He closed his eyes, seemingly in effort, shook his head: "Mere noise and shadow." He picked up the knife. "But this one," he said. "I remember his face. A rich man. A big house. I knocked on his door, and when he looked through the crack I shot him through the door with a shotgun. I went inside and shot him again." He told Luz that the man died right away, which was not as common as one might think. In the hallway behind the man was a glass case full of artifacts. The knife was there. "It was beautiful. I knew I needed it. I needed it and I took it and now it is mine." Cicatriz smiled, the white furrow rigid. "Anyway," he said, tapping the packages again, "your home, Las Monarcas, is their plaza. Eat your toast."

He stood, his boot heels rapping against the tile. Luz wasn't hungry.

Cicatriz patted the stack of parcels. "A good haul," he said. Nodding. With the knife he slit a package open and dipped his pinkie finger in, and then he held his fingernail to his nostril and snorted. He shivered. "I worked for them, now I rob them." His smile was brilliant. "I am a Robin Hood." He pointed with the knife and ordered her again to eat her toast.

Luz stood up. Her head was heavy and her limbs were loose, wobbly. Cicatriz was not much taller. She said, "I didn't know Robin Hood kidnapped women."

Cicatriz spun faster than she could react and he had her against the corrugated wall, a two-by-four crossbeam in the small of her back. The knife blade was to her throat and his other hand gripped her between her legs. His face was inches from her own and he squeezed, pushing into her groin. "I would," he breathed, rancid. "I would. Just to take you." The blade pressed against her larynx, threatened to puncture. Then he let go and backed away, and she collapsed, drawing herself into the corner.

His arms hung at his sides and he shook his head and seemed somehow disoriented. He sheathed his knife and picked up the plate and the cup, and he flung the bread from the plate onto the floor. "Eat your fucking toast," he said and walked out. The chain banged against the tin, and Luz pressed the heels of her palms to her eyes and cried.

8

LUZ LAY ON HER SIDE, SWEATING OUT ALL HER WATER AND watching the light under the door whiten. In the suffocating heat of the shed she slipped in and out of a half-delirious, choking slumber. The vehicles fired up and tore away, and she nodded unconscious and heard them return, men whooping and hollering. In her dream she fluttered along, one among many others on a never-ending journey, and she woke remembering a jog with Jonah. They ran from his house to City Park. He started off with too aggressive a pace and she urged him to take it easy, to run for the distance, but he couldn't seem to understand, and soon he was dragging, heaving for breath, saying he might throw up. She laughed and encouraged him, come on, come on, there's always a way through it, and eventually they reached the park. They were walking along the fenced gardens to cool down when a monarch butterfly slipped through the iron bars and wobbled across their path, and Jonah said, Look, and tried to catch it. Luz placed her hand on his arm to stop him. She understood the butterfly for the lost one that it was, a member of a larger migration somewhere out there. In her childhood she'd known clouds of monarchs, and her mother letting one land on her palm and passing it to Luz's own, and saying, They are here for you, my daughter, they are here for you, my Luz.

She was lying where she'd urinated, and she sat up, gasping. Her head ached, the shed smelled terrible. Every breath was like a dollop of something rotten. She remembered that butterfly. There was something important about it, something she could have shared with Jonah then but didn't. I should have, she thought.

Luz rested her head against the packages behind her. The light beneath the door softened as the day progressed. Men were coming to get her. She was to be sold. And what could she do? She remembered that night in the Quarter when she and Jonah were held up at gunpoint. Jonah's futile anger afterward. I shoulda done something, I shoulda done something. Luz had told him there was nothing he could have done, but she was in the dark, sweating against packages of cocaine, and she whispered to herself:

"You have to do something. You have to try."

She stood up. She leaned against a clear piece of wall and stretched her calves. If Cicatriz returned again, alone, perhaps she could surprise him by being on her feet. She reached for her toes, stretched her hamstrings, a good feeling ruined by the rush of blood to her head and the aching cut over her ear. If she could somehow get past him and get out of the shed, perhaps she could outrun him. She lunged to one side and then the other. She wouldn't be able to run full speed with her wrists bound, though. And if she did get past him and she did outrun him, where would she go? There was no way of telling what was out there.

She sat down again, woozy and wondering if she had a concussion. She'd never been hit in the head before. She thought of the fights at school. Her near invisibility in that place, the worlds she lived between. In New Orleans her thoughts began arriving in English, and though she had returned to Mexico her thoughts continued to arrive in English. She was still something different. The shed walls seemed to collapse on her and draw away, like the respiring of a black lung. She was hungry and thirsty and her mind raced. And underneath all of it still was her pregnancy and its claims.

Pain seared through her fingertips—she'd been nervously scratching at the mortar between the tiles in the floor. The grout, damp from her sweat and urine, had crumbled a bit. She scraped at it again and felt the hard edge of one of the floor tiles.

Her fingertips sang and it wasn't long before blood slicked the groove. She smelled the iron, saw Papá bloodied on the couch. How could she have said no to him? There had been no other option. The mortar came away in pebble-sized chunks. The nerves in her fingers howled. She worked her nails beneath the tile and pried until she thought she'd lose them, and then she scoured the mortar again, feeling her nails break. Water filled her eyes. She wedged her fingers beneath the tile and it popped loose, skittering off across the floor into the dark. When had it gotten dark?

Her pulse throbbed in her fingertips. She crawled, patting the ground until she found the tile. It was flat and hard edged, about the size of a saucer. She put it in her lap and scooted on her ass to sit alongside the door and wait.

9

LAUGHTER. A BURST OF MUSIC, A DOOR SLAMMING. SHE JERKED where she sat with her ear to the tin and stood, holding the tile at her waist. A pair of boots shifted and crunched in the grit outside. The chain rattled and clanged and then the door swung open, the orange glow of the yard. In came a flashlight, beam bursting and banishing the shadow from the back of the shed. Next came a clay bowl, some beans and rice. In stepped Cicatriz.

Luz swung from her shoes, putting all of her behind the tile, leading with its hard edge into the bridge of his nose. His face knocked the tile from her hands. She didn't feel a crunch, didn't feel an impact at all, but the food erupted from the bowl and he dropped in the doorway. She crashed into the wall with her momentum. His hands were to his face and he rocked on his shoulders, and she leaped over him into the yard.

A barren stretch of brown grass and dirt. A woodpile and a long-handled ax. Music pumped from the adobe house. Smoke shifted pale over the roof.

Cicatriz grabbed her ankle. He was rolling, trying to get up. Wet grunts coming through the black smudge of his face. Blood roped to the dust. Luz pivoted and kicked him, heel to ruined nose, and he flopped onto his back.

She picked up the flashlight. She saw the big knife on Cicatriz's hip, and while his hands were over his face she bent and drew the blade—heavy, awkward in her bound hands along with the flashlight—and she turned and sprinted to the back of the house. She slid along the wall and crouched beneath a windowsill.

They were listening to hip-hop inside. The smell of woodsmoke and roasting meat. She switched off the flashlight and peeked over the sill. Men sat at a table playing cards, firelight against the cards fanned in their hands.

A moan. Cicatriz rose to his knees. Luz took off, running, leveling the knife and the flashlight ahead of her.

The pickup and two Jeep Wranglers were parked next to the house. The Jeeps sat on tall off-road wheels, and their racks of roof lights bristled like the hackles of angry dogs. She sprinted from the sphere of light around the house, and the stars descended.

In the wash of moonlight, the desert filled with nebulous shapes. Scrub trees and agave and cacti, rushing out of the dark. A distant cordillera existed because the mountains themselves were not filled with stars. Her ghost runner sprang to life. Cold and growing. She felt she could hear him breathing, gaining on her. Run. Her legs were weak, her breath thin. She had grown out of shape and she was beat up.

She was perhaps three hundred meters from the house when she heard the vehicles roar to life, one after the other. She glanced, saw the manifold high beams, and felt her ghost runner brush past her face. Something like a brick—the paddle-shaped limb of a cactus tree—slammed into her shoulder and spun her. She hunched, pulling scorching breaths. The air tasted like blood. A heavy burning in her shoulder from the cactus. The vehicles climbed into gear, a sound fleet and menacing over the desert. Luz wedged the flashlight into the crutch between two limbs of the tree and flipped the switch on. Then she turned and ran in the opposite direction, parallel to the mountain range.

The vehicles angled toward the flashlight. When Luz stubbed her foot against a rock and fell, she rolled to avoid impaling herself on the knife. She retched, bile stringing from her lips. She wiped her mouth and got up and ran. Come on. Push.

Another fifty meters and she paused. The vehicles had converged on the flashlight, and shadowed figures moved through the high beams.

Luz scrambled on, bear-crawling up an outcrop of stone, shins banging against rock. The headlights swung like distant alien spotlights, but once she crested the stone they vanished from view. She gasped into dust. The air was suddenly cool, soaking into her skin. She dragged herself through a sandy wash and then down the bank of a dry arroyo and onto the parched bed.

She sat with her back against the embankment. Listening for engines, for voices. A deep, slow breath helped a little. She squeezed the handle of the knife between her knees, placed the twine around her wrists against the blade, and sawed up and down. Her bindings fell away and the air tickled her numb wrists. Somewhere, a creature yipped.

V

I never hear you say anything.

1

THE RESIDUE OF THE NIGHTTIME SLUGS GLEAMED LIKE VEINS OF quartz in the sidewalk as Jonah walked out to the truck. He had determined that they'd stop to see Dex at the camp, and as Jonah turned the ignition he contended with memory. He had truly been a little boy then. It was the day Dex had been booted from the high school basketball team. Bill was still alive, but war was suddenly imminent; they would see him maybe once more before he deployed, and that would be the final time they'd ever see him. Dex had been fighting at school. Now he'd been caught smoking pot in the school washroom, too, and it was more than likely that he'd be expelled. Dex and Pop were screaming at each other. Jonah stood by and watched the old man drop Dex, felt the thump of his brother's back against the floor. Dex ran out, and Jonah followed. Dex sat behind the wheel of the truck, blood trickling over his lip. The same truck Jonah now brought to rattling life. They drove to the camp, Jonah and his brother, and in the morning they boated out to a blind and hid with their shotguns. Jonah had shot a duck—the first of his life—and it crumpled and fell out of the fog, splashing dead in the water, and Dex had clapped him on the back. The words Dex had said branded themselves into some secret place and Jonah could still hear them: You crunched it!

Colby came out of his house with a gym bag under his arm and jogged to the truck. "She was still asleep," he said. "I left her a note."

"You okay with that?"

"Yeah."

"What'd you say to her?"

"That we was going on a road trip, I'd be back soon." Colby pulled a roll of rubber-banded bills from his pocket. He shrugged at Jonah's look. "We might as well use it for gas."

They lifted out of downtown on the interstate. The tall buildings and gigantic sun-drenched bulb of the Superdome. Next came the concrete suburbs, then soon enough the second-growth cypress swamp. Limbless trees, gray and dead looking. Far off, the spines of a chemical plant bristled. The massive bridge over the river assembled in the haze ahead, rising up and up out of the low-lying pastures. Colby remarked that the bridge was weird and scary out here in the country, without a city around it. At the apex they saw ships chugging upriver or unloading containers onto barges. The truck descended to sugarcane fields. The two-lane highway seemed unchanged. Jonah pulled off into a half gas station, half casino.

While he pumped gas he asked Colby if he'd ever been to a duck camp.

"Big-screen TV and sexy serving chicks, right?"

"You got it."

"What's your bro like?"

"Dex," Jonah said. "He's kinda tough, right. I mean, he lives alone in a swamp and makes his living hunting all year. Gator, duck, deer. Whatever."

"What he say about us coming?"

Jonah shrugged. "He doesn't know we are."

Driving again, Colby scrolled through radio stations. He settled on a zydeco channel and danced in the passenger seat. Jonah knew his friend was trying to make him laugh, so he laughed. Colby paused.

"You think Luz will be happy to see me?"

"Yeah." Jonah glanced at him. "Course she will."

"I mean, she won't be bummed it ain't you alone?"

"Nah, man. She loves you."

Jonah recalled Mardi Gras day. Luz must already have known she was pregnant. Colby had knocked down that coconut that was going to hit her, and then she had kissed him on the cheek. Jonah watched Colby place a hand along his face, as if to hold the feeling there. Jonah had waited for Colby to start teasing him, but his friend never said a word.

2

THE UNPAVED ROAD RAN PARALLEL TO A NARROW CHANNEL beyond which began the intricate mesh of waterways and spongy islands, shallows where speckled trout and redfish swam. Individual camps were built along the bank. Low structures of clapboard or vinyl siding stood on cinder-block piers or floated in the water on pontoons. Pickup trucks with steel gun cabinets in their beds were parked in the driveways.

The old McBee camp had new siding, and there was a satellite dish bolted to the roof. A shiny Dodge Ram was in the driveway. Jonah pulled the F-100 in and parked. His head felt light and he closed his eyes for a moment.

"You cool?" Colby asked.

"Yeah. Yeah. Let's go."

They shouldered their bags and knocked at the camp door, but nobody answered.

"Musta stepped out," Colby said.

"Out on the boat, maybe."

Around the back of the camp they sat on a bench butted up against the wall. A large nest rested in the upper tangle of a cypress tree across the channel. Jonah searched and found the eagle, circling in a thermal. He nudged Colby and pointed it out. Colby whistled. "Nice out here." He slapped at his forearm. "Except the mosquitoes."

"All you can do is ignore 'em."

A grass-and-weed lawn sloped down to the channel. There was a cleaning shed and a grill. A footpath furrowed the bank at the water's edge.

"We used to have a dog," Jonah said, "when I was a kid. A black Lab, you know, to retrieve the ducks. I'd race her up and down that path."

"What y'all call her?"

"Girl."

"Girl?"

"Yeah. When we got here, Girl would be so excited she'd jump out the truck and dive into the water. I was always scared a gator would get her." Jonah chuckled, shook his head. "Stupid."

After a moment Colby asked, "That how she die?"

"Old age. Couple years ago."

"Oh. You sure you good?"

Jonah nodded, and then he saw his big brother coming up the footpath.

A dog, a puppyish black Labrador, trotted at Dex's heels. Dex wore rubber muck boots and camouflage overalls and a long-sleeved thermal shirt. Brown hair spilled out from the back of his baseball cap, and his eyes glared within the telescoped bill. In one hand he carried a cooler and with the other a plastic grocery bag. A fabric rifle case was slung over his shoulder. He halted, briefly, when he noticed Jonah and Colby.

Before Dex was within earshot, Colby asked, "When you see him last?"

"Last year."

Dex neared. "Jonah. Hey, man."

"Hey, Dex."

Colby jumped to his feet, extended his hand, and introduced himself.

Dex set the cooler down and shook but didn't say anything.

The Lab bounded to Jonah and tried to bait him into a fight but settled for a scratch behind the ears. "What's his name?"

"Donald," Dex answered. "Donald the dog."

Jonah glanced at his brother. "Named him after Pop?"

Dex grinned quick, small. He cleared his throat and hefted the grocery bag, which was full of things that looked like long, withered carrots. "Gotta go turn these in."

Colby asked what they were.

"Nutria tails."

Colby's face went stricken.

"Lemme let y'all in," Dex said.

After the Dodge fired up and pulled out, Colby cried, "The fuck he got a bag of nutria tails for?"

"You get paid by the tail," Jonah said. "Five bucks apiece. Didn't know that?"

"People use them things for something?"

"Invasive species, man. State's got a bounty on them. Tails are proof."

"Five bucks," Colby said, "to touch one of them things?"

The interior of the camp had not changed much in the few years since Jonah had been there. A ratty couch and armchair, linoleum floor, wallpaper made to look like wood. Donald leaped onto the armchair and fell asleep. There was a new gun rack by the door, as well as a new coffee table with three picture frames propped on it. The first photo was the one of Jonah and his two brothers, the same one he had up at home. The second frame held two photos, cropped to fit. They were the shots of Jonah's father and mother, the duck blind and the river. Lydia, Jonah thought, and it felt strange to think his mother's name. He hadn't thought it in a long time, maybe. Colby tapped the third photo, a smiling blond woman before a pastel backdrop, and asked who she was, but Jonah had no idea.

When Dex returned, Donald woke and leaped from the couch. Dex patted the dog on the head, set his keys on the coffee table, and then went down the hall to change clothes.

Colby whispered, "Hey, do your bro like black people?"

"He's just quiet, man."

Dex returned in jeans and a T-shirt. He sat in the armchair. "So."

Jonah held up the picture of the blond woman. "Who's this?"

"My girlfriend. Sharon."

"You got a girlfriend?"

Dex nodded. "She's a nurse in Houma. Comes over here on the weekends."

"That's nice," Colby tried.

Jonah looked around the camp. "I haven't been here in a long time."

"I know it," Dex said.

"Surprised?"

Dex shrugged. "Come anytime you want. It's your camp, too."

Something twitched in the pit of Jonah's stomach as he stared down the uncompromising depth of history.

"School's not out yet, right?" Dex went to the fridge, retrieved a beer, and cranked the cap off.

Colby answered when Jonah didn't: "Long story."

"Huh." Dex sipped the beer. "I caught some nice specks today. Gonna grill 'em up. Jonah, come help me out back. Beers in the fridge, Colby."

The sun failed quickly. Dex flipped on the floodlight that cast an alley down to the water. Some creature's eyes gleamed and vanished with a splash.

Inside the shed, Dex removed three good-sized speckled trout from the cooler. Bodies curved and stiffening. The light of the lone bulb in the shed ran through their green-purple skin. He set them on a cutting board next to a long, thin-bladed knife. He hefted a bag of charcoal from the back of the shed and asked Jonah to fillet the fish while he got the grill going.

Jonah placed his hand around one of the cold bodies. His palm came away coated with fish slime. He looked at his brother.

Dex answered: "You'll remember how. Keep going."

Jonah worked the knife in behind the gills and sawed toward the tail.

Charcoal clinked against the grill bottom. "So, what's up?"

It felt funny to try to explain it to Dex, brother or not. "You're gonna think I'm crazy."

"That's all right."

Jonah pared the skin away from the fillet and flipped the fish over. "There's a girl."

"Okay."

"She's gonna have a baby."

Jonah waited for Dex to say something, but Dex didn't speak.

"My baby."

Dex kept quiet. The fish on the board was head and spine and guts and tail.

"She's Mexican. I mean, like, straight up from Mexico. Her pops sent her back when she told him she was pregnant. Anyway, " Jonah said as he bent to work on the next fish, "I'm on my way to Mexico."

"Mexico."

"Yeah." Jonah finished the fillet, dropped the knife, and turned toward Dex. "Gonna visit, but eventually"—and he felt his stomach seize with doubt as he said it aloud to his brother—"I'm gonna bring her and our kid back to the States. I got a plan."

Dex nodded slowly. Then he entered the shed and gathered the fish parts in both hands. "We'll wait a minute for the grill to heat up." He walked out, and Jonah followed.

When Dex tossed the scraps into the water, an enormous garfish emerged almost immediately, rolling over and snapping up the guts and then vanishing from view.

"Dex."

"I'm not gonna tell you what to do."

"I don't want you to."

"Good." Dex started for the camp but stopped. "What's her name?"

"Luz," Jonah said. "Her name is Luz Hidalgo."

"That's pretty," Dex said. And he went inside.

3

AFTER DINNER THE BOYS SET UP SLEEPING BAGS ON THE CAMP floor. Jonah dreamed of the footpath by the water, the path upon which he used to race to the dock and the flatboat. In his dream he walked the path alone in the night, feeling the living things around him. Trout hovered in the lightless, still water. Out through the marsh, blue crabs wandered into the crab pots or were lucky enough not to. The teal and the wigeon and the mallard huddled together, pulling their feet and necks into their bodies where they slept on patches of grass. And the nutria swam the dark surface of the water, leaving their silent wakes, propelling themselves toward food. The young ones followed and learned. A foreign species, doing what they do in a Louisiana swamp same as a South American swamp. The swish-swish of their claws was heard beneath the surface only, where in the dark and the deep a gator thrashed its tail and watched through clear eyelids those webbed claws kick. And if there was any understanding of this creature on the part of its prey, it was that this was the thing always there in the dark, always there in the deep.

4

THE PERCOLATING COFFEE ROUSED JONAH IN HIS SLEEPING BAG. He got up and sat on the couch with his elbows on his knees and waited for his mind to galvanize out of slumber. While Bill was deployed, Jonah used to stare at his shoes and see the duck-blind floor beneath them, or the boards of their back porch, or the grass, or the gravel. And he'd wonder what kind of ground was beneath Bill's boots in Afghanistan—he'd always imagined sand for some reason, but there was snow in the videos he'd looked up. He couldn't know. He thought he'd feel better if he could know, but there was a wall there he'd never be able to see through, and it made him want to scream. Now he thought of Luz, and what did she see beneath her sneakers? He pressed his thumbs into his eyes until he saw stars, and then he went to Dex's bedroom door and knocked.

Dex was slipping a shirt on over his tattooed chest. Jonah hadn't known that his brother had tattoos. Dex looked at him and pulled on his baseball cap. "Up early."

"Heard the coffee."

"Was trying to be quiet."

"I was wondering if we could go out with you today."

Dex sat and pulled on socks. "Huh?"

"Like, could we help and maybe you could give us a few bucks?"

"Oh." Dex stood and opened his palms. "Okay. Wake up your buddy. He lazy?"

"He's all right."

Jonah poured coffee and kicked Colby gently in his sleeping bag. Colby grunted and Jonah said, "Get up, dude. We're working today."

"I don't drink this shit," Colby said when Jonah handed him the mug.

"You'll do shots of mouthwash but won't touch this, that right?"

"Fuck you," Colby grunted and sipped the coffee.

They dressed and followed Dex and Donald the dog down the path. The mosquitoes could be felt but not seen this early. Dex carried the .22 in its case, and a satchel of other supplies. He had a cigarette in his mouth trailing smoke. A structure materialized in the shadow ahead. Jonah halted.

"Dex. Where's the dock."

Where the dock used to be—long and rickety, a tin overhang—stood a sheltered, narrow wharf and half a dozen plank jetties. Moored flatboats and pirogues.

"Washed away in Hurricane Gustav, year and a half back," Dex said. "All of us with camps out here ponied up the cash for this. Now they call it a landing." Dex sighed and flicked the cigarette into the water. "A landing."

Dex clomped to the family flatboat and Colby followed, but Jonah was rooted to the spot: Wake up, Little Dude. What Bill always called him. They raced down to the dock. Bill carried the fishing gear and he let Jonah win the race, and at the end of the dock Jonah came face-to-beak with a blue heron. Thing's taller than me, standing there. Small, fierce eyes. Bill came up and the heron turned and lurched over the water, rising through the fog with prehistoric wing strokes. Never seen a bird do something like that, Bill said. Like it wanted to be friends—Bill smiled—or maybe eat you.

5

DEX STEERED SLOWLY DOWN THE BAYOU, SWINGING THEM INTO a wider channel flanked by marsh grass. He said, "Hold on," and laid into the throttle, and the wind obliterated all sound except for the smack-smack-smack of the flat hull against the chop. Dex throttled back as the route became more tangled, overgrown.

Jonah arched and knuckled his lower back. "You should get a new boat."

Dex grunted and lit a cigarette while the sky went orange.

"Mickey-Bee," Colby said. He looked hungover and he was rubbing his back, and he slapped at a mosquito that landed on his neck. "I feel good enough to run through a brick wall, johnson first."

A quick snort of laughter escaped Dex. He glided the prow into a patch of spongy earth where the cane was yellow and trampled. A yard back from the water stood a wooden stake with a neon-pink ribbon tied around its top. Connected to the stake was a loop of wire, and caught in the snare was a nutria. Big as a beaver. Orange buckteeth and a long ratlike tail. The snare had one of its hind legs, and the creature scrabbled in the muck, straining for the water.

"Oh, no," Colby said, standing.

Dex smiled behind the glow of his cigarette. He hefted a wooden baseball bat from the deck and hopped onto the island.

"All right, Mr. Nutria," Dex said, and clubbed the rodent's skull. A dull clunk.

The thing toppled, one leg kicking. Dex undid the snare and lifted the nutria by its tail. He swung the heavy creature back once and heaved it into the boat, where it landed against the metal hull with a thud. Donald didn't even rise to sniff it.

Dex had snares all over the swamp. If the nutria were large enough to butcher he'd toss them into the boat. If they were too small he'd simply remove their tails with a cleaver and set the carcasses to float for the gators.

"All this shit out here looks the same," Colby said, waving at the green tangle along one bank. "How you remember where you got the traps?"

"Spend enough time out here and you'll remember, too." Dex pitched a cigarette butt overboard. "Give me a hand here any time you two feel like it."

At the next trap Jonah asked Colby if he wanted to handle it, and Colby's eyes grew wide. Jonah laughed, took the bat from his brother, and hopped onto land. His boots squelched an inch into the muck. The small nutria's claws churned up mud. Dex passed the cleaver down to Jonah.

Jonah raised the bat one-handed and brought the barrel down on the nutria's skull. He felt the connection in his fingertips, like a fastball cued off the end. The nutria toppled. Then it stood up again, rigid and staring. Brain-dead.

"Give him another," Dex said.

Jonah swung again, hard. Too hard. The animal collapsed, and there was a small spatter of gore on the bat's sweet spot. Dex nodded, once. Colby covered his eyes. Jonah bent, drew the warm tail taut, and lopped it off with the cleaver.

The day was still and hot when the boat entered a long manmade canal. A small outcrop of rusted machinery rose from the water. "Gauges and such," Dex said. "While back, a gas company dredged all through here, laying pipeline. Right underneath us. If you could see the swamp from above . . . It's all cut up." He chuckled. "Wonder if you could pop a few executives, turn in their suit tails for five bucks each."

Colby said he didn't get it.

"You saw how that grass was all dead where the nutria were at?" Dex asked. "They dig out the roots, and the land starts to wash away. Any time you chop up the land, a little bit more of the wetlands dissolve. That's what the bounty's all about, trying to control the damage they do." Dex motioned up and down the expansive canal. "I've never seen a water rat dig a trench this big, though."

"But ain't nobody gonna tell the gas company to stop," Colby said.

"You got it." Dex nodded. "Eighty or ninety years ago, some dumbasses imported the nutria from South America. You know, put 'em on farms, try to sell 'em. But who wants rat meat, rat fur? They let 'em all go." Dex smiled ruefully. "So I got a job now."

He shoved the throttle forward and a flock of snowy egrets launched from the forest in a single cascade.

The final trap of the day had been sprung, but the nutria had escaped.

"There," Colby said, pointing to a spot some seventy yards off through a stretch of dead cane. The nutria hunched at the edge of a seep, gnawing on something.

"Good eye," Dex answered.

He unzipped the .22 and put the rifle to his shoulder. He sighted from where he stood, cigarette dangling from the corner of his mouth. "Poor stupid fucker," he muttered. Fired. The report sieved through the swamp with a sound like the fluttering of wings, and the nutria flopped over.

Colby whistled. Jonah crossed the distance, trudging through the mud.

The nutria's limbs were outstretched, claws splayed. The round had entered just behind the shoulder, straight to the heart. Blood like dark water soaked through its coat. Jonah lifted it by the tail—had to be twenty-five, thirty pounds—and trekked back.

He leaned and held the creature out. "Take it, Colby. You ain't done shit."

Colby scrunched his face.

"Don't be a pussy." Jonah put a boot in the water, stretched. "Fucking grab it."

Colby reached over the water, short armed. He sighed and lowered his arm and shook it out, and then he leaned again, bracing himself with a hand against the edge of the hull. His fingers closed around the tail. When Jonah let go, Colby's hand fell, like he slipped or was surprised by the weight, and then he was in the water. Splashing, flailing, shouting. Not more than a foot deep. He was up and back in the boat almost quicker than he'd fallen out of it. He pitched the nutria two-handed like a basketball into the prow and said, "Fuck holy fuck!"

Jonah laughed, hands on his knees. Dex smiled around his cigarette.

"It ain't fuckin' funny!" Colby cried. "A gator coulda got me!"

6

THEY TIED UP AND CARRIED THE NUTRIA AND THEIR TAILS down the path. Colby dropped his load at the shed and made for the camp, a change of clothes, and the beer.

"I don't know how to clean these," Jonah said.

"That's all right," Dex told him. "I'll take care of it. Things smell terrible when you cut into 'em."

Inside, Colby stood in a pair of boxer shorts drinking a beer. Jonah told him to get some clothes on. After a while Dex brought strips of meat in on a plate and put a new case of beer into the refrigerator. He made chili with the nutria meat, and they ate and drank late in the quiet of the camp. Colby was drunk, talking. When he paused, Jonah spoke up, something on his mind.

"Dex, remember that night we came over here? When I was little?"

Dex stared into the neck of his beer.

"The night just me and you—"

"I remember."

Did Dex think of the way Pop hit him? Jonah remembered the thud of Dex's back against the floor. Jonah gestured at the frames on the table. "I'm glad there are some pictures in here now."

Dex smiled, slightly, without looking at him.

"Do you still believe what you told me that night?"

"I don't know. What did I say?"

Jonah picked at the label on his beer. They had been sitting in this very room. Earlier that same day, Jonah remembered, some boys at school had been talking about the country going to war, going after the terrorists. Jonah was worried about Bill having to go, potentially, and he wanted to talk with Dex about it. "You told me"—Jonah cleared his throat—"we only lose the things we care about, so it was better if we didn't talk about him or think about him or anything."

"I said all that?"

"Yeah." Jonah wanted to know if Dex still believed it. Luz was out there, and they were going to have a kid, and Jonah didn't know where she was or what she was doing, but he wanted to think about her, he wanted to talk about her.

"Hell." Dex drained his beer, got up. "I was only eighteen. I didn't know shit."

Jonah strangled his bottle. When he glanced at Dex, Dex looked away.

Dex returned with new beers and handed one to Colby: "You got any brothers or sisters?"

"I got a brother. Jamal."

"What's he do?"

Colby drank a lot of the beer quickly, set the bottle on the coffee table, and slid off the couch onto his sleeping bag. "Jamal been locked up in Angola for almost four years." He closed his eyes but continued to speak, voice faltering as he neared slumber. "Nobody used to mess with me. People were scared of Jamal, ya heard? Nobody fucked with me. But he gone now." His voice trailed off, and Jonah thought his friend had fallen asleep, but Colby spoke up again, smiling dimly. "I told people I knew kung fu. Ha. They didn't believe me. I don't. I don't know kung fu."

Colby's breathing evened out and there was silence in the room. Jonah got to his feet. "I'm going for a walk." He carried his beer out back and set off down the path.

He walked to the landing, and this newer and grander construction made him feel like a stranger to his own history. He sat in the old boat and drank. His eyes burned. He drained the beer and watched the moon rise and bore through the sky like a lode of silver, and he got up and hurled the beer bottle at it. The night swallowed up the bottle as soon as it left his hand. The glass spun somewhere out there until it splashed, a feeble sound.

"Hey." Dex appeared on the jetty alongside the flatboat. "I wonder if Jamal knows Uncle Dexter."

Pop's brother, the one for whom Dex was named, was also in the penitentiary. Their other uncle, for whom Jonah was named, had died long ago in Vietnam, and they only knew stories about him. Once, Jonah heard Mom tell Pop that it was a curse, so many boys in the family. Sometimes he figured his mother had been right.

Dex sipped his beer and stepped into the boat and sat across from Jonah. "Do you remember," he began, "that night Pop went looking for the guy who crashed into Mom?"

"What?" Jonah said. There was nothing there, an awful vacancy. "No."

"Yeah. Month, maybe two, after the funeral."

"I don't remember."

"Pop drank most a bottle of whiskey, then got in his truck. He'd found the man's address. I tried reminding him that the dude was in jail, me and Bill did. Pop was crazy, wouldn't listen. I kept thinking he was so drunk he'd kill someone looking for the guy who killed Mom and how the fuck would that ever make sense. Something like that never woulda dawned on Pop, I thought, so it made me hate him more—I could imagine it, see what I mean, and I was only fifteen years old. But then Pop didn't come home and we didn't know what the hell had happened. Me and you and Bill were alone all night. When Bill wasn't looking I tasted Pop's whiskey and about coughed my guts out."

"I didn't know any of that."

Dex bobbed his shoulders and drained his beer and set the empty in the boat.

"Where was Pop?"

"Got pulled over on the way there. Spent the night in jail himself. Lost his license for a while."

A frog trilled. The boat was moored, but Jonah felt adrift.

Dex started to get up. "I think I'll go to bed."

"Wait—"

Dex paused on the boards and turned, eyebrows raised.

"What's the point?"

"Of what?"

"Of that story."

Dex put his hands on his hips. "I don't know what you mean."

"Why'd you tell it to me?"

"Didn't know if you remembered, I guess."

"You think I'm doing something dumb, don't you, going to Mexico."

"I didn't say that."

"Yeah, but you think it."

"Hell, Jonah. Did you hear me say that?"

Jonah stood in the boat, felt it pitch. "I never hear you say anything, Dex."

His brother shook his head. "It ain't my place to tell you what to do."

There were words on the tip of Jonah's tongue: Shouldn't it be somebody's place? There's no one else but you, Dex. What are you so afraid of?

But Jonah balked and swallowed the sentences. He couldn't bring himself to ask for his brother's advice. Stubborn, but also hurt and angry. And now Dex turned and went, and Jonah stood in the boat and listened to the swamp.

VI

...está allí para siempre.

1

A REMOTE GROWLING STIRRED LUZ AWAKE—A JET, SCRATCHING its contrail across a pale sky. She sat up, terror clutching her when she realized she had failed to keep watch. Her heart slowed; she was alone in the creek bed. She let go of the knife—she had held it all through the night—and flexed her stiff fingers and thought of her mother's hands. The jet crawled across the sky. There were people up there.

Luz's skull ached. A wicked thirst in her throat. It seemed that red ants had bitten her while she slept, and her ankle was on fire. She stood and peered over the rim of the arroyo and saw nothing but scrubland folding into hills and the green ridge beyond. A shadow of cloud crested the hills, galloped toward her, and then passed, leaving the sky clear and blinding. Distant telephone poles came into focus. She climbed from the dry creek. The adobe house must be nearby, but she couldn't see it anywhere.

The hardpan road beneath the power lines was empty, dusty. A radio or perhaps cell tower rose in the hills and she set out for it along the road, hoping a phone might wait in that direction.

She was so thirsty, thirsty like she had been those nights after crossing the river—and God, how the river had stunk, her uncle's clothes reeking of it. She'd borne her gallon of water, feeling it lighten. The thirsty men all around her. Word came back that it was time to walk again. A rind of moon caught in the sunset, the world out of order. An old man didn't get up. He lay with his head against a rock, holding his hand out to all who passed. His mouth moved, no words. His lips looked like wax, like the coagulated rings around the candles in the church grotto where Luz and her mother prayed for Papá. There was a little water left in her jug and she started for the man, but her uncle yanked her back, shouting at her. She begged him, she was crying. In some deep place she knew that the man was going to die, but it didn't matter—she could give him what she had left. You need it, Luz, her uncle said, you alone. He dragged her, sobbing, through the Texas brush, and in truth Luz finished the water before midnight and she was still thirsty. Her uncle told her to listen for frogs. If you hear frogs, then you know there is water. But they never heard any, and Luz now wondered whether this had been meant to occupy her, to take her mind from the dying man. She still had dreams about his colorless lips, and the guilt gnarled beneath her breastbone.

A high whining. Luz only heard it now and looked. A small vehicle was coming fast down the road behind her, a plume of dust. A four-wheeler. She could see it and the man riding it. The flat scrubland around the road offered no place to hide. He would have seen her, regardless. Acid bubbled in her throat and her limbs grew cold. She squeezed the knife handle in her fist and stepped off the road.

The driver decelerated, finally braking and rolling to stop even with where she stood. The four-wheeler was black and streaked with mud, and a curved hunting knife was sheathed along the steering column. A headless rattlesnake was wound around the handlebars, its tail and rattle pendulous with the idling motor. The driver turned out to be no more than a boy. He wore jeans and boots and a flannel shirt, and a pump shotgun was slung across his back. Sweat glistened on his smooth face. Neat, combed hair. He let go of the throttle and rested his hand on his knee, and Luz noticed he only had four whole fingers—his middle finger ended at its first knuckle. He looked at her and then he looked at the knife. Under his gaze she felt the abrasions around her wrists, the scrapes on her fingers, the blood that had dried down her jawline. She stepped backward and raised the blade. The boy was stone-faced.

"I know that knife," he said.

Luz tried to speak, but her arid windpipe seized and she could only croak. The boy stood. She waved the knife at him and shuffled farther off the road. He shook his head and removed a metal thermos from the compartment beneath the seat. He held up his four-fingered hand as if this should calm her and tossed the thermos. She caught it against her body with her free hand. The thermos was slick with condensation.

"Water," the boy said.

With the thermos clamped in her armpit she twisted the cap off and dropped it and then drank until a cramp stitched across her belly. She watched the boy, kept the knifepoint raised. She tossed the thermos back and said, "Are you with them?"

His eyes moved over her, intuiting her ordeal. "No," he said. "I am not with them."

"You said you know the knife."

"How did you get it?" When she didn't immediately answer, he asked if the man who owned the knife was dead. Luz shook her head. The boy turned his head down the road, toward the mountains. "I live that way. I can bring you there. My grandmother will help you."

Luz looked. "Can I use your cell phone?"

"I don't have one." He swung his leg over the four-wheeler and beckoned. "Come on. My grandmother will be angry with me if I leave you here. She can help."

The muscles in Luz's arm quivered. The knife was heavy. Her mind raced. "What is your grandmother's name?"

"Armanda."

"What is your name?"

"Felipo." A weary smile. "I am fifteen. I live in San Cristóbal, there"—he pointed down the road—"with my grandmother and my brother. I am not lying to you." He patted the seat and swung the shotgun around so that it rested across his lap. "Come with me. You don't want to stay here."

There was nobody else around. No vehicles. The road lay empty and still in the heat. Her clothes were stiff with salt and dirt and some rust-colored blood. She didn't want to get onto the four-wheeler, but she didn't know what else she could do, either.

She sat down behind Felipo and he told her to hold on. She placed the knife along his ribs under his arm and said, "If I see the narcos' house I will stab you." She hoped he didn't hear the tremor in her voice. He snorted and throttled up, and as the four-wheeler leaped forward Luz almost fell from the vehicle. The big silver knife tumbled from her grip and she squeezed Felipo around the waist. She glanced, wind filling her ears. The silver knife glared in the road like a sliver of sun.

2

THE ROAD RAN THROUGH LAND POPULATED BY A HERD OF THIN, bug-eyed steers. They entered a wide gulch, the slopes of the hills rising at either side. Maguey and other scrub plants. A campsite of nylon tents and parked dirt bikes. They crossed a muddy creek on a stone bridge. Deeper in the hills, the pueblo of San Cristóbal terraced up the slopes on switchbacking dirt trails. A solitary church bell rang, a bright sound.

A pack of dogs burst from a copse of evergreens and ran out into the road, a slobbering mesh of snapping teeth, and Felipo accelerated past them. An anvil-shaped escarpment, dead ahead, sheared off the sunlight. They passed a store with a canvas awning. In the gravel lot, a boy sitting on the lowered tailgate of a truck waved.

Felipo turned up a path and parked alongside a small brick home. Behind the house, two horses hung their graying muzzles over the top slat of their pen. A small barn and shower stall. A gas generator chugged, and Luz smelled the greasy exhaust. The fumes twisted into her guts. The dead snake swung from the handlebars, its red severed neck. Felipo was saying something about the horses, and Luz tried to stand but nearly fell. Her head weighed a thousand pounds. The world around her ran like melting wax. "My head hurts," she managed.

She leaned on Felipo as he helped her through the front door of the house. The aroma of ground corn and woodsmoke. Felipo called out for his grandmother. It was hot inside the house, and Luz's stomach churned. Once, she had gotten drunk with Jonah and Colby and felt like this, and she'd thrown up in the kitchen at Jonah's and was embarrassed, and where was he now? "I need a phone," Luz said to the older woman waddling toward her. The woman squinted through glasses and took Luz's face in her hands. "I need a phone," Luz said again, and then she fell to her hands and knees and vomited water and bile onto the floorboards. "I'm sorry," Luz wheezed.

Felipo and his grandmother helped her up. "It is okay, dear," the old woman said.

"I'm really sorry."

"Quiet now." The grandmother smiled, warm. "Everything is okay."

"I need to call my father, and my—"

"There will be time." She began to lead Luz somewhere. "Let me help you."

She took Luz down a short hallway into a bedroom with a mattress on the floor. A crucifix hung on the wall. A vanity that looked like it came from a much larger home took up most of another wall. Holy santos huddled on the windowsill. The old woman lit a candle among them and whispered something about or to San Judas Tadeo.

Luz watched herself in the mirror, a stranger staring back. She was filthy and red-eyed. More blood than she had imagined was dried down the side of her face. Felipo's grandmother filled a basin with water from a clay pitcher, wet a cloth, and helped Luz clean her face. She dabbed at a spot over Luz's ear. Pain darted and crackled.

"You hit your head very hard," the old woman said.

"I'm sorry," Luz again said, not really knowing why.

"You should rest. There will be time to take care of everything."

The old woman gently prodded Luz toward the mattress and blankets. She didn't want to lie down. She needed to call her father and she needed to call Jonah. But the blankets looked nice, and Luz was so, so tired.

"You have nothing to worry about," the grandmother said.

When Luz lay down, her heavy head seemed to anchor her to the mattress while the rest of the room orbited around her. For the first time she noticed the little boy holding on to his grandmother's skirt and staring at Luz from around the old woman. His big, dark eyes. He didn't speak, he only stared.

The old woman took his hand and turned. "Come away, Ignacio." The boy watched Luz even as he left the room.

Luz closed her eyes and tumbled into a dream about the boy. No. A boy very much like him, but different yet. This boy had blond hair, like his father. He wandered from place to place, knocking on doors. At every door he knocked they told him, You don't belong here. They told him, You don't belong anywhere.

3

A RATTLE SHOOK, SHOOK, SHOOK. SNAKES COILED IN THE BED with her, their scales not slimy but rough against her legs. They warned her, rattling: she'd fallen asleep in the wrong place—but she couldn't move, and she woke with a start to a headache harpooning her from temple to temple. The little boy, Felipo's brother, stood at the foot of the mattress, shaking the rattle severed from the dead snake. Candles flickered among the santos on the windowsill. The boy turned and ran from the room. Luz wrapped her arms around her knees.

Calm down. We're okay here. The cut over her ear throbbed. Felipo's grandmother had set a change of clothes out for her, a pair of slacks and a linen shirt. She put them on. They were roomy but clean.

Something smelled good. Places had been set at the kitchen table. The little boy, Felipo's brother, sat at the table and examined the rattle. The grandmother turned from the stove and pulled out a chair for Luz.

Luz thanked her again and added that she should get in touch with some people who would be worried. "I could call, or even e-mail them if there is a computer nearby."

Felipo entered, bearing an armload of wood for the stove.

The grandmother asked, "Does Rafa's have a computer?"

He set the firewood down and said he didn't know. When Luz inquired further, he explained that Rafa's was the store they'd passed on the road into the village. "I can take you there after dinner. If no computer, somebody will have a phone."

"I'd like to go down there now, if that's okay."

"There will be time," the old woman said. "First you must eat, you must drink."

Luz's stomach groaned and she knew she must also be dehydrated. She sat, drumming her fingers on the tabletop. The little boy was watching her. When she asked him his name, he scrunched his face and shook the rattle.

"He is mute," the grandmother said.

"Oh. I'm sorry."

The old woman turned, wiping her hands on her apron. She smiled at Felipo's brother. "It is okay, yes, Ignacio?"

Ignacio nodded once, very adult, and returned to scrutinizing the rattle. Their grandmother set bowls down on the table in front of them. A stew of snake meat, potatoes, and corn. They bowed their heads and the old woman uttered a quick prayer, mentioning Luz and her deliverance along with the gift of their supper.

They ate and drank in silence. The stew was spicy, good. The grandmother asked Luz about herself. Luz cleared her throat. "I was on my way home to Las Monarcas, to my own grandmother's." She told them she had lived in America for the previous six years.

Felipo snorted. "You should have stayed there."

"Felipo," the old woman hissed.

"Sorry," he said, spooning another bite.

"Las Monarcas is only a couple hours east from here," the old woman said. She smiled. "We will get you to a bus in Monclova in the morning."

"Thank you." Luz didn't wish to tell them anything else about her circumstances, but she looked at Felipo as she remembered: "You knew that knife. How?"

A glance passed between him and his grandmother. He looked at Luz and shrugged and lowered his eyes. "Everybody knows that knife."

4

FELIPO WALKED WITH HER TO THE STORE AFTER DINNER. THIN moonlight. Stars thicker than she'd known in years. Down the road, the store floated in a hazy sphere of light. Banda music crackled from speakers. There was a lone lamp on a telephone pole, as well as a string of white Christmas lights wound into the flowering branches of an anacahuita near the store. The music pumped from a boom box sitting in the truck bed. A couple danced casually, each of them holding a brown bottle of beer. Elsewhere a group of men sat in a circle, playing some kind of game. When the song ended, Felipo got the dancing man's attention. He came over, grinning, and Luz felt his eyes creep over her.

"Good evening." The top snaps of his shirt hung open. He wore silver and turquoise jewelry. Rafa, the store owner. There was a phone with which she could dial internationally. "It is an emergency?"

"I need to reach my papá in America."

Rafa's eyebrows bumped. He adopted an engineered forlorn look. "That will be an expensive call."

When Felipo saw Luz's face fall, he said he'd cover the cost. Luz thanked him.

"Very good." Rafa flashed white teeth. "This way, please."

They passed by the men circled on the ground. They were sitting around something. One of them jolted and the others laughed, jeered.

Inside the store, the shelves bore crates of soda pop and bags of chips. Behind the counter, a curtained portal seemed to be the entrance to Rafa's home. The phone sat on the counter next to the register. Rafa opened a cooler and handed an unlabeled brown bottle to Felipo. The boy cranked off the top and sipped the beer. Luz went around the counter to the phone, recalling the sparse calls to her father when she was a child. Her mother waiting for his calls in between. He had even sounded far away, voice thin in the earpiece. Luz lifted the phone. Rafa remained, smiling. Felipo nodded, holding the beer. "I'd like to be alone," Luz said. "Please."

"Of course," Rafa intoned, bowing his head, and they left the store.

She dialed her father's cell, her chest stitching tighter with each digit. It didn't even ring, the cold computer voice of his voice mail toning. If he had answered, she would have tried to keep her voice tight. She would have been angry, and then she would have been sorry. It would not have gone well. But now she heard the beep and reigned it all in: "Papá, it's me. Everything is okay. The car broke down in Monclova and I couldn't reach you until now. I'm in a hotel. They think the car will be ready again tomorrow, or they'll put me on a bus. Will you please call Abuela and let her know?" She paused, thinking about telling him she loved him. "Okay," she said, and hung up.

She lowered her face and closed her eyes and breathed. She could hear the men laughing outside. She began to dial Jonah's number, but stopped and hung up the phone when a cold feeling spidered up her legs. If he answered her call, she'd begin to cry. She wouldn't know what to say. She decided she'd call him once she was in Las Monarcas, with her grandmother, once there was nothing extra to make him worry.

Luz left the store and found Felipo and Rafa hovering over the shoulders of the men on the ground. The lone woman sat on the truck's tailgate, kicking her feet and drinking her beer.

There was a length of rope circled on the ground in the midst of the men. Some of them leered at Luz as she approached. A rough-looking bunch. Each of them had a hand pressed flat on the ground just inside the rope circle. One of them held a glass upside down in the center. A brown scorpion flailed under the glass, trying to scramble up the inside of it. The man counted down from three, and then he lifted the glass. The scorpion, claws raised and tail flexed, spun and shot toward a set of fingers. The man yelped and yanked his hand from the circle before the little scorpion could get to him. The others laughed, high, nervous cackles. Another one pulled his hand away. The objective seemed to be to keep one's hand in the circle longest. Luz watched. There was something about that inescapable loop. Something about the hands of the men reaching, coming and going as they pleased. She found herself rooting for the scorpion to sting one of them. Felipo nudged her and jerked his head in the direction of his home. Luz nodded. He finished his beer and gave the bottle back to Rafa, and they walked from the lot. Rafa said something by way of a farewell but Luz didn't listen, and she could feel his eyes on the back of her neck.

They returned through the dark up the hill to the house. "Did you get a hold of the right people?"

"Yes," Luz said.

Felipo turned to her in front of the door. "You can have my bed tonight. I'll share with my brother." Luz started to protest, but he raised a hand. "It is okay. And tomorrow we will—" But he stopped talking, eyes on something over her shoulder. She looked, and he said, "Shit. Oh, shit."

The vantage from the slope allowed a view down the road. A vehicle approached, coming fast. Its manifold roof lights swung and bounced like the beams of some exploratory ship. And Luz remembered the knife, the big silver knife etched with the Chichimec designs, lying and shining next to the tire tracks on the road to San Cristóbal.

5

A N HOUR LATER, THEY HALTED NEAR THE TOP OF THE ESCARP-
ment. Monclova burned far out on the plain, a red-orange grid,
like the earth's crust had cracked with geometric precision. Immediately beneath her vantage, down in the darkened gulch where San Cristóbal lay, the lights were sharp: Rafa's store, a few warm window frames,
and the high beams of Cicatriz's Jeep—diminutive now—where it was
parked near Felipo's home.

It had been his grandmother's idea that they take the horses and flee
up the mountain trail. There was little doubt that Rafa or one of the
others by his store would confirm Cicatriz's suspicions, and there were
only minutes to spare. Las Monarcas would be a day or two away by
horseback, the grandmother said, and Felipo could get her there. "Our
family knows Cicatriz better than most," the old woman said to Luz,
"and so you must go, now." Luz didn't understand, but there wasn't time
for clarification.

The old horses were breathing hard, stamping their hooves. Luz had
never been on a horse before, and she'd expressed her fears while Felipo
rushed to saddle the old animals, Pegaso and Canguro. He explained
that his family used to run a ranch and these were the last of their horses.
The horses had been raised handling tourists who'd never ridden a day
in their lives. "Just get on and hold the reins," he said. "They know what
they are doing." And he'd been right.

The great heaving of Pegaso's rib cage beneath her knees, the nimble
yet powerful strides as he found the solid spots in the steep mountain
trail—it amazed Luz. She hadn't needed to do anything as Pegaso followed Canguro up the rocky switchback. But now she watched the Jeep's
lights below and guilt overpowered any other emotion. Felipo's grandmother was still down there, and so was his brother, Ignacio. The little
boy had been asleep. They hadn't even said good-bye.

Felipo's face was stoic in the dark. Canguro tossed his head and snorted. The Jeep began to move, and soon enough the vehicle crawled out of the village along the road.

"What," Luz ventured quietly, "did your grandmother mean when she said your family knew Cicatriz?"

Felipo shook his head. "Let's get a little farther." Pause. "I don't think he'd hurt them." Before Luz could say anything, Felipo turned Canguro away from San Cristóbal and Pegaso stepped to follow.

They stopped for the night on the far side of the mountain, on the way down. San Cristóbal was gone, as was Monclova, out on the plain. Eastward, the valley lay in shadow. A twinkling homestead here and there. The twinned headlights of an automobile on an unseen highway, arcing silent as a satellite. A warm wind blew, and Felipo found them a little stone flat, sheltered by a fist of rock. He took care of the horses, and Luz busied herself unrolling their blankets. They lay down in silence.

Luz looked at the sky and felt lost, afloat in an ocean. She closed her eyes and saw the woman in the cab, the unreal emptying of her skull, and she opened her eyes again and kept them open. Her pulse jumped in her neck and she clasped her hands together and reached for her mother.

"My grandmother," Felipo started, a quiet voice in the dark, "she says that if El Narco touches a place, it is there forever."

Luz listened, jaw muscles tensing.

"I think she is right, but it came to our home a long time before you did, Luz." The boy sat up in the starlight. "Cicatriz," he went on. "His real name is Juan Luis Medina. He is my cousin."

Now Luz sat up and stared at Felipo.

"I will tell you a story," he said. "Don't worry. Please."

Luz looked out to the never-ending dark of the valley. *Where am I . . . and where am I running to now?*

Felipo waved his four-fingered hand to the south. "Our horse ranch was in the hills between Saltillo and Monterrey . . ."

6

FELIPO WAS TEN YEARS OLD. IGNACIO WAS VERY YOUNG. THEY lived with their parents, and in the other homes on the property lived the ranch hands as well as another family, including the teenage Juan Luis Medina.

They bred horses and accepted reservations from tourists who wanted the real caballero experience. Felipo's family took the tourists riding in the mountains and along the riverbed. They stopped for a lunch of cold marinated steak, tortillas, and beans packed by Felipo's mother and his aunts. They stopped on the trail where it overlooked the valley, and far down there an ancient pyramid stood. The pyramid was brown, awash in sunlight. One could see this and feel the ancient ones, hear their enduring murmurs.

The teenage Juan Luis hated the ranch life, and he began making visits to Monterrey on the weekends. Word eventually reached the family that he'd become an halcón—a lookout—for a gang of narcos tied up with the Gulf Cartel. When the men of the ranch accused him, Juan Luis denied it. They knew it was true, but they let Juan Luis stay because somehow boxes of toys started arriving for the children on the ranch. Then more boxes, of clothes, and of fruits and vegetables. It was the cartel, of course, giving those things. Generous souls. But it wasn't long before Felipo's father woke in the night to a commotion and found a group of men unloading packages from a truck and carrying them into the Medina house.

Felipo's father grabbed Juan Luis by the shirt, and one of the other men wrenched him away from the boy, telling him to go back inside, old man. Into his own home. The next day Felipo's father tried to banish Juan Luis from the property.

Days later, a noise like a wind woke Felipo. He opened the bedroom door, and the hallway was full of smoke. He ran to Ignacio's bed, where the mute child sat with arms extended and face contorted in soundless wailing. Felipo lifted his brother and ran from the house.

And Felipo would always see this, imagining it over and over again. How it must have happened.

They were there. His mother and his father, on their bellies in the dirt. The lights from the truck were on them. Their blood, black and glistening and soaking into the earth. He could not see either face but it was them and they were dead.

Ignacio squirmed, mouth agape. The truck tossed soil and fled down the drive. A towering crash—their home's chimney collapsed through the roof tiles and the beams. The whole house would burn.

Felipo passed his brother off to one of the others who had gathered with the commotion. He got the shotgun from behind the seat in his father's truck. The truck keys were melting in the house, so he sprinted to the stable and saddled Pegaso and set off at a gallop after the fleeing vehicle. The taillights were specks and then they were gone, headed east, toward Monterrey. Felipo kept the heading, riding until the sun broke, piercing over the hills.

He rode through an outpost of sorts—a gas station and a few other bunkers of cinder block. Still miles yet from the Monterrey–Saltillo highway. A truck was parked outside one of the blocky structures. Felipo dismounted, hitched Pegaso to a fence post, and went to the bunker's wooden door. He put his ear to it but didn't hear much. He opened the door and stepped through, shotgun at his waist.

There were five or six men in the room. Most of them were asleep in various spots on the floor. Felipo's memory of this would always be blurred, the images strangling down to a constricted view of the two men who were still awake, where they sat at a table with beer bottles before them. One of these men was Felipo's cousin. Juan Luis turned toward him. Juan Luis watched Felipo raise the shotgun, watched him take aim. And then someone grabbed Felipo from behind, pulling the gun so that he blew a hole in the ceiling. The man was large—or much bigger than a ten-year-old, at least. He wrested the gun away from Felipo, and the other men, rudely awakened, began to laugh.

Felipo did something then, a stupid gesture he'd seen in an American movie, something he understood only marginally. The men laughed all the harder, and one of them seized the finger, and they held him over the table, hands clamped and pinning his wrist, and Felipo remembered the pressure, the incredible pressure, only.

He woke to them cauterizing the wound with cigarettes, and he passed out again. When he woke the next time he was alone in the house and bruised and bloody. He tasted blood in his mouth. He got up and hobbled out onto the empty and dusty road. They left Pegaso alive, thank God.

7

L UZ HELD HERSELF, SUDDENLY COLD. FELIPO WAS QUIET. "I'M SO
sorry," Luz whispered.

Felipo lifted his face, ghostly and eyeless in the dark. A small shrug.

"No," Luz said, hoarsely. "I'm sorry you found me on the road. That it was you, not somebody else."

Felipo sighed. "I am glad we can help. That's all."

But Luz saw the dying man in the desert so long ago, felt the heavy sloshing of the water jug in her hand. A regret like poison for the rest of her life. The horrible paradox of one's duty to survive and the choices God still made you make.

"Thank you for this," she said. "No," she said when Felipo tried to wave her gratitude away. "Thank you."

After a while Felipo went on. "Ignacio and I, we moved to my grand-mother's after that. It is not hard to imagine what became of the ranch."

Luz imagined the sweltering shed where they held her, the packages of narcotics stacked against the walls. "Your cousin doesn't work for them anymore, does he?"

Felipo shook his head. "I heard sometime he'd become a sicario for them. A, you know, assassin. But then he fell out of their favor. There were different stories."

"What are the stories?"

Felipo grumbled. "They aren't pleasant."

Luz said, "I don't care."

The boy sighed again. "One story says the Zetas bought him and paid him to kill his own boss, but he failed." Felipo drew a finger across his face to explain the scar—punishment. He began to say something else, trailed off.

"What."

"I don't want to use some of these words in front of you."

It was a ridiculous notion. "It's fine," she said.

"I heard," Felipo continued slowly, "that my cousin likes boys instead of girls. One day his boss, who considered himself a righteous man, caught Juan Luis with another man's cock in his mouth, and so—" He paused. "I heard this from some other guys, you know? Not my grandmother."

"It's okay," Luz told him.

"So his boss killed the other man, but first he measured the man's cock across Juan Luis's face with a knife." Again, he drew his finger across his face. "Cicatriz."

There was quiet on the mountain. The deep sky, the apprehended universe. "Why didn't his boss kill him, too?" Luz asked. Then she clarified: "Why let him live, I mean, if either story is true? He's like a renegade now, he robs them, right?"

Felipo shrugged. "Like I said. They are just stories. The stories are everywhere, about everyone." He lay down on his blanket and exhaled. "Who can say what is the truth?"

Luz thought about stories. About stories and what they could do, and of course it was only what they could do that mattered. She wondered whether Cicatriz would keep looking for her. As if Felipo read her mind, he spoke up.

"I think you'll be safe now. It was probably easy enough for him, a short drive, once he saw the knife in the road. But now. I don't know. He'll have other concerns."

"I hope," Luz said, "he left your family alone." Her imagination ran with the thought. A septic guilt.

"Don't worry," Felipo said.

"I hope your grandmother just told him we ran up the mountain. I hope she just told him what he wanted to know and he decided to give up."

"I know," Felipo said.

"I'm sorry for getting you and your family into this. I'm sorry."

"Stop."

"But I am. I worry for Ignacio."

Felipo didn't say anything at first. He shifted on his blanket. Then he answered:

"I worry for my brother, too, but not because of this. I worry for him because he will grow up and be unsurprised that things like this happen, and happen all the time. That is not your fault."

8

SHE WAS RUNNING. SHE WAS RUNNING AND BEARING LEFT AND left. This track, a circle without escape. Her ghost runner gained. Cold and clawing. The breath burned in her throat, in her lungs. There needed to be an exit—but she never came to it and she couldn't stop for the spirit gaining on her. As she'd never done in her waking life, she glanced to see the shape of her ghost runner and saw that it wasn't a man at all but an enormous hand, a man's hand with cracked fingernails and silver baubles jangling around his wrist. The hand was large enough to crush her. Her legs dragged but she pushed on, running. The walls hemming her in were made of rope, coarse rope thicker than she was tall. Rope threaded from fibers that cut at her arms and face like saw grass. Another hand descended ahead of her, ready to pluck her from the ground and crush her to jelly, and she had no claws and no stinger with which to fight. She couldn't stop but there was no escape, and so she ran toward that waiting grip.

9

IN THE SUNRISE SHE WATCHED A FREIGHT TRAIN SMOKE ACROSS the valley. They rode the horses into the hills and onto the plain and crossed the now-empty tracks. The power lines overhead buzzed. Felipo kept the horses at a walk, not wanting to push the old animals. They went along a country road concurrent with wire-fenced cattle pasture. The land undulated again, gently. An irrigated field. A blue cordillera in the distance. Las Monarcas must be somewhere in the foothills, Luz thought. They rode, passing Felipo's water thermos back and forth.

They halted around midday and approached a stand of juniper. The tree bark reminded Luz of the alligators she'd seen with Jonah in the New Orleans aquarium, their rough hides. The trees cast marbled shade on the rock, and water bubbled and ran over the stone into a small, sediment-colored pool. The horses bent to drink and Felipo unpacked the food his grandmother had hastily gathered for them.

"My favorite," he said, "was at the end of the rides, when we let the tourists race."

"Even if they were like me?"

He gestured at the horses with a wedge of tortilla. "You see how good they are. They all were." He smiled, wistful. "There was a flat grassy stretch near the end of the day's ride. A field. We lined them up to race, a pair at a time, but if there was an odd number of riders my father had me race the final tourist."

Pegaso lifted his mouth from the water, sneezed, shook his head.

"I was the better rider, but I would give them a race, do you see? Pull ahead and then slow down and fall even. I could see it in their faces. The thrill. And then I always let them win. They threw up their arms and shouted."

Luz smiled. "Always?"

"Most of the time." Felipo shrugged. "Not if they deserved to lose."

Luz laughed, and then a rush of color and noise swept through the juniper trees—monarch butterflies, thousands of them, surging into the oasis. They rose in a whispering gyre, wing strokes brushing against skin, and began to settle, blanketing the trees in a shimmering quilt of orange and black. All the while, the migration thickened. A grotto of wings. A monarch wobbled onto Luz's palm, then fluttered off again.

"I remember this," she said. She smiled. "I'd almost forgotten." There was the hill somewhere in Las Monarcas, the hill with the big oak tree at its crown. The monarchs came every year, soon after Easter. Soon, now, she realized. Her mother used to lead her by the hand up the winding trail, just a thin scratch in the hillside. Luz's calf muscles burned from the hike. Her mother helped her along, pulling with her hand rough and chapped from the scalding water and the lye. They crested the hill into the susurration of so many wings. They are here for you, my daughter.

And now, in this living grotto, Luz looked to her own hands, her dishwashing hands that were not soft, either. Her bloodied fingertips and broken nails. She saw her future, her new future, charted like a course on a map. She would be home in Las Monarcas, and she would have her own child. It would be the same migration, one year and then the next, and she would repeat the same ritual, one year and then the next.

That is your life. It is determined. Can you do it, Luz? Can you do it? She looked at the monarchs where they rested, and fear filled her.

VII

You leave those feelings alone.

1

BEFORE THEY LEFT THE CAMP, DEX OUTFITTED THEM WITH TUP-perware containers of leftovers and gave them a hundred dollars for their help. Hardly an unnecessary word passed between Dex and Jonah while they packed, and Dex watched them back out of the driveway but never raised a hand in farewell. They drove west through the Atchafalaya Basin, one great primordial sweep of water and earth and flora. By midmorning they had crossed the Sabine and entered Texas. They passed through Beaumont, and then Houston reared up, serpentine tangles of overpass and exit ramp. They crept along in the six-lane gridlock.

"This as far as I been from home," Colby said. "After this, it's all new."

"Y'all evacuated to Houston, too?"

"Yeah. Me and Mom and Jamal." Heat danced over the cars. Colby spoke to his window. "He's been gone to jail since before I met you."

"What he do?"

"What he had to, I guess."

"Huh. I got an uncle in Angola."

"So you know what I mean, then."

Jonah shrugged. "The second time in there for him. Dumb-ass."

"What he do?"

"Busted parole. They found him in a Biloxi casino with a bunch of money wasn't his."

"Ha. What about the first time?"

"Know the difference between manslaughter and murder?"

"Yeah."

"Manslaughter." Jonah punched the horn and immediately felt stupid for doing so. He looked at Colby. "Like you said. What he had to do."

They lurched forward before taillights flared through the column of cars.

"That's how Pop explained it, at least," Jonah said. "When my uncle got out he was gonna come live with us, so my dad tried to explain it to me. I was a kid. I asked if he was a murderer. I didn't know the fucking difference, you know? I still don't, not really. But Pop smacked me across the mouth and I ran out to the backyard."

Colby listened, face placid.

"Jamal ever tell you that crying was for pussies or anything like that? I got that shit all the time. So I just stand there, holding my breath. Don't fuckin' cry, I say to myself. And Pop comes out and stands behind me. He says sorry. He always said sorry. I dunno. He grabs my shoulders and turns me around and looks me in the face and goes, Jonah, listen to me. I'm telling you this because I love you. What your uncle did was an accident, yeah, but he had to protect himself. He wouldn't be here at all—alive, I mean—if not for this."

Jonah paused, cleared his throat.

"Pop brings his face real close and tells me: If you're ever in a fight, you beat him until he's fucking retarded. Or else as soon as you turn around, he'll get up and kick you in the back of the head." Jonah snorted, a kind of laugh. "I was, like, nine." Jonah glanced at Colby. "Then Pop picked up Uncle Dexter and he lived with us for a while and then he got caught in Biloxi. What you think about that?"

Colby shrugged. "It makes sense."

Jonah recalled the fight that had gotten him kicked out of his second high school, the expulsion that had brought him to Luz and to Colby. This second high school was full of second-chance white kids—teenagers who'd been booted from previous private schools for drugs or cheating or fighting or, as in Jonah's case, breaking zero-tolerance policies. It was the last stop on the private side of education, and it was a school full of bullies and wannabe tough guys. The kid had been picking on Jonah and wouldn't stop when asked. Jonah broke the kid's nose there in the hallway. He knew it when he hit him. The kid never imagined what it would look like, his own blood speckled across the lockers. That had been his problem. There was blood on Jonah's fist, too. Even before the kid fell to the ground, a hush coursed through the boys looking on, all the private-school boys wearing their shirts and ties. None of them had foreseen such an outcome, either, not from a fight they urged on and did indeed wish to happen. The reality of the redness. And when the teacher arrived, he saw Jonah's knuckles and regarded him as one might regard an animal. Jonah remembered that look.

"I used to cruise with Jamal." Colby said it softly.

Jonah looked at his friend.

"Not all the time, you know. But he asked me to come along sometimes. Me, I was just a boy. He had this red Grand Prix, and he'd play the music real low, just a quiet little pulse. If I went to jack up the volume, Jamal would say, Naw, naw. That was how he liked it, real easy like. I loved cruising with him. Never told him that, though. You leave those feelings alone."

"Right," Jonah said.

"We'd roll past this house or that house where some boys were chilling on the steps. They'd be just staring at us, all hard like. And Jamal, he say, Don't you smile now. Give 'em that look right back, ya heard? Finally we'd stop at this pink shotgun, his boss's house. He'd run inside, leave me in the car. Afterward, he'd drive through the daiquiri shop. Always had these crisp new twenties. I remember that. Jamal was a tough dude—still, he loved him some strawberry daiquiris." Colby chuckled.

Jonah smiled. The traffic started and stopped. The sun glared against the Houston skyline. He thought about the month he spent here with his father after Katrina. They stayed at the camp in the months after that, until they could return to New Orleans. It would have been during that time that Luz had arrived with her father, when all the work was just beginning. Almost five years ago. Jonah and Luz, they'd been hardly more than children. "I never need to spend any more time in Houston," Jonah said, believing Colby would take his meaning.

"Me, I liked it here." Colby watched the tall buildings glint.

"Come on."

"We stayed with some cousins for almost a year." Colby grinned. "It was the first time I ever seen black kids and white kids playing together. Here, in Houston."

"Really?"

Colby told him about an outdoor basketball court ringed with chain-link. Jamal and Colby would go down there with their cousins. It was mostly black guys playing pickup, sure, but there were white boys, too. Colby stood on the sideline more often than not, watched everyone play. It was good pickup—some shit-talking and you better have some grit, but it was honorable, no cheap fouls, no whining. Sometimes Colby got in and ran around the unpainted arc, hoping someone would dish him the ball so he could chuck one up. "Right after the storm," he said, "I saw my brother smile more than ever before."

Back home, the water still hadn't receded. Once it was clear they weren't returning to the city anytime soon—and maybe never, according to the news—Jamal's people, the crew from the pink house, turned up in Houston. "After that," Colby said, "Jamal didn't have time to play no more. It was back to business." Colby, though, kept playing ball at the court. He found himself thinking about their New Orleans neighborhood, and the strange white family on their street, the only white family he knew of on their side of St. Charles Avenue. "It was y'all, Mickey-Bee," Colby chuckled. He told Jonah how when he was young and sitting with Jamal and his friends on the porch, they used to see one of the older white kids walking along the street, under the cemetery wall. "It was your brother Dex," Colby said. "We just thought he was weird."

Jonah laughed. "No shit."

"Yeah. So you know, that's why I said hi to you when you showed up in school last year. I recognized you from around the way."

"Huh," Jonah said, gripping the wheel. Traffic picked up and he kept his eyes on the highway.

"I think about it," Colby went on, " . . . maybe I never woulda said hey if I didn't play with all kinds of kids in Houston."

An uncomfortable feeling took root in Jonah's gut. He'd never considered that their friendship began with something akin to an act of pity on Colby's part. He pushed the conversation in a new direction: "You talk to Jamal ever?"

"Me and Mom write him letters." Colby bumped his shoulders. "See, what happened was we came back to New Orleans in August, a year after the storm. Jamal got a second possession charge, right off the bat, and they tacked something about an illegal gun to it, too. The city was fucking crazy that fall. Everybody coming home and carving out territory all over again. Judges weren't playing."

"Yeah."

"I figure they probably wanted him to flip on his crew, but that ain't Jamal. After a while, somebody come looking for me, wanting me to help out to pay Jamal back. But you know, Mickey-Bee, I ain't never hustled like Jamal. I never been in that pink house. I never wanted to climb like he did." Colby sighed. "I ain't cut out for it the way my brother was."

Jonah glanced at his friend, but Colby was looking elsewhere. "I get it, bud."

2

THEY REACHED SAN ANTONIO IN THE AFTERNOON. THEY PULLED off the interstate toward downtown, and Jonah was looking for Luz's cathedral. He recalled the weight of her head on his chest, the soft words she spoke, the fragile memories shared. After he brought her back to New Orleans, he thought, they would take a road trip together to San Antonio. She could show him around. He saw it. They'd push a stroller around.

"You all right?" Colby asked. "You missed, like, four parking spots."

"Yeah," Jonah said. "Sorry. Thinking."

"Something's been bothering me," Colby said.

"Huh?"

"We going to visit Luz. And you say we're gonna come right back, graduate, and enlist. You gonna be cool with that? I mean, saying hey to Luz and coming right back?"

"Well," Jonah said, "no."

"So . . ."

"I'd like to be with her and help when the baby gets closer."

"But you can't. Not if you wanna be able to bring her back."

"I guess not. Gotta get back to graduate and enlist. That's where the money will come from. But if I can look at her, you know?—see her in person and make a plan, I think it'll go over better. Don't you?"

"Sure," Colby said.

"I can't get her on the phone, anyway. Not unless she calls," Jonah said. "This way, I can see her and make her a promise."

"Yeah."

Jonah parked the truck along a small park. A lot of people were out and about. They opened the cooler Dex had given them and took out the containers of chili, and they set off following the crowd. Signs directed them toward the PASEO DEL RIO / RIVER WALK. The street wound gently downhill and ended where the narrow green river passed through the shade of the buildings. Trees grew from cutouts in the flagstone. Shops and restaurants hemmed in the water. People sat at outdoor lunch tables. There were water taxis and tour boats. Music, somewhere. A tour guide's voice buzzed from a loudspeaker as a boat passed, and the boys crossed the river on a skinny arch of stone steps.

"This is sweet," Colby remarked. "Luz tell you about this?"

"Once or twice."

Jonah stopped a man and asked for directions to the San Fernando Cathedral, and the man jerked his thumb in the direction the crowd was moving.

"Mickey-Bee, a church?"

"Like a historical church."

"But this is nice down here."

"Something I wanna see. Come on." And Colby groaned, but he followed.

The crowd led them to an open plaza where the stone cathedral and its boxy spires rose above the throng. A martial drumbeat built: one . . . two . . . one-two-three-four.

"Hear that?" Colby said.

The beat drummed up images in Jonah's memory—the marching band in its regalia tromped in step beneath the boughs of the live oaks, snare drums counting it out and bass drums punctuating. The dance team sashayed and the steppers walked it out. A whistle shrilled and the brass jumped in—trumpet, trombone, sousaphone. The three of them shook it in the street, laughing. Jonah saw Luz. Hold onto this: she dances, eyes downcast but a smile on her face. She backs against the night, the parade. The flames of the marching flambeaus glow all around her. Then they pass and the costumed folk on stilts move in the shadow over her shoulders, and Jonah sees her.

Jonah and Colby pushed to the front, near the cathedral. Jonah waited for the music, for the brass. But nobody danced, nobody smiled. The band wore red and gold plumed helmets—a drum corps only. They marched slowly. In their midst a man wore a ragged and bloody piece of linen and bore a wooden cross, the crux of it over his shoulder and the foot of it scraping along the cobblestone behind him. Blood dried in the creases down his face, beneath his crown of thorns. Other men dressed like Romans cracked whips and shouted, but they shouted in Spanish. The cross clattered to the street and the soldiers swarmed the man, whips flailing. After a while, they got the man back up and he dragged the cross onward.

"That real blood?" Colby asked.

A man nearby whispered, grave, "Sí."

Jonah nudged another man. "That real?"

"No." The man shook his head.

The drum corps slid by, one . . . two . . . one-two-three-four.

They backed out of the crowd. Colby was troubled. "I forgot it was Good Friday."

"Me too."

They made for the River Walk and sat on an iron bench next to the river, the leftovers from Dex in their laps.

"Easter's the only day of the year I go to church with my mom," Colby said. He stirred food, spooned a bite, dumped it back into the container. "Fuckin' water rats."

Jonah, chewing, nodded to the narrow green waterway. "Ain't much of a river."

"Nah," Colby agreed. "Luz liked this place, huh?"

She had loved it. Why? The gruesome parade told Jonah nothing new about her, though he sensed some truth of hers in this place, thrumming just out of reach beneath the flagstones. The way the river had been beaten down to this narrow dribble suddenly infuriated him. "Let's go," he told Colby.

VIII

El que nada debe nada teme.

1

LUZ AND FELIPO HALTED IN THE LEE OF AN OLD STONE WALL. IT had been something once, but this *L*-shaped corner was all that remained. Luz unrolled their sleeping bags while Felipo tended to the horses. He wanted a fire but there was no wood to be found. With a lighter he lit handfuls of dry grass that flared brief and oily then shriveled to ash.

Luz sat, thinking of a good day, when she had walked with Jonah to a small park near his house. They carried baseball gloves he'd pulled from a closet. Hers was a soft and supple thing, dark leather. Along the thumb she saw his brother's name, Dexter, written in faded permanent marker. She lifted the glove to her face, examined the pocket, sniffed the leather. She liked the smell; she liked the feel. She had never worn one before, but it slipped easy and snug and comfortable onto her hand. Jonah slapped the pocket of his and said he wished their school had a team.

He positioned her in the park where the grass had been worn nearly to dust, backed away, and lobbed her the baseball. She caught it, took it from her glove, and fired it back. Whoa! he cried. You're a natural! She laughed. They settled into a rhythm, and the silence and the proficiency with which they received and returned held her mind steady.

They were sweating when they left the park. He told her how he had wanted to play baseball for his first high school, but he hadn't been there long enough, and he'd not been allowed to play at his next one. By the time he was old enough to have a serious catch with his brothers, Bill was gone and Dex had moved to the swamp. His father played with him back then, but that faded, too. Luz reached and squeezed his shoulder, and he looked at her, a reflective smile on his face, and she understood what they had shared, tossing the rawhide baseball back and forth. I can be this for you, she thought. I will be this for you. She believed it right then, had faith in it.

Luz wiped a tear from her cheek. How the moment makes us forget what we know of providence. The horses snuffled. Crickets sang in the chaparral. The stars were thick enough to seem like a net strained with sky.

"Do you think," Felipo suddenly asked, "it has always been like this?"

Luz cleared her throat. "What do you mean?"

"El Narco."

Luz searched her memory but found only blank spots. "I don't know. I don't remember what it was like when I was a girl."

"I forgot that you grew up here."

"Do I seem different?"

"A little, yes."

"Sometimes," Luz said, "I think the world has always been one way and I never noticed. Other times I think I do know the world, but moments make me forget."

Felipo tapped a stick against the weathered stone wall. "My grandmother tells a story that several years ago she drove to Monterrey with a friend, and along the way they came to a barricade. An old truck pulled across the road. Robbers came to the car and took a silver bracelet and some money. That was all they had. One of the thieves, she says, bent to the window and she saw herself in his sunglasses like mirrors, and he smiled and had a gold tooth. Here." Felipo tapped his canine.

"They go on to Monterrey and stay with a friend for a day or two and then start back for San Cristóbal. They come to a municipal police checkpoint, where the policemen check all the cars for contraband. And my grandmother says that as they pulled even with the sandbags, one of the police smiled at her, and he was the robber, wearing a uniform, holding a rifle. The same gold tooth. She saw it."

Luz asked if his grandmother ever told anyone, or tried to.

"Who to tell?" Felipo answered. "The good and the bad, there is no such thing. They all do what they want." He sighed and tossed the stick off into the night. "How can one person fight any of it? There are too many men like my cousin. They set so many evils into motion that you can only find a seam to hide in. But eventually that closes up, too."

He grew quiet. He was thinking of San Cristóbal, perhaps, of his grandmother and his brother, and of seams closing.

2

PEGASO AND CANGURO PLODDED ALONG, FOLLOWING PARALLEL dirt tracks through farmland. At this pace, Felipo thought they could reach Las Monarcas by the next morning if they rested only briefly that night and got started early. They shared the canteen, and Luz lost herself in the sound of the horses' hooves. There was no traffic on the country road. Luz's headache had begun to fade and the cut over her ear itched. The scrapes on her fingers burned when she wiped the sweat from her brow. She stank and she needed to brush her teeth, but none of that mattered right now, and Luz realized she was having a good time, in a way, on the move through the country on horseback.

A short wall of piled rocks, who knew how old, separated the trail from a field. The irrigated earth was a rich brown. Small green shoots in the rows. Corn, maybe. They crested a slight bump in the trail and passed the edge of the cornfield, and the rock wall fell away. Felipo halted Canguro, and Pegaso stopped in turn.

Staked sheets of black mesh shadowed an acre of land. Absurdly green bushes grew beneath the mesh. Luz recalled in an instant the time Colby handed her an open ziplock and told her to sniff it. Good, he had said, huh?

"Mota," Felipo said. Marijuana. He rested his forearms on the saddle horn and grimaced at Luz. "This is a special farm."

3

THE TRAIL BECAME AN UNPAVED ROAD AGAIN OUT IN THE FLAT. For fear of traffic, Felipo led her away from the road and up a ridge to camp out of sight against the pine forest at the foot of a hill. As promised, they were up before sunrise. The horses were fidgety and recalcitrant as Felipo saddled them. "Do you smell that?" he asked Luz. And she did. Smoke. They set out on foot, leading the animals along the ridge with the reins in their hands. The scent grew stronger.

"Maybe the army burns the mota," Felipo ventured. "Maybe the farmers burn back their own crops. You can't be sure if it even matters. Do not worry."

But as the light rose, so did a column of black smoke, ahead and to the south, drifting with the wind. Midmorning, they discovered the skeleton of a barn situated on a dirt road, down across an expanse of arid ground. The distant frame beams were charred, and fire had licked into a wheat field beyond it, carpets of flame so hot they were nearly clear.

A black pickup truck was parked in the foreground near the barn. The truck's doors hung open. Four dark heaps lay on the ground around the truck. The bodies were far off—Luz estimated nearly three hundred meters—but they both saw it, clearly, when one of the forms raised an arm, as if to wave to them.

Felipo looked at Luz, then began to lead Canguro down the ridge toward the barn and the truck and the bodies.

"No," Luz hissed.

"One of them is alive," he said. "Maybe they had an accident. Maybe I can help."

"Don't," she said. And her own firmness, her willingness to believe it, surprised her: "They are dead."

Felipo glanced again. The fire behind the bodies. Luz saw it in his face—the memory of the evening when his house had collapsed in flames and his parents lay dead on the lawn. "I'm sorry," Felipo said. He shrugged and started down the loose slope of the ridge, pulling the horse. "Wait here if you like."

Luz watched him go. "Shit," she said in English, then she tugged on Pegaso's reins and followed.

The heat was monumental. Grasshoppers fleeing the fire pelted against them, stinging Luz's face and arms and sticking to her shirt. Pegaso shook his head and snorted and began to resist her pull. She whispered to him, tried to sound confident, but cold slipped between her ribs as it became clear that there had been no accident. The truck's windows circled the vehicle in glass beads, and a sequence of narrowly spaced bullet holes checkmarked the body of the truck.

The low roar of the fire canceled out most other noise, and she didn't hear the truck still idling until they were almost next to it. A handgun lay on the driver's seat. Of the bodies, which were off a short way behind the truck, she couldn't tell which one had waved. They all seemed to be dead by now. The nearest man lay cruciform, head twisted toward them, sand caked against his bloody rictus and the fresh red laceration through his lips.

"I'm sorry," Felipo said. "I thought they could be the farmers. I'm sorry, Luz. You were right." Felipo was pulling Canguro around, starting back for the ridge and the hills and the pine forest.

Something snapped overhead, a quick atmospheric twitch. Luz felt it as much as she heard it. Another snap. The briefest whistle of split air. Luz's memory toned before the reports reached her. She dropped facedown in the dirt. Felipo pointed and shouted. Her eyes rolled heavily toward the Jeep tearing down the next hill, returning.

She got to her feet and pulled on Pegaso's reins, but the horse wouldn't budge. The big animal locked his knees and stared into some other place. Luz pulled on the reins, but it was as if they were lashed to a boulder. She saw the blood on the horse's breast, rich and nearly black, spreading through his gray coat. She reached and grabbed hold of the bridle but the horse wouldn't move, wouldn't turn his skull. Felipo shoved her and she stumbled and straightened and looked at him.

She heard a sighing deep in her eardrums, like air being let out, and then something popped in the center of her brain, and all the sound around her crystallized—the low roar of the fire, the snap and bite of another rifle round, Felipo screaming:

"Run, Luz, run!"

She turned and accelerated into her sprint, her ghost runner a step behind. She sensed him reaching, extending his arm, grasping at her in an effort to trip her up. She lengthened her strides. Her soles found tenuous purchase in the dry crust of earth. Her heart thumped at a quicker rate than she could recycle her feet. It was a discordant, out-of-order feeling.

The Jeep leveled onto the trail. Dust plumed as it raced toward the skeletal barn and the bodies.

Head turned, Luz sprawled, full body crashing into the slope of the ridge. She scrambled to her feet. Felipo wasn't with her.

He had remained with the horses, still yanking on Pegaso's reins, attempting to get the wounded horse moving by throwing his whole body into it. She screamed his name, and a cramp razored across her lower abdomen, crooking her spine and folding her in half. A hot swell of nausea.

The Jeep skidded to a stop near the barn. Three men leaped out. Felipo let go of Pegaso's reins and broke for where he had his shotgun sheathed along Canguro's flank. He was pulling it free when the first man hit him, spearing him to the dirt. The gun spun away. The other men arrived and fell onto the boy, fists rising and falling.

Luz groaned. The pain in her stomach unclenched and she straightened. The men pulled Felipo to his feet. The boy hung limply between them. One of the men raised an arm in Luz's direction, and another began loping toward her.

4

THE MAN HAD CROSSED THE FIRST HUNDRED METERS BY THE time Luz clawed up the loose shoring of the ridge and ran into the pine forest. Dried needles crunched beneath her sneakers. She needed to get far enough into the forest for the trees to obscure her from the narco's view once he topped the ridge. She estimated the distance and guessed she had about fifteen seconds.

Shut up. Run.

She grasped at a tree and swung herself in a new direction. Her ghost runner tangled his feet and stumbled, and she pushed ahead. The webbing of her lungs strained. Her abdominal muscles knotted tighter.

Through the trees she saw the ground fall away. She slowed, halted, and stood, gasping at the edge of a *U*-shaped cliff, its arms stretching away. Rock hills crinkled into the distance. Buzzards turned in the smokeless air. She fled along the curve and faded back into the trees.

Her stomach convulsed. She was going to throw up. A brief but clear image of the narco in pursuit finding her vomit and tracking her made her hold it in for a few moments longer, and she found a depression within the pines, a little crater lined with pine needles. She fell to all fours, sharp broken rock beneath the needle bed, and she retched, the bile burning in her throat, and she stifled her vocal cords and strained, and then it was done and she collapsed onto her side. Her limbs were stone themselves, no feeling, but the pain in her stomach was like a boot stamping into her abdomen. She lay there. Get up, she told herself. Get up. But she couldn't.

Felipo. They had him. The laceration through the dead man's lips blazed in her mind. She had gotten away, and shitty luck ran her right into them again. Why, why. The cramp spiked. She scrunched into a ball and clutched her knees.

There was silence except for her own raging pulse and the rustling when she shifted her weight against the needle bed. Inches from her face, a gray spider burrowed. She rolled to her back and gazed past the trees to the white sky. She narrowed her lips and forced slow breaths and willed against the pain in her gut.

Footfalls, boots on stone. The man was whistling a happy little ditty.

Luz held her breath, rolled gingerly onto her stomach, and crawled to the edge of the crater, where she could peek through the bottoms of the evergreens.

The narco was there, taking in the view over the valley. He wore a western shirt and jeans and cowboy boots. He held a pistol at his side. His other fist dropped into view, a cigarette trailing smoke. He whistled again in awe.

Luz dug through the pine needles, closing her fingers around a loose rock. If the man turned, he might see her face. He might press through the trees and level that pistol, and the rock would do her no good.

She pulled the shard free and squatted and held it. Gray and jagged. Dirt caked to it. The man dropped his cigarette and ground it out with the toe of a boot.

Now, she thought. Now, or he will turn and see you and you will be dead.

She stood and pushed through the pines.

The narco wheeled, startled, but quickly a pleased expression melted across his sweating face. He was older than Luz had expected. Deep wrinkles and gray-flecked hair. He grinned. "Hello—"

Luz reared back and hurled the rock across the few short meters.

The rock pelted against the narco's eyebrow with a wet solid smack.

The man clapped his free hand over his eye, and he stepped backward and dropped from sight.

No sound. He had been there. Now he was not. No sound at all.

Adrenaline sucked away from her, and the next breath brought absolute pain wrenching from beneath her navel, knocking her to the ground. She was a live and quivering bait shrimp impaled and forced to the curvature of a steel hook. She pressed her forehead against the sun-warmed rock and cried out.

The pain crashed and rushed away, but it was still within sight and would return. She dragged herself into the crater and hid while the hurt racked her. Her very molecules howled. It subsided, leaving a blue and pulsing afterimage. Water leaked from her eyes. Luz knew what was happening even before the blood started seeping through her slacks.

She managed to unbutton her pants and pull them down, and she lay there, clinging to the pain.

Jonah, she thought. She reached. Mamá, please.

She held onto silence by the thinnest of shreds. Voices passed through the trees. Hunters. She tumbled through the hours and the falling dark, and the universe swung over the tops of the pine trees. A bottomless sky threaded with drifting smoke.

The future—everything she had come to accept, everything to which her life would shape itself—bled away. It bled away and went home to the earth.

5

Luz's muscles quaked, her limbs trembled. Raw and exhausted. There was nothing to do and nothing to think and there was no one else, but Luz heard dogs. Faint, growing louder. Yes, she decided, the dogs were real. They were coming. They smelled blood, and they were coming. She got to her feet and pulled her pants up, and she scrounged and found another rock fragment, flat and sharp. She held it at her side and waited, slumping.

The pack darted into the trees. No preamble. The first dog came in low, white teeth and dark body. Luz swatted at its jaw with the flat of the rock. Saliva burst and roped. The blow reverberated through Luz's finger bones. The dog spun and slunk away, and Luz braced herself. The pack bunched, a writhing mass, teeth popping. A dog tunneled its snout into the pine needles. She kicked at the animal, as if there was something left to protect. But there wasn't. And there was no reason to run. I am going to die. For the first time, the thought entered her mind. I am going to die.

Wind gusted into the crater. The pines thrashed. Needles whipped and whirled. The dogs yelped and cowered, and a roaring wash of light swung over them all.

A man appeared behind the dogs. A craggy face. A collection of leather leashes knotted around his fist. Only now did Luz note that the dogs wore collars. The man hefted a knobby walking staff in his other hand, and he used it to beat his way through the animals, toward Luz. She retreated, brandished the rock. The man dropped his stick and showed his palms, mouthing inaudible words. Luz wobbled on her feet, and with this slight damming of the torrent coursing through her she lost her balance—the world flickering for a breath—and started to fall. The man rushed and caught her.

He helped her from the trees, leading her back to the ridge and the flat expanse toward the barn. The dogs trotted alongside, weaving over and around one another, nipping and fighting among themselves. The spotlight illuminated their path, and then the aircraft slid out over the clearing and landed in a billowing of dust. Out in the field, patches of fire smoldered like magma. There were people everywhere. Men in black uniforms and flak jackets held weapons. They stood like statues of men, but their round eyes were bright and quick in the eyeholes of their balaclavas. Lights shined on everything. Big trucks painted in pixelated black camouflage. Another helicopter bottomed out of the night and unzipped a cascade of water over the weakening flames.

A dark hump—Pegaso. No sign of Canguro, no sign of Felipo.

Ahead, a man in a suit leaped down from the helicopter. His tie lashed in the downdraft like a wine-colored snake. He shouted something she couldn't hear. The dog man let go of her and shouted something into the official's ear, and the official took a folded rain poncho from under his arm, shook it out, and put it around Luz's shoulders. She held it shut at the front, concealing her bloody clothing.

The official helped her into the helicopter and buckled her into the bench seat. He gave her a headset and put one on himself. She watched his mouth move and heard the words thinly in her ears: "You are safe, miss. We will be off soon." She waited, holding herself beneath the poncho, while the commandos returned to the helicopter. When the aircraft finally lifted from the ground, her stomach swooned and a cramp radiated through her abdomen. The glowing earth rolled away and the dark rushed past.

6

THEY LANDED SOMEWHERE NEAR MONCLOVA. LUZ WALKED with the official into a squat, square building. She clutched the poncho shut. The ceiling lights spiked to the back of her eyeballs. A woman in uniform rose from her desk. Something flashed over the woman's pudgy features when she looked at Luz—fascination or concern or even horror. But the woman composed herself and smiled.

"Marta," the official said, "please assist this young lady—" He paused and glanced at Luz, and she provided her name. The man smiled, white teeth. Gray at his temples and a cleanly shaven face, even in the middle of the night. His name was Garza. "Marta, please take señorita Hidalgo to one of the rooms so that she may refresh herself. Find her some clothes, shoes . . . anything else she might need. After, I would have a word with her."

Luz went with Marta down a long, linoleum-floored hallway. The last light panel in the ceiling flickered, and the hallway's terminus alternated in and out of existence. Reality itself came into question. I am here . . . I am here.

Marta opened a door. A spartan barracks room. Narrow bed with papery-looking sheets. Bedside lamp. Particleboard wardrobe. A door opened into a small washroom with a sterile-looking shower stall. Luz entered and sat wrapped in the poncho on the narrow bed. The cramp beneath her navel ebbed. She thought she was still bleeding.

Marta returned with a stack of things in her arms and set them on the mattress. A folded towel, a bar of soap, a small bottle of shampoo. A pair of gray sweatpants, an olive-green T-shirt, and a gray sweatshirt. A pair of white socks and some cotton underpants. A box of maxi pads.

After Marta departed, Luz stood and stripped out of the clothes Felipo's grandmother had given her. They were stiff and disgusting. She balled them up and threw them into a corner. The washroom floor was cold against her bare feet. The light fixture hummed. She was there in the mirror. Naked, cold, trembling, and alone. Her face was filthy, striated soot in her dried sweat. But her eyes in the midst of it all were sharp, and she ceased shivering by focusing on them.

The pain in her abdomen heaved back. Luz gripped the sides of the sink and forced herself to remain upright. All those times as a girl she had imagined the Guachichiles, the ancient warriors who came before her mother, before herself. As a girl she looked in the mirror, dreaming of that lineage, and envisioned the warrior who might stare back like a hawk. Luz gripped the sink and shouldered through the pain. And now the warrior was there, watching in the mirror. She was held in the eyes. She existed. A thought—a memory, perhaps, something Mamá once told her—arrived in Spanish: El espíritu está vivo a causa de la justicia.

7

SHE TOWELED OFF AND DRESSED IN THE FRESH CLOTHES. A brand-new pair of running shoes had been set outside her door. She laced them up, light and comfortable. When she straightened, a quick spasm lanced from hip to hip. She steadied herself and stowed a few of the maxi pads in the sweatshirt pocket. She clutched the length of her wet hair and flipped it over her shoulder.

The buzzing of the fluorescents in the hallway made her uneasy. As she neared the lobby she heard the hushed tones of a television, melodramatic voices and affected music. She found Marta watching a telenovela on the small set on her desk. Her mother used to watch telenovelas, when there was time, with Luz curled up against her. Mamá would explain the plot as it unfolded, predicting what came next with a chuckle. What does it say about me that I enjoy this garbage? Laughing to herself, not caring that she did enjoy watching. Luz's grandmother would pass through the room and say something. After she'd left, her mother would screw her face into a grotesque imitation and mimic Abuela's tone, and little Luz would giggle.

Marta noticed Luz and punched the power button on the television. She jumped to her feet and took Luz in, saying, "You look beautiful."

The old woman in the taxi had said that to Luz, as well. Luz saw the woman's head snap back, and she put the vision away like replacing some kind of file, and the ease of this shocked her more than the vision itself.

Luz thanked Marta for her help, then followed her into a dim, square room full of cubicles. Garza was in an office partitioned from the room by a glass wall. He waved them in. Steam tendriled from a coffee mug atop the heap of papers on his desk. There was a large map of northeastern Mexico bolted to the wall. Luz sat across from the desk and Marta took the other chair, producing a small notepad and pen. Garza poured a glass of water from a pitcher atop the cabinet and handed it to Luz. She drank it all in one go.

"You are very tired," Garza said, "very distressed, so I am sorry. I will not keep you long, Luz. But you need to help me understand why we found you where we did."

Luz merely looked at him.

"To begin," Garza said, bumping his shoulders, "tell me what you know about the destroyed barn."

Luz clutched the drinking glass in her lap. "Cicatriz," she said. "He was there."

Garza folded his hands on his desk. "And how do you know this?"

"The cuts," she said, and pointed to her lips.

Marta's pen scratched. Garza drummed his fingers on the desk. "What did you see?"

"They took my friend," Luz said. Any calm she had felt a moment before now fractured. She was here, and where was Felipo? The ache in her abdomen pulsed. "You have to do something."

Garza's mouth opened and closed. He sipped his coffee. "I am truly sorry for whatever you have endured. Tell me what happened, and we will do what we can for your friend."

Luz wiped her eyes. "It was bad luck," she said, "running into the fire. I was trying to get home. Felipo was helping me."

She started with the car ride, the cross fire, and her abduction.

"Cicatriz and his men ripped off what we assume was a cartel supply truck," Garza offered, "six days ago, south of here, in the manner you have described."

Luz swallowed and continued. The dark and the heat, fleeing into the desert.

"You," Garza interjected, "were at his headquarters." He gestured to the map on the wall. "Can you point it out to me?"

Luz shook her head. "I was blindfolded. Somewhere near San Cristóbal, Felipo's village." She told Garza how Felipo and her grandmother cared for her, saved her. "You have to help him. Please."

Garza's expression was difficult to read. "You saw them take your friend?"

"They had him when I ran. They were chasing me."

"You didn't see them take him, though. Put him in the Jeep and drive away."

"No."

"Forgive me, Luz, but my position has made me a harsher man than I once was." Garza's jaw muscles flexed. "How do you know that he has been taken?"

She stared back, under the full weight of his meaning: "You found his body?"

"No. Be that as it may, Luz. 'One who owes nothing fears nothing.' What would Cicatriz want with your friend if he owed nothing?"

"He owed nothing," Luz said. "He owed nothing aside from helping me." She left out Felipo's familial connection to Cicatriz because it didn't matter, it shouldn't. Rage punched like a hatchet through the cramp in her gut. "But it isn't true," she said.

Garza cocked his head, and Luz didn't realize she had spoken in English until Garza replied in English himself: "What isn't true?"

"'El que nada debe nada teme.' It is a lie." She closed her eyes. The list tabulated. Those others in the taxi. Felipo's mother and father. Jonah's brother. Jonah's parents, señora McBee. Mamá. And the life, the future, lost to Luz forever. What did any of us owe? She opened her eyes and glared at Garza. "Tell me what I owed. I was on my way home. What did I owe?"

Something sparked in the pools of Garza's eyes, and Luz sensed his need to push back. It only made her angrier. Garza's eyes flicked to Marta and now back to Luz, and he returned to Spanish: "Apologies, Luz." He got up and came around the desk. "I have become an insensitive man. Another glass of water?"

"No."

"Perhaps you should rest, then."

"What are you going to do for Felipo?"

Garza pursed his lips. "It is a terrible thing, Luz, but events like this occur all the time. Every single day. I know that doesn't help any, but it is true. We will scout San Cristóbal and the surrounding area. We will do what we can in order to find Cicatriz, as well as your friend." He smiled, but it didn't touch his eyes. "You, however, must return home. You have been through too much."

Luz stood and turned for the door. Garza said, "Ah, I nearly forgot."

He opened a drawer, removed a photograph, and handed it to Luz. It was of a man with salt-and-pepper hair, and somewhere in the space between her eyes and the photo Luz watched him fall beyond the rim of the cliff and vanish, silent as the void.

Garza straightened his tie. "Along with Cicatriz, this man is a former CDG member turned renegade. He, however, is also a former federale, and I care to have a few words with him. Do you recognize him, did you see him at the farm?"

Luz looked at the photo. The eyes. She saw him smile and she saw him die. She lifted her face to Garza. "No," she said.

8

THE MILITARY DOCTOR WAS A SHORT MAN. HE BLINKED THROUGH rimless glasses. He scribbled Luz's succinct answers onto a clipboard. She lay on the table, paper crinkling under her, and stared at the brilliant fluorescents in the ceiling.

"Eight weeks," she told him, "maybe nine."

The doctor hummed and scribbled. "I believe," he said, pausing, testing his words, "it is over. I am sorry."

The ceiling lights burned into Luz's corneas.

"There may be some cramping," the doctor mumbled. "Some bleeding. But that will end soon." He told her he could offer pain medication. The lights sizzled in the silence. "Nevertheless, you will want to see your own doctor when you return home."

Luz closed her eyes.

"Do not worry, young lady." His voice was softer now. He was trying to make her feel better. "When your cycle returns, you and your husband may try again."

IX

Tell me you understand what I'm saying.

1

IT WAS DARK BY THE TIME THEY REACHED LAREDO'S SPRAWL, AND they ran smack into gridlock as the interstate funneled toward the international bridge. Taillights stretched clear on, presumably halted all the way across the bridge. "Shit," Jonah groaned.

He eased them off the highway and onto an access road. He turned west into an older neighborhood, wheels drumming against the brick surface. There were shops and boutique hotels and restaurants separating them from the grade toward the river. They parked and went into a nearby Tex-Mex diner and got a booth. A young waiter with a heavy accent arrived and they ordered water, and Jonah asked the kid about the traffic.

"They close the bridges all the time." The kid twirled his pen. "Sometimes there's fighting across."

Colby wanted to know if it happened often. "Fighting, I mean."

The kid held his hand out and wobbled it.

"Is that where you're from?"

"Nuevo Laredo? No, man. I'm born in Laredo. I'm American. Got a sister and a nephew, they live across. She thinks things will get better. But I don't know." He shook his head and walked away.

2

THE AIR OUTSIDE SMELLED LIKE A THUNDERSTORM. THEY walked the alley alongside the diner to the tall chain-link in order to take in the view. The long swoop of the bank fell toward an unlit road and the river. The reeds were still in a windless moment. There was no moon, and the lights from the bridge guttered in the water. Across the way, Nuevo Laredo blinked. An enormous Mexican flag billowed like a sailcloth high over the city. Thunder grumbled. The taillights still sat locked across the bridge. Jonah hooked his fingers in the fence and watched.

Something flashed in Nuevo Laredo, near the bridge's foreign end. A silent orange blossom that was there before it folded into itself and vanished. Like that. Jonah almost wondered aloud whether it had been there at all, and then the sound of the explosion rolled to them like a distant thunderclap. The hush that followed filled with car alarms, quiet blips out there in the dark.

3

THEY STOOD QUIETLY IN THE ALLEY FOR A LONG TIME. THEY were on the border but Luz was no closer, and Jonah knew to certainty that if he couldn't get to her their worlds would change forever. Hers would alter in a way, he imagined, that would no longer accommodate his. He needed to see her, to promise their future. To be a part of things.

"We just saw that," Colby said. "Right?"

Lightning pulsed, silent.

Jonah said, "It coulda been anything," but it sounded and felt stupid. Whatever the cause, there had been a big explosion.

"Let's think for a minute," Colby said.

But Jonah turned, paced to the end of the alley, and put his hands on his knees. Old brick beneath his boots. What did Luz tread, and where?

Colby appeared next to him and put a hand on his shoulder. "You gonna see her again, Mickey-Bee."

Jonah stood up straight. It was as if one word was chained to the next, each yanking its successor from his throat, and he hated them but he couldn't stop: "How the fuck do you know?"

Colby's face flashed. He said, "Be reasonable, man. Shit looks a lot rougher than you probably imagined. Plus I don't speak Spanish, and 'less you learned it in secret, you don't speak it, either, so that's two strikes. But the bottom line is, I ain't going no farther." Colby added, "You ain't, either."

"I can't go back to New Orleans."

"Wake the fuck up, Mickey-Bee. This—" Lightning burst nearby, and Colby flinched with the immediate thunderclap.

Failure seared like a brand. Jonah heard Colby's logic, but he couldn't relent. If he returned now, he'd pull off the interstate into New Orleans and he'd be even less than he was now.

"Come on, man. I get it. I'm worried about going back, too. I mean, shit, you think folks ain't been wondering where I been? Davonte gets got and then I up and disappear? If I'm saying I'd rather go back home than cross that bridge, that ought to tell you something." Colby paused before whispering the next part. "She ain't called you. She wanted to, she woulda. I'm sorry. We gotta face the facts."

"Fuck you," Jonah said. Colby was calm, but Jonah was shaking. He had never told Colby to fuck himself before and meant it. Jonah was rebelling against the fact that she hadn't called, sure, but what really pissed him off was Colby's implication that the facts somehow suggested that matters would improve. That things would work themselves out. When did things ever get better on their own? No, this was Jonah's chance to do something. To help etch the path ahead rather than to dumbly accept what was offered, what was denied. He needed to be there, to look her in the eye and tell her that he was bringing her back to New Orleans. "Don't tell me to face the facts," he went on. "You never see how fucked we are. The army, that's gonna be all fun and games and shit, right? You just keep hoping for that."

Colby bit his lip and let his fists hang. He turned and looked at the river, and Jonah thought he might, for the first time, see his friend get truly angry. He imagined Colby pivoting to swing at him, and the image blunted the edge of his own anger.

But Colby only sighed. "I came on this trip for you," he said, "because I knew you needed it. I'm trying to be positive for your ass. But there ain't no point because you right, just like always. I never realized how shitty tomorrow looks. I'm that fuckin' stupid. You right, Mickey-Bee. Thanks." Then he walked to the truck.

Jonah remained behind. A spasm seized his stomach. He took a few breaths. All the things he had assumed, all the ways he'd sold his friend short, all while believing he owned some special kind of knowledge about the world and the way it worked. It had been nothing more than a way to think he was better than Colby. That was what it was. That and nothing more. It began to rain then, cold and stinging.

4

JONAH JOGGED TO THE DINER AND GOT SOME DIRECTIONS FROM the Latino waiter. When Jonah returned—sopping wet from the downpour—Colby was sitting with his arms crossed. Jonah started the truck and drove out of the old town. Colby glanced at him when he turned away from the bridge, still gridlocked, but he didn't say anything.

The bus terminal wasn't far. Colby said, "Mickey-Bee—" but Jonah snapped, "I'm not going home yet, Colby."

"Stupid ass," Colby muttered. "Just being stupid."

They counted their funds. The booking agent, a friendly woman named Jessica, quoted them a price of more than two hundred dollars for a one-way ticket to New Orleans, the bus leaving early in the morning.

"Nah," Colby said, "we only need one ticket."

"That is one ticket, sugar." Jessica was smiling, chewing gum.

The air went out of Jonah. They didn't have enough, considering the gas money Jonah would still need. He backed away from the counter and went and sat in one of the plastic seats. He glanced the room over. A few Latino families seemed to be waiting for a bus. That was it. Colby sat down next to him. They didn't speak for a while. Then Colby said, "You gonna leave me in Texas, then?"

Jonah closed his eyes and the fluorescents burned through his lids. He was so tired. He rubbed his face and looked at Colby and sighed. He said, "Hang on," and then he went to talk to Jessica again.

He asked her if she knew anything about the buses in Mexico.

"Yeah," she said, smacking her gum, "I got family that lives across. Mexican buses are nice. Luxurious. For real. They do express routes on the federal highways, too, no stops."

"Are they more expensive?"

"Nah. They're nicer and way cheaper."

"Really?"

"Yeah, really. But it depends where—"

But Jonah had already told her thanks and started off. Colby asked what was up, but Jonah only motioned for him to follow and they walked outside. They stood under the overhang, watching the rainfall.

Jonah took his keys out of his pocket and held them out. Colby looked at them before he reached, timidly. "Jonah . . ."

"You can do it."

Colby tried handing the keys back. "The fuck I can."

"I know you can."

Colby lowered his face, and Jonah could see that his friend remembered that big empty lot, the hulking and abandoned roller coasters. Just the two of them, whooping and hollering. Colby drove, they laughed. There was no one else around. A good day.

And that was what Jonah said to Colby: "It was a good day, wasn't it?"

"Yeah." Colby looked away. "It was."

"You can do it." Jonah spoke softly. "I can't go back, man. Not yet. And I can't make you come with me, either, even if I want to. This is best."

"What you gonna do?"

"Get a bus ticket over there. Lady said it was way cheaper."

Colby tried giving the keys back again. "I can't do this."

"It's easy," Jonah said. "Just get back on the highway, and when you hit San Antonio follow the signs for Houston and then keep going. Stay in that right lane if you're nervous." Jonah slapped him on the back. "You're a great driver. I seen you."

Colby hemmed and hawed, and Jonah told him that this was the only way he was getting home, short of hitchhiking. "Just drop me back off at the bridge first." He chuckled, trying to keep it light. Colby cursed.

He accelerated and braked jerkily a couple of times just getting out of the lot. Jonah encouraged him, telling him to ease in and out.

"It's like riding a bike," Jonah said.

"Real fuckin' funny." Colby shook his head. "Gonna have to pump gas and shit."

"You can do it."

Soon enough, they were back by the river.

The wipers whipped back and forth. "Gotta drive in this shit," Colby said.

"Why don't you wait a minute for it to slow?"

"Why don't you just wait with me?"

"All right," Jonah told him.

When the downpour finally ebbed, Colby prompted, "How you gonna get back without your truck?"

Jonah snorted a laugh. He hadn't thought about it until just then. But an exciting feeling bubbled, something to go along with the necessity of it all. The feeling had something to do with this final and utter commitment to the journey itself. This severing of escape routes. He smiled at Colby. "I don't know."

Colby said, "You look like a crazy person."

"I'll be all right. I'll call you, let you know what's up."

Colby shrugged. "I still wish you'd come with me," but there was resignation in his voice.

"I know. You drive safe."

Colby held out his hand and they shook, and Colby pulled him in for a quick embrace. Jonah got out and shouldered his backpack. "I'll be back before you know it," he told Colby.

"Be good, Jonah man."

Then Jonah stood in the drizzle and watched the bleary taillights of his father's truck, his brothers' truck, his own truck, shrink away.

5

THE TRAFFIC HAD STARTED MOVING ACROSS IN FITS AND STARTS. The drizzle had strengthened again, and Jonah stood at the beginning of the bridge, sheltered. He didn't notice the man in uniform until he spoke: "You ain't going across right now?"

Jonah looked at the man. Tall, pink faced. A hat with a round brim. Jonah shrugged and said, "Yeah."

"I'd advise against that, kid. Not a good time."

"I got to see somebody important."

"Wait till the sun comes up, at least. It's the middle of the goddamn night."

Jonah decided he didn't want to wait for the rain to let up. He didn't want to be here talking to this man. He readied to dash out from shelter.

"Christ's sake, kid."

Jonah told him he was sorry, he didn't know why, and ran out into the rain. He set to jogging along the walkway, his backpack bouncing. He paused in the middle of the bridge, where the plaque beneath an orange light identified the border. Jonah straddled it, and what struck him was the weight of the two countries to either side, infinitely falling against each other, and the line between them that was infinitely small. Invisible. He looked out through the fence and tried to imagine what Luz might have thought when she crossed, years before. But it was dark and raining and he couldn't see anything, not even the river.

6

THERE WAS A MOTOR POOL AHEAD AND SEVERAL MILITARY-TYPE vehicles, one with a heavy machine gun mounted to its back, but Jonah didn't see any soldiers. The traffic crawled, tires sighing against wet pavement. There was no other pedestrian traffic. A man in uniform appeared and motioned him inside the guardroom.

There were two other men inside. A ceiling fan spun at full tilt, the fluorescent light behind the blades lurid and flashing. The smell of burned coffee and cigarette smoke. Jonah was freezing in his soaked clothes. The guards spoke Spanish among themselves and glanced at Jonah, and one spoke in English.

"You are running from police."

"No," Jonah said, feeling it come out too quick, too high.

"Then why you cross now, hmm?"

"I'm going to see a sick friend," Jonah said. He didn't know where the lie came from. His heart thumped, and he half worried the men would hear it. "It's an emergency."

The guard frowned. "Your friend lives in Nuevo Laredo?"

"Yes," Jonah lied, again. He was intimidated and he felt like that was the answer the guard had wanted. He hoped the man wouldn't press him further.

The guard asked for Jonah's passport. Jonah looked young in the photo, fourteen or fifteen. He was worried it would pose a problem. His initial passport had been part of a ploy by Pop in order to get little Jonah to be okay with Bill going overseas. We can visit, Pop told him. It was all bullshit, of course. But his father had been sweet when he'd wanted to be.

The guard handed the passport back and asked to see Jonah's bag. He opened it and removed some scrunched, dirty shirts to peer deeper into the backpack.

"Okay." The guard flashed a number with his hands: "You stay in

Nuevo Laredo for only this many days, three, then you go home. You understand?"

"Yes." Jonah repacked his bag under their eyes, pressure rising as he fumbled with his things. When he walked out of the guardroom the feeling in his chest eased, and he entered Mexico.

7

THE RAIN THINNED. HE TRUDGED AWAY FROM THE BRIDGE through small globes of weak streetlight. The cars returning to the country whooshed past, spraying puddle water. One- and two-story brick apartment houses pressed in on the street. Well-lit billboards over the darkened buildings. He paused at the next intersection in front of a stucco facade covered with bright, hand-painted Spanish words. A padlocked door.

The lamp overhead was out, and the intersecting street had been blocked off to the left. A congregation of police cars and black trucks and a fire engine. Men, faceless in balaclavas, held weapons. Others, dressed in suits and ties, slouched beneath umbrellas. The flashers of the different vehicles cast the scene in a halting progression of blue and white, red and yellow. Jonah couldn't tell what, if anything, had been blown up.

The traffic hummed. A driver rubbernecked and turned slowly in front of Jonah, away from the roadblock. The headlights bored through the dark. The power seemed to be out for a block, but there was a working stoplight at the next intersection. Jonah found a tavern sandwiched between taller structures, a small neon sign in the tinted front window. He wanted to get out of his wet clothes and ask for directions to the bus station.

The air-conditioning in the silent barroom soaked into his skin. The walls were painted a deep red color and seemed to absorb the dim light. A short bar and a few tables, and a jukebox mutely flashing. The lone patron at the bar rested his forehead on his forearms. The bartender, a wide-faced, mustached man, watched Jonah but didn't speak, and Jonah crossed directly to the washroom.

The smell assaulted him. Graffiti on the walls. Boots scuffed against the tile inside the stall. Jonah put his bag on the counter, stripped out of his clothes, and put on a pair of shorts and a T-shirt that were filthy but dry.

The stall door creaked, and the man who came out said, "Where the hell did you come from?"

Jonah stammered.

"American, aren't you?" The man wore jeans and a long-sleeved T. He had carrot-colored hair and a beard. His eyeballs swam.

"Are you?" Jonah asked.

"Hell yeah, brother." The man zipped his fly. "You must be a writer, huh?" He bent to wash his hands. "Name's Kurtis." He glanced at Jonah to emphasize: "With a *K*."

Jonah introduced himself and asked about the bus station. "I've got a map," he said, "but it's not real good with the local stuff."

"Sure, man. Not far. Buy you a beer first." Kurtis started for the door.

"Uh," Jonah said, "I'm kind of in a rush."

"Shit." Kurtis grinned. "Rookie, huh? You're not walking across town right now, and you ain't taking a cab. I'll get you there. Come on, beer first. We'll trade notes." He punched the swinging door open and clopped out.

Kurtis ordered beers in Spanish and told Jonah he was from California but hadn't been back in years. Two beers in clear bottles arrived without the bartender uttering a word, and Kurtis slid money across the bar. "Where you say you were from?"

"I didn't," Jonah said.

"Well, where?"

"New Orleans."

Kurtis's throat jumped while he drank. "I was there in oh-five, reporting."

Jonah sipped his own beer and it tasted a little skunky, but here he was, in a Mexican bar, having a drink with a journalist. Luz felt slightly more within reach.

"So," Kurtis said, "you're down here for the car bomb, too. I asked around, but nobody's saying shit." He grinned, his eyelids half-closed, and spread his arms. "So here I am." He sipped his beer. He whistled. "A car bomb. That is some new shit, I tell you what."

"I saw it from across the river," Jonah said.

Kurtis nearly spewed beer, laughing. With awe: "Fuck."

"Who blew it up?" Jonah asked. He noticed the other patron lift his head from the bar and cross the room to the jukebox.

"Hell." Kurtis waved his hand. He scratched his cheek through the bramble. "Could be anybody. They all know each other."

The jukebox started to pump American rap music. Kurtis made a face like something stank. "Can't get away from this shit." He drained his beer, set the empty on the bar, and got up to go, and Jonah, at a loss, followed.

Kurtis listed down the sidewalk and made a spectacle of peering in either direction before pissing on somebody's door.

"So, the bus station," Jonah said after Kurtis had composed himself.

"Hotel's this way," the journalist replied. "I'll take a gander at your map, but let's get off the fuckin' street."

Around the corner, the old hotel took up much of the block. A four- or five-story stone building. Palms grew from cutouts in the sidewalk. The lobby was varnished floors and crimson rugs. The kid at the desk nodded in sleep.

"Nice place, huh?" Kurtis said. "Magazine I wrote for used to have their headquarters here."

"Used to?"

"What I said, brother. I'm freelance, now, all the way."

Clothes everywhere in his room. An overflowing ashtray on the dresser. A laptop with a darkened screen sat on the desk, papers stacked alongside it. The sound of a motorcycle climbing through gears came up through the open window. The damp glow of the city. Kurtis went to the window and sat on the sill and peered out at the rooftops.

"Kurtis."

The journalist jerked like he'd fallen asleep. "You probably want a beer, huh?" He went to the small refrigerator and withdrew a couple bottles and tossed one to Jonah.

Jonah set the bottle down and took off his backpack to rummage for his map. "Maybe you could—"

Kurtis raised a hand, asking for silence. "Listen," he said.

Wind. A car engine. Tires through rainwater.

"I love it," Kurtis whispered. "The way this place sounds at night, peaceful when nothing's going off." He returned to the window and peered earthward. "Not as exciting, sure. But you need the quiet moments. You need both."

Jonah spread the map on the foot of the bed. "The bus station?"

Kurtis lifted away from the window and bent over the map. He tapped. "We here. Bus station's here." Only a handful of blocks away by the look of it, near the nexus of a couple of highways cutting west and south. "Where you gotta get to, anyway?"

"Las Monarcas."

"Never heard of it. Some little shit dump?"

"I dunno."

"Show me."

Jonah pointed it out, across the state line into Coahuila.

Kurtis covered his mouth with a fist and belched. "You won't be getting a bus there, bro. Maybe to here—" He tapped a place called Lampazos de Naranjo. "And that's a maybe. Once you're in Lampazos, you better hope there's another bus, or else you gonna have to hire a car service or rent a car or something, if you got the scratch. Must be some story you're sniffing. I figured you were here for the car bomb."

It took Jonah a moment to understand Kurtis's meaning. He started to correct him when several distant but sharp reports rang out, and Kurtis raised a finger. "Ah," he said. "You know how to tell the difference between firecrackers and gunshots?"

Jonah did, but Kurtis didn't give him the opportunity to answer.

"You gotta know the difference, because there's a shitload of both. Place is a trip." He smiled and swigged his beer and walked to the window to peer at the city. He went on: "A rifle shot is like brr-app. Brr-app. The shot and the noise the round makes splitting the air, a little echo. Fireworks just pop. That's it. Pop. Pop."

Jonah refolded his map and shoved it back in his bag.

Kurtis shook his head. "Them cartel fuckers are smart, man. When a fight breaks out, you get buses hijacked to block the roads. Then the federales or the army, or the Marines if someone's serious, can't get to the fight." Kurtis glanced at Jonah and then looked at the street below again.

"But you gotta know, too, all of Mexico isn't crazy like this. It's like your home, bro—America isn't as crazy as New Orleans. I'm talking about pockets, you know, areas in Mexico. The border, the gulf. The Pacific. But I could live here for a long time, man. Good people. The violence isn't random, I promise you. Extreme, no doubt, but it isn't senseless. Well. Not most of the time. People like me and you, we find out the why. We dig out the truth, that's our job, right? So here we are, where shit happens. The frenetic edges. You know what I mean." He lifted his bottle and glanced as if to toast something. "Outposts of progress. Why would you want to be anywhere else?"

Kurtis spun from the window and saw Jonah slinging his bag over his shoulder. "You're new in country," he went on, "so here's what I'm going to do. I'll go with you. We'll bus to Lampazos and I'll find us a way to Las Marcas or whatever your shit dump's called. Hell, maybe we can work together on your story. I speak español if you don't, hombre. Who you say you write for again?"

"I don't write for anybody," Jonah said. "I don't write at all."

"What?"

"I never told you I write."

Kurtis pushed away from the window. "You told me you were a writer," he said.

There was a gleam in his eye that Jonah didn't like. "No, I didn't."

"Did you lie to me, bro?"

"No."

Kurtis pointed at Jonah. "I invite you up to my home and you"—he pointed to his own chest—"you fucking lied to me?"

Jonah backed toward the door, frightened even as anger stirred.

Kurtis advanced. "I can tell you don't get it. You think you're a writer because you got some story down here, but you don't fucking get it. It ain't gold we're talking about here, it ain't ivory. It's truth, man. Nothing more valuable than that. People crave it. And if you want the real stuff, if you want the good shit, you gotta make that place your home."

Kurtis stopped in front of him. He was very close. Jonah's backpack pressed into the door. It wasn't a good position to be in. He tried to anticipate Kurtis's first move. They were about the same height and the journalist was drunk—favorable details. Jonah balled his fists at his sides and said, "I'm not here to write."

"Do you get it?" Kurtis whispered. "Tell me you understand what I'm saying."

"Yeah," Jonah said. "Sure."

"Good." Kurtis nodded. His face slackened and warped into a smile, and he seemed very relieved. "Good, bro." He turned and went to the dresser and took out a glass pipe and a baggie of pot. "Wanna smoke?" Jonah didn't answer and Kurtis didn't look at him as he went on speaking: "You know how I learned that about gunshots, how they sound?" He pinched some of the weed out of the baggie and tapped it into the bowl with his pinkie. "I was out on this story when a fight broke out. They just happen, no telling when. Like the fights are all part of one thing, one amoebic thing, just waiting in the doorways, the windows." He gestured grandly: "It rises out of the sidewalks. I had a big beard, bigger than this. And, dude, a stray fucking bullet goes right like this. Zip. A high fastball under the chin. I heard the shot and all. Took off some of my beard. Had to trim it down." He laughed and finally looked at Jonah. Red, gleeful eyes.

Kurtis walked again to the window with the pipe and a plastic lighter. "If you want to get all you can out of this place, you got to let it take you." He held the flame to the bowl and inhaled and blew the smoke out the window. He stared at the street below and spoke quietly. "You got to let it swallow you up."

Jonah yanked the door open and ran out of the room, dashing down the hall. He shouldered the exit open and bounded down the stairs.

He stopped at the bottom, breathless and sweating. He felt Kurtis's voice on his skin, a crawling, wormy residue. He didn't hear anything; Kurtis never called out, never came into the hall after him. Jonah gathered himself and crossed the lobby.

The kid at the desk had disappeared and Jonah jogged into the wet night, listening for sharp, distant reports, but he didn't hear any. The city was peaceful.

X

...un círculo sin salida.

1

L UZ LAY AWAKE IN THE BARRACKS ROOM. WHEN SHE STARTED running track in the ninth grade she had been terrified of veering from her narrow lane, careening into the other runners. She had nightmares about embarrassing catastrophes. But her worry had been needless. She discovered that her feet stayed locked within her lane. With the sound of the starting gun, her soles found the path and she couldn't have left her lane if she wished.

She had felt her ghost runner stumble in the trees, near the fire. But she imagined she hadn't left him behind completely. Where was she running to now? The only thing that hadn't changed was the shape of the track. "Esta pista," she muttered, "es un círculo sin salida." It was a path born from neither her hopes nor her wishes, yet she found it soldered to her feet all the same.

2

THE OLIVE-COLORED FORD LOBO SPED ALONG THE HIGHWAY east of Monclova. Marta had volunteered to drive Luz home. Luz sat in the passenger seat, and a young soldier with stubbled cheeks sat in the back. There was a dull ache in Luz's abdomen, and she held herself and rested her forehead against the window and watched the clear day. A haze hung over a distant steel factory. The outlying shacks clustered along the road were painted red and yellow, advertisements for Sol beer and Coca-Cola. The two-lane highway ran straight through the valley. Heat danced. Luz dozed to the Ford's droning.

She jolted awake, warm wind blowing through the cab. The soldier exhaled cigarette smoke out the open window. Sweat ran down Marta's chubby cheeks. Luz looked ahead and blinked. Several hundred meters out, three black vehicles blocked the road, parked from shoulder to shoulder.

Marta kept her eyes forward, and the soldier offered nothing, face passive.

"Marta," Luz said, but the woman seemed to ignore her and sped toward the blockade. "Marta, turn around."

Marta squeezed the wheel and glanced at Luz. "It's not what you think."

In English: "Turn the fucking truck around, Marta."

Marta shook her head, wiped sweat from her forehead, and readjusted her grip on the steering wheel. The vehicles were clearer now, big Chevy Suburbans. There were people standing in front of the SUVs, fanned across the highway.

Luz reached across the center console for the wheel, and the soldier in the back grabbed her around the seat, an arm across her chest, pinning her. She thrashed, cursed at him and at Marta. She cursed in English and Spanish. This was all a joke. It had to be. She kicked at the dash and bucked against his grip and then bowed her head, exertion orbs raining before her eyes.

"It is not what you think," Marta said. "I promise."

Luz shook her head.

"Don't worry," Marta tried one more time. "We'll be on the move again soon."

She braked and brought them to a stop. There were seven of them standing in the road, wearing soccer jerseys and T-shirts. There was one woman, dressed entirely in black, hair pulled into a ponytail. They held rifles. The lone unarmed man stood in their center. He wore a crisp lavender oxford, gray slacks, and gleaming shoes. His hair adhered to a precise part. He had his hands in his pockets and he rocked on his feet from heel to toe, and he started forward alone toward the Ford Lobo. He came to the passenger window and looked at Luz. He smiled, jaw muscles standing out. In his upper row of teeth, a gold canine twinkled.

The soldier let go of her, and the man with the gold tooth opened her door. "Hello, Marta," he said. To the soldier, "Nóe, good day to you." He looked at Luz for a long moment and then said, "I am Oziel Zegas y Garcia, but please call me Oziel. I am very happy to meet you, Luz Hidalgo."

Luz smelled his cologne. He spoke slowly, meticulously. He offered his hand, but she didn't take it. "I only wish to speak with you," he said. "Please, walk with me."

Luz didn't move and Marta began to say something, but Oziel silenced her with a glance and beckoned with a hand. "Please," he said kindly.

Luz shot a glare at Marta, then swung her legs out and stepped down onto the hot tarmac. She followed Oziel, away from the Ford and the other vehicles, off the shoulder and onto the hardpan alongside the highway. A cordillera floated on the plain.

"Beautiful country," Oziel said, "no?"

"What do you want."

Something like humor passed through his face. "I regret the nature of this stop, should we have startled you."

"I've been through worse."

"Of course." He smiled and looked toward the mountains. "I understand that you know the location of the safe house belonging to Juan Luis Medina. Cicatriz, as they call him." He turned to Luz. "I need this information."

Luz said, "I don't know where the house is."

"I was told you did."

Luz could see Marta leaning across the seats in the truck, straining to get a view. "Marta told you wrong," she said. "I was there, but I don't know where it is."

Oziel rolled his hand through the air, suggesting she elaborate.

"It is near San Cristóbal."

"In what direction does it lie?"

Luz began to speak, but she stopped and changed course. "I need something from you first."

Again the flicker of amusement. "Enlighten me."

"Cicatriz took my friend, Felipo. If I get you to the safe house, you have to rescue him and get him home to his village."

Oziel shrugged. "Done. Tell me where the house is."

Luz shook her head. "You're not going to help."

"Señorita," Oziel groaned. He spread his arms. "My strategy is unknown, as is the location and layout of Juan Luis's camp, as is your friend's status. And so how can I promise that I will shape my plan to accommodate this Felipo, to whom I owe nothing?"

"You would owe me."

"I do not think you understand how this works." The gold tooth flashed.

The narcos on the highway—not one of them had moved. Luz felt only exhausted. She couldn't think of or identify a thing in her future that she would be sorry to lose or to never see again—nothing that might be leveraged against her, not even her own existence. She spoke in English, turning toward Oziel: "You can try. You can try to make me tell you. You can do whatever you want. But I promise I won't tell you a fucking thing. I will keep my mouth shut and you can hurt me, and I'll be quiet and then I'll be dead."

The man's eyebrows bumped. A small smile played on his lips. He replied in English. "You are an unusual young woman."

Luz sighed. "I'm just tired. I'm tired of everything." She returned to Spanish. "I can't say which direction from San Cristóbal. North, south, I don't know. If I was there, I would know. I could take you there. And that's the only real option."

Oziel shook his head. Almost gravely. As if something about her proposition saddened him.

"But," Luz added, "you would have to help me rescue my friend. You would take him home to San Cristóbal, and then you would take me home to Las Monarcas."

"Do not offer this," the man said.

Luz was thinking of Felipo. Helping him now was the only thing to do. Any other option felt vacuous—how would she live with herself, after all he'd done for her? "I will only be riding with you to help my friend."

"No." Oziel looked at her. "There is no such thing." He swept his hand toward the vehicles and his crew. "Your choice aligns you with us."

He withdrew a flat leather case from his chest pocket and lifted out a cigarette. He held it toward Luz and tapped the white foam filter, making sure she saw. Then he lit the smoke, drew deeply, and exhaled. He held the filter toward her again and tapped the yellow-stained foam. "So it is with this kind of decision. Do you see? We will draw the breath of our business through you. There is no undoing it." He shrugged. "You must be certain. Think more on it if you must."

Of the men and the woman standing on the highway, most of them weren't even looking her way. Marta still strained to watch, a pale round face. Farther up the highway, a jalopy crawled to a wary stop and then executed a two-point turn and drove away. Luz looked at Oziel and imagined him tumbling silently from view. "I understand what you say," she said, "but it is too late for me already."

He sighed, dropped the butt, ground it out. "Very well."

Luz started for the vehicles, but Oziel did not immediately follow. He punched a number into a cell phone and put it to his ear. He listened and said, "Good to go, yes," and hung up. He smiled humorlessly when he noticed that Luz had heard him.

"I have the autonomy I require in the way I run my plaza. But my duties are not without their challenges, and certain things are expected of me. Cicatriz used to work for me, and he lives in my plaza still, and so that makes him my problem." He gestured for Luz to walk with him. "Please."

They crossed the hardpan and he gave quick orders, and the crew scattered. Luz followed Oziel and the woman dressed in black to one of the Suburbans. Marta leaped from the Ford Lobo and called out.

"Señor Zegas? You said only a talk."

Oziel said, "Ask the girl."

Marta turned to Luz, and Luz answered before the woman uttered a question.

"You," she told her, "are a coward." She pointed to the soldier in the back of the truck. "So is he."

Oziel chuckled quietly as he held the SUV door open for Luz. "Yes," he whispered, just for her. "They are."

3

THE WOMAN IN BLACK DROVE, RESTING HER RIFLE IN THE passenger-side footwell. Her name was Cecilia. She was Oziel's niece. She had a smooth face, no lines from smiling or worrying. Dark eyes and dark eyebrows and dark hair. She was pretty, but that had not been Luz's initial observation. When Cecilia acknowledged Luz with a wordless glance, the woman's eyes were steady, serious, and unsurprised by anything. The way she looked at you made you remember that the ability to breathe was only a temporary condition. She was a killer. This had been Luz's immediate thought.

Luz sat in the middle with Oziel. He crossed his legs and locked his fingers behind his head. "Your English is very good," he said. "Where did you learn?"

Luz shrugged. "It doesn't matter."

"Yes, it does. I am curious."

"No."

He watched her. "You are beautiful and you are a fighter. Descended from old warriors, perhaps." Luz looked at him. His skin was paler than hers. He looked less Mexican than he did white, European. He tapped his fingers on his knees. "It makes no sense to me that anyone should disregard or attempt to scrub away his own history. It continually asserts itself. It lives on. One should embrace it."

Luz squeezed her eyes shut. Old warriors. She had always wanted to believe her mother's stories.

"And 'Hidalgo,' of course," Oziel went on. "There must be royalty somewhere in your ancestry. Disregard any who use your history to insult you, Luz. I believe that you are Mexico yourself, every part of her history—a fighter on every side." He paused, then added, "And let us not forget Miguel Hidalgo, whose head once adorned the Alhóndiga in Guanajuato and inspired us to independence. Yes, yes."

In the driver's seat, Cecilia sighed but said nothing.

"People are useful, each in their own ways," Oziel said, "at the proper times. Juan Luis was a sicario for me. I gave him a crew in Monterrey. But he had always been shortsighted and a slave to impulse. I should have seen it coming. He is not only an abomination, but a traitor, too. An enemy offered him something sweet and he turned his gun on me." Oziel touched Luz's shoulder so she would look at him. "I am telling you this so that you understand what you are doing. Juan Luis turned his gun on me, but I survived. The only regret there can be is that we let him escape with his life."

Cecilia's eyes flashed in the rearview.

Luz faced the window. "I'll help you get to the house, then you take me home."

"Home." He hummed. "Of course."

4

CICATRIZ ALLOWED HIS MEN TO SAMPLE WHAT THEY HAD RIPPED from the storehouse at the farm, and they partied through the night and most of the day after. It seemed that the same bitch had appeared and bested them again, and so they toasted the man who had been a federale. It was a surprise, running into her at the farm. Cicatriz had almost put her out of his mind, but there was no doubt it had been she, for his whelp of a cousin had been with her. Cicatriz sat and thought about the girl, breathing through his mouth because of the impasse of his ruined nose. Men and women slept all over the room. Naked brown bodies, the rise and fall of snores. A connection in the city had driven a van of Saltillo whores to them. But tonight the liquor ran dry, the perico ran thin. He sat awake and alone, naked, buoyed by some last chemical pulsing. Once he pushed the bitch from his mind, dead faces formed in the ether of his thoughts and he wished them gone. He stroked himself and watched the dark snatch of a sleeping whore, the limp cock of one of his men. He had had lovers in his life, but he had once had a friend, as well—a true friend, he thought, one of the few—and it was the friend he missed the most. He thought of her, his friend, and held on to her face in defense against the others.

5

THE CONVOY OF SUBURBANS LEFT THE BLACKTOP HIGHWAY FOR the dusty track Luz had been walking upon when she met Felipo. The ridge rose up ahead, the anvil-shaped escarpment that loomed over San Cristóbal. The sun fell behind it. The convoy halted on Oziel's order, spoken through his cell phone walkie-talkie. He pointed and said that San Cristóbal lay ahead, in the mountains. Luz nodded.

Luz instructed them to turn off the road onto a dirt path that ran parallel to the mountains. She had no way of knowing if it was indeed the right turn, but she knew that the house would be in this direction. Dark swallowed dusk.

Their Suburban led the way, crawling, with only the weak glow of the fog lights. The remaining SUVs drove without their lights on. Nothing specific in the landscape spoke to Luz, but it was reminiscent in a formless way. Nebulous shapes of scrub and rock. The black wall of the mountains. Cecilia drove carefully, both hands on the wheel. The vehicle lurched and rocked. Insects whorled in the fog lamps. Luz felt sick, the same way she used to feel in the hour leading up to a track meet.

Some dark feature of the landscape passed. Luz spied, burning down in the valley, a small cluster of orange light. She pointed. "That's got to be it."

"Well done," Oziel said.

Luz hardly heard him. Be okay, Felipo.

The house lay not on their particular road but farther away from the mountains. Cecilia eased the Suburban off the dirt path toward the house. The others followed. The SUV bounced and pitched, even though she kept it under five kilometers per hour. Oziel ordered a halt perhaps four hundred meters from the house, and Cecilia killed the engine. There were vehicles next to the house, within the orange globe of light. The Jeep and the pickup, but also a large passenger van. There was the shed behind the house—Luz could see it. A voice in the dark, fingers on her skin. The tile hitting him in the face, the crunch through her wrists.

The narcos gathered around Oziel, boots and sneakers grinding in the earth. There was no moon, a darker night than when Luz had escaped. No sound trickled out from the house in the distance. Cecilia and the men held their rifles and waited for Oziel to speak. One of the narcos donned a black knit ski mask, red grinning lips embroidered around the mouth. Oziel whispered—Luz, standing off away from them, couldn't make out his words. And then they all let their weapons hang from their shoulder straps and joined hands and bowed their heads, and Luz, creeping closer, heard Oziel pray to God and to San Miguel el arcángel. Renewal through blood, amen.

They broke their huddle and five of them set off, walking briskly behind Cecilia. The figures of the narcos faded into the dark, and they reappeared as thin silhouettes against the lights of the house and then vanished again as they dipped into some low spot.

Luz watched them go and wondered whether Cicatriz might be holding Felipo in that shed as well. If Felipo was alive. Please.

Oziel and the remaining narco, a boy with a rifle, stepped behind the SUVs, putting the vehicles between themselves and the house and the gunmen. They sat on the ground, and he whispered for Luz to join them. She peeked around the fender, watching the shadows of the narcos diverge into two groups.

"Stay hidden," Oziel said. "Be careful."

Luz nodded, extended one leg, and brought the instep of her other foot to her knee in a hurdler's stretch. She held it and straightened, and the men watched her with mild confusion. She switched legs and bent again at the waist.

"What are you doing?" Oziel said.

Four hundred meters. She had once run that distance in just shy of sixty seconds.

"Luz," Oziel said, but gunfire unseamed the night.

Luz jerked, a reflex, but she forced herself to look around the edge of the Suburban. Muzzles flashed. It was difficult to tell, but it seemed that the groups of narcos were firing into the house at different angles, all facing away from her location.

When the firing paused she heard Oziel shouting, jumbled words. A hand—the young narco's—landed on her shoulder, and she shrugged it off, leaping to her feet and breaking into her sprint.

The stretch of desert. The adobe structure that now seemed darker. Already the smell of cordite. The sound of her breath and the impact of her footfalls and the cold presence of the ghost runner on her hip—she hadn't left him behind after all. She heard no shout from Oziel, and the ghost runner pressed in on her, as did the fear that the narco might simply rise and shoot her in the back. She pushed, drew a step ahead.

She could see the shadowed forms of the narcos joining up in front of the house. They would go inside, and there would be more shooting. Luz knew that even her best time for this distance was still a very long time to be so exposed when the bullets began to fly. She focused on swinging her arms faster, forcing her legs to catch up.

The windows in the house flashed, staccato and arrhythmic. The reports were louder. Luz was face-first in the dirt, holding on to the earth. She wasn't sure how she'd gotten there. She was petrified, something icy pinning her down. She didn't think she'd been shot—she was trapped inside a body that wouldn't respond. In a lull someone screamed, so quiet. Come on, Luz thought. "Come on," she said. And now she was screaming, getting up, willing her limbs to motion. Screaming and running again, sprinting toward the house. She flinched with the next burst and waited to be shot, but she kept her legs going. A cramp squeezed beneath her belly button. There was no ghost runner on her hip, but she wasn't outrunning anything, she realized—she was running into it.

She slid on her knees into the rear wheel of the pickup truck as a round bit into another tire and the truck sank toward the earth. The window overhead exploded into hail. Her numb eardrums pulsed. Shouting surfaced. The quick belch of a three-round burst. The cramp sliced from her belly to her oblique, a raw and red fault line. She'd been holding her breath and it started over again all at once, ragged.

Her hands were cold and unsteady. Her quadriceps quivered. She got to her feet and ran leadenly around the vehicles. The windows of the house lay broken in the yard. What light there was collected, glimmering, in the shards. Dust coughed from the adobe wall and a round bored through the air a few feet ahead of her, all in less time than a single step, and she hadn't heard the report.

The shed door was chained, padlocked. She grabbed the chain and yanked futilely. She banged on the tin door and shouted for Felipo. No response.

The rear door of the house flew open.

A naked, potbellied man leaped into the yard, running. His splayed toes reached for purchase, his torso awash in black blood. He was even with the shed when Cecilia stepped into the open doorway and raised her rifle.

The naked body went slack in midstride. Blood and tissue roped from his chest. The corpse tumbled into the woodpile at the back of the yard. The long-handled ax fell across his hip, the handle like an exposed, polished bone. Cecilia aimed and fired once more into the man, and the body briefly animated.

Luz's stomach convulsed. Cecilia pivoted toward her and then lowered the rifle. The sicaria cocked her head, disappeared back into the house.

Luz exhaled, dashed across the yard, and grabbed the ax handle. Her knuckles brushed the damp skin of the corpse's hip, and she could smell him, smell the odor of his body and the metal in his blood. She hefted the ax.

The noises were distinct now. A laugh. A spoken line. The single pop of a gunshot. Don't look into the house, she told herself. Don't look. She ran to the shed.

The ax head glanced off the chain, and the ineffective clang vibrated up through her fingers. She was trying for the padlock, but she missed again. On her third attempt the blade deflected and punctured the tin door. She remembered: the walls of the shed were supported by two-by-fours, but the door was of a single piece.

She put her face to the cut in the door and shouted, "If you're in there, get away from the door!"

She reset her feet and swung the ax like a baseball bat and buried the blade in the tin. She jerked it free and swung again, fighting through the cramp that stiffened her trunk with each hack. She had opened a dark cleft a foot long. She peered into the space and called Felipo's name. A four-fingered hand rose and fell through the beam of light. "Oh, God," Luz said. "Hang on, Felipo. Hang on."

A narco appeared in the open door of the house, black ski mask scrunched up onto his dome. He watched her. His rifle hung at his side. He gestured at her and said something to somebody over his shoulder. Luz ignored him and hacked with the ax, widening the cut.

She chopped vertically at it and then hammered the edges of the opening with the flat of the ax blade. Her shoulders burned and her forearms were shaking. She squatted and managed to slide sideways through the gap.

Felipo sat slouched against the back wall. He didn't speak, and Luz had to help him up. His face, passing briefly through the light, was a pulp of purple flesh.

"I'm sorry," Luz said as he leaned on her. "I'm sorry."

At the rift in the tin he tottered and ducked into the opening, sliding through and collapsing in the dirt. Luz followed him out and with her hands in his armpits got him to his feet again. One of his eyes was completely shut. "Luz," he rasped.

"It's okay now," she said. "It's okay."

6

THEY CAME AROUND THE HOUSE. OZIEL AND THE OTHER YOUNG narco had driven two of the Suburbans down and parked them in the path. Four naked corpses were lined up—two men and two women, dirt plastered to wet spots. There were another five people, also naked, sitting with their legs crossed and their hands bound behind them. Two were women and three were men. Oziel's crew stood over them with casually aimed rifles. Oziel watched Luz and Felipo approach. He smiled slightly and shook his head. As they passed, Oziel bent and seized the hair of one of his captives and jerked the man's head back. The rolling eyes found Luz and narrowed. A sneer split the white furrow through his lips. He wore a blood-soaked splint taped over his nose.

"Remember this young lady?" Oziel asked.

The cords stood out in Cicatriz's neck. He began to cough, and Oziel shoved his head away. Oziel turned to Luz and pulled something from his waistband. It was the knife, the silver knife with the Chichimec designs, that Luz had dropped in the desert. It was now sheathed in a simple leather scabbard. Oziel held the knife out to her. "Would you like to have this, a memento of the occasion?"

Luz stared at it. Her mind was fuzzy and she was very tired.

"Take it," Oziel urged, pressing it into her hand. Then he looked at Felipo, squinting into his disfigured face. "You are in good hands, young man."

Luz led Felipo to one of the vehicles. Cecilia was sitting on the bumper, smoking a cigarette. Strands of black hair stuck to her forehead with sweat. Her rifle was propped next to her. She stared somberly at Luz approaching, and Luz nodded back, but Cecilia didn't respond. No. Cecilia wasn't looking at her. Luz followed the woman's gaze. The sicaria and Cicatriz were looking at each other. Cicatriz laughed to himself, rueful, and lowered his face.

After Oziel's men had recovered what stolen product was left, he ordered them to load Cicatriz and his followers—both the dead and alive—into one of the SUVs. Then he produced a set of car keys and jingled them in front of the women's faces. One of the whores shivered and cried, saliva stringing from her mouth, but the other was stoic. Oziel gestured toward the bodies of the dead women. "I am sorry for your colleagues," he said. "Unavoidable. I do, however, have a proposition for you two, should you care to avoid joining them in the corner of hell reserved for whores. Would you like to hear my proposal?"

The crying woman was hysterical, shaking. The other stared at Oziel. He jingled the keys again. "These," he said, "belong to your van over there. The two of you will drive back to Saltillo. Go as you are. You will tell every soul along the way that Cicatriz is finished. His men are dead. There is now no question—this plaza is mine, as it has always been. You understand me?" The stoic woman glared and the sobbing woman nodded. A narco bent and severed their bindings. Oziel dropped the keys to the dirt. "Now. Go."

The sobbing woman got up and ran toward the van. The other scooped up the keys. The van came to life and drove away, and Oziel turned to Luz and smiled, as if seeking her approval. Felipo leaned heavily on her, and she opened the door to the unoccupied Suburban and helped him in. One of Oziel's men exited the house and threw a red plastic jug aside. He struck a match and tossed it through the doorway, and flames began to eat up the house.

7

MORNING BROKE RED OVER THE MOUNTAINS. THEY HAD stopped at a crossroads where a decrepit arena hulked. Rusted scaffolding. Warped wooden grandstand. Around the arena's upper limit, old streamers flicked like dried eel skins. An aluminum sign over the clay parking lot depicted a matador dodging a bull, all in faded graphics and rattling in the wind. In the distance lay the jumbled haze of a city.

Oziel's men dragged the dead renegades from the back of a vehicle and arranged the bodies on the clay of the arena's lot, just off the highway, where they would be seen by travelers in and out of the city. Next they made the three surviving members, still naked, stand in a row next to the corpses. The men were bound around the ankles and wrists. Cicatriz leveled his gaze at Luz and Felipo where they stood, the boy leaning against her. Cecilia placed a silver pistol in Oziel's hand, and he walked to the first of the surviving narcos. The man's softer spots jiggled.

"Get a hold of yourself," Oziel told him. "You made the choice that brought you here. Surely this possibility did not escape you." Then he raised the pistol and shot the man through the forehead. Blood and bone and brain matter spurted, slopped to the clay, and the man collapsed in a heap alongside his dead comrades.

Felipo jumped. The report ricocheted in tinny fragments off the ancient bullfighting arena and vanished out into the waste.

The next narco in line tried hopping away but fell almost immediately. Oziel groaned and gestured. Two of his men came forward and hauled the man to his feet. Oziel gripped the man's shoulders and squared him up. He gestured toward the arena. "Think of the strong creatures that must have died in this place. Draw inspiration from them." And he shot the man through the forehead as well.

Cicatriz was last. He held still, watched Oziel. Cicatriz's body was lean, almost starved looking. A small dark tattoo on his pectoral. Very little hair. He seemed young, and Luz supposed that he was.

"And here we are," Oziel said. "Forgive my lack of ceremony, Juan Luis. I am merely glad to get this over with."

Luz heard shuffling and glanced to see Cecilia pivot away from the scene, leaning against the Suburban and watching the red valley.

Oziel raised the pistol to Cicatriz's sneering face. But he did pause, dropping his arm and spinning. "Wait!" he exclaimed. He strode to Luz and Felipo, extending the pistol by the barrel to the boy. "I am happy to let you finish this. For what he's done to you."

Felipo lifted his weight away from Luz. He glanced at her. His swollen and purple face, his one visible eye.

"Truly," Oziel said, "it makes no difference to me who pulls the trigger at this point."

Felipo took the pistol, held it in his hands. It gleamed. Luz watched. I have imagined it so often, Felipo had said, how it must have happened. His parents dead on the ground outside his home. He gripped the pistol and limped to his cousin.

Oziel followed close behind Felipo and said, "You see, Juan Luis. You are nothing, and you will soon be nothing forever, and no one will remember you."

Felipo raised the pistol. The sign over the parking lot creaked and rattled in the wind. Felipo extended his arm, aimed at his cousin's face.

Cicatriz licked his lips. He spoke to Oziel, words quick and high. "I am nothing, but so are you." Felipo's arm was shaking and he didn't pull the trigger.

Oziel turned to one of his men and held his hand out. The man placed another pistol in it.

"I won't be alone," Cicatriz said to Oziel. "Nobody will care for you when you are gone. What you've done will be swallowed along with all the rest. You—"

Oziel stepped around Felipo, who was still leveling the silver pistol at his cousin's face, and shot Cicatriz through the temple.

Cicatriz crumpled. Felipo's arm dropped.

Luz could see the blood soaking and thickening into the clay, a red halo. She watched it near the toes of Felipo's boots and she wanted to scream at him to move, but the words were stuck. Luz swayed on her feet, and she put her hands on her knees and took a deep breath and stared at the ground.

Oziel was saying something. Apologizing to Felipo. Luz felt a hand on her back. It was the boy. She straightened and he put his arm around her shoulders. "I couldn't," Felipo wheezed.

"I know," Luz answered.

Oziel returned the two handguns to their owners. He drew a jack-knife from the pocket of his slacks and locked the blade open.

"I will tell you why Juan Luis was wrong." Oziel pointed at the corpse with the knife. "I will tell you why we are not going anywhere. The hand where the dollar originates may be hidden, obscured by agencies and borders and skin color, but that dollar does end up in our hand." He held out his palm to demonstrate, splaying his fingers. "You see, the hand where the money originates hides. It is complicit, but it protects itself, cowering. It is afraid of dirtying itself. But my hand? Well." And then he bent over Cicatriz and went to work with the knife.

Luz averted her eyes. It took Oziel a while. He straightened, yanked the piece of skin free, and kicked dirt onto the red-faced corpse. He exhaled, resolute. A narco came forward with a cooler, and Oziel placed the trophy inside. He spread his arms like a magician, the sun glistering on his wet palm, on the wet blade. Then he went over to an old hand pump next to the arena and opened the flow, rinsing his hands and face under the torrent. He returned dripping and grinning.

Oziel addressed the men: "You know the drill."

The narcos disappeared into their vehicles and drove away, leaving Luz and Felipo, Oziel and Cecilia behind, with the corpses in a swirling of red dust.

"I feel like a new man," Oziel proclaimed, opening the door to the remaining Suburban. "Shall we?"

8

A STATUETTE OF LA VIRGEN WAS GLUED TO THE DASH OF THE Suburban, and a wooden rosary swung from the rearview. Luz hadn't noticed either before. Cecilia parked on the road into San Cristóbal, and Oziel told Luz they'd wait where they were.

She walked with Felipo into the ravine where the village lay. A hot afternoon. Crickets droned in the brush. They crossed the stone bridge and passed Rafa's store. The village was quiet. A face hovered in the shadowed opening, vanished. Alongside, on the wall of the store, a black *C* with a white slash through it had been painted.

"It is over," Luz said, but the words felt insubstantial.

The boy bowed his head and tears slid through the dust on his face. "What now?"

Luz couldn't tell if the question was for her. Regardless, she didn't think she was capable of providing an answer. She put her arm around him as they walked. "Thank you for everything," she whispered.

Up the hill, the doors of the small chapel opened and the priest exited, wearing a red stole. The scant congregation followed. There was no music, no joyous babble. The small bell tower stood silent. Luz waited with Felipo in the road as the families dragged their feet past, eyes downcast and repentant. Felipo tugged Luz's wrist and they went to wait on the front step of his house.

His grandmother arrived hand-in-hand with Ignacio. The old woman saw them and let go of the boy's hand and covered her mouth. But she smoothed her face as she neared, wrangling her emotions and burying them down and out of sight.

A small noise escaped her throat when she hugged her grandson. She didn't ask what had happened, and she didn't seem surprised, either. She seemed relieved, somehow. She reached for Luz's hands. "I am sorry, dear," she said.

Luz shook her head, a lump in her throat. "I am. I am sorry. Whatever wrong turn I made, I would not want to live had it led to—"

"Hush," the old woman said. "Often, the wrong turn is the only route offered."

Felipo went stiffly to a knee and embraced the mute Ignacio. Their grandmother asked Luz to come in and rest, to pray with them. But Luz told her she couldn't; she had a ride home waiting for her. Last, she told the grandmother that Cicatriz would never hurt them again.

The old woman closed her eyes and turned her face to the sun. "My grandson, then, has come to the end he designed for himself."

Luz walked out into the dusty road. The parishioners still passed in silence. She raised a hand to Felipo and his family. "Thank you," she said.

The family went inside. Ignacio reached and took his brother's hand, and the door closed.

Luz returned through the village. Nobody looked at her. The villagers walked with hands clasped, contemplating sacrifice. Luz moved beyond them all, across the stone bridge, and onto the last stretch of trail, where she was alone. The insects sang. She was sweating in the still heat. She put one foot in front of the other. A peace settled into her, a peace like she'd not felt in weeks.

9

THEY FOUND THE HIGHWAY AGAIN AND TACKED EAST, THREAD-
ing out of the mountains and slaloming between acres of rolling
scrubland and pasture. Hills on the horizon. What had taken two days
on horseback with Felipo took a couple of hours by SUV. Luz didn't
speak, and neither did Cecilia while she drove. Oziel made phone calls
and drummed his fingers on his knees.

Cecilia took the turnoff toward Las Monarcas, and the town appeared—a collection of shimmering structures among sun-soaked foothills. The sicaria pulled the Suburban over to the side of the road and
parked. Luz could see the dome of the church. A silver radio tower. The
place had been her home, and it would be again. Somewhere in there
grew the monarch tree, but in her memory this was the only detail in a
picture that had been all but scrubbed blank. Las Monarcas was there,
right there, but it didn't move her. She had spent years assimilating to
another place, after all, which meant effacing her home's context—her
former life.

"I hope you don't mind if we let you walk from here," Oziel said.

"That's fine."

"You seem less than happy."

"I'm all right."

"Luz. Permit me to say something before you go on your way."

"Okay."

He took out his cigarettes and lit one. He smoked and tapped the
yellowed filter and smiled. "You are a special woman, Luz. Like she is."
He pointed to his niece. Cecilia didn't turn to look. Oziel went on. "I
can feel your potential. Welling up, searching for an outlet, like a spring
in a mountainside." He exhaled smoke and let his arm hang out of the
open window. "What I am saying is, though I do not know your history,
I can see that going back to this home of yours is not the best thing for
you. Particularly if you have not been back in a long time."

He waited for a response, but she didn't say anything.

He continued, "I predict that you will be unsatisfied unless you can find some venture that actively challenges you and your being, therein offering the opportunities you will require for constant vindication. You are like us." He pointed to himself and to his niece. "It will be as I said to you when we met. There is no going back. There is no such thing as being along for the ride."

Luz let his words wash over her. "Thank you for helping me with Felipo. I just want to go home."

"Very well." He sighed. "Do me this favor—" He produced a blank business card and wrote a phone number on it. "Call in the event you need something more."

Luz put the card in her pocket but didn't say anything. Cecilia turned her head and briefly nodded good-bye. Luz opened the door and got out.

"Ah!" Oziel said. "Do not forget this!" He was holding out the large silver knife in the leather sheath.

Luz looked at it for a moment, then numbly reached and took it. She rolled it up in the army sweatshirt and put it under her arm. She shut the door and started off. The vehicle turned and pealed away behind her, clawing through gears. It was gone soon enough.

10

SHE TRUDGED UP THE INCLINING COBBLESTONE, WAITING FOR some unremembered image to flare. A girl whined past on a four-wheeler and Luz stepped aside, nearly putting her foot into the crevice of the narrow, deep rain channel between cobblestone and sidewalk, and there it was. She once sat at the front gate of her grandmother's, during a downpour, thinking of her father who was so far away, and she watched the rainwater flood the channels and course down the street itself like a river.

The low buildings hedged in the street, smashed up against one another, and staggered up the grade, creating a steppe of rooftop laundry lines and flowerbeds. Sunlight twisted through the glass shards embedded in wall tops. The street flattened into a roundabout holding a dry, moldering fountain in its center. A bald man sat on the fountain's rim and sang through his mustache, singing for the empty street.

The street climbed toward a *T* in front of the Spanish church with the tall, varnished doors. Its dome shouldered the sky, and pigeons lined the crossbar of the copper cross at its apex. A woman who seemed as ancient as the building sat on the steps, palm held out and head bowed. Her eyes were hardly open and her thin lips quivered with indecipherable whispers. Luz remembered her mother waking her and dressing her on Sundays, then leading her down the street. Her mother always pressed a few pesos into the beggars' palms, and it confused Luz—her father had left because they needed money. But her mother would take her into church and they'd sit, waiting for Mass, and Mamá would recite the parable about the camel and the eye of the needle.

Toward the east the street dived eventually from sight, and within the bounded scope of the Las Monarcas rooftops the plain arced toward the horizon. To the west the street climbed higher, and the bisecting streets climbed higher yet, north, into the hills. The homes, blue and yellow and red, seemed to stack atop one another. The monarch tree, Luz figured, was somewhere in that direction.

Squashed paper cups littered the street, empty soda bottles. Luz realized she'd missed the recent Passion parade. Memory swarmed, thick as the monarch clouds. She remembered the parades of her youth, standing gravely with Mamá. She knew that the church, inside, would be quiet and smell of incense. She recalled the dioramas situated within the entranceway, little glass-encased visages on pedestals. The scene at Golgotha and the Last Supper and the martyrdoms of various saints— Sebastián lashed to a tree and pincushioned with arrows, Esteban bloody and broken in the street. Above the altar, Christ would be hanging crucified in a gleaming, realistic replica. His blood had seemed perpetually wet. All that holy violence—she was made to know it even as a child. And Luz recalled the alcove that housed the iron framework of candles flickering in red glass. Luz and her mother used to go to the grotto after Mass for her father. We lit candles for you, Papá, so far away. She had stared at those flames dancing solitary in their glasses and prayed, as hard as she was able.

But that had been a long time ago, and Luz was tired, too tired to go into the church and see what, if anything, had changed. She turned from the steps and from the beggar woman and walked uphill, toward her grandmother's. She was thinking about opposing yet simultaneous worlds. The knowledge she had now versus the knowledge she used to not have, for instance. That as a girl she could kneel and pray for her father, while he, unaware, slaved on a scorched rooftop.

11

THE GATE WAS SET INTO AN ORANGE STUCCO WALL. IT SQUEALED open. She walked into the courtyard, gravel sloshing under her shoes. Wooden wind chimes clacked. A sprawling vine flowered along one interior wall. The center of the courtyard contained a thin tree, an iron table and chairs, a few potted plants. Doors were set into the walls, a total of four separate apartments. Luz remembered. Her grandmother's door was in the highest corner of the courtyard, amid the flowering vine.

A vacant hummingbird feeder hung from the eave, rotating in the breeze. It slowed and reversed direction. Luz moved toward the door, feeling strangely detached. As if she was physical form only, all motion and no spirit. A homemade wreath encircled the door knocker. Luz knocked, and the door opened almost immediately.

Her grandmother was short and thin. Long slacks folded over her feet, bare toes sticking out, and a linen shirt draped loose past her waist. Her silver hair was cropped close and ruffled. Her eyes blinked through their spectacles. She stared at Luz, and Luz could smell the leather goods, and the spices from the kitchen—the ground corn and the dried chiles that would be strung on twine across the window above the sink—and there was another scent, too, something more difficult to name. The scent of years, perhaps, of a childhood. Something unremembered until now, and yet still no memory gave it a face. But it was there. This was where she had lived.

"Luz," her grandmother said, water glistening in the corners of her magnified eyes. She pulled her inside and embraced her, and Luz felt her sharp bones.

Abuela brewed coffee and told Luz that she'd waited the entire first day and night, sitting up and worrying. Her father had called, saying he'd heard nothing, and finally two days later called to say that Luz had been delayed because of an auto problem of some kind. Her grandmother had waited in the apartment each day since then, not going to the market, not going to Mass, fearing that Luz might arrive when she wasn't home. And as the days stretched, her grandmother began to fear much worse things. She had called Luz's father. He knew nothing.

The living room was painted a bright blue. Sunlight slanted in through a skylight. There were plants on the windowsill and a water-cooler in the kitchen and woven rugs over the concrete floor. A sagging couch, a couple of rattan chairs, a small table. A miniature crucifix on the wall. In an alcove at the back of the living room, her grandmother kept her workbench and tools and strips of tanned leather hanging from hooks. Luz remembered a television, but there wasn't one anymore.

Her grandmother brought coffee to the table. "I'm sorry for thinking such terrible thoughts while I worried," she said. "But you are here now."

Luz smiled weakly. She lifted the coffee mug to her face, felt the heat on her lips, and her grandmother jolted and said, "Wait!"

Luz set the mug down and her grandmother took it and shuffled toward the kitchen. "My mind," she muttered. "I'm sorry. I don't know what I was thinking. No coffee for you." She slung the coffee from the mug into the ceramic sink. "I will pour you some juice. That is good. Very good."

Luz got up and crossed to the kitchen entrance, stood barefoot on the cool cement.

"I have orange juice," her grandmother was saying, peering into the refrigerator.

"Abuela," Luz said. "I can have the coffee."

"No, you cannot." She shook her head.

Luz stepped toward her and gently gripped her shoulders. Luz looked her in the eye and spoke slowly: "I can have the coffee."

Her grandmother blinked through her glasses. She swung the refrigerator door shut. Her grandmother opened her mouth, closed it again. Luz let go of her and returned to the table. Through the front window she watched the hummingbird feeder turn, refracting sunlight. Two birds blurred into view.

When her grandmother shuffled back to the table, her question was a whisper. "What happened, Luz?"

Luz shrugged. Tears welled and burned beneath her lids. She pulled her hair back over her ear, where her scalp was sore to the touch even as the cut itched and healed. "Do you see this cut?"

Her grandmother leaned and squinted. She shook her head, reaching tentatively for the spot Luz indicated. "I make my works by feel now."

"Don't I look terrible?" Luz asked. "Can't you see?"

The old woman seemed on the verge of weeping. "You look beautiful to me."

In the window, a collection of large red hornets zipped toward the bird feeder and harassed the hummingbirds until they flitted away.

"Have you been to a doctor?"

"In Monclova. Yes."

A hummingbird timidly returned, and a hornet zoomed after it. There was silence in the apartment.

"It was a car wreck, Abuela," Luz said. "I only told Papá the car broke down. I didn't want to worry him. I'm okay now."

"I don't understand," her grandmother said. "A car wreck a week ago. Are you sure you are all right? If it was violent enough to induce—"

"Well." Luz swallowed. She sought an answer. "I was in the hospital."

"Luz! Nobody called—"

"I'm okay now," Luz said. "Please, Abuela. I'm okay."

Her grandmother sighed. "You should have called, Luz. Or the doctors should have." She looked out the window, but Luz doubted that the old woman could see the hornets ransacking her bird feeder. She sat and watched her aged and battered hands rest in her lap. "Maybe I should not tell you this," she said.

"What?" Luz asked.

"I told your father not to send you back here."

"You did."

She nodded. She removed her glasses and wiped her eyes. She left her glasses off while she spoke. "When you left me six years ago, I was devastated. But I knew it would be for the best. I knew you needed to be with your father."

The bird feeder spun and the hornets scrabbled over the sugar-water trough.

"And I told him, two weeks ago, that you needed to stay in New Orleans. To be near this young man whose child you carried. If, of course, you did indeed love each other." She put her glasses back on and looked at Luz. "Your father had no answer for that, or he wouldn't talk about it. He was adamant. New Orleans was more awful than I knew. I told him he had forgotten the trouble one can find here. The truth, of course, is that every place has its trouble. There is no perfect home. He insisted that you must be with me, that I could help. It wasn't feasible for you to stay, he said. I told him that mistakes do happen, but their outcomes are not always what we expect. Mystery, Luz, shrouds God's plan. If we are true, then our mistakes might be made useful. But there was no talking to your father. He wouldn't even tell me the young man's name."

Luz swallowed. "Jonás."

Her grandmother hummed. Repeated his name. "Did he love you and did you love him?"

"Yes," Luz answered, though it seemed a very long time since she'd seen him. "I believe so."

Abuela took hold of Luz's hand. "Then I am truly sorry." She turned her face to the window. They sat. "Well," she said after a while.

The bird feeder spun. The red hornets, vile looking, clung to it. To this thing that was not made for them. She wished for the hummingbirds and their furiously pumping hearts to return, for the hornets to vanish. She wished for it in a desperate way she couldn't quite understand.

12

HER GRANDMOTHER DIALED THE NUMBERS, AND LUZ PUT THE cordless phone to her ear and listened to it ring in another country. Her lungs constricted. Her pulse quickened. When her father answered he stuttered, said hello twice. Someone was shouting in the background, shouting in Spanish. It sounded like preaching. She could hear traffic, too. Car engines. Somebody honked. Luz knew where her father was—outside the home improvement center, in the heat and the sun, hoping for work.

"Hi, Papá."

"Luz," he said. "Thank God. One moment." And he was breathing and walking, the background noise receding. "Are you all right?"

"I'm okay, Papá."

"What happened, Luz? Something must have happened."

"Everything is going to be fine," she told him.

"Luz—"

"I love you, Papá," she said, and she held the phone out to her grandmother, covering the mouthpiece. She said to her, "You tell him, it's okay." She placed a hand over her stomach. "I can't."

Her grandmother took the phone. Her father's voice was quick and frantic in miniature. Luz lifted her rolled sweatshirt and the concealed knife from the tabletop and walked down the hallway. "Moses," her grandmother said into the phone.

Three doors at the end of the hall: her grandmother's bedroom, a bathroom, and the room Luz had shared with her mother and her father, when he had been around.

She shut the door behind her, muting her grandmother's voice. The room was warm, sunlight filling the lone square window. The walls were painted a peach color, but she couldn't remember if they had always been. A bed with white sheets. A crucifix on the wall. A wooden wardrobe. Nothing more. They had shared this bed.

Luz set her sweatshirt down atop the wardrobe and opened the doors. There were women's clothes hanging inside it. Luz went weak in the knees. She lifted out a white linen dress. Something nice and light. Something she saw her mother wearing in the spark and flare of remembrance. Luz held it out in front of her, and the sunlight made it glow. She held it against her own body. It would fit. In life Luz was the same shape as the memory she held of her mother. She sat hard on the edge of the bed, the dress across her lap, and she put her face in her hands and cried.

The bedroom door opened. Luz wiped at her eyes and sniffed and got up and put the dress back into the wardrobe.

"I thought—" her grandmother started, "I thought you'd like to have them. I thought—I don't know what I was thinking."

"Thank you, Abuela." Luz went and hugged her. "Thank you. I am not upset because of them."

They sat together on the bed. Luz asked how her father had taken the news.

"Your father," her grandmother said, shaking her head and trailing off. Now she looked at Luz. "Did you see any stray dogs on your way into town?"

"I don't think so."

"Do you remember when Las Monarcas was overrun with stray dogs?"

"Not really."

"Well," her grandmother said, "it was. But there are fewer strays now, and this gives me hope."

"Abuela. What are you talking about?"

"A growing willingness, perhaps, to see choices through." She smiled wistfully. "Nevertheless. Your father, as a boy, went out to play, and he returned home with a stray puppy. Something small and precious he found near the walking market. Have I told you this story before?"

Luz didn't think so.

"Okay. So. Your father brought the puppy home. I was furious. Your father had already named the puppy—I forget what—and he kissed it on its snout and begged me to keep it. I told him he did not understand how much work it would require. Feeding and training and watching. I said, Sometimes you will not be able to go play with friends because you will need to stay home with your dog. He pleaded, he promised. I understand, Mamá, I understand. And so I told him, Okay, Moses, but you must understand one thing. I said, You must remember that if you have this dog, you are responsible for it. You are responsible forever." Abuela waved her hand and made a sorrowful sound.

"The poor dog. He was very good to the puppy at the start. But the best intentions always fade, hmm? Moses would come home from school, and I would tell him, You cannot go out right now, you need to feed and walk your dog. It became a chore, you see? Your father would groan." She paused, clasped her hands together. "One day I came home from the market, and the puppy didn't greet me at the door. So I asked Moses. Your father said the dog ran off, the dog got away from him outside and ran off. But I had seen that puppy with him. It would not run away, not back to what he had rescued it from. I said, Moses, you are telling me the truth? And he swore it. He swore he was telling the truth. But later that night I passed by his room. Well, this very room, I suppose. And I heard him crying from within. Not crying like he merely missed something. Do you see?" Abuela looked at Luz. "I never told him I heard him crying like that, that I knew he was lying."

The dresses hung in the wardrobe in silence. Luz rubbed her eyes.

"My mind," her grandmother said. "I was certain I'd told you that story before. It is an important lesson." She patted Luz's knee. "I will get started on dinner."

Luz sat there alone, something sticking in her mind. The story, in the end, had seemed very familiar. Perhaps her grandmother was right. Perhaps Luz had heard it before.

13

SHE TRIED TO CALL JONAH, BUT IT WENT STRAIGHT TO HIS VOICE mail. After the beep her mouth worked in silence, and then she hung up. She went to bed. She was exhausted. She woke sometime during the next day, hot and racked with thirst. The room was bright. Abuela had placed a glass of water on the nightstand for her. Luz drank from it and fell asleep again. She didn't get up until that night.

While they ate supper, her grandmother asked if she'd like to attend the Easter vigil that evening, but Luz shook her head. "Mass tomorrow, then," her grandmother said. "On Monday I'll return to work, and we will figure out something for you to do."

The evening was quiet. Luz heard the muffled tones of conversation in the courtyard. The church bell tolled the hour. A small sound. She returned to bed and fell again into an exhausted and dreamless sleep.

When morning rose, Luz wouldn't get out of bed. Her grandmother attended Easter Mass without her. Later, her grandmother prepared dinner in silence.

Luz asked, "Do the monarchs still return this time of year?"

Her grandmother blinked. "Perhaps. I never make that hike anymore."

Luz couldn't stop thinking about the migration, corralled, circling on the hill.

XI

La cuenta, por favor.

1

THE BUS JONAH NEEDED WASN'T ONE OF THE LUXURY LINERS THE woman had described but rather a utilitarian regional conveyance. When it pulled out, he sat in the hot vehicle crowded with Easter-weekend travelers and watched the land roll by through the rhomboid window. Beige and green and flat, the gray mountains floating on the horizon. A new landscape. The highway was a narrow two lanes. He fell asleep, exhausted, and he woke up in Lampazos de Naranjo in the late afternoon. He stepped off the bus into the old town. His transfer to Las Monarcas, unfortunately, wouldn't leave until the evening of the next day. He didn't know what to do so he started walking, and he felt good, imagining that he drew closer to Luz with each step.

When dark began to fall he feared he might get lost, so he made his way back to the bus station by trial and error. He went inside and found a bench against the wall. He clutched his backpack to his chest and closed his eyes. A worker nudged him awake at some point in the night, quizzing him in Spanish. Jonah didn't understand but he showed him his ticket, and the man groaned and went away. Jonah nodded in and out of a fitful sleep, waking for good when the sun was full up and flooding the station with warm light.

He stretched and checked the time. He walked outside and followed bells to a square. People streamed from the church. A band, dressed in white, was just beginning to play in the gazebo at the square's center. Jonah watched an older couple dance. A stray golden retriever appeared, licked his hand, and then departed in search of someone with food. Jonah's stomach growled.

At the edge of the square he spotted a café with outdoor tables. The young waitress gestured for him to sit. A young man in slacks and a collared shirt drank coffee at the adjacent table. He was reading the middle of a newspaper, and Jonah could see the front page and its color spread. The headline in big, bold type: EL SAQUE DE ESQUINA DEL VIERNES

SANTO. The image beneath it was a close-up of what appeared to be a soccer ball with something wet and dirt-caked stretched across it. Jonah stared and, as with one of those illusional pictures generated by computers, the hidden content coalesced. On the soccer ball was the skin of a human face. Eyeholes and lips. Nostrils, stretched to gruesome diameter.

The young man lowered the paper and looked at Jonah over the top of it. He said, "You can borrow it when I'm done if that's what you want." He had a Texan drawl.

Jonah hardly heard him. He asked what the headline said.

The man folded the paper shut and looked at it. "You don't read Spanish?"

Jonah shook his head.

"They're calling it 'The Good Friday Corner Kick.'"

"What?"

The young man rolled his hand through the air. "Some renegade narco. Cartel killed him, stitched his face onto a soccer ball, and kicked it down the street." He chuckled grimly, shook his head.

"Jesus," Jonah said. "That happen here?"

"Nah. Couple hours west, in Monclova." The man lifted his coffee mug and sipped. "I'm actually gonna take a ride over there today, before I head back to the States. Do some research—"

They were interrupted by the waitress, who asked Jonah something. He didn't understand the words, but he knew what she wanted. On the menu Jonah pointed to *café*, which he knew was coffee, and then to the cheapest food item, whatever it was. The waitress smiled and bowed her head and disappeared. The man had gone back to his paper. Jonah stared at the face on the soccer ball.

The waitress brought the coffee, along with a little cinnamon bun. He'd eaten it and picked the crumbs from the plate when he waved off his third coffee refill. Then he sat there and waited. The waitress passed by and smiled, but she didn't say anything and she didn't bring the check. Jonah tried to look like he needed something, needed to get somewhere, but still she just smiled politely and brought him no bill.

"You have to ask for it, you know." The man folded the newspaper into his lap. "She won't bring it otherwise. She doesn't want to be rude."

The next time she passed, the man made eye contact with her and said, "La cuenta, por favor." She came back with his bill and he said something else to her that made her look at Jonah and grin. "Now you try," the man said. "Go on. It's all right."

"Uh. What was it?"

"La cuenta," the man repeated, "por favor."

Jonah smiled at the waitress and did the best he could. She said something, laughing, and walked away. "Attaboy," the man said. He put the newspaper under his arm and got up.

"Hey," Jonah said, "will you wait a sec, tell me how much I owe?"

The guy raised his eyebrows but he came over to Jonah's table. "You eat cheap."

"Well—" Jonah held up his American money.

"For future reference—now, understand, I'm just trying to be helpful—you want pesos. Some places can't make you change. For now, just leave that five." Then the man walked out into the square.

Jonah skinned the bill out from what he had left and folded the rest into his pocket. He jogged after the man, caught up with him, and told him thanks.

The man looked at him sidelong for a moment. "Glad I could help. You take care."

"Hey," Jonah said. "You said you were driving west—think I could get a ride?"

The man only glanced at him.

Jonah held up his hands. "I'm sorry to ask, but if I'm on your way I'd really appreciate it. I mean, my bus doesn't leave for hours, and I'm getting anxious to see my girlfriend. That's what I'm doing—I'm visiting her. And it seems lucky that I ran into you. You know what I mean? Isn't it crazy we'd both be sitting there?"

The man shrugged. "It's the twenty-first century."

2

HIS NAME WAS VICTOR AND HE WAS FROM DALLAS, BUT HE WAS in graduate school for history in Austin. He told Jonah to wait for him in the square while he went to say good-bye to his grandparents, whom he'd been visiting for the Easter holiday. He returned in a green, old-model Land Rover with Texas plates. It smelled like coffee inside, and the leather upholstery was cracked. They passed a warehouse, walls striated with rust. A gas station with one pump sprawled on the concrete like a dead tentacle. A small cantina, facade painted green and yellow into an advertisement for a beer called Indio. Victor turned on the radio and let the Spanish music play real low. The country highway stretched on ahead, into the hills.

"Thanks again," Jonah said.

Victor waved it off.

After a while Jonah spoke up. "You come to Mexico a lot?"

"A few times a year, yeah, to see family."

"You said you've got research to do, too." That face stitched onto the soccer ball.

"For my dissertation." Victor nodded. He continued in a different timbre: "You see, history won't allow itself to be separated from violence. Regardless of place. It's true in Mexico, it's true in Texas, and I'm sure it's true wherever you're from."

Jonah thought about that. He recalled Davonte's shooting at Colby's game. Other things one heard about daily, and other things he'd seen. All of it commonplace. Kids from school, murdered or convicted of murder. A backyard barbecue—a child's birthday party—strafed in a drive-by, all because the birthday girl's uncle had some kind of feud with the gunmen. It had happened right around the corner from Jonah's home. There were shootings at second-line parades, at memorial services. Luz's father getting mugged, and the fact that it wasn't surprising. Jonah thought of the drugs sold at school, and Colby, a good guy, who had his own role in that. Jonah sat in the Land Rover and watched Mexico slide past, and he felt slightly untethered—Mom and Pop and Bill, Dex who preferred to be alone, and Luz. He couldn't untangle any of them from the violent place he came from. Where we all came from, or where we met. This coupling with violence, it was a truth that had always existed, just beyond Jonah's periphery.

"It's easy to think it's all out of control," the graduate student continued, clutching the wheel. "Too easy, which makes me think that's not the right way to look at it. Still, it's difficult to remain positive, to feel like you can have an impact. One man, when El Narco's got such inertia."

"You get worried coming down here?" Jonah asked. "I mean, scared. People are, like, rolling faces down streets."

"That kind of stuff just looms so large. It's all you hear about. But, sure. You try to be as smart as you can, but sometimes it's not up to you."

"Shit just reaches out and finds you."

"Precisely."

Jonah exhaled. "I don't get why there's a drug war at all."

"Well." The graduate student sounded like he'd begin a lecture. "We can start with the nineteenth century, when the Chinese brought the poppy to Sinaloa. Or let's start with the hemispheric vacuum after the Colombian cartels fell to pieces. Something had to fill it. We can even make the argument that Mexico's move toward democracy let it happen, because if there's one thing an autocratic regime can do, it's suppress a drug trade. But then what other freedoms have to be surrendered? A ridiculous option. And let's not forget our American appetites. There's money behind it all, man. Lots and lots and lots of money. An infinite engine drives this thing. Some of the cartels recruit Guatemalan commandos to join them, for instance. We're talking about killers just as bad as they come. They're here only for this—" Victor rubbed his thumb and forefinger together.

"What I'm more interested in academically," he continued, "is what Mexico will become. What new shape will emerge."

Jonah looked at him.

"From the violence, and from the idea of it," Victor explained. "Because, don't get me wrong, Mexico is still here—generous people and good food and the beauty of it all. You know?"

"I guess I do," Jonah said. He knew Luz, and Luz was beautiful.

"The violence, okay," Victor said. "We've got a new war on our hands; the CDG and the Zetas have turned on each other. The violence can be extreme. But what's so unusual about that? The thing is, periods of really widespread violence eventually run their courses and peter down to the stream we won't ever be rid of—what's natural to us being us, if you follow. Of course, we could be talking about years and years, but that's how it works when you look at great big whacks of history. Rampant violence regenerates its place of origin into something new. The shedding of blood doesn't come cheap or easy, but it eventually creates even as it destroys. It's terrible right now, no doubt. And when I say terrible, I mean worse than you can imagine. That's why a face on a soccer ball gets a joke headline, for Christ's sake. But Mexico will survive, and what will it become? What will it be?"

Jonah watched some flying insect flicker against the windshield. Something was off-putting about the graduate student's opinion, and Jonah decided it was because the man had overlooked an important distinction. It was weird to think of violence as merely an idea. He thought about his brother Dex again, and Luz, and even her father. He thought about himself. And that was it: violence didn't make over places; and it wasn't structure or order, whatever those words meant, that got rearranged, either. The real changes happened inside, Jonah thought. Violence changed people, not places. He asked Victor: "So is that what you're writing about or something?"

The graduate student seemed suddenly sheepish. "Yeah."

3

VICTOR DROPPED HIM AT LUZ'S GRANDMOTHER'S ADDRESS AND drove away. The street was incredibly steep. Dim lamps coming on in the dusk. A few lights twinkled out on the plain, beyond the rim of the neighborhood. The cobblestone was uneven and hard beneath his soles. Jonah felt the urge to let Colby know he'd arrived, then remembered that his cell had been dead for days. He looked at the iron gate in the wall and opened it.

Four doors in the courtyard. Nothing else to do—Jonah went to the first one and knocked. He was tired. He smelled bad. His heart bounced against his ribs like something caged, like something hitched to her and invigorated by proximity. The door never opened. He waited and it never opened and he went to the next door. No one answered there, either. The third door did open, creaking slowly.

A surge of nerves.

A little old man looked out, a pungent smell wafting from within the apartment.

"Luz?" Jonah said. "Is Luz Hidalgo here?"

The man wheezed, bringing a fist to his lips, as he backed away and shut the door.

Jonah walked to the fourth and final apartment. A hummingbird feeder hung from the eave, lazily rotating. There were no birds, but while he watched, a monarch butterfly wobbled into sight and rested on the lip of the feeder. It was there for a moment, and then it fluttered away. Jonah breathed deep. He raised his fist and knocked.

INTERLUDE

They rinse the earth with shadow. They blanket oak and cling to milkweed. They gather and rest with slow and metronomic wing beat. By some secret do they lift and surge again. Thousands of miles yet to go. The destination is the north, the destination is the south. The journey ends nowhere, and this is their part in it. If they do have a purpose on this earth, it is the fulfillment of this act. This migration. The necessity of it is born into each of them. The shape of it is perpetuated and honed through the generations it serves, and their resting places will each be found along the way. They are always arriving, a circle without escape. As it was and as it will be. They are travelers and must keep going.

XII

Es común, pero no es fácil.

1

THE DOOR OPENED. IT WAS LUZ, AND HE SAW HER AS HE FIRST had. He saw her as he had that day when they went out to the Mississippi, when she held his hand and shared the beginning of her story. Her hands rose to her face, and she questioned, "Jonás?" Hardly above a whisper. The sound on her lips made him smile even as it sapped him of his last energy.

"Hi," he said.

She said something in Spanish. Then she said, "You are really here."

She stepped through the doorway onto the step. She wore drab sweatpants and a white T-shirt. He could imagine her figure and he wanted to gather her to him, hold her, inhale her. She was looking at him and the question was on her face but she didn't ask it and Jonah threw his hands up: "I needed to talk to you. I wanted to see you. I didn't hear from you and I couldn't take being in New Orleans anymore. Colby was with me." He stopped. She neared and there was a certain puffiness around her eyes and the yellowing of a bruise creeping out from her hairline. She must have seen the worry cross his features because she lowered her face. He reached and took her hands and saw the healing scrapes on her fingertips. The bruising around her wrists and forearms. "Luz. What happened."

"I'm okay." She raised her eyes now. "I can't believe you are here."

"What happened?"

"It's a long story, but everything is fine."

"I want to hear it."

"Okay." She came to him now and laid her cheek against his breastbone and he put his arms around her. Then she said, "You stink."

"I know. Sorry." He grinned.

"Luz?" Her grandmother peered around the doorframe. She was short and industrious looking, squinting through spectacles.

Luz pulled quickly away from him, turning toward her. "Jonás, Abuela."

Her grandmother stared.

"Sí." Luz laughed, clipped. She shrugged. "Estoy tan sorprendida como tú."

"Hi," Jonah said, thinking he'd been introduced. "I'm Jonah."

Her grandmother waved, one slow movement with her hand. She looked perplexed. Then she said something to Luz, chuckled, shrugged.

"What did she say?" Jonah asked.

"She says to bring you inside."

Her grandmother was beckoning with her hand as she turned.

"I," Jonah tried, "I woulda told you I was coming if I could. I even tried to see your pops—"

Luz was shaking her head. "I've only been home a few days, Jonah."

"What do you mean?"

"I told you. It's a long story. I tried calling you."

"You didn't leave me a message." He tried to meet her eyes, but they fled. "Are you okay, Luz?"

"Come inside," she said.

"I want to kiss you."

"I know. Just come inside."

2

HER GRANDMOTHER GAVE HIM A GLASS OF WATER AND SHOWED him to the bathroom. She was saying things to him in Spanish, but he was grateful for her friendly tone. He tried telling her thanks, but she waved it away and shut the door behind him. He heard their muffled voices through the door. He couldn't understand any of it. He turned on the shower.

When he came out, they were sitting at the table, having finished eating. Her grandmother got up and brought him a plate. She gestured for him to sit, and he said, "Thanks." Beans and rice, some sautéed vegetables. "This looks great." Her grandmother smiled at him.

He took a bite and they watched him in silence, and then he set his fork down. He looked at her grandmother and figured she wouldn't understand him anyway. To Luz: "How have you been feeling?"

Luz's face fell. Jonah just caught it. A deeply sorrowful expression. But she lifted her eyes and looked at him so quickly that he thought maybe she hadn't heard the question.

"I mean, you been getting sick or anything? What can I do to help?"

She said his name, quiet.

"I'm not, like, an expert or anything," he said, chuckling, "so I don't really know how it all works, being pregnant. But I'm gonna read up on it and learn. I know I can't stay long, but I wanna help however I can. Okay? I wanna help. And I've got a plan for the future. I need to talk to you about it. We're gonna do it together."

"Jonah," she repeated. Something wrestling behind her eyes. A deep breath. Her face went calm, as he was accustomed to seeing. She said, "I lost the baby."

A soundless, thoughtless, breathless pulse. He blinked.

"I had a—"

"A miscarriage."

"Yes."

"Luz."

"While I was trying to get home."

He got up and went around the table and dropped to his knees next to her. He clutched her hands with his own. He looked at the scrapes on her fingertips. He wanted to understand. He wanted to comfort her.

Her grandmother made an inquisitive noise. Luz replied, "Le dije que perdí el bebé."

After a moment her grandmother said, "¿Jonás?" Short in her chair, eyes large in her lenses. "Lo siento," she said. "Es común, pero no es fácil."

Jonah looked to Luz.

"She says she's sorry. She says it isn't easy to go through this."

Luz squeezed his hand, and Jonah knelt there. And then he realized that they were the ones trying to console him. He hurt for Luz. He wanted to do something, be helpful to her in some way. But there was a bitter taste in the back of his mouth and he was knotted up with his own uselessness. His anger toward her father crackled underneath it all. How pointless this had been. How goddamn pointless.

3

AFTER HER GRANDMOTHER RETIRED FOR THE EVENING, THEY SAT in the living room. Luz lit a few of the candles in the window. Somebody laughed out in the street as they passed. Jonah told her that he had missed her. She smiled—sadly, he thought—and said she had missed him, too.

He waited. He could hear the candlewicks burning. "What happened," he finally managed, scooting a little closer to her.

She glanced at him. "I don't want to talk about it just yet. Is that okay?"

"Yeah. Of course." His desire to understand roiled within him, but he told himself that he was here. He was here, and he would be here. "I'm sorry."

"It's almost funny," Luz said, but there was no humor in her voice. "What it took to leave Mexico, when I was little, was hard. Really hard. I didn't think coming home would be harder. I never thought I'd be back at all." She paused. "Colby was really with you?"

"Yeah. All the way to the border. He turned back there, though."

"Why?"

"They had the bridge closed because there'd been, well, there'd been a car bomb on the other side of it. Colby didn't want to cross. I mean, I'm glad he didn't. I couldn't make him come with me after that." He watched her, but she didn't flinch or react in any way. "He should be home by now, I guess. Back in school tomorrow."

Luz smiled, but her eyes were distant.

"We stopped to see Dex, too."

"Oh?" She patted his hand. "That's great, Jonah."

"Luz," he said, "I been real worried. About you. I mean real worried."

"I know." She let go of his hand and got up. "I'm sorry. I'm exhausted."

"Okay," he said, and followed her through the apartment to the bedroom. He knew he wouldn't be going in with her, because she stopped and faced him in the doorway. "Listen," he began. "I know I can't stay that long. But I want you to come back with me. Or . . . or if that doesn't work, just hang tight, and once I make some money I can figure out a way to bring you back and we will work everything out. I'm enlisting with Colby and—"

"Tomorrow, Jonah," Luz said. She rose and kissed him lightly on the lips. "I'm happy to see you, I promise, but let's talk tomorrow." Then she went into the room and shut the door.

Jonah stood in the dark hall and listened to her footfalls, just on the other side of the door. He returned to the living room and lay down on the couch and closed his eyes while his mind raced. He did not understand a single thing.

4

JONAH WOKE TO LUZ'S GRANDMOTHER SCRUBBING A POT IN THE kitchen. She was watching him. She shut the water off and shuffled down the hallway and returned with a satchel over one shoulder and a wooden pole in her fist. She went to her workbench and loaded her wares into the satchel. She held up an ornate belt for Jonah to see and then dropped it into the bag. She said something in Spanish that Jonah didn't get.

"Can I help you carry your stuff?" he asked.

She blinked at him.

He gestured at her things. "Can I help you?"

"No, no." She walked to the front door and said, "Gracias, Jonás," before exiting.

He drew a glass of water from the cooler in the kitchen and drank it and brushed his teeth. He stretched, yawning, thought of Luz in her bedroom.

He eased the door open. The sun rising through the canvas shade colored the walls peach. A single bar of sunlight slipped between shade and window frame and lay across her brown shoulder. He watched the subtle rise and fall of her breathing, and he stepped into the room and shut the door with great care. He got into bed with her and held her. He closed his eyes and dreamed of the evening in the French Market with Luz, her laughter, her words resounding in his head: We will be responsible for each other.

5

LUZ FELL THROUGH THE DREAMLESS DARK AND WOKE LIKE SHE hadn't slept a minute. She was very warm. Thirsty. Where? Somebody's arm lay heavily over her.

She shrugged the arm off and sat up, and there was Jonah waking up next to her.

"God," Luz said, pressing fingers into her eyes.

"I didn't come in till after your grandma left."

She had a headache in addition to the persistent dull throb in her abdomen. Sore muscles. "We're really here." The plaster ceiling looked like some sharp moonscape.

Jonah snuggled closer, but she got up and slid over him and went to the kitchen for a drink. Then she took a shower and returned to the bedroom with a towel wrapped around her. Jonah watched from the bed.

Luz opened the wardrobe and took out one of her mother's dresses. Something light. She let the towel fall and stood with her backside toward Jonah as she slipped the dress over her head and then smoothed it over her stomach. It fit well, and she was dizzy.

"You look beautiful," Jonah said.

Luz turned to him. She was on the verge of breaking apart. She had the deep urge to tell him everything that had happened, but she didn't know how to say it, how to begin.

"I'm hungry," Jonah said, saving her.

They walked down the hill to the church and then down to the roundabout, which was much busier today. A pickup laden with boxes of produce fumed around the circle. A green taxi. A policewoman in a black uniform held a rifle and lounged against the jamb of an open doorway. They passed a grill, corn husks blackening on the grate. Stray fibers glowing orange like wire filaments. A woman with a wilted face stirred chicharrón in a greasy, smoking pan. Pork fat sizzled and popped.

The garage door of a warehouse was open, and Luz led Jonah into the crowded space, her eyes adjusting to the shade. There were stands of avocados and lettuce, mangos and bananas and melons. Vendors hawked shoes, straw hats, luchador masks, cheap electronics. There were woven rugs from Oaxaca. Silver jewelry from Guanajuato.

"This is like the French Market, sorta," Jonah said. "Remember that day?"

And Luz did, feeling a stab of guilt. She wondered if Jonah was here, in Las Monarcas right now, because of what she had told him that day. She realized, suddenly, where those words had come from—her grandmother's old advice and the story of her father and his stray puppy. She had indeed heard that story as a little girl. A sensation came over her, like her being itself was unfolding, flattening, lengthening. There was too much to remember and too much to get a handle on. Her grandmother called out to them.

Abuela had suspended the wooden post between two large flowerpots and looped the leather bracelets and belts around it, some already with designs branded in, others that were plain and might be customized upon request. Luz asked if she could borrow some money for lunch. Her grandmother opened a tin box, took out a handful of ten-peso coins, and gave them to Luz.

"Thanks," Luz told her. She looked up and down the crowded market. Some girls sat on a step making cloth dolls by hand. "Is there a daily Mass?" Luz asked.

Her grandmother smiled and confirmed and told her the time.

They walked away, and Jonah hollered good-bye back at her grandmother.

Out in the circle, Luz selected two ears of corn from the woman with the grill, and the woman peeled back the burned husks and rolled the ears in mayonnaise and chili powder. Next Luz bought a plastic container of fresh, sliced melon.

After she finished the transactions, Jonah said, "I shoulda learned Spanish."

Luz shrugged.

"Novia." He smiled. "I know that one."

And Luz wanted to be there, present in the moment with him, but she heard her own laugh and it was a distant, automatic sound. As if it came from someone else.

They ate on a bench near the church. Jonah tried to feed a piece of melon to a stray dog, no luck. They didn't talk, and Luz watched the questions like living things beneath the surface of Jonah's face. After they ate, she asked if he'd go to Mass with her.

"Sure," he said. "Whatever you want."

The church was cool and empty, and it fit her memory of the place almost precisely. The graphic dioramas. The lifelike crucifix. The grotto where, for all Luz knew, her prayers for her father still lived on in the candle flames, in the smoke drifting heavenward. Jonah made a noise. He was looking at the crucifix, the gleaming blood. Luz felt compressed between this place out of her past and this boy out of her present. She ran her fingertips over the smooth grain of the pew, trying to steady herself.

"I almost forgot to tell you," Jonah whispered. "I saw the Good Friday parade in San Antonio."

"You did?"

He turned his face to her. "I wanted to see the place you loved."

"Did you like San Fernando?"

"It was neat, yeah. The parade looked pretty real."

"Yes," Luz answered.

The daily Mass began in silence, no music. An old priest walked out from the sacristy, flanked by altar servers hefting tall candles. The priest's words diffused into the big, muted space, and Luz's mind wandered, stumbling back across the highways and the hills and through the night-time sky to the farmland and those trees and that cliff face.

A woman shuffled to the lectern to commence the first reading. She spoke in a monotone voice, never pausing for emphasis or pace, but something about the words gathered Luz in. The woman read the epistle of Santiago straight through:

"Be doers of the word and not merely listeners who only deceive themselves. If any are listeners and not doers they are like those who look at themselves in a mirror and upon going away immediately forget who and what they are . . ."

Luz's breath shortened. The muscles in her legs twitched. When she had seen herself in the mirror, finally, in the Monclova barracks room, her face stared back from some ancient place. How many people had told her who she was and what she must do and how she must live? All the thoughts and words of others. Panic clogged her lungs, and the woman continued:

"But those who look into the perfect law and persevere—being not listeners who forget but rather doers who act—they will be blessed in their doing."

Luz ripped her hand from Jonah's and got up and ran to the doors, and the last thing she heard were words concerning bridled tongues and self-deceived hearts.

6

JONAH SAT THERE IN A STUPOR WATCHING HER EXIT THE CHURCH before he got up to follow.

She was outside, hunched with her hands on her knees. The way he'd seen her at the end of a race. Worn down, nothing left. He approached timidly, and hated his fear.

Slowly she straightened. She drew a deep breath and exhaled as she collapsed to sit on the church steps. "I don't know what's wrong with me."

"Was it something in that reading?" Jonah sat next to her. "I couldn't understand the Spanish . . ."

Luz shook her head, and Jonah waited for more but the wordless space between them hardened. He still needed to talk to her about his intentions to make a life together in New Orleans, but he'd never felt so nervous around her. A cab smoked in the street. Sun-blasted faces passed, eyes focused only on the bricks ahead of their feet. Jonah didn't know what to do with his hands and he crossed his arms and then uncrossed them and gripped the hard edge of the stone step beneath him.

"I'm just," Luz began, and relief leaped inside Jonah. He found himself leaning toward her, grateful for whatever she was going to say. "I'm just—" She paused again and shivered. She seemed like she was fighting something.

"It's okay," Jonah tried. "It's okay, Luz."

"Something bad happened to me," she said.

The words were sudden. She glanced at Jonah and her eyes were red and ringed with water, and she looked quickly away.

"When I was on my way back. That's why it took me so long to get here."

"What happened?" His windpipe constricted with the dread that sails ahead of tragic news. "What do you mean?"

She crossed her arms on her knees and pressed her forehead against them. "I'm all right now." She lifted her face. "Please, Jonah. You need to know that. I'm all right."

"Yeah, but—"

She shook her head and reached, taking his hands. And he looked down at them and saw again her healing fingertips and the yellow-purple bruising around her wrists and then he met her eyes, trying desperately not to cry himself, though he had nothing to contend with yet but his own imagination and the suggestion that the woman he loved had been wounded.

"My cab from the airport," Luz said, "got caught in a shoot-out."

"Jesus, Luz," Jonah whispered. "Like a drug war thing?"

Luz nodded. "The car wrecked. Really bad."

"The miscarriage, is that when . . . ?"

"Later. But maybe. I don't know."

Jonah waited.

"I saw—" she said, closing her eyes as if she was still seeing whatever it was.

She was holding her breath, it seemed. She exhaled slowly. And again. She didn't finish describing what she had seen. She gripped Jonah's hands and he felt her rough fingers sliding over his palms. She opened her eyes.

"Some men, they took me. They tied me up."

All the world drained away from them, all sound and sensation, where they sat on the steps.

"I'm okay," Luz said. "All right?"

"Okay," Jonah heard himself.

"They didn't do anything to me. Not that, you know? They wanted to sell me to somebody, I think. They locked me in a shed."

"Christ."

"I got away," she told him. "I ran." A long, granite silence ensued. There was more there, Jonah could tell, much more there, but finally she said, "The military found me."

Luz let go of his hands and rubbed her palms on her thighs and sighed. She looked off up the hill, away from Jonah. He thought she started to say something more, but her voice clotted. She wasn't looking at him.

"Luz?"

"I don't know how to explain the rest," she said, turning toward him.

"What do you mean?"

She shook her head, lowered her eyes.

"It's fine," Jonah said, scooting nearer and putting his arm around her. He thought she meant that she didn't know how to tell him what it all felt like, how it had changed her. He wanted her to know that he was with her, that he could help her bear her pain, somehow. "I understand," he said. He knew it must be hard for her to talk about because it was hard to listen to, as well. "I do."

Luz leaned into him.

"I'm so sorry, Luz."

She sniffed. He felt her ribs rise and fall. They sat for a long time.

When the church doors opened behind them, Luz stood as though she'd been startled. Parishioners began to exit, and Jonah got up and followed Luz down the steps. He wanted to pursue the conversation, but what to say?

Luz halted and Jonah stopped alongside her.

"Can I show you something special?"

"Okay," Jonah said. "I'd like that."

They passed her grandmother's building and climbed the street. Jonah glanced over his shoulder, where the steep grade sank away, offering the illusion that the city existed on the summit of some collisional world. Luz led them into a park, a shaded trail switchbacking through the trees. All quiet. Not even the thrum of insects.

"I thought I'd forgotten the way," Luz said.

Jonah noted that her tone had changed. There was something breathless in it, something excited. It was a comfort, a sense of healing.

"Remember when we went out to the levee the first time?" Luz asked him.

"Yes."

"You said your family used to go out there, that your mother took you."

"Yeah."

"This place where we're going. It's like that. Mamá took me here, when I was little."

The path climbed a hill and the trees fell away and the trail narrowed to a scratch through the dry grass. This, Jonah realized, is it. This was the truth he'd sought in the dark of his bedroom with Luz, and this was what he'd searched for in San Antonio. He had come to Mexico to find this. This was what they needed between them. This would carry them together into the future.

7

THEY CRESTED THE HILL, BOY AND GIRL HAND IN HAND. THOU-
sands of monarch butterflies orbited the solitary, enormous oak.
More blanketed the tree in a shivering veil. She closed her eyes against
everything, both reality and memory, and stepped forward into the del-
icate cloud, extending her arms with care. And the boy understood—it
would be a crime against something unseen to move about too heed-
lessly. He joined her, closing his own eyes, and eased into this gentle
and inborn sway of the world. In this moment they could brush together
against the vermiculated tapestry woven by every living thing, boundless
when encountered by a single human mind. The thread of each life approached every other infinitely, so that they seemed to touch or intersect
but never did, and yet still they made one thing. Of the shape it was in
the beginning, the size it will always be.

XIII

. . . the border will always be there.

1

THEY HAD A GOOD NIGHT, WALKING THE CITY. JONAH KISSED Luz and she kissed him back, there on the street against the brick facade of a building. He felt her opening to it. He felt his hopes coming into focus. He determined that what Luz had been through—the ordeal with the men and the loss of their baby—shouldn't change what he hoped for, shouldn't alter his design. He wouldn't let it. They kissed against the brick until she had to pull away, smiling, saying, Come on, and pulling him toward the apartment. Not here, not yet, she seemed to say, but there will be time. There will, Jonah believed.

2

THE NEXT MORNING JONAH WALKED THROUGH THE APARTMENT, glass of water and toothbrush in hand. He entered the bathroom. He was rehearsing in his head, considering how he would frame his plan to Luz, when something small and dark on the tile caught his eye and the words flew from his mind. It was a scorpion, little and brown but scary looking—he'd never seen one before. He chucked the water from his glass into the sink, and, moving quickly, he dropped the glass over the scorpion and trapped it. The thing's legs flailed in a blur as it circled and tried to climb. Jonah watched its stinger striking harmlessly against the glass. He called for Luz, and she came running with the urgency in his voice. He was holding the glass down and saying, Look! She stopped in the doorway. Then she came forward and knocked his hand away and lifted the glass. The scorpion shot out, and Jonah yelped, leaping away. The arachnid bolted behind the toilet and disappeared. Jonah looked at Luz, but she had already turned and walked out.

3

THAT AFTERNOON, HER GRANDMOTHER ASKED THEM TO DO something and handed Luz money, and Jonah followed her out. Luz explained that they needed to pick up something from the carnicería, the butcher shop. They walked over the cobblestone in silence, and Jonah couldn't figure out what he'd done wrong, what had happened, with the scorpion. Luz didn't talk as she trudged ahead. Please, Jonah thought.

They turned a corner, and the sounds of a parade entered the street. It was led by a flatbed truck crawling down the hill, and the speakers latched to the roof of the cab blared music and cracked and hissed. Wooden slats fenced in the bed, where people stood, waving and dancing. Some of them held cardboard posters, portraits of a smiling woman, over their heads. A small mob danced alongside the truck, and children ran after it, playing some kind of game in which they ran forward and slapped the bumper and fell back. A man in the bed hung over the tailgate and launched bottle rockets from a glass bottle. The rockets screeched and popped in white puffs among the cable lines tangled over the street. People came out onto their roofs or balconies or front steps to watch. A stray dog howled and flinched.

Jonah and Luz backed against a building. The marchers chanted, punching the air with emphasis. Jonah spied the woman from the posters standing in the truck bed. She braced herself with one hand atop the cab and shouted something into a megaphone she held with the other. The music, the chanting, the shouting, the bottle rockets. Jonah knuckled his ear and grinned at Luz as the parade grated past.

"She's campaigning for mayor," Luz shouted.

Jonah tasted the acrid smoke. "Wild."

The parade turned off the street and the music broke up. A dim final pop and a drifting wisp. The need to reach for something good swelled in Jonah's belly.

"Hey," he said, "remember Zulu? When Colby caught the coconut?"

A slight smile. "I remember that."

"Colby was pretty proud of himself."

"Feels like a long time ago."

The street lay deserted now, quiet like there'd never been a parade. "I dunno," Jonah said. "It was only, like, two months ago. No, not even."

Luz shrugged. "Feels like a long time to me." She gestured in the direction of the departed campaign parade. "She was saying the guy she's running against is connected to the CDG."

Jonah had heard that before, CDG. It took him a moment to remember. The graduate student who gave him the ride. The initials meant a drug cartel.

Luz turned and started up the sidewalk. "She'll be in trouble, talking like that."

Jonah watched her pull away from him. He was stunned by her flat voice, by the dispassionate way she had delivered such a grave declaration.

He marched after her, uphill, working hard to catch up.

4

HER GRANDMOTHER STARTED DINNER WHILE THEY SAT IN THE living room. Luz seemed withdrawn, no longer the person who had opened up to him. He was furious for her, for what had happened to her. But it was an impotent fury, anchored with a deep and abiding sadness. He watched her chew on her lip, watched her think. He wanted to understand. Let me try. He wanted to scream it.

Luz stood up and said she was going for a jog. "I need to burn some energy. I'm jumpy."

"I'll join you," Jonah said.

"No. That's all right."

"I mean I want to," he said. The needy edge to his own voice pissed him off.

"I'd better go alone. Just to think about some things."

"Sure," Jonah said. "Sure."

"I'm sorry."

"It's all right," Jonah answered. The words were automatic. He didn't feel all right about anything. Luz gave him a quick hug, and she said something to her grandmother and left.

Jonah wandered into the kitchen. Luz's grandmother raised her eyes from the onions on the cutting board and arched an eyebrow.

"Can I help?" He went through a chopping charade.

"No," she answered, smiling.

He lingered, listening to the blade strike the board. Then he said he was going to go for a walk as well. Her grandmother looked at him, and he made a walking motion with his fingers. She nodded and waved, and he left, passing through the courtyard into the street. He looked one way and then the other, but he didn't see her anywhere.

He entered the park, trudged up the path. The sun fell among the slopes to the west. He reached the hilltop. There was the massive oak. It took him a moment, however, to realize that almost all the monarchs had gone, and it took him another moment to realize where they'd gone to: their forms lay across the hilltop, tangled in the grass or scoured by the sand or blustered up against the trunk of the tree, crammed between the roots. Lone monarchs here and there still rose, but they seemed so much frailer on their own, winging jerkily above the rest of their expired migration. They weren't long for the journey themselves.

Jonah squatted and examined the dead things all around him. Slivers missing from wings like panels punched from stained-glass windows. With a breeze, the dead monarchs tilted and settled. Jonah imagined that this was a place where the journey ran aground, where a fraction of the larger migration corralled itself, disoriented or mistaken in some way. Misled by the shape of the oak or the taste of the air, and by the time the monarchs realized this was not the place they had thought it to be, it was too late. Year after year, he imagined, they arrived and they circled and they never left.

Jonah brushed a wing with a fingertip.

The dry thing broke apart into weightless flakes, like a dead leaf.

5

THE EVENING DARKENED, AND LUZ JOGGED CAREFULLY ALONG the steep Las Monarcas streets. She slowed her pace, feeling the stress of the decline in her shins. She was good and warm, sweating and breathing hard. Her head cleared. Some perspective wasn't far off, and the events of the past few days settled into their proper context.

She remembered the late nights spent washing dishes in the chrome kitchen of that New Orleans restaurant. The scalding water and the sauces crusted to the plates. And she remembered how Jonah would wait for her outside the service entrance. A smile, a laugh, a pair of arms. She remembered it and knew it had been real. But she could not summon the way it had felt. She could not summon the good feelings as she could summon past sorrows and fears. Those she could call forth. She could sink into despair. Cold breath in her lungs, a prickling in her fingertips, a frightening voice in the darkness. It was as if the good moments had happened to a person who no longer existed. How could she reconcile the fact that good things had indeed happened with the fact that there was no longer any evidence of them? Maybe Jonah, here in Las Monarcas, was the evidence of those good times. Then again, if she couldn't react in the same way to his presence as she believed she once had . . . But that, she knew, was no failing of his. And so she slowed when the street leveled out at the town bus terminal. She leaned against the wall, stretched her calves. She shook her legs out and let her breath slow before she went inside.

It was a small place full of Formica chairs. The windows were smudged. Luz took a pamphlet from the ticket counter and looked at the destination and fare charts. The ticket agent, a bored young man with acne-scarred cheeks, watched her. There was no one else in line and he didn't say anything to try to hustle her along. She turned. A pay phone, its black receiver shining with grease, was bolted to the cinder-block wall.

6

WHEN LUZ RETURNED TO HER GRANDMOTHER'S, JONAH WAS waiting in the wash of a streetlamp, sitting against the wall adjacent to the gate. He got to his feet when he saw her.

"Hey," he said. He put his hands in his pockets. "I went to the hill again."

He didn't have to say it because Luz remembered. "It happens every year," she told him. "It's like they get lost here." And that was part of the problem—when it came to God's vengeance and its dispersal, the worst were spared but the simply lost were not.

Jonah bounced on the balls of his feet, and Luz sensed the words piling up. She wanted to tell him that she had killed a man, wanted to describe the wet slap of the rock against his eye, the final sound of it. She needed Jonah to understand that she had orchestrated that finality, and for that knowledge to help explain, in turn, the gathering distance between them. But she didn't think he'd be able to understand—she didn't think anybody ever would—and so what she said instead was, "One day we'll look back, I think, and see that all this made us who we are."

He sighed. "I love you."

"I know." And Luz still loved him, too—she thought she always would—but not in the sense that he meant or wanted. Her love had become a kind of fossilized thing. She would never be able to deny the love's existence. She would never wish to deny it. But it was no longer something she felt capable of acting upon.

"I still want you to come back to New Orleans with me," Jonah said. "I want to take care of you. I want to build a life with you."

Luz averted her eyes because there were no tears in them.

"We can make it work. I'm serious, Luz."

"I believe you."

"But you don't think I can."

"It's not that," Luz said. She remembered well Jonah's despair the evening they'd been robbed at gunpoint in the French Quarter. She knew that the losses in Jonah's life made him feel incapable, but he wasn't that. "I've never believed you were helpless, Jonás."

"Let me prove it. Come back with me. Or let me bring you back soon."

"It's not about that, either," Luz said. She met his look, then cast her eyes up the quiet street. Her ghost runner had arrived, heavy and cold, and the soles of her feet began to itch. Luz thought through their origins, through their histories. As she had done times before, imagining their love in older, improbable eras. The millions of things that had to happen over the millennia just to bring them together for a little while in New Orleans. It was good fortune, and she was grateful for it. She really was. But that period was at an end, and she could not separate them each from the places they came from or the places they had yet to go. "I'm a runner," she said. "I think I'm always going to be."

"It doesn't have to be that hopeless," Jonah tried.

"Hopeless isn't the right word for it." Luz had been pregnant, and the landscape that would have been her future had formed and forced itself to her feet, and she had prepared herself for the long journey because there was nothing else to do. But now that it was over, it was as if that landscape had eroded. It was still there, only unrecognizable.

She had placed her hand over her stomach; she let it fall back to her side. There were no more cramps. There was no physical reminder left at all.

"We can make something good happen. I'm going to go into the army—"

"Oh, Jonás," Luz said, hearing her voice rise in spite of herself, "you don't want to join the army. I know you don't. And you don't need to, now."

"Well, okay, I mean—maybe now there's just no hurry. I can start working on McBee Auto, I'll get it working . . . We can go back to how things were."

"I don't want to go back," Luz said. "There's no going back for me, Jonah, that's what I'm telling you."

"Forward, then!" Jonah cried. "We used to talk about it. I know you dreamed about it, too. I'll reopen the shop—damn it, you made me start thinking I could!"

"You still should," Luz said. "But you don't need me to do it."

"Then what's the fucking point, Luz?"

"Think of your mother, Jonah. Your father. Your brother. Speak to them. Do it for them. Do it for yourself. Build the life you want."

"You are part of the life I want," he answered.

Luz was sorry. More sorry than she'd ever been. Sorrier than when she didn't give the dying man in the desert her water. Sorrier than when she'd brought Felipo home, beaten and battered, to his grandmother and brother. But perhaps it was merely the same old guilt. The same guilt regenerating into new spaces and new regrets. Here was Jonah, standing before her in Las Monarcas, waiting for her to speak.

Luz said: "I can't go with you. Not anymore. I'm sorry I can't explain. I do love you, Jonah. I'm glad I know you. I'm glad I met you. But I don't belong in New Orleans."

"Luz," Jonah said, "you can't want to stay here, not after what's happened."

"That's what I'm saying, Jonah. I don't even belong here anymore. I don't know where I belong. I'm sorry. I don't know what else to say."

"You told me I was responsible," Jonah said, teeth clenched. "Remember?"

"I meant it when I said it."

He looked at her. "What were you saying to me that day out in the street, in Spanish, when you were saying good-bye?"

"I was telling you to forget about me."

"No, you weren't. That's not true."

And it wasn't true. But they were where they were, now and only now. What she had said to him then didn't matter. It was better for him to not even know.

"Forgive me, Jonah." And she went in through the gate.

7

H E THOUGHT HE WOULDN'T BE ABLE TO SLEEP, BUT HE DID eventually. He woke up on the couch, early in the morning, and he could hear her grandmother speaking loudly and rapidly from down the hall. He got up. Luz's bedroom door was open. The old woman was in there, talking to the sky, shaking a handwritten note she clenched in her fist. There was another piece of paper folded on the bed with his name written on it, and more words written on the inside. Luz had left in the night.

8

Jonah—I will always care for you. I'm sorry. It isn't your fault. We are like our countries, you and me. It doesn't matter how close we are to each other, the border will always be there. I don't know what I'm looking for. I don't even know where to find it. But I've got to keep going. I will let you know that I'm okay. Promise me you'll keep going, too.

—Luz

XIV

. . . sometimes you come back with less.

1

H E READ THE LETTER AGAIN AND AGAIN. HE REFOLDED THE note and put it in his pocket. Her grandmother was sitting in the living room, slumped, hands clasped against her breastbone as if she was praying. The look on her face said she blamed herself. She said something in Spanish, her tone suggesting she wasn't completely talking to Jonah.

"Thanks for letting me stay," Jonah tried. "I don't get what's going on, either."

She looked at him.

"I wanted to help. I wanted to protect her." He wouldn't let himself cry in front of the old woman, but he couldn't help the words, knowing she couldn't understand: "But I should know better than to think anyone cares what I want."

She couldn't answer, so she lowered her face and watched her feet.

"Sorry," Jonah said. He felt lousy for feeling sorry for himself. He shouldered his bag and drifted to the door. "Adiós," he tried.

Luz's grandmother unclasped her hands and opened a creased palm in farewell.

2

H E WALKED ALL MORNING. NO SIGN OF LUZ, THOUGH HE hadn't held out much hope of seeing her. He found the bus terminal by the afternoon. It sat on a cracked concrete patch at the edge of town. After some difficult discourse with the ticket agent he handed over most of his dollars. Then he sat and waited, numb. He thought: This is the end of it. An utterly listless feeling, both spiritual and physical. How the hell was he going to get home once he reached the border? He supposed he could call Dex, but he reflected on his brother's intimations that this was a fool's quest and he dreaded it. Jonah hated that he had failed. He hated that Dex had been right.

A man in sunglasses with mirror lenses drove the bus. He smiled around his toothpick. Nearly every seat was taken. A lot of blank stares. Men with sleeves rolled to biceps. Women with whimpering children. A man had propped his snakeskin boots across the aisle, and Jonah waited for him to put his feet down so he could pass. The bus lurched and he stumbled, but he found a seat near the back. With his backpack on his lap, he stared out the window, sinking into himself.

The tangled sheets of his bed. The quiet light falling through the window. Church bells from St. Charles Avenue, clear and beautiful. She stops him with a hand placed on his bare chest and says the border will always be here.

3

AFTER THE LATE-NIGHT TRANSFER HE WAS RESTLESS. EXHAUSTED and uncomfortable, a continuous smog of half-lidded stupor.

He dreamed of a burning car on the roadside. A blackened frame smoldering within. He dreamed of masked men with rifles, and the bus lurching to a stop, and a man coming aboard, his cloaked skull turning and his eyes glaring from the eyeholes. His mouth hung open and his cheeks puffed with breath as he stared at each passenger, one at a time, and Jonah waited for those eyes to fall on him, alone and lost in his seat.

When Jonah awoke, the bus was silent and frigid with air-conditioning. They sped through the dark. He had a headache, and his dream had frightened him.

4

Jonah disembarked from the bus in Nuevo Laredo, unable to latch onto coherent thoughts. Another passenger approached, an American. He wore a T-shirt and cargo pants and hiking boots. A large camping bag rose above his shoulders. The man had combed brown hair, sunburned skin, and a scruff of beard on his square jaw. He stood in front of Jonah, a grin on his face, and said, "We're a couple of lucky gringos, dude."

Jonah's skull throbbed as he stared back and waited for the words to mean something.

"The narco and the bus driver knew each other." The man shook his head with wonderment. "Can you believe that shit?"

Jonah blinked. The burning car, the man in the mask. It came to Jonah's recollection truly as a dream. But he hadn't dreamed it; he had witnessed it. Past and present shimmered. What was real leached into what was not. The burning car was impressionistic in his mind, and as he tried to grab detail, more slipped away.

"Christ, we're lucky sons of bitches." The man turned and beckoned. "Come on, let's get a cab together. Better that way."

Jonah hardly spoke. The man said he'd been down south, attempting to climb a mountain. He'd had a friend with him who'd become ill and had to fly home. But Jonah's mind wandered as the cab ferried them to the border. He would have liked to tell Bill about this trip. He imagined that his brother could have told him something that would help, but Bill wasn't anywhere. A small voice—Luz's voice, maybe—told him to reach, to pray, but instead he silenced his mind and knuckled his tired eyes.

The cab stopped in a turnaround near the bridge. Jonah had only three dollars to contribute to the fare, and the climber picked up the rest. When Jonah said thanks, the climber replied: "I know a thing or two about going down old Mexico way. Sometimes you come back with more, sometimes you come back with less. Don't sweat it."

Jonah followed the climber into the foot traffic returning stateside. Fencing rose high overhead, hemming in the pedestrian lane. Jonah trailed his fingers along the chain-link and looked out at the river below. There were the city lights ahead and the city lights behind. It was not as dark as the night he had first crossed, but much of the river lay in interminable shadow. Except for the marker on the bridge, the border was still invisible.

Jonah wondered about Luz crossing the river as a child. He believed she'd swum across with her uncle, but he didn't know the whole story. It was a memory she had never fully shared, and the way she guarded it made him too hesitant to ask. Perhaps with that memory resided an answer, something that would now remain forever unknown.

The globes of streetlight standing on the fence over the lane were a pale yellow. Not much automobile traffic this late, but a fair number of walkers. The line bunched and slowed as they neared the border station.

"Things been pretty wild here lately," the climber said, turning to Jonah. "Must be why the wait. The customs dudes will be turned up to Max Hard-Ass, I'm sure." He slapped Jonah on the shoulder. "But with our luck we shouldn't complain, eh?"

Jonah said, "Yeah," but he couldn't recall the unreal occurrence on the bus as vividly as he wished. More detail would equal fear, and more fear would engender gratitude, and more gratitude would mean that the experience had been useful to him in some way. But the memory was too hazy. What he needed just wasn't there.

Jonah gripped the bridge fence and tried to imagine how harrowing Luz's crossing might have been. He waited in line with the others returning to America and it struck him that the ease with which he could return was part of the problem, that it was one of the things that kept the border between him and Luz. What might Jonah discover if he simply turned around, went back to Mexico, and tried to find a place to swim across?

He could imagine it. Willows thrashing in the wind. The wet mud smell of the river. Moonlight fragmenting in the gentle chop. The current tugging at his jeans. Is it shallow and slow and easy? Is it deceitfully lethal, like the Mississippi? He could reach the American bank and identify with Luz anew, based on their shared experience. This would be the hope, that the risk alone might rend the veil from all he couldn't understand. And, perhaps, she might still want him then.

Shoes scuffled forward. The American bank passed beneath the bridge. The first dark treetops. The river looked swollen tonight.

Luck, the climber called it. Jonah had never thought of himself as a lucky person, but depending on his vantage point there was luck to be found in his life. Meeting Luz when he did and where he did—that had to be luck of some kind. Looked at one way, it had been a good conclusion at the end of a long, unlucky sequence of years.

Before entering the border station he glanced back at the river, one last time. No, he thought. Swimming across wouldn't help him understand Luz any better than he already did. Her crossing had been necessary, as had been the method. There was no separating those facts from the experience itself. To extend himself into harm's way for personal proof—well, that offered just another false promise.

But. He could create something, build something, restore something. The revelation filled his lungs. These were actions made of meaning. These were endeavors with which he could vindicate his own existence. He walked into the air-conditioned border station with visions of McBee Auto in his mind. The old place renovated, repainted. Doors open, all personal automobiles welcome. McBee Auto would be a business for the neighborhood to rally around. There was pride there, for him and for others. He would be responsible for all of it.

There, Jonah saw, was something earned.

He walked forward, bolstered with purpose.

5

THE AGENT WAS A YOUNG MAN WITH WHITE-BLOND HAIR closely shorn around his ears. He wore a baseball cap pulled low over his eyes. A patch on its crown read in gold script:

US CUSTOMS AND BORDER PROTECTION

He chewed gum behind thin lips, the muscles in his temples bulging, as he examined the identification of the travelers who passed through the lane alongside his kiosk.

The climber stepped forward and handed over his passport.

Jonah heard the agent's question: "Are you an American citizen?"

"Yes, sir," the climber replied.

The agent flipped through the pages of the climber's passport, handed it back, and waved him through. "Welcome back to the United States," he said.

The climber turned and nodded a farewell to Jonah.

The border agent held his hand out and Jonah rummaged in his pack for his passport. Finally he located it and placed it in the agent's hand. The man had blue eyes deep within the shadow of the curved bill of his hat.

"Are you an American citizen?"

"Yes."

The agent turned the passport photo toward Jonah. "How old are you in this photo?"

"Uh. I don't know."

"You're not sure?"

"I don't remember exactly. It's not expired yet, I checked."

"Is there anything in your backpack you wouldn't want me to find, Mr. McBee?"

Jonah stuttered. "What? No."

The agent pursed his lips. Sweat trickled down Jonah's sides. The agent's blue eyes swiveled. Jonah was aware of the wrinkled, dirty clothing he wore, the sleepless circles beneath his own eyes. He had a vague sense of guilt, as though he had a secret.

"Where do you live, Mr. McBee?"

"New Orleans."

"Did you leave your automobile in Mexico?"

"No—no, I walked across."

"What was your business in Nuevo Laredo?"

"I passed through on my way to Las Monarcas. To visit a friend."

"In Coahuila state?"

"Yeah."

"Did you return your FM-T at customs in Mexico?"

"My what?"

"Your tourist visa."

"I didn't know I needed one . . ."

The agent frowned. He set the passport down and rested his fingers on the keyboard of his computer. "What is your friend's name? The one you were visiting."

"Luz Hidalgo," Jonah said.

Keys clacked. The agent looked from the screen to Jonah to the line waiting.

"Mr. McBee, did Miss Hidalgo accompany you to the border?"

"What?"

"Is she with you?"

"No."

"She remained in Las Monarcas while you returned to the border?"

"Well, no, but she didn't come with me."

"Okay, Mr. McBee." The agent pointed toward the wall. "I need you to step over here and wait a moment."

"What?" Jonah's hands went cold. "Why? What did I do?"

"Please do as you are asked, sir."

"Come on, man. I'm just trying to get home."

The agent came around his kiosk and held his hand toward the wall. "Step aside and wait here, Mr. McBee. Please remove your backpack, as well."

Jonah turned and glanced at the travelers waiting in line behind him. White and Latino faces alike, they averted their eyes, as if connecting with him might tempt fate.

XV

Tú nunca hablas.

1

THE DRIVER DID NOT WISH TO SPEAK WITH LUZ. IT WAS JUST AS well. A bright, hot day, and Luz hadn't slept. She leaned her temple against the window glass and watched the town crawl past. The Honda slowed around a bend, and there alongside an open-air café was Cicatriz's sign—the red *C* with the slash through it. This was the same street, the very same spot, but no evidence suggested the cross fire. The graffito was like a fish skeleton in a cliff face, an insignificant artifact. Luz saw the old woman die, felt the tires leave the blacktop, and she remained calm. The horror of that day no longer seemed like an occurrence that had merely happened to her—to think of it in that way would be to enslave herself to fear and worry. Instead, that day and those following had become something interwoven with her being: I am the woman who crawled from the ditch; I am the woman who escaped in the night; I am the woman who has survived.

On her lap she held a grocery bag tied shut and packed with a change of clothes and a few of her mother's dresses. Her jean leg fit snugly over the silver knife, which she'd strapped to her calf. The hilt started just below her knee and the point came to just above her ankle. She thought the bulge was only noticeable if one really looked for it. She had considered leaving the knife behind, but what was the difference? Discarding it wouldn't rid her of the memories associated with it. And should this new path reveal itself to be another circle without escape, she figured she better be able to sting.

In the Las Monarcas bus terminal the night before, she had replaced the bus-company pamphlet on the ticket counter and then gone to the pay phone. She had the card with Oziel's phone number in her pocket.

Somebody had picked up after the first ring but uttered no greeting. Luz said, "Señor Zegas?"

A man demanded, "Who is this?"

"Luz Hidalgo."

Silence. She was going to hang up, but then he was on the line: "And here you are." The sound of a cigarette burning quietly to ash. "I had hoped to hear from you. In truth, I feared I would not. Tell me—was I right in what I said to you?"

Luz sighed. "I need to get out of here, that's all. I want to go somewhere else, and the buses are too expensive."

"I can bring you here. To me."

Luz looked over the bus depot. All the travelers. "Where is 'here'?"

"Perhaps you can understand my trepidation in telling you, over the phone, where I can be located."

"Well. I can go somewhere else from there. Yes?"

"We will work out an arrangement. I have great respect for you, Luz."

The seconds had ticked. Her guts had fluttered. She had squeezed the receiver and shut her eyes and pressed her forehead against the wall. "Okay," she had told the capo.

In the car, Luz looked at her driver. He wore sunglasses and didn't smile. Every now and again he rolled open the window and quickly smoked, as if there was no enjoyment in it. He was doing a job and wished to be done with it. He looked young, but he had a family—a wife and three small children. Luz knew because Oziel had given her the driver's Las Monarcas address over the phone. The driver's wife, a smiling and round-faced woman, had answered the door even though it was the middle of the night. She held a slumbering baby. There were two other children in pajamas, sitting on the couch and watching cartoons; they'd been woken up simply to greet Luz. The mother was uncomfortably nice, sitting up with Luz for most of the night. She had asked if Luz worked for señor Zegas as well, but Luz didn't know how to answer. She slept on the couch eventually, only briefly. The man returned home late in the morning—from whatever task he'd been assigned last night—kissed his wife, and waved for Luz to follow. Then they got in the car and hit the road. Luz surmised that today was supposed to have been his day off, a day with his family.

On the way out of Las Monarcas, Luz was thinking about Jonah. She had watched him during supper, after they talked in the street. He didn't touch his food. Luz felt wretched, but she didn't speak. She didn't know what else she could say to him. When it was time to go to bed, she looked at him a last time, where he stood watching her with his hands in his back pockets. She knew that this would be the last time she ever saw him. She acknowledged it, and she understood that she would think about him for years to come. For maybe all her years. But she also knew that there was nothing new about this kind of feeling. She smiled at him sadly, tucked the image of him away, and went into her room and shut the door.

She could hear her grandmother snuffling in her sleep. She listened for something to indicate Jonah's slumber, but he had never snored. Sometimes he mumbled, little frightened utterances—she'd heard him when they napped on slow afternoons and on the few nights they'd managed to stay together. She heard his footfalls while he paced, but eventually there was nothing, and she waited until all was quiet for a long time. When she crept through the dark front room, she could only see his vague form on the couch. Could just hear the sound of his breath.

Good-bye, Jonah. Good-bye.

She walked then down the empty street, looking for the driver's address. A dog threw itself, snarling, against the bars of an entry gate. She jumped. Then she resolved to stand there and watch the source of her fright until it held no power over her. Soon she moved on.

2

THEY CAME TO A CHECKPOINT CROSSING INTO NUEVO LEÓN, A neon orange arm lowered over their lane. Off on the shoulder stood a small particleboard hut and a sandbag bunker. As the Honda rolled to a stop, a young soldier with dark circles beneath his eyes and sweat standing out through his fatigues came to the window and told them to get out of the car. The man glared at the soldier but opened his door, so Luz followed suit. The soldier ogled her. Luz smelled marijuana, smoked in the small hut, perhaps. The soldier looked away when she glanced at him. He bent to peer into the car. He opened the door and searched the footwell.

Another three soldiers had stopped a white passenger van going in the other direction. Its doors were open and its passengers stood around, looking unsurprised. The soldiers separated an old man in a flannel shirt from the group. A bulging plastic bag dangled from his fist. One of the soldiers poked at it with the barrel of his rifle.

Luz's driver pulled a cell phone from his pocket and punched a number and held it to his ear. The soldier straightened and shouted, "What do you think you are doing?" hefting his rifle and striding around the hood. Luz slid a step away.

The other soldiers were laughing, but not at them. One grabbed the plastic bag from the old man, reached in, and withdrew an orange.

"Did I say you could make a call?" the young soldier demanded, blowing past Luz. "Put that fucking thing down. Now."

The driver didn't acknowledge him and spoke quietly into the phone.

Across the highway, the soldier with the orange crow-hopped and hurled the fruit. The others broke up laughing when it landed. The next one seized an orange.

"I will make you sorry," the soldier said. He raised a palm as if he'd slap the phone from the driver's hand, but the driver turned and presented the phone: "He wants to talk with you."

The soldier halted. He cocked his head. "You think you—"

The driver reached with the phone. "You must listen."

Across the road, the second orange arced through the air. They waited for it to land. The old man's shoulders drooped.

The soldier reached and took the cell phone from the driver and placed it to his ear. He seemed about to speak, but then he stopped and turned while he listened. Luz watched his eyes jump back and forth. Then he held the phone out, looked at its screen, and ended the call. He never said anything. He tossed the phone back to the driver.

"Okay," he said. "On your way."

He whistled in the direction of the hut and twirled a finger. The security arm over the highway rose. They pulled through the checkpoint and accelerated. Luz watched through the rear window. The young soldier crossed the street toward the others with the oranges. "Fucking snakes," the driver said, eyes flashing to the rearview.

3

NIGHT CAME ON AS THEY PASSED THROUGH THE MONTERREY suburbs, and then the city was there in its crown of mountains. A flash of memory: Luz and her father, on their way into New Orleans for the first time, had passed by the chemical plant out in the marsh. All the yellow and orange lights marked the shape of the stacks and the scaffolding. A world burning in the darkness. This was how Monterrey looked to Luz from afar.

The highway took them alongside an industrial gulch built around a swampy waterway. To the south the lights climbed the hills, and the city sprawled to the north. They crossed a bridge and sat in traffic, moving in fits and starts. The avenue was named for a long-dead general and bordered a plaza, one illuminated monument after another rearing up. A palatial construction of marble and columns anchored the end of the plaza. They turned onto yet another street named for a general and came to an old quarter of town. The narrow, bisecting cobblestone streets were blocked off against vehicles. Crowds were out. Street artists and vendors had set up on the sidewalks. The aged facades of the buildings wore neon signs, and competing rhythms pumped from the clubs.

The driver pulled over to the curb. He dialed someone on his cell, said, "We're here," and hung up.

He rolled down his window and lit a cigarette. They sat. Luz wanted to ask what they were waiting for but was nervous, and a moment later someone rapped on her window. Startled, she turned and found Cecilia, Oziel's niece, looking at her through the glass. The sicaria wore all black, as Luz had seen her before, and her hair was done into one long braid. She beckoned with her hand.

Luz glanced at her driver, whose eyes rolled toward her. "Good luck, girl."

Luz clutched her belongings to her chest and followed Cecilia down the street, through the crowd. A man whistled. Luz glanced out of reflex, then felt a mild and confusing regret when she noted that Cecilia ignored the catcall altogether.

The woman produced car keys, and a black Durango chirped on the curb. Wordless, they got in and Cecilia drove them out of the neighborhood. No radio, just the hum of the engine. Luz asked where they were going but received no answer. Cecilia drove through the city to a parking garage. They got out and went down a couple of flights of stairs into the lobby of a chain hotel. Cecilia blew past the check-in and the concierge to the elevator. Their room contained two large beds, soft and welcoming. Cecilia's bag was already unzipped at the foot of one bed. She swept an arm over the room. Make yourself at home. Then she went into the washroom.

Luz set her bag on her bed and crossed to the window. The room was several floors up. Black mountains shouldered the starless sky. Down in the city a neon cross glared blue atop its steeple, branding the shadow. Luz stared at it long enough that she could still see it when she blinked.

Cecilia reentered the room in a white nightgown. It was peculiar, this killer in her pajamas. Luz went to the washroom herself, unbuckled the scabbard from her calf, rolled the knife in a dress, and hid it in the plastic bag. She splashed some water on her face and used one of the complimentary toothbrushes. When she came out, Cecilia was in bed, already sleeping on her side, rolled away from Luz.

Luz lay in her clothes in bed for a long time. She felt sick, thinking about Jonah. His kind eyes and his sincere attempts to listen. The way she ran when the time for it came. She did love him. I did, I do—there was no difference. Luz needed to speak, to hear the story in her voice. It boiled inside her, this need to own the truth. The red numerals in the digital clock ticked toward morning. She wanted to talk to Cecilia, but the sicaria's sheets rose and fell gently as she slept. Luz could not put her finger on the reason she thought the woman might understand, but she wanted to talk to her.

Restless, Luz wrapped a blanket around her shoulders and returned to the window. There were islands of light down there, monuments and statues in the plazas and the roundabouts. Heroes hedged in by darkness. Of course, the heroes would merely have been enemies to many others in

history. That was how it worked. Luz could remember some of the monuments in New Orleans—statues of men she'd learned about in school,
men who had been traitors. She looked again to the glaring blue cross and
recalled the tiny blue cross she'd held, quaking, in her fist before the race at
that Uptown high school. So much had happened since then. The blinking lights of a jetliner crawled down the sky, slipped toward the airport
behind the mountains.

Luz turned away from the window. Cecilia was sitting up in bed and
watching her. The sicaria spread her arms then jerked her thumb toward
Luz's bed. She put her hands together, placed them along her cheek, and
closed her eyes, pantomiming sleep. Luz had admired Cecilia for the
quiet kind of confidence she possessed, her calm and resolute bearing,
but for the first time, this charade gave Luz pause. She realized:

"You never speak."

Cecilia sat there a moment, staring at Luz. She sighed and waved
Luz over. Luz sat on the edge of her own bed, facing the woman. Cecilia
rubbed her eyes. She sighed one more time and then opened her mouth,
wide. She had no tongue. There was the stem of it, not raw or painful
looking but smooth where it had been severed from her mouth.

"Who did that to you?" Luz whispered.

But now Cecilia chuckled. Silent, sardonic. She put her head on the
pillow and rolled again away from Luz.

4

LUZ FLOATS ON THE FRONT STEPS, BUOYED WITH THE NOTES HER father draws from his guitar. The words to old songs travel through her, though they originate somewhere else—from the place her mother learned them, and from somewhere deeper than that, too. The old street lies in shadow. The light posts are charred candlewicks. The wind tumbles down the street, something dark and granular in it, whorling like silt. And the people, the crowd now passing by, their faces smear when the wind touches them, like a tongue wiping their features away. Dust that cannot be reconstructed, whipping away in the flow. The faceless drone, plod. But when the first old words leave Luz's throat, the wind recoils. It twitches like a struck nerve. Now the wind again reaches for the marchers. Luz sings. The wind parts, folding into itself like a murmuration of starlings. It is your voice, Luz. It is your voice. The wind that is shadow whirls and descends, relentless in its effort to blind the sojourners. To nullify them, each in turn. And Luz sings, so that they may pass in safety. The wind bends a finger toward her with the sound of a freight train. The words stumble in her larynx, and her father's guitar grinds to powder. The silver tuning pegs hover for a moment, then spin into the wind like six wayward nickels. Her father is eaten, too, granulating into nothing. Gone. The music ceases. The lyrics lodge in her throat. The wind-shadow licks a face clean in the street. And now Luz sees them: there is Jonah, there is Colby. There is Felipo, and there is the mute Ignacio riding on his shoulders. They shuffle in the midst of the crowd. And in the crowd are more faces she recognizes: there is the dying man in the desert to whom she could not give her water, and there is the uncle who made her drink the water. She calls to them, but they don't hear her; she must sing. She sings to protect them. She understands that she cannot stop. My voice must be infinite. The wind gropes toward her, and she sings against it, and the crowd of people marches. She must keep singing, and so she tries she tries she tries—

5

CECILIA SHOOK LUZ AWAKE. LUZ WAS CHOKING ON SOMETHING, but there was nothing in her throat, and she sat up with her windpipe burning and with water in her eyes. Cecilia sat on the edge of the bed and tapped her own throat to ask what was wrong. "I'm okay," Luz said, and wiped the spaces beneath her eyes.

The room was bright. It looked hot and clear outside. Cecilia was dressed in black, packed and ready to go. Luz went to the washroom and showered. She hefted the knife, slid it from its sheath. It shined in the fluorescent lights. Luz looked at herself in the mirror, holding it. She tried to imagine the warrior but only saw her flicker, and then she felt ridiculous. She rolled the knife in her clothes and stowed it in the grocery bag.

Cecilia led her back to the parking garage, but this time they got into a midnight-blue Silverado. The truck roared out of the garage and into the sunshine. They left the city and angled farther into the highlands. The city haze sheared away. Cecilia kept both hands on the wheel and eyes firmly on the road. She was a diligent driver.

Luz ventured, "You've worked for your uncle for a long time?"

Cecilia nodded.

"What do you think he expects of me?"

Cecilia raised her eyebrows, glanced.

Oziel had tried to tell Luz she was special, but he had also told her she was beautiful, and that was perhaps the easiest explanation. It would make sense. Still, it felt somehow more complicated to Luz than something merely lustful, but she didn't yet see how. "I only needed a ride out of Las Monarcas," Luz said. "I told him that."

Cecilia huffed. Luz turned to watch the unbounded air beyond the edge of the mountain highway. She caught a glimpse of the narco slipping from view. To her palm she summoned the weight of the rock. Its sharp edge. And—Luz thought—I need to make sense of some things. I need to figure out where I'm going next.

6

THE HIGHWAY CONVERTED TO SIMPLE TWO-LANE BLACKTOP. IN the middle of one cinder-block village a gaggle of children blocked the road. They danced and made obscene gestures. One of them mimed firing a gun at the Silverado. Cecilia gunned the engine and stopped short to make them scatter. Later, she turned through a gate onto a rocky path. The suspension groaned. Pebbles banged against the skid plate.

They rumbled over a cattle guard into an old ranch. Stone buildings, grim among the cholla. The path climbed. A pasture, a solitary horse. As the unpaved road plateaued along a ridge, the vantage sloped and bottomed out. The cordillera shaved the afternoon sun into the valley, where down in the distance stood a brown pyramid. Hazy, like an apparition. Luz's heart pumped. She imagined horses racing in the valley. A young boy rode the lead animal, but he fell back to let the others win. It was a world that once existed, gone the way of those versions before it. Those who trained horses and those who built pyramids.

The trail switchbacked up a forested slope and evened out into a clearing. There was a big adobe house with a red tile roof. The windows glowed. Another smaller house squatted alongside. Several vehicles were parked out front—trucks and SUVs. Cecilia parked and turned off the ignition. The mountain air was a little cooler, a little drier. Luz smelled woodsmoke. A man sat on the porch in a rocking chair, creaking back and forth while he smoked. He held the barrel of his rifle, its butt resting on the porch boards. He nodded to Luz and Cecilia as they went inside.

Someone was cooking, and it smelled very good. An antelope-horn chandelier hung in the entranceway, and the heads of white-tailed deer stared from their wall mounts. Black marble eyes. A woman wearing a grease-stained apron appeared from the kitchen, smiling, wiping her hands with a rag. Gray wisps of hair frizzed around her face. Cecilia gestured to the woman, then briefly gripped Luz's shoulder and left the house. The cook introduced herself as Ninfa, the help around the house.

Luz followed Ninfa upstairs, the old woman's slippers shuffling against the oak floor. Paintings filled the walls, icons of saints with gold halos.

Luz's room contained a four-poster bed and windows with a view over the treetops to the sweep of the valley beyond. Another door opened into a bathroom of white tile. A folded towel had been set atop the bedsheets. Ninfa told Luz that señor Zegas was away on business. Luz was free to come and go as she pleased. If she was hungry, something would be prepared. Luz thanked her. Then Luz stood at the window and watched the light fail over the valley, over the pyramid.

XVI

Tell us what happened.

1

WHETHER YOU'RE AN AMERICAN CITIZEN IS NOT THE ISSUE AT hand." The speaker was a big man called Connelly. The light twisted and ran in his pink scalp.

"Quit hassling me, then." Jonah's stomach groaned. They'd kept him waiting a long time, and he was exhausted. He needed a shower and he needed food and he needed sleep, but he was still so far from home.

Connelly chuckled. The door opened and the other agent, Gonzalez, reentered bearing three Styrofoam cups. He set one down in front of Jonah, steam snaking out from the coffee. Gonzalez was the younger of the two. A smooth and serious face, sculpted black hair. He sat and folded his hands on the burnished silver tabletop. A slender digital recorder sat on the table between them.

"You"—Connelly consulted his notes—"left New Orleans to visit a woman named Luz Hidalgo in Las Monarcas, Coahuila."

"She was my girlfriend." Jonah wiped grit from his eyes. "That's like the fourth time I've said it. Please. Either tell me what the hell is going on or let me go home."

"Okay, here's the hang-up." Connelly was slate-colored eyes in a pale face. "A Luz Hidalgo from Coahuila recently blipped on our radar. Nothing significant enough for us to worry about, but it seems she helped some cartel boys pull off a massacre. Bunch of bodies, a face stitched onto a soccer ball—an instant classic. We've got her name on a little list of narcos now and everything."

Jonah looked at the two agents and started laughing. "Come on, man. I saw that face thing in the news down there."

Connelly grinned. "Unmentioned in a newspaper doesn't mean her name hasn't gotten around."

"You're joking. You have to be."

"Not in the slightest, Mr. McBee."

"It's fucking impossible. I just saw her. I mean"—Jonah shook his head—"there's gotta be millions of Luz Hidalgos."

"I'll grant you that." Connelly spread his hands. "But understand, I don't give a sincere rat's ass what your girlfriend is into. I care about you showing up at my border looking—well, let's just say it—looking like shit. You're flustered by harmless questions. And the first name out of your mouth is a girl hooked up with a drug gang."

Jonah exhaled and looked into the corner of the room. White painted cinder block.

"I don't want to make this a bigger production than it has to be, but I need some answers first." Connelly tapped his pen on his notepad. "Show me how this all adds up."

Jonah sighed.

"I'm going to read you some names," Connelly went on, "and I want you to tell me if they mean anything to you."

"Fine."

"Juan Luis Medina."

"Nope."

"How about Cicatriz?"

Jonah waited for more. "Is that a name?"

"Cecilia Garcia."

"No."

"Oziel Zegas y Garcia."

"No, man," Jonah said. "Look, I just want to go home. I haven't done anything wrong."

"Help us believe that." This was the other one, Gonzalez. A measured tone. "Earlier, you said Luz lived in New Orleans but she recently moved back to Mexico. Tell us what happened."

I'm not afraid—Luz had said that to him in the dark of his bedroom that night. When all the possibilities began to chip and fray. I'm not afraid. Jonah understood less now than he did then about Luz, though her fearlessness seemed to remain. She couldn't have done the things these men were saying, but there was the matter of her kidnapping. At best these men had it backward, and that was a stretch. But Jonah didn't tell them so. It wouldn't matter, and they didn't deserve it. Jonah just had to get out of here. He had to keep going. He had to get home and start building something. The lights in the room sizzled and swelled.

2

HE BEGAN WITH HER FATHER SENDING HER HOME, TELLING them the facts, sparing what detail he could. Here and there, the men interrupted with questions—serious questions about the timing of the trip and the places he'd been, and lighter questions about the things they simply didn't understand.

"Never heard of a nutria," Connelly said.

"Neither have I," Gonzalez echoed.

"Maybe Texas doesn't have 'em." Jonah was weary. They'd brought him a glass of water and he slugged some, cold and numbing.

"I wouldn't know," Connelly said. "I'm from New York."

"New Mexico." Gonzalez shrugged.

"People hate them, but they're not bad," Jonah said. "You think about them long enough and you start to feel bad for them."

"The nutria?"

"It ain't their fault where they are."

"Sounds to me," Connelly answered, "like that's got nothing to do with it."

Jonah looked at the man, then lowered his eyes. With a fingertip he traced a line on the metal tabletop. A smudge of condensation spreading. He wiped the heel of his palm across it, but the smudge remained.

A while later, Connelly went to take a leak. Jonah pressed his thumbs into his eyes until he saw stars. He leaned over the table. An impression of himself reflected in the metal, striated with the residue of some kind of cleaning product.

Gonzalez suddenly spoke. "Your oldest brother, where was he in Afghanistan?"

Something clenched and twisted in Jonah's chest, but the feeling had no temperature and it didn't hurt. It was a rote reaction, one that reminded him, as always, of how he used to stare at his sneakers and try to imagine the places Bill walked. All the videos on the Internet Jonah had watched, hoping to discover something, some answer. Jonah folded his arms on the table and rested his chin on them: "I never could remember the name of the place."

"He was there in oh-two?"

"Yeah."

"He must have been one of the earliest guys we lost."

Jonah shrugged.

"I was there," Gonzalez said, "in oh-three. Less than a hundred dead by that point, I think."

"How many by now?"

"I don't know. A lot more."

The door swung open and Connelly reentered, buckling his belt. "So," he said, "tell me about this drug-dealing pal of yours, Colby. Why'd he need to get to Mexico?"

"He's just my friend. He's got nothing to do with any of this."

"The drug dealer doesn't matter?"

"He's not here. He's never been here. He's a kid in New Orleans who doesn't know about any of this."

"I promise you," Connelly said, "he connects. Maybe not directly, and not in a way that matters to us in this moment. He's probably got no idea, but I promise you he's connected in some way to everything that's happening south of the border. Where else you think that shit he's selling comes from?" Connelly looked at Gonzalez and seemed to be searching for something. "What do they call it?"

Gonzalez raised his eyebrows.

"Degrees of separation." Connelly snapped his fingers. "That's it. Anyway, go on, Mr. McBee."

Jonah sighed and kept talking.

3

JONAH WAS WORN OUT BY THE TIME HE FINISHED. HIS LIDS WERE heavy. The two agents exchanged a long look before Connelly shrugged, reached, and turned off the recorder.

"Well," he said. "You're either a magnificent liar or a certified idiot. Either way, you must have a horseshoe up your ass." He lifted his big frame out of the chair. "You handle him?" he asked Gonzalez.

"I will," the subordinate answered, and Connelly walked out, saying no more.

Several breaths passed, as if Gonzalez needed time for the story to settle.

"All right," he said. "Come with me."

Jonah followed him to a room with a couch, a vending machine, and a coffeepot. Gonzalez gestured at the couch.

"You just wait for me a minute here, okay? Let me finish up a couple things."

Jonah didn't have the energy to question what was happening. He sat down, and the next thing he knew, Gonzalez was shaking him awake.

Jonah grunted. Gonzalez had keys and a pair of sunglasses in his hands. He beckoned for Jonah to follow.

They walked out into the searing morning light, and with it came a headache. Jonah recalled a time when he and Colby had snuck into a Bourbon Street bar and stayed longer than they had intended, drink after drink. When they exited, the sun had covertly risen and it made him feel disoriented and strange. Like he'd left himself and everything he knew behind and been reborn as an aching, awkward, and dumbfounded thing.

Gonzalez led Jonah through a fenced-in concrete parking lot packed full of official vehicles, to a black SUV. Jonah asked where they were going.

"Well," Gonzalez said as he cranked the air-conditioning. "You're out of money, aren't you?"

"Yeah."

"And your truck, you said, is back in New Orleans?"

"Yeah."

"Then I better help you get home, don't you think?"

"Oh." Jonah blinked, didn't know what to say.

"You got a cell phone?"

"The battery's dead."

Gonzalez removed a smartphone from his pocket and passed it to Jonah. "Call your brother," he said. "Tell him you'll be on the next bus to—what's the closest city Greyhound will get you to, you think?"

"Baton Rouge, probably."

"All right, tell him that."

The camp phone rang four times and the answering machine picked up. No recording. Just the beep.

"Dex. It's me. Jonah. I'm getting on a bus soon from Texas to Baton Rouge. I don't know how long it'll take. Dad's truck is okay, don't worry. Colby drove it home. Uh, I'll call you soon as I can. Hoping you can come get me." He hung up and handed the phone back to Gonzalez and said, "Thanks."

"Don't worry about it," Gonzalez answered, shifting the SUV into gear.

"Why are you helping me?" Jonah asked.

Gonzalez shrugged in a way that suggested he was thinking of a response, but then he said nothing and they drove in silence to the same bus station where Jonah had said good-bye to Colby. The heat rolled in waves from the pavement as they walked toward the entrance. Again, Jonah tried to tell the man he appreciated the assistance.

"You know," Gonzalez said, "my great-grandfather fought with Zapata. That's what they say, at least."

Jonah didn't understand, but he listened.

"I guess it could be true. Anyway, my mom likes the thought. You ever heard of Zapata?"

Jonah told him no.

"Well," Gonzalez went on, "don't worry too much about what Connelly had to say. He can be a dick."

"Okay. Thanks."

Gonzalez opened the door and looked south, past Jonah. "History," he said, "proves all of us wrong, sooner or later."

4

JONAH SLEPT FOR MUCH OF THE FIFTEEN-HOUR RIDE, WAKING FOR the transfers and not talking to anybody. A crick cinched up the side of his neck. He allowed half-asleep ruminations, dreaming of future things. I'll run specials on oil changes. I'll do discounts on realignments, help you deal with all the goddamn broken streets. He woke when the bus crossed the Sabine in the dark and he remained alert as it ascended over Lake Charles, the void opening beneath the bridge. The bus stopped briefly in Lafayette, and Jonah got out, plugged his phone into an outlet in the station, and called his brother.

Dex was waiting for him in Baton Rouge wearing a ball cap, T-shirt, and jeans. The air in his Dodge Ram blew cool and strong. The swamp suggested itself, flashing past in dark bursts along the unlit two-lane state highway. Thinking of Luz's midnight departure, of the incompatibility of their visions, of Luz's kidnapping and what it must have been like—it all made dread stir in Jonah's gut. Jonah didn't want to tell Dex what had happened. And how to explain to his brother what he wanted to do next? As of this moment, the auto shop was just an idea. Just a figment. To put actual words to the dream required knowledge, figures, plans. Without that, Jonah didn't yet have the confidence to utter it—as if hearing it aloud would reveal it, too, as just another foolish and ultimately heartbreaking enterprise. He could imagine the subtext of Dex's reply, whatever the actual words might be—What the hell do you know about making something like that happen, little Jonah?

Eventually Dex broke the silence. "You look rough."

"I know."

"Sharon's at the camp. You'll get to meet her." Dex paused. "I figure we can go there for a night or two, and I'll get you back to New Orleans for school on Monday."

"Okay."

The outside seemed to repel Jonah's focus. The engine hummed. He saw Dex reflected in the window, watched him glance between him and the highway.

"Luz lost the baby." Jonah said it without turning from the window.

There were no words. His brother's eyes were on him, then they slid to the highway again.

After a while Dex said, "There's gonna be a cookout tomorrow. Might be good. Take your mind off things."

Jonah didn't answer and so Dex went on.

"I shot this hog. You know, one of them feral things. They migrate to where the food is. Killed all a neighbor's chickens. Whole mess of blood and feathers. You shoulda seen this thing, real big son of a bitch. Three-, four-inch tusks. Had to flag down a guy on the road to help me get it in the truck." Dex chuckled, glanced at Jonah. "Anyway, dude a few camps over has this Cajun microwave, so we're gonna roast the meat under that charcoal and have a little party."

"Cool," Jonah offered. It was just a word to say.

"You'll like it," Dex tried.

"All right."

5

FRAGRANT CITRONELLA TORCHES BURNED AROUND THE YARD IN an effort to keep the mosquitoes in check. People from up and down the bayou were gathered. There was music and beer and laughter. Frogs trilling in the swamp. The sky in the east deepened, a dark indigo rolling across heaven toward the last tangerine wreckage of the sun. The roasting hog meat smelled good. The old boy who cooked wore an apron and an industrial-looking oven mitt. The Cajun microwave looked like a coffin with a tray of glowing coals on top of it.

Jonah sat in the grass at the perimeter of the party, patting Donald the dog. Dex's girlfriend, Sharon, sat with him. She was tall, about the same height as Dex. Short blond hair she tucked behind her ears. A soft Cajun accent. She held a cigarette with long slender fingers.

"You know, your brother's told me lots about you."

Jonah's difficulty imagining that must have been apparent.

"Really," she said. She tapped ash into the grass. "Dex reminds me of my own brother, in a way. Like, other people are always gonna know him better than I do, my brother."

Sharon told Jonah that she and her brother were a few years apart and had never been close growing up. She told him about their roughneck father, who had worked his life away offshore. Her brother was a former marine, like Bill. He'd survived three tours in Iraq. But he had a drinking problem now, and he'd been wrestling with it for a couple of years. "He got a job," Sharon said, "on a shrimp boat, finally. It's a tough living, but he seems to like it. It seems to help." She paused to finish her cigarette, and then she spoke through an exhalation of smoke: "That's all you can hope for, really, for the people you care about. Don't you think? That they find a way to be that gives them peace."

Jonah nodded, turned a little inward. Donald rolled onto his back and pawed at the air, and Jonah patted his belly. Sharon opened her pack of cigarettes.

Jonah said, "Think I could have one of those?"

The corner of her mouth turned up. "You smoke?"

"Nah, not usually."

She glanced around. "Just one. Don't let your brother see."

Jonah puffed lightly, tried not to cough. After a bit he got up. Donald stood, too, wagging his tail, waiting for orders. "Think I'll go for a walk. Wanna come?"

"No, thanks, Jonah." She held her hand out and Jonah helped her up. She nodded at Dex, where he stood with a beer, talking to the cook. "I'll check on that grump."

Jonah walked with Donald down the trail along the bayou's edge. The mosquitoes descended as soon as he left the halo created by the torches.

He reached the new landing and all the moored boats. Donald ran forward, nails clicking against the boards. Electric lights were on under the overhang. The space against the ceiling was turbid with moths. Jonah looked at the grander structure of the landing and thought about rebuilding things.

"Don't look natural on you."

It was Dex, arriving along the path behind Jonah.

"Smoking, I mean." Dex waved his own cigarette.

"Oh," Jonah said. "Yeah." He dropped the butt and ground it out.

"Sharon told me you were down here."

"Yep."

Dex was holding two bottles of beer in his other hand and he offered one to Jonah. He took it and sipped and didn't look at Dex.

"You wouldn't remember this," Dex said. "You woulda been only three or four." Dex stepped forward and leaned against one of the landing's support posts. "Bill wanted to go play catch on the levee, you know, like down past where the St. Thomas projects used to be. He had Pop's old glove. Pop gave it to him. Did you know that?"

"No."

"So Bill was like, Come on, let's go. Holding his glove like this, like a football. I didn't want to go. I was playing Nintendo or something. Dumb. I can't even remember now. And he kept being like, Come on,

Dex, come on. And I said no. He got annoyed and said he'd just go by himself. And I said—" Dex paused and shook his head. "I said, How are you gonna play catch with yourself?"

Dex drained his beer and set the empty standing on the boards.

"Bill just walked out. He came back later, real upset. His eyes were all red. And I remember he had dirt stains here, on his shoulder. He got down to the levee and a group of bigger kids roughed him up and they took Pop's glove and they threw it in the river. I mean in the goddamn river."

Faint music wafted across the water. The wind shifted and all was quiet again.

"I don't know," Dex went on, "if it woulda made any difference if I went with him. Probably not. I was smaller than he was. But that's not what bothers me. We played catch again. Lots more times. We were fine. But eventually the days when we could play catch came to an end, right? And it's not the good days I can think about anymore."

Jonah kept quiet. The hollow space in his chest tightened.

"When you passed through with Colby," Dex said, "you asked me if I remembered saying something to you a long time ago."

"Yeah," Jonah said.

"Well," Dex said. "I lied. I do remember. You asked me if I was worried, too, about Bill getting sent to war. I told you we shouldn't talk about him because you only lose the things you care about. Like if we pretended we didn't care about him, he'd be all right or something."

Dex exhaled.

"I mean," Dex continued, "yeah, you do only lose things you care about. The loss of something you don't give a shit about isn't a loss at all."

"No."

"But I was wrong when I said we shouldn't talk about him." Dex rubbed his hands together as if he were cold. "I turned mean because I missed Bill. I was worried about him. We all missed him. But Jonah, man, we didn't blow up that bomb. And maybe I didn't go with Bill to the levee that day, but I didn't throw Dad's glove in the river. And, okay, things didn't work out with Luz—but you didn't send her back to Mexico. You did your best."

Jonah rubbed his eyes.

"There are other things at work out there," Dex said. "That's what I think now. Things that only want to take the special stuff away from us. I don't know if they're from God or if they're just, like, ghosts or something. I don't know. I'm not smart enough to know that part. But I do know that soon enough they catch up to you, and they take something you care about away from you, and you realize you never did a good enough job with that thing when you had it. What I'm trying to say, Jonah, is, I'm sorry for a lot of things. I'm sorry."

Jonah was looking at his brother. In a low voice, not quite a whisper, he said, "Thanks."

"I been thinking I shoulda gone to Mexico with you. Ha."

"Yeah?"

"Or I shoulda done something like it once. I feel—I dunno—like maybe I missed my chance at something. To help me figure out who I am, what I am."

"I know what you mean," Jonah said, and an answer occurred to him. "But I know who you are, Dex. I know what you are, too."

Dex shrugged and looked away. For a moment he seemed overtaken. "Anyway," he started, clearing his throat. "I'm glad you're here, Jonah." He came forward and put his arm around Jonah's shoulders. "Come on, let's get back."

Jonah said, "I been thinking about what I want to do next."

"Okay," Dex said.

"I want to fix up Pop's old business, get it running again."

Dex halted and glanced at him. "McBee Auto?"

Jonah nodded. Waited.

Dex said, "That's a hell of an idea."

"I think I could do it," Jonah said, "I think—"

"I do, too," Dex answered. "I think you can do it."

Jonah let the thick air into his lungs, and Donald the dog brushed against his leg, making for the camp and the smell of the barbecue, and outside the light of the landing, night had fallen, complete and pulsing and full with the promise of tomorrow.

"I just don't know how to get started," Jonah said, "like in a money sense."

"Oh, we can take care of that," Dex said. "First thing, we gotta clean the building out. Then we can take a loan out against the house. I can set that up when the time comes." They started moving together, away from the landing. "It puts the house at risk if you can't pay the loan back, but you'll get the business going, I know you will. And I'll help, too. But first thing's first, we gotta spruce the place up. I haven't been there in a long time. How's it look?"

"Like shit," Jonah said.

Dex laughed. "So we got work to do."

"Yeah."

The brothers returned together to the party, and the next morning they drove to New Orleans.

XVII

...y será infinita mi voz.

1

SHE WATCHED MORNING RISE THROUGH THE VALLEY. THE PYRA-mid was there, beyond the tops of the foregrounded juniper and piñon. Physically, Luz felt good. Well rested. She took a shower and buckled the knife to her calf and put on the same clothes she'd worn the day before. She looked at the closet and gave some thought to hanging up her mother's dresses, but she did not intend to be here very long—she just didn't know where she'd go yet, or how—so she left the dresses rolled up in her bag. She did not want to feel as if she were moving in.

Ninfa had prepared eggs and black beans with fresh salsa and warm tortillas. There was good coffee in the pot. Off the kitchen was an alcove with a square table, where Cecilia sat drinking coffee. She was dressed in her customary black. There was an assault rifle propped against the wall behind her. Ninfa bustled in the kitchen, wished Luz a good morning, told her to sit. A morning news program babbled on the wall-mounted flat-screen between two mounted deer heads.

Cecilia, examining football scores in a paper open on the table, didn't acknowledge Luz when she sat. Ninfa brought her a plate. The salsa ran around the rim. Cecilia folded her paper and sat back with her coffee. By way of a greeting she finally looked at Luz and winked without smiling.

"Your uncle isn't home yet?"

Cecilia shook her head. She rolled her hand through the air and held up fingers: Two days. Then she drained her coffee and scooted out from the table. She hefted her rifle and left through the front door.

Ninfa came out from the kitchen then, and asked if she might join Luz.

"Of course."

The woman sat. She stirred milk into her coffee. "I have worked here for five years, since this has been señor Zegas's home. It will be nice to have someone else around." She leaned forward, cupped an old hand around her mouth, and added quietly, "Someone I can speak with, I mean." Terror flashed on her face and she added, "Please do not tell Cecilia I said that."

Luz waved her concerns away, more interested in the notion that Ninfa believed she was here to stay, for a while at least. But she held onto this, decided not to prod further. Instead she asked the housekeeper about the home, who came and went.

"Oh," she said, "this is señor Zegas's house alone. His niece works in Monterrey, but she stays in the house when she visits. I also make my quarters here, naturally. But the men rotate in and out, and they bunk in the other cottage." She paused, sipped her coffee. "I always assumed señor Zegas kept his girlfriends in other places. It will be very nice having you here." Again, that quick look of terror: "My mouth runs now that I have somebody to speak with—forgive me."

Luz crossed her arms. The coffee settled hot in her belly, making her feel sick. "Did somebody tell you I was his girlfriend?"

Ninfa's features scrunched. "Aren't you?"

A heavy pause. Luz didn't answer. She asked how Ninfa came to be there.

She began to clear the plates from the table. She spoke over her shoulder. "My husband once worked with him, too, but he passed, and señor Zegas has treated me well."

Luz said she was sorry. Ninfa's tone indicated that it had happened a long time before, but Luz couldn't help seeing the man with graying hair, hand clapped to his eye, tumble into the void beyond the brink of the cliff.

2

Luz WALKED OUTSIDE IN THE AFTERNOON. ANOTHER NARCO was rocking in a chair near the door, holding his rifle between his knees. He rolled his eyes toward her lazily, uninterested. Cecilia sat at the other end of the porch, smoking a cigarette, staring someplace else.

Luz approached and asked if she might borrow a pair of athletic shorts. Cecilia didn't look at her, but she flicked the cigarette out into the dirt, got up, and motioned for Luz to follow. They returned through the living room, passing beneath the mounted trophies with the marble eyes, to a first-floor bedroom. Cecilia's bag was open at the foot of her bed. She propped the rifle against the mattress, rummaged, came up with a pair of black gym shorts, and tossed them to Luz.

"Thanks," Luz told her. "I need to get some new stuff, I guess."

The sicaria shrugged and walked away. Luz wished to hear her speak, wished to hear her express something unique. But Cecilia was a mute soldier. And Luz grasped that Cecilia's refusal to express an opinion or any kind of perspective had less to do with her physical muteness than it did with the way she'd been silenced in a much deeper way.

Luz left the house again a few minutes later and passed the narcos without a word. She passed the cottage and the other vehicles and entered the rocky track that came up the mountain. The trail continued to rise past the clearing. Luz heard a jingling, a clopping of hooves. An old man in baggy clothes, huaraches, and a straw hat shuffled alongside a mule laden with split firewood for sale. The leñero lifted his face and spotted Luz. He raised his hand in greeting. Luz turned and started up the mountain. Before turning out of sight she glanced back to see the old man and his mule bear into the clearing, heading for Oziel's house.

Luz began to jog, feeling her hamstrings and calves loosen. Her ankles were stiff and they ached until they warmed. It was a relief to run only because she wanted to. The road was hard and steep, and so she didn't push herself but rather picked her steps carefully, relishing the

slow burn smoldering in her quadriceps. The trail ended at a dilapidated
shed, collapsed upon itself and rotted. There was nothing there. Black,
scorched rock where fires once guttered. No smell save for the pines.
The clear air.

She pressed on into the forest, ascending. Here there were no stark
white borders. No shouting and screaming parents, no jangling cowbells.
There was no Papá, separate from everybody, clutching the chain-link
fence and looking in from the outside. This was no track at all. She could
run where she pleased. She felt free. The breath in her lungs tasted sweet.
But only for a moment, for she recognized that at the end of her run she
would return to the big house in the clearing—indeed, this was another
loop, after all.

With the thought, her ghost runner sprang to life behind her, and
so she had to outrun him, climbing the slope, her soles finding the stone
beneath the dried needles and pulling her forward. He was there, cold
and gaining. She was tired of him. She wished she had the knife with her
so she might turn and slash, cut his smoky form to wisps and scatter him
to nothing. But she was unable, and his pace was relentless, so she pressed
on, spurred on by him.

Her mind wandered as she settled into the work of running. She saw
a boy, a young child. He was quiet and content, but he would speak and
have much to say if need be. He wouldn't be muzzled, and he naturally
accepted this as the right way—he would have no reason to question it.
He was special because of the histories that made him, the crossing of
borders that made his life possible. He had parents who loved him, who
loved each other, and who could live with him. Luz saw it: a world that
could have been.

No. Not that could have been. She was breathing hard and climbing
through the pine forest, and this was what she thought: It was a world
only to be imagined, now and forever—but of what use is the imagining?
Luz needed to determine this, or forbid herself from imagining it again.

She came through the last of the forest to the ridge. She halted,
ribcage heaving. Ahead the mountain dropped, diving toward a frothing
stream at its foot and an adjacent flat of lush-looking grass. From there
the earth crimped into a serrated panorama, sprouting entire forests that

were nothing more than tufts at this remove. In the waning light a flock of something rose from the pines, a fluttering shadow, and though they were likely bats Luz imagined them to be monarchs, traveling as they were meant to. Luz turned to the east and walked along the ridge to the edge of the outcropping, where the valley bottomed out far below. Down there, horses had once galloped, and the pyramid stood small and distant, hardly there.

3

IN THE MORNING LUZ WOKE FROM A DREAM IN WHICH SHE'D BEEN
pursuing somebody along a dark, dry alluvial plain. Cracked earth
underfoot. Silent, faraway lightning uncloaked mountains, like perpetually frozen swells just shy of crashing upon the plain. She found the
remains of her quarry's fires where they couldn't be buried over in this
place. Ash and the fine, blackened bones of rodents. They were out there
ahead of her somewhere, flying in the darkness, but Luz didn't think they
were actually prey. They were somewhere ahead, with another fire and
with other stories, and she needed to sit with them and to hear them and
to share her own tales. She needed to ask them something important. But
when she woke, she didn't know what it was. She was hot and it was late
in the morning, and she got up and crossed to the window and looked
at the valley and the pyramid and desired to see the structure up close.

She put the borrowed gym shorts on again. She left the knife rolled
in her mother's dresses. She told Ninfa she was going for a hike and
walked out. She didn't see Cecilia anywhere. The narco on the porch
looked at her, at her legs. She stared at him until he averted his eyes. On
the trail, she turned down the mountain.

She walked on her heels against the decline, where it ran away and
slalomed like some petrified creek bed. The general quiet clung to her,
and she listened to the thrumming of grasshoppers, the squalling of a
squirrel somewhere overhead. A steady jingling interrupted it, and the
leñero with the mule came into view, headed once again up the trail.
When they passed, the old man lifted his face—white whiskers and dark,
drooping patches beneath his eyes—and grunted, "Blessed day, miss."
Luz nodded. The jingling and clip-clop faded, and she was alone again.

Where the rocky road ran off the mountain, Luz found a divergent
path, narrow, fit for a horse or mule or four-wheeler. It scrawled straight
on into the valley, toward the hazy suggestion of the pyramid.

Luz flung her feet forward. She was lathered in sweat. She'd been walking for an hour, perhaps, when she came to a brick hut roofed with sheets of corrugated tin. A stack of firewood against the side of the home lay protected beneath a staked blue tarp. A rusted car sat wheelless on cinder blocks behind an empty livestock pen. Luz hurried her pace, not in the mood to be harangued if someone was home.

The pyramid glimmered like an apparition. She took in the valley, the earth scything into sky on either side. A contrail diffused over the ridge. She wondered where among the hills Felipo's family had lived. Would the burned bricks and charred beams still mark the place? They certainly had not lived in a manor like Oziel's. But somewhere nearby, they'd called this place home. As had Cicatriz, when he'd been Juan Luis Medina.

And it struck Luz with a bolt of electricity—an explanation, an idea, a story.

Ninfa had told her that Cecilia worked in Monterrey, and Cicatriz, when he'd held Luz in the shed, stated that he had worked in that same city. That he'd run a team or crew or something there. Luz recalled the rueful look between Cicatriz and Cecilia while he sat naked and bound in front of his hideout, and it was clear to her: once upon a time, Cecilia and Juan Luis Medina had been friends.

Luz marched on through the heat, the dust coughing up from beneath her sneakers and coating her legs. She squinted through the glare. The pyramid seemed farther away now than it had from the top of the mountain. Luz watched her feet and built the story.

Cecilia and Juan Luis were friends—not in the same sense as Jonah and Colby, for instance, but in the only way the sicarios could have been. They could not have been lovers; the story could not have gone this way, though they might have wished it at times, for their own reasons. They cared for each other, each the other's lone friend. Each outcasts in their own regard, and each talented at a terrible thing. They had a mutual empathy for a complex way of life, for all the guilt and their methods of management. For their inability to free themselves, for the horrifying truth that they enjoyed themselves and their work much of the time, and for their consequent and shared self-hatred.

Yes, Luz thought. Sometimes this truth waited for them in the quiet:

the glistening, pulsing, awful heart of the truth—and so they wouldn't want to be alone. Cecilia and Juan Luis sat together in the evenings. At his apartment, perhaps, and he would place the silver knife on the tile between them where they sat on the floor and spin it, watching it flare and glint in the light. He had no scar yet. Still a smooth, young face. They drank tequila straight from the bottle, passing it back and forth and chasing it with cold beer. He would tell her on these nights stories he told no other, stories of his old family and the land where they raised horses. He had hated it, the backbreaking work and the negligible profits. But there were moments—galloping alongside his cousin, perhaps, the creek water splashing to either side and the wind filling his shirt—when he knew that it was a good life, a true life. A life that, he now knew, would never resurrect itself.

And Cecilia would open to him, as well. She understood that Juan Luis had run toward a life he thought offered something more, but that was not her history. Instead, she'd been pulled into it. She told her friend—for her voice was still hers—of growing up in Monterrey, of her policeman uncle who'd promised to take care of her and her mother after her father had died. Her uncle delivered envelopes of cash to their home. As Cecilia grew, he took her on ride-alongs and she saw and understood certain things. Sometimes he left her in his car with a handgun in her lap for protection while he went into a store or office or other nondescript structure to collect. She learned to appreciate the weight of the gun in her hand, the feel of it, the promise of it. She learned to appreciate how her fear excited her, if she was afraid at all. When the day came for her to make a living of her own, she needed only to ask her uncle, whose true existence had come into the light by this point and would be the single life he led.

These were the stories they gave to each other. Theirs were lives filled with many things, not the least of which was regret. There would be no forgiveness—not of themselves nor from any other—and they could love each other for this.

Inevitably the world, and what it determined, interfered. As it must, as it always does. Cecilia was caught between her friend and what amounted to her family. She was the force and they were the immovable objects. The product was her silence. The infinite engine that had swallowed them both spewed them out no longer whole. It continued to churn. Their lives crawled on in the last manner left to them.

Luz imagined the story while she walked in the heat, throat sticky with thirst. Cicatriz's team, with the exception of Cecilia, had defected, become renegades—they would blaze out. Though newly scarred, he'd never grow old enough for his otherwise smooth face to be touched by the tobacco, the alcohol, the drugs. Cecilia herself had become both rat and failed assassin. Sometimes the wrong turn is the only turn offered. Luz hiked toward the distant pyramid and understood, in a way, that this imagined story was similar to her mother's old stories. She could not know whether the story was true; all that mattered was what the story could do for her. There were, however, two details she could accept as fact: Oziel had first tempted Juan Luis, and Oziel had used up Cecilia.

Luz halted in the dust. She was bushed. The pyramid, spectral on the horizon, had grown no closer. She thought it might be unreachable. She pivoted and started back.

4

LATE IN THE AFTERNOON SHE NEARED THE BRICK HUT. NOW A mule stood in the pen. Smoke tendriled from the stovepipe in the roof. The mule bayed and its bell jangled. The leñero appeared, stooping to get through his door. He wore the same baggy clothes and huaraches, but his straw hat was gone and his white hair flared like a crown around the brown dome of his bald head. His jowls jumped as if he needed to limber up his throat: "Good afternoon, miss."

Luz smiled politely. Great, she thought. She was woozy in the heat.

The old man swiveled and looked toward the pyramid. "One moment," he said. "You must be thirsty."

He disappeared into his home and returned with a clay cup in one hand and a plastic gallon of water in his other. He shuffled toward her, pouring into the cup. Luz was parched, and the water made a chugging sound, and she saw the dying man in the desert, but here he was giving her the water instead, and she wanted to refuse—I don't deserve this, let me die—but she was thirsty, too thirsty, and she accepted the cool cup with both hands. She sipped, and everything came into firmer focus.

"Thank you," she told him.

The old man's name was Onofre. "Please," he said, gesturing to a folding chair on the dirt in front of the hut, "sit with me while you finish your water."

He disappeared once more into the house and reappeared dragging a wooden stool. Onofre asked if she had hiked to the pyramid, and if so, what did it look like?

The folding chair shifted in the dirt beneath her. She shook her head. "It's a lot farther away than it looks."

Onofre chuckled, whiskers bristling and eyes glittering. "Yes. I have never seen it up close, either. Sometimes I wonder if it is actually there at all." He was holding his own cup and the jug, and he poured himself some water and set the jug on the ground. "I have heard that a family owns the land where the pyramid sits, so they own the pyramid itself. There is some dispute over what to do with it—open it for digging, turn it into some kind of tourist attraction. But there is no agreement, and so nobody visits." He sipped his water, waved his hand. "There are other pyramids—larger ones, popular ones. There is no hurry, and God will decide in the end."

Luz's water was silty but satisfying. Sweat slid down her ribs. "I like the thought," she said, "of nobody ever getting close to it."

The sliding sunlight swallowed the distant structure. The mule wheezed, stamped a hoof.

"There is no hurry," Onofre repeated, "and God will decide in the end."

Luz grinned, finished her water. He asked if she'd like some more, but she declined. She didn't get up, though. She didn't feel like moving yet. The old man was right. No hurry.

Onofre swirled his clay cup as if aerating a fine wine. He twirled his finger to indicate the surrounding land. "I sell my firewood to everyone in these hills, and I have never seen you before. Now I have seen you twice in two days. Once coming down the hill, and once returning."

"I am just passing through," Luz said.

Onofre raised his brow. "Is that what you believe?"

The question had the flavor of accusation. Luz did not like the way she'd so easily let her guard down. She would learn, though. She would learn to stop doing that. She stood, placed the cup on the chair, and started away.

"Please," Onofre said. He pleaded with his hands. "I do not mean to upset you. I know who lives on the mountain—"

Anger sparked in Luz's belly. She spun: "You would save me, old man?"

"I wish nothing of the sort. I certainly do not wish to cross my neighbor." His eyes were large in his drooping face. He kept his hands out, splayed. "But I am telling you that if you do not wish to stay in that house forever, you will go from here. Right now. You will take some water from me and you will start walking and you will not turn around. You do not need him"—he pointed up the trail—"to go where you need to go, but if you return to his house now, you will never leave."

Luz placed her fists on her hips. The trail ran to the road that snaked up the mountain. The sun had truly begun to set. The old man had articulated her fears; she admitted this to herself. But her mother's dresses were still in the house, and Oziel wouldn't return until the next day. The thought of abandoning her mother's things was unbearable.

"Do not," Onofre said, as if to sway her thoughts, "confuse God's time with what we may deem as urgent. You must go."

She looked at the leñero. He hunched toward her.

"I know," she told him, "I'm sorry," and she walked away.

A hundred meters or so down the trail, she finally looked back. He remained on the stool, elbows on his knees, hanging his head.

5

Luz hiked up the road, listening to insects sing as shadow gathered. Onofre was right, she knew it. But she could still grab her mother's things and leave, as long as Cecilia and the other narco guard didn't try to stop her. But what if they did? They'd see her bag, ask questions. The leñero's voice rang in her mind—turn around and go right now. Fear needled the nape of her neck, made her want to run. No, she thought. No. I can't, not yet. She would just have to figure something out; she had before. There would be another way out of the house, a back door or a window, and she could hike to the top of the mountain, find a path down the back slope.

The trail swung around the mountain. There was a figure in the road, Cecilia, dressed in black and holding her rifle. Upon seeing Luz—and Luz had the distinct impression that the sicaria had been waiting for her—she lifted an arm and waved Luz in, beckoned to her: Come on. Molten lead filled Luz's stomach and cooled, but she willed herself to walk calmly, to keep her pace. As she neared, Cecilia reached and gripped her shoulder. She pointed at the house. "I understand," Luz said.

There was a new narco on the porch, rocking in the chair, smoking a cigarette. They passed him and went inside. Spanish music played softly in the house. The smell of roasting green chiles. The antelope-horn chandelier swayed and cast a discordant light show onto the wall. Cecilia gestured toward the kitchen: You first.

Luz walked to the entrance. Oziel was there, bent over the cutting board. He wore an apron and wielded a chopping knife. His gold tooth shined.

"Greetings, Luz!" He spread his arms. "I gave Ninfa the night off, as I shall make you dinner myself." The point of the knife veered toward her before he returned to dicing an onion.

"It smells good," Luz said tactfully. "I thought you were gone until tomorrow."

"Business concluded early." He glanced at her, at her legs where sweat had dried in a delta through the dirt. "Why don't you shower, put something nice on. I'll have dinner ready shortly. I have a story to tell you, one I think you'll enjoy." He rolled the knife through the air. "I would worry Cecilia might have spoiled the surprise, but alas."

Luz flinched as if she were the one without the tongue, but Cecilia gave no outward indication of having been offended. The sicaria gestured with her eyes to the stairwell, and Luz pivoted and marched.

While she showered, she wondered if the leñero had seen Oziel's car return, if that was why he had told her to run. She wrapped her hair in the towel, then laid her mother's white linen dress out on the bed and looked at it for a while. Luz wasn't sure anything would have changed, though, if Onofre had mentioned the car. She still would have come back for the dresses.

She finished toweling off and slipped the dress over her head. It was soft and it fit well. The hem reached her ankles, but the fabric rested loose and airy. She stood in front of the mirror and smoothed the dress over her stomach. She sighed and watched the breath move through her body. She turned to her things and hefted the silver knife in its leather sheath. She put her foot up on the bed, raised the dress, and placed the scabbard on her calf. Her hands were shaking, and it took her a couple of tries to work the buckles. When she stood straight, the dress completely obscured the knife.

In the mirror she narrowed her eyes like a hawk. There was a flash, nothing more than a glimmer, of the old warrior. She could use the right words with Oziel, she could make him understand with all possible respect and without giving offense. She'd sit with him and eat his food and hear what he had to say, and then she would thank him for his generosity, thank him for getting her out of Las Monarcas, and then firmly indicate that she intended to move on soon, to be on her own.

The thickening tension in her gut, the anticipation tingling in her fingertips. She grinned sardonically at herself and went through her prerace stretching routine, twisting her trunk and loosening her back, touching her toes and warming her hamstrings. She finished, raised her face.

Mamá, she prayed. A breath. And you, too, señora McBee, if you can forgive me.

She had no nice shoes to wear with the dress, so she descended the stairs barefoot. Oziel was in the kitchen, scraping green meat from charred chile skins.

"You look lovely," he said, dicing the chile meat and adding it to a large pot on the stovetop. He untied his apron and hung it on a hook. His dark shirt was open at the neck. His sleeves were rolled. He wore charcoal slacks and gleaming black shoes.

"I will make you a drink," he said. It wasn't a question, but Luz wanted to reply as if he had asked whether she wanted one, so she said, "Sure." He sliced limes and made vodka cocktails and suggested they sit outside on the porch while dinner finished cooking.

The guard got to his feet. Oziel told him to go somewhere else and gestured for Luz to take his rocking chair. Then he dragged the other chair over and sat next to her. The guard had stopped in the shadow alongside the smaller cottage. His cigarette glowed. Oziel said, "Go somewhere where I cannot see you," and the man dragged his feet out of sight. Oziel exhaled and settled, rocking chair creaking. "Pretty night," he said.

The pines walled off her view of the valley. The stars bobbed close on their unseen tethers. The porch light, a single bulb in an enclosure meant to look like a lantern, buzzed overhead. A slight tapping. A trapped moth juking against the bare bulb.

"You wanted to tell me a story," Luz said.

He crunched an ice cube in his teeth. "I will save that for dinner. Let's talk about you for a moment."

Luz politely put her glass to her lips but didn't swallow. "What do you want to know."

"What happened in Las Monarcas?"

"More or less what you suggested," she said. "I worked for my grandmother, walked around town. That's about it." She'd keep Jonah hidden; he was hers alone.

"And that was all it took for you to call me."

"No. The last thing was something I heard."

He asked for more by raising his eyebrows.

"The reading at Mass."

"Really."

"Yes." Overhead, the moth fluttered, clicking against the glass fix-ture, not realizing it could simply escape out the bottom. "From Santi-ago."

Oziel smiled to himself, sipped his drink. He hummed. "Be doers of the word."

They sat in the quiet, and something screeched out in the valley.

"Well," he said, "I believe it is time to eat."

"Sure."

As they got up, Luz felt something soft on her head. She ran her fingers through her hair and came away with the moth, the life burned out of it.

6

"JUST THE TWO OF US TONIGHT," OZIEL SAID AS HE SET PLACES AT the table off the kitchen. The music played in hushed tones. He set out a bowl of rice and a plate stacked with tortillas, and then he ladled them bowls of the chile verde. Luz smelled the spice and the roasted pork. He sat against one of the alcove walls, and Luz sat with her back to the open expanse of the kitchen. It made her feel a little exposed, but nobody else was around. She crossed her legs beneath the table.

Oziel scooped a bite, halted. "Do you wish to say grace?"

"No," Luz said, "thank you."

His features registered slight surprise but he only said, "Okay."

The food was good. The heat eased something in her skull. She was careful not to eat too much or too quickly, though. In each moment she tried to remember to measure her own actions, thoughts, and words. "Your story?" she prodded.

"Yes." He swabbed the rim of his bowl with a tortilla and tore a bite with his teeth. "You will appreciate this."

"I'm waiting."

He chuckled. "You must remember your meddlesome federale friend, Garza, the one from the base?"

Luz did.

"How shall I put this . . ."

"He's dead," Luz finished.

Oziel looked at her. "I was going to say something more clever, but yes, he is."

"Is that the story?"

"No. As you know, I have people in his outpost."

Luz placed her spoon in her bowl and crossed her arms on the table.

"I order them to study Garza, so they do. They can tell me when he takes a smoke break, a coffee break. When he goes to the latrine, when he arrives, when he leaves every day. I have my eye on him because he is a pain in the ass. And you must understand this now, Luz—in this business it is no longer a matter of simply removing obstacles from the path ahead. Certainly uncreative brute force still has its place—as you have seen—but methods must now be found in order to distinguish oneself. So. I learn that Garza takes his cigarette breaks outside the garage on the base, and I engineer an accident with some gasoline." He winked, spooned a mouthful of chile.

"And that killed him?" Luz asked. She thought of the moth on the porch.

"I confess it would have been more elegant. I understand he was burned very badly, but as he rolled on the concrete, some mechanic managed to douse him with a fire extinguisher. Still, he was critical."

"So he's not dead?"

"No, he is dead. I sent a sicario to the hospital to finish him."

"Oh."

"Yes." He shrugged, ripped another tortilla in half. "When the departed is someone of his stature, people naturally assume that something more than an accident has taken place. This works in our favor. We hang a banner from a Monclova bridge, stating, 'Righteous flame consumes the unrighteous,' and sign it, and then there can be no mistake. The people, the plaza—they know we are resolutely in charge. Any memory of Cicatriz and his minor run of terror is forgotten. Good, no?"

Luz stirred her chile, watched pink bits of pork emerge and submerge. "You consider yourself to be righteous?"

He cocked his head and didn't immediately answer. "How do you mean?"

"I mean—" She paused. Think, Luz. "I suppose that I am confused. I saw you pray with your men. But your faith cannot be why you do this."

Oziel mopped the bottom of his bowl with his tortilla, smiling again to himself. "You are a smart woman, I have told you this before." He lifted his eyes. "Much of my aesthetic is mere posturing, for the sake of my men and for effect in the plaza. Many of them need this baseline, you understand. But do not trap yourself, Luz, with such antipodal strictures. This game is a business like any other. I provide for many families with

what I earn—is there no element of righteousness in that? And surely
there are degrees of, oh, call it evil if you must. There are many who are
worse than me, who offer nothing to those whom they should protect—I
speak of those we war with, for example. There are degrees, and there
are always counterweights, and righteousness falls somewhere on this
spectrum. My own righteousness is something I determine, no one else."
He paused, teeth gritted. "And yourself? Are you righteous?"

"No," Luz answered. "I have done things that prevent it."

He waved, as though batting away a fly. "If that is what you believe."

"I thought," she said, "maybe you didn't believe in God."

"I have no tolerance for atheists," he started. "Liars, cowards. Who
else would argue with you concerning the existence of something they
deny in the first place? But it is not their unbelief that I hate, Luz. It is
their cowardice. The denier and the blind believer are one and the same
to me. It is cowardly to refuse complexity. One must not be afraid of the
unknown. I believe that you get my meaning. If I am at all right about
you, then you understand what I am saying."

"I do," Luz said, but she was being pulled into a conversation she
could not have. She needed to tell him she was leaving. It did not matter
whether he was right about her.

"God," Oziel said, "can be either very cruel or very sad. If he does
not intercede when Cicatriz opens fire on a street crowded with the
innocent—"

—the dead woman, the old man screaming, the life still inside Luz—

"—then God's failure must be in his own refusal. But if God's absence is not by choice, then there is no such thing as his omnipotence. He
may only watch from afar and hope we make the right choices. If God
is not here, then we must therefore say that the devil exists at a remove,
as well. That leaves Man to stand alone. All the evil and all the good, it
belongs to us. It is up to the individual man to mete out the portioning.
Are we agreed?"

Bells crashed in Luz's head. Tell him you're leaving. Thank him,
be polite, try to get out. She said: "I see only the absence of God's vengeance in the world."

"Yes." He grinned. His gold tooth blazed. "There have always been men like me. There are more every day. But at this juncture, Luz, God's vengeance is beside the point, and I must deal in practicalities. I know our enemy well. I must gather those who are capable, those who are not cowardly, those who understand. I must rally them to my purpose. And you are talented, Luz. You are special. I could use you."

Luz's heart murmured in her chest. She clenched her fists, felt feeble. She looked at them and saw her mother's hands and willed them to be strong.

"Voices rush to fill the void," Oziel said. "So many of them, clamoring to be heard, that they create a void of another kind. To be heard, you must silence those others."

And Luz understood, in this moment, what he wanted with her. There was nothing sexual about it, as his workers assumed, and neither was he after her skills—whatever they were—no matter what he said. In Luz, Oziel saw somebody who was strong. He saw somebody who was unafraid. He saw a voice. He saw a voice, and he needed to silence it.

Tell him now. If you are going to get out of here, you need to tell him right now that you aren't staying. Do it now.

"Who," Luz whispered, "silenced Cecilia?"

Oziel blinked. He furrowed his brow. A confused kind of smile crossed his face.

There was no music playing. There was no sound at all.

"Did I hear you correctly?" Oziel asked.

Luz stared at him. "Your niece's tongue. Who cut it out?"

He looked like he was waiting for a punch line. Then, "You must know the answer to your question, Luz."

She gave no reply. She was not who he would have her be.

"You are smarter than this, or I have misjudged you."

She didn't reply. Oziel's end-of-the-day stubble stood out sharply. The pores in his skin. Excruciating detail.

Luz thought: I am not Mexico and I am not America. I am something else, and my voice will be infinite. She smiled at him sadly and said: "I am no mute woman."

His eyes narrowed. The room was trapped in warped miniature, twisting in the gold veneer of his tooth. His lips closed, and that version of the world ceased to be.

Her lungs filled with oxygen. Adrenaline fizzed in her limbs. As if she were crouched at the starting block, awaiting the sound of the gun. The lanes arced ahead, stark and white, ending where they began. The track seemed inescapable.

Oziel's eyes opened wide. They shined with revelation. Luz gripped the hilt of the knife where it was strapped to her calf beneath the table.

Oziel lunged from his chair, arms outstretched, hands seeking her throat.

She jerked the knife free. It was a heavy thing. Too heavy to bring up in time.

He hurtled over the corner of the table, smashing into her. They went backward in the chair. Her head slammed against the floor. Stars detonated. His weight compressed her ribcage, and breath left her. And then he somersaulted past, and she lay in a dully throbbing bubble, all the world sparking and roaring at its fringe. She could have lain there forever, mind afloat. She found herself, tiny and untethered, somewhere in her own skull. Swim, she thought, and she surfaced into the bellowing world.

She was wheezing, great involuntary grabs for breath. A hot and sick feeling spread beneath her navel. She rolled to her side, pushed to her hands and knees. Her wrist burned cold, and the thought that it might be broken flitted through. But she still clutched the knife. She couldn't feel her fingers, and she couldn't sense how much strength remained in them. With her good hand she shoved the toppled chair aside and got to her feet. Her bare soles slid in the spilled chile. An ankle also seemed to be injured. She wrapped her good hand around her knife hand and squeezed, gripping the hilt with both. She put her weight on her uninjured leg and gathered what breath she could.

Oziel was on the kitchen floor, rocking to his hands and knees. Dinner was splattered across the varnished floorboards. Ceramic lay in shards. It would only be moments before Cecilia came running. Oziel got to his feet, facing away from her. Luz leveled the long knife. He turned, eyes down, hands to his stomach. When he took them away, his palms were slick. The wet fabric of his shirt clung to him. Luz looked at her blade. Red, as was the belly of her own dress. But it was his blood, not hers.

Strands of hair hung in Oziel's face. His skin was pale, glistening. He glared at her and brushed his hair away, leaving a red swipe on his forehead. His eyes darted around the kitchen. The counter ran parallel to where they faced off, and the sink yawed between them. Inside the basin, the wooden handle of the chopping knife leaned against the chrome. She was still closest to it but her ankle howled, pulled like an anchor.

He charged for the chopping knife. Luz shuffled to intercept, propelling her knife ahead of her. The thrust was sluggish and inept, with the same terrible feeling as in the nightmare when her legs wouldn't work well enough and her ghost runner gained. Oziel opened his hands as if to catch the blade rising toward him, but his fingers let it pass and he clamped onto her wrists. He swung her to the side and drove her into the kitchen cabinets. They were glass, crosshatched with wood. Everything—inside and out—burst, bright and soundless. She threw herself sideways, trying to get around him. A shard of glass stuck in its frame bit into her triceps—pain lanced from there to her brain stem. Oziel had her wrists in a vise grip, and he swung her back, pressed her into the broken cabinets. He forced her arms to bend, directing the blade toward herself. Her wristbones wailed. She was going to have to drop the knife. That was the only way, the only turn offered, and then it would be over.

She lunged one last desperate time, and her injured ankle gave out. She went down around Oziel's foremost leg, spinning as she fell and pulling him on top of her. His full mass pinned her, and a wide smile split his face. She couldn't move. Then blood spilled through his teeth, the ivory and gold alike. Luz turned her head. It splashed hot along her cheek, her neck, her earlobe.

Her arms were trapped between their chests, and the blade had sunk into the underside of his jaw and gone through the roof of his mouth. His entire being, the unfathomable weight of it, trembled around the knife blade. His grimace widened. A soft squalling in his mouth. His eyes were large and clear, quaking in their sockets. A viscous mixture of blood and drool slipped slowly from him. Words scuffled in his throat. They never made it out.

Luz rocked on her shoulders and rolled Oziel onto his side. She got up, and her fingers wouldn't unclench from the knife. It slid free from his jaw. A spurt of nearly black blood. He twitched, fell onto his back. The heels of his shoes clicked against the floorboards. He was staring at her. Then he wasn't there at all.

The blood on Luz's skin plunged from hot to cold. She shivered uncontrollably. She saw shards of glass glinting on the floor and she would have to be careful not to step on them, but she thought she'd fall over if she tried to take a step. Then Luz saw her.

Cecilia stood in the kitchen's entrance. Her rifle hung across her chest. The mute sicaria looked at her dead uncle. Now she looked at Luz and the wet blade in her hands.

There was nothing Luz could do. Thought blazed, phosphorescent, but her muscles were utterly unreachable. Nothing to do.

Cecilia wore a flat, indeterminable expression. She reached and lifted the rifle's strap off over her head. She set the rifle down, barrel against the kitchen counter. She looked once more at Luz, turned, and walked through the front door.

Feeling came back. Pain like thawing flesh. Luz slipped carefully through the kitchen and hobbled upstairs, leaving red footprints. She clutched the knife in her good hand. Her other was unresponsive. Blood ran from the back of her arm, trickling past her numb wrist and fingers.

In the bedroom she moved as quickly as possible. She took off her mother's dress and held it out before her. Sweat-damp and bloody. Her breath came in nearly hysterical respirations and she squeezed back tears and dropped the dress to the floor. She took the towel from earlier and wiped her feet clean. In the bathroom she wet another towel and cleaned off the rest of her as best she could, but she knew she couldn't wipe it all away, rushing. The laceration on the back of her arm wouldn't stop bleeding. She probed it with her fingers and retched, nearly vomiting. She returned to her grocery bag and removed her dirty jeans and T-shirt. Getting dressed was difficult with one hand, but she managed it. She slipped one sneaker on easily, yelped when she had to put the other on. The knife lay bloody on the bedspread. She thought about leaving it, but instead she took the towel, wiped the blade clean, and sheathed the knife again against her calf. She tied shut the grocery bag containing two more of her mother's dresses and exited the room.

The house was quiet. An absolute, suffocating quiet. She hopped down the stairs, using the railing and avoiding her injured ankle. She didn't look into the kitchen; her stomach revolted at the thought. She opened the front door and limped into the porch light, shuffling as quickly as she could out of the house.

There was nobody else. The guard had apparently stayed hidden after he'd been ordered to. Luz stepped off the porch and crossed the clearing, eyes adjusting. The night was loud with life twittering in the pines. She heard men laughing inside the cottage.

Luz found Cecilia standing in the dirt road out on the slope. Hands on her hips. Watching the stars. She nodded as Luz drew even with her and held her gaze. Untold memories, inarticulate thoughts. But Luz knew her story. She could see it shimmering in her dark pupils. Cecilia pivoted and began to hike up the trail. A few steps out, she raised a hand in farewell.

Luz took a deep breath. Then she started down the mountain.

XVIII

Be thankful. Don't look back.

1

COLBY'S MOTHER ANSWERED, BUT ALL SHE SAID WAS, "HANG on," and shut the door in Jonah's face. Colby appeared a few moments later. "Mickey-Bee!"

They walked together through the neighborhood, swatting at the flies roiling over the decomposing palm fronds stacked on the curb along with somebody's trash. Jonah told him about the burning car and the masked man and how he thought it had been a dream. Colby stopped, looked at him. "You fuckin' crazy, you know that? I'm glad I came back." He reached into his pocket and produced Jonah's keys.

"You did all right, then, driving? I told you."

"Took me forever." Colby shrugged. "My mama, she's mad at you."

"Mad at me?"

"Yeah. But she was pretty mad at me, too, so don't sweat it."

They walked for a long while, crossing the streetcar tracks, past the bars and restaurants on the avenue, and then past the finer homes on the other side of the street. A man selling watermelons from his flatbed. A taco truck, empty of business. They reached the levee and sat on the steps overlooking the river. A massive container ship had paused in the process of either taking on cargo or unloading it. Colby finally asked him:

"The suspense is killing me, Mickey-Bee. What happened with Luz?"

Jonah scratched an imaginary itch on his forearm. "Didn't go too well."

"You got there? She was home?"

"Yeah." But what else to tell him? How to tell him? "We broke up."

"Shit." Colby let the word out slowly, like a sigh. "What about . . . ?"

Jonah said, "She lost the baby. Before I got there."

Colby squinted at him in the sunlight. He opened his mouth, closed it. He left it unsaid. He scooped a handful of gravel and rolled it down the levee slope. A cyclist blew past on the levee trail, dinging his bell. Way out in the river a tug labored against the current. Downriver, the bridge reached out of downtown. The cruise ships must all have been out at sea. Colby leaned over and elbowed Jonah. "She missed me, didn't she?"

"Yeah. I think she did."

The river was still there, broad and brown. It seemed calm. Jonah knew it wasn't.

"You coming back to school?"

"Yeah," Jonah said. "I guess I better. See if I can graduate."

In the lull, Colby plucked a desiccated cicada shell from the step beneath them, palmed it, and showed it to Jonah. "I'm leaving right after graduation for Georgia."

"Georgia."

"Yeah," Colby said. "Fort Benning."

Jonah looked at him.

"I signed up last week."

Jonah shrank back into his own head. Didn't know what to say.

"I ain't been selling shit, neither. Gave it up." Colby folded his arms, rested his elbows on his knees. His eyes were on the river, but Jonah sensed that his friend looked somehow through it. "The other day," Colby said, "I'm sitting in the back of Mr. Sise's classroom. He was up front with a few kids, watching something on the computer. Me, I'm just spacing out. Thinking about you, probably, hoping you weren't dead." He grinned, then went on. "There's this kid at the desk next to me. I'm not really watching him, but he thinks I am. See, he's sitting there thumbing through a stack of bills. Like, a lot of money, Mickey-Bee, and you know how he been earning it. And he's staring at me, thinking I been watching him, and he go, 'What you looking at, nigga?' Said it like a threat. I got my ass up and went to the front of the room, and the dude goes on counting."

"You didn't know him?"

"Nah, man. That's the thing. I didn't know him at all. Felt like I'd never seen him before. I had this sense all of a sudden of the whole game, just how fucking big it is. Swelling from New Orleans and Mexico and a million other places, all of it connected. I saw it, right then."

Jonah had the sensation that he was looking at his friend from a great distance.

"You know," Colby continued, "I was nervous coming back. Thinking about Davonte. He vanished, and first time he pops his head up, blam. I didn't know what to expect. I was gone, hadn't been selling. I was scared."

Colby shook his head, then looked at Jonah: "Shit, I get back, and it was like nobody even noticed I'd been missing. Except my mom." Colby paused. "I got it finally, how big the business was I had my fingers in. I saw how little I actually pulled from it. Not enough for motherfuckers to even notice. Might as well have been nothing. Made me realize it's like I'm buried under this whole city, all of it just pressing down on me. I'm down here getting chewed up in the guts of it all. I ain't nothing more than a bit of fuel. So I gotta get up and get out. There's a lot of world out there. I hope there is."

"I'm sorry, Colby. I'm sorry I'm not going with you."

"I understand, Mickey-Bee. The army stuff was all just talk for you anyway."

Gulls rose and fell all along the levee, their lonesome cries.

"You know," Colby said, "they, like, made the Mississippi go where they wanted it to. With all the levees and shit, they forced it to flow just the one way so they could build all around it. But that ain't how rivers work. Not supposed to, at least." He swished his hand to illustrate. "Gotta flow where they want, else you end up with problems."

Jonah looked slantwise at him, grinning. "Where'd you learn that?"

"School, I guess." Colby smiled. "What you getting into next?"

"Well," Jonah said, "I got a business plan."

"Listen to you. A business plan."

"Yeah, man. You broke right now?"

"You know it."

"Wanna make some cash?"

"What, you paying?"

"I am."

Colby narrowed his eyes, tried to figure out the joke.

"I'm serious. I'll pay you to help me out with something."

"Pay me with what?"

"My brother's working it out. He's here."

"Dex is in New Orleans?"

"Yeah. I told you. We're going into business."

"How much?"

"We'll figure out the details."

Colby grinned. Looked out at the river. An airliner quietly thundered high overhead, going someplace. Colby turned to Jonah. "What do I got to do?"

Jonah shrugged. "Might have to sweat a little bit."

2

JONAH FELT GOOD, HAVING DEX AT THE HOUSE WITH HIM. ON Jonah's nineteenth birthday, Dex sat up with him late into the night drinking beers and talking, making plans. Dex looked at the photographs on the walls, told stories. Donald the dog made himself at home on the couch. They were family, under one roof.

The next week, an oil rig in the Gulf exploded. It was all over the news. Nobody talked about much else. Eleven had died. The rig sank, and now crude geysered from the seafloor with no sign of stopping. Jonah and Dex watched the news, images flashing in silent catastrophe. Dex wondered aloud whether he'd known any of the workers.

"Everybody down the bayou either works out there or knows people who do."

A graphic on the screen showed potential currents and drifting slicks, miles long.

"Fuck," Dex breathed out, slow.

Sharon arrived at the house Friday night. Jonah met her out front with Dex. She had planned to come over and help them get started on the cleanup of the McBee Auto building. The three of them talked well into the night. She was worried about her brother, now that the shrimpers were being docked due to the oil pumping toward the surface and washing inland. "All the shrimp fleets are coming in," she said.

Jonah understood the problem. Workless days were no good for those who had good reason to be restless. He said, "Tell him to come up here and help with the renovation."

Sharon and Dex looked at him.

"I mean, I gotta get help eventually anyway. Maybe could hire him to do some work once the bank money comes through. What do you think, Dex?"

"Hey." Dex shrugged and raised his beer. "You're the boss."

3

COME THE MORNING JONAH WAS UP EARLIER THAN HE MEANT to be, willing his headache away, pacing the kitchen. While he sipped coffee he went out back with Donald the dog and watched the light kindle through the canopy of the ancient live oak rising over the roofs.

Dex and Sharon came downstairs soon enough. There was a somber air about them. The news said that the oil was still gushing. All attempts to stave it off had failed so far, and the next option wasn't yet clear.

They ate a quiet breakfast and loaded the truck bed with sledge-hammers, breathing masks, hedge clippers, a weed eater, a couple of crowbars, an electric sander. Some of the tools were old, having sat in the backyard shed for years. Some were new. Some were Dex's, from the camp. Jonah also had a box of contractors' trash bags and a gallon of herbicide for the tall grasses growing through the cracks in the sidewalk. He'd need many more materials, but he'd learn as he went. There was something exciting about that.

Warm wind blew through the open windows and filled the cab. It felt good to all of them. So did the movement, so did the promise of sincere and honest work. They could each imagine a day well spent, and it took their minds off the Gulf and the oil.

Colby showed up soon after they arrived. He struck a pose with his fists on his hips. He watched Jonah unloading materials from the truck. He looked the whole structure over and whistled. "You know, Mickey-Bee. It ain't too late to enlist."

Jonah grinned, passed him the hedge clippers, and said, "Why don't you get to work on them vines?"

"Shit," Colby said. He grabbed the clippers and moved toward the facade, calling over his shoulder in jest, "Figure out what you paying me yet?"

"We'll talk over a beer later."

"All right." Colby said to Jonah's brother, "What up, Dex," and Dex nodded back.

Jonah leaped to the sidewalk, crowbar in hand. Movement caught his eye. An elderly woman in a nightgown had come out onto her porch and sat in the shade to watch what was happening. Jonah waved to her and she waved back. Then Jonah went to the shop's front door. It had been glass, though now there was just a sheet of plywood bolted over the frame with stripped and rusted screws. Layers of graffiti slashed across it. Jonah looked at the old X code painted alongside the door. Then he wedged the tapered end of the crowbar under an edge of the plywood, braced himself, and heaved the first fresh breath into the place.

4

Jonah was there to see Colby off at the bus station when it came time for him to depart for Georgia. Jonah embraced his friend. They were in the middle of downtown New Orleans. The bus idled and the air was hot.

They'd gotten drunk together the night before. "You better hope that hangover wears off before all the push-ups start."

Colby patted him on the back, then pulled away. "You be good, Mickey-Bee."

Jonah wished his friend luck and told him to keep in touch. Then he stepped aside and let Colby's mom say good-bye. Moments later, the bus pulled away.

Jonah drove by the shop on his way home. There was still a lot of work to do. They had put new plywood over the windows, but he needed money before he could cut new glass. He'd have to order replacement garage doors. The inside was gutted, awaiting renovation, including electrical and plumbing work. The vines and weeds were gone. A fresh coat of primer had dried over the graffiti. Lots of work to do, but it was looking brighter. It was looking better. Jonah had decided to let the X remain alongside the door. Might be a nice thing—a reminder of times past, holding at the center of everything he would build in the future. He thought maybe he'd construct a frame and bolt it down around the X, like a little work of art. He looked at the shop, on its way to new life, and he thought: This, right here. This is me reaching for them. Mom and Pop and Bill. Remembering them and moving on still.

He parked in front of the house and went up the steps. Dex was also departing today, going back to the bayou. The authorities were hiring folks who owned boats to lay boom and skim oil along the wetlands. The only money to be had at sea these days. Dex thought he should get in on it. The loan money will come through shortly, Dex told Jonah, and I'll be back soon as I can to help with everything.

Inside, Dex was shouldering his bag. He pointed to a short stack of mail on the coffee table. "Showed up while you were out," he said.

Jonah lifted two bills and a postcard. The postcard was a battered-looking thing, an old photograph of a tropical beach. Breakers roll in. Thunderheads loom on the horizon. Along the bottom of the photo, in cartoonish orange print: Golfo de México.

Jonah flipped the postcard over. The only thing in the white space was a simple line drawing of a butterfly. A monarch, Jonah was certain. A few pen strokes, no words.

"What?" Dex asked.

Jonah shook his head.

"That from Luz?"

"Yeah," Jonah said.

"Listen to me," Dex said. "Did y'all make the most of it when you had it?"

"I think so."

"Then be thankful," his brother said, "and don't look back."

"Be thankful," Jonah repeated. "Don't look back."

He walked Dex out, watched him get into his truck. A moment of vision-warping déjà vu, like dancing waves of heat. But everything steadied, and Jonah waved to his brother. Dex called back that he'd see him soon, and then he shifted into gear and drove away. And Jonah lingered on the porch for a moment and closed his eyes, and the morning sun warmed his face. He thought again of Mom and Pop and Bill and felt a tentative urge to offer something not unlike a prayer. Then he turned toward his door, turning toward home.

XIX

...sino una mujer.

1

SHE HAD LIMPED OFF THE MOUNTAIN AND REACHED THE TRAIL toward the pyramid before she heard the vehicles. She lay flat in the dirt and watched the headlights pass in the road. Then she got up and dragged herself on. Onofre answered his door when she knocked. The old leñero seemed neither surprised nor relieved as he waved her inside. One room, a low ceiling, a cot with a thin mattress. The floorboards lay directly on the dirt. Onofre built a fire and boiled water and sterilized a needle. He produced a spool of thread. He had Luz sit on the stool in front of the fire so he could clearly see her triceps.

"Do not worry," he said. "I have performed this surgery on Magdalena many times." Magdalena, Luz found out, was the mule.

Onofre insisted she take his cot, and he made a pallet for himself on the floor. His son would arrive from Saltillo in three days' time in order to make his weekly delivery of groceries. Luz could leave with him. Onofre insisted that she stay hidden in the meantime, and only leave when she needed the outhouse. Onofre loaded up Magdalena each morning, made his rounds, returned, and made supper. On the second day, he reported that the large house on the hill still stood empty.

2

ONOFRE KNELT BENEATH HIS WINDOW, A LONE CLOUDY PANE OF glass, before bed each night. A Virgen de Guadalupe santo stood on the sill, a short candle beside it. Luz sat on the cot and watched him mumble through his devotions.

The evening before she was to leave, he asked if she'd like to pray with him. Luz declined with thanks, but she liked to listen. So Onofre said his prayers. He got to his feet. He seemed more hunched than usual as he raised a finger. "God," he said, "cannot be understood because God belongs to the good man and the evil man, one and the same."

Luz thought about this. Something resonated, though she couldn't quite pinpoint it in her blurred memory. The conversation with Oziel had become a film of static.

"You see"—Onofre lowered his finger toward the statuette on the sill—"it is the mother we can understand. People forget this. The mother is who we must contemplate."

Luz sat with her elbows on her knees. She looked at her hands. Mamá's hands. This makes you strong, my Luz. She closed her eyes and reached for her.

3

Luz walked the market in Saltillo, attempting to sell the knife and sheath. She didn't want to—for some unnameable reason—but she had no choice. She needed the money. The vendor at a jewelry stall looked the knife over. He was a short man with a lazy eye. He glanced at the shoppers in the market quickly, nervously perhaps, and Luz knew that the man wanted the knife. When he lowballed an offer, Luz leaned in and told him that the knife had belonged to Cicatriz Medina, and that it was the same knife that killed Oziel Zegas. The jeweler said, "And now I know you are lying, for Cicatriz was finished before Zegas died. Anyway, I heard it wasn't one of Cicatriz's men who killed Zegas at all but a woman." And Luz stared at him until something dawned in the eye that watched her, and he bought the knife for a good deal of money. She hurried out of the market after that, feeling ill and cheap. She took the first bus south.

4

SHE STAYED A DAY IN ZACATECAS. SHE WAS SITTING IN A CAFÉ having an espresso when shots rang out in the street. They were loud and close enough, through the open-air front of the shop. Single reports, pistols. A few people whimpered in the café, and the waitress ducked behind the pastry counter. Minutes later, Luz placed pesos on the counter and left. In the street there was no sign of violence at all. A motorbike fumed through the intersection.

5

TWO DAYS LATER SHE WAS IN THE CITY OF GUANAJUATO, STATE of Guanajuato. The city was built on the slopes of opposing hills. It was beautiful. Not just another place, Luz felt, but one to really look at. Impressive cathedrals. Old musicians played guitars on corners where the streets bent and turned at ridiculous angles and couldn't accommodate vehicles. She bought a container of sliced mango and wandered, pausing to read the signs denoting the city's history. She stopped at the hulking square Alhóndiga, and considered the corner once festooned with the head of a man also named Hidalgo. She followed a hiking trail out of town to an abandoned antique mine. This city had been Spain's cradle of silver. The entrance to the mine gaped in the ground. A guide with a group of Canadian tourists offered to take her a kilometer down the lightless column for only twenty pesos, but she refused the offer. What she wished for was the knife; she wished she could hurl it back, send it clattering down the mine shaft to the place of its birth as though this might undo something. Fall, slashing, to sever the knot where all borders are anchored.

6

IT RAINED FOR FOUR DAYS AND FOUR NIGHTS STRAIGHT. HER wrist and her ankle had begun to feel better. The cut on her triceps itched as it healed, and she washed it each morning and evening. During the deluge she holed up in a youth hostel while the Guanajuato streets flooded. She met a European traveler, a young German named Lukas. A mop of curly sun-bleached hair. He spoke some English. He claimed to be an artist. Lukas wanted to know a lot about her, but she deflected the questions and asked about him. He was overly willing to discuss himself. He was on a pilgrimage to some bizarre sculpture garden in the jungle. He hated his family, and he had been in Mexico for weeks. He rolled joints and continually offered her tokes, though she always declined. He hadn't been to the art installation in the jungle yet and he couldn't say when he'd finally get there, but he claimed it was near enough. After the rain passed, Luz split a cab ride with him, east to San Miguel de Allende.

7

THE DRIVER POINTED OUT A LOW SKY-BLUE LAKE ON THE WAY in. "It is only there when it rains."

Luz translated for Lukas and watched the city assemble in the hills. Dusty red structures, some buildings she could identify as churches from the highway.

Lukas had the address for another hostel. The cab dropped them in a working-class barrio, on a street named for a military school. The neighborhood contained a chapel, a few discreet liquor stores, a small school. Roosters crowed in the morning. Lukas slept all day in the hostel room—a small space with sets of bunk beds in which two American college students were also staying. Luz came and went through the hostel's iron door. She read placards in the jardín at the center of town. Mexican independence had grown from here. There were a lot of foreigners in the city. People who sat outside the restaurants and conversed in Spanish, English, French, Italian. Artists sat in the jardín with canvases and easels, painting the red stone cathedral. She told Lukas about them, but she never saw him trying to create any art himself. He was a listener, not a doer.

One night she accompanied Lukas to a bar full of hard looks. Not another woman in the place. Poor erotic paintings hung on the walls. Ratty couches. Men wreathed in cigarette smoke. She heard the malevolent whispers around them, and she worried more for the abrasive blond foreigner than for herself. Lukas drank shots of tequila and refused to get up until Luz attempted to leave alone.

They walked through the quiet city. The streets were steep, cobblestone. Channeled with rain gutters. It reminded her of Las Monarcas. She thought about her grandmother and she thought about her father.

A series of dim pops punctured the stillness. Firecrackers somewhere in the barrio. Lukas, however, thought they were gunshots. He wanted them to be, it seemed.

"I am glad," Lukas slurred, "that I see this country before it all goes to fucking shit."

Luz felt like hitting the fool, but she tamped down the urge. She thought about Jonah and felt very alone.

8

SHE WOKE IN THE PITCH DARK, ON THE BOTTOM BUNK AGAINST the hostel wall. Someone was hunched over her in the compressed space, touching her breasts. Warm, rank breath. She was in the shed again, heard the voice in the dark, her arms were heavy and bound behind her. No. She reached and grabbed the groping arms and flung them away. Lukas said, "Baby, baby," and his pale hands floated out of the shadow.

She grabbed him by the bicep and threw her weight, and Lukas banged into the concrete wall, grunting. She rolled out of the bed.

"Hey—"

She hissed at him in Spanish: "I could have killed you."

"Luz, hey."

She needed to get away, to keep on the move. She'd kept her clothes packed, and she knew where the bag was in the dark. She slipped on her sneakers and left the hostel. She started jogging on the damp cobblestone. Her ghost runner kept pace.

9

OUT OF THE SIERRA, INTO THE TROPICS. STATE OF VERACRUZ.
She had a backpack now, containing several changes of clothes, a
toothbrush, a stick of deodorant, and some travel-sized soaps and sham-
poos, and she shouldered her pack and disembarked from the bus into a
beachside community that seemed as right a place as any other. Night
climbed from the east on the shoulders of rain clouds. She was thinking
of Jonah, and she bought a postcard from a stand in a little snack shop.
She wanted him to know she was all right, and she wanted to believe he
could hold this postcard from her in his hands and be all right, too.

Luz received directions to the nearest youth hostel from the shop's
cashier, but first she wanted to see the Gulf. She had never seen the sea
before. The air smelled like a storm and saltwater. Orbs of humidity
gathered to the sodium-vapor lamps. There were no stars, no moon. The
wall of cloud silently pulsed with lightning, teasing out its depths. She
crossed the final street and took off her sneakers and squeezed the cool
sand beneath her toes. She could just begin to see the white spit of foam
in the black gulf when torrential rain began to fall.

Luz ran to shelter beneath a wooden gazebo. She sat at the picnic
table beneath it and watched the storm. Luz had seen the news, knew
what was happening off the Louisiana coast. Thinking about Louisiana
made her think of her father. She hoped he was okay. She hoped he was
finding his way. The cardboard and glass detritus of people's lunches lay
scattered across the picnic table, and Luz reached and spun an empty pint
of whiskey, watched it come to rest parallel to the shoreline, pointing
south.

10

IN THE MORNING, THERE WERE EGGS AND COFFEE IN THE HOSTEL'S kitchen. The owner of the place, a youngish man who lived in an upstairs apartment, promised to mail Luz's postcard for her. He nodded to her drawing on the card as she handed it to him.

"¿Una mariposa?" he asked.

"La mariposa monarca," Luz told him with a shrug, "en su jornada."

The young man nodded with appreciation. He wished Luz well on her own journey. She thanked him and left the hostel. The day was bright and clear.

She made her way back to the beach to see it in the light. She took off her sneakers and tied the laces together and hung them from one of her backpack straps. The sand was white and glaring and soft underfoot. Warmth that spread from her soles up through her body. Small waves rolled in. There were distant container ships and tankers. Nearer were the fishing vessels and party barges for vacationing tourists. One Jet Ski chased another, tossing tall spumes of water. There were families on the beach, children screaming with glee. Sunbathers and couples walking hand in hand. Near the water, two young girls—Luz guessed they were sisters—held a footrace. Their brown legs churned, and the spray of water and sand sparkled as they went. Somewhere, dance music beat from a stereo, and everybody everywhere was going on with their lives. It was a beautiful day. From a certain vantage point the day existed by itself, independent of the days before and not yet leaning toward the days to come, and Luz saw this and made herself at home in it, now and now and now again in the spaces between her breaths.

Luz walked to the damp sand where the water slid ashore and rushed away. She followed the shoreline south. She shielded her eyes and watched the families where they kicked footballs or dozed in the sun or molded sand castles. She came upon the two young girls who had been racing. They were breathing with their hands on their knees, and now they were lining up to race again. They were deeply tanned and shining in their bathing suits, their black hair braided into long pigtails. They waved to Luz and called to her to race against them, laughing, not thinking she would. Then they were off and Luz leaped to run alongside, and the girls seemed both pleased and surprised, not saying anything but grinning and pushing themselves all the harder. They were running for no reason other than the pleasure of it. Luz's backpack bounced and she loved the burning in her calves as her feet recycled through the wet sand. She kept her pace close to that of the laughing sisters, falling ahead, falling behind, pulling even and making a race of it. There were no lanes here—just the open beach stretching on, knitted with the continual surge of the sea, relentless even as it was dependable. Luz kept running, pulling past the sisters as they tired and slowed and shouted to her. Luz spun and backpedaled and waved to them where they stood, smiling and waving after her. Luz spun forward, focusing on the way her hamstrings stretched, the way the muscles in her lower back loosened. She settled into a rhythm. She thought she could keep it up for a good long while. She reached to find her ghost runner, and it was only now that she realized he was not there.

EPILOGUE

MOSES HIDALGO TOOK HIS TALL BOY OUT TO THE FRONT STEPS and sat, resting his guitar on his knee. He lifted the can and sipped, cold and good. Rodrigo had been the only one to get a job that day, and he'd kindly purchased the evening's six-pack. The sun fell behind the overpass, funneling the light up the street. Moses closed his eyes against it and played, striking the nickel strings with calloused fingertips and feeling the notes resound in the body of the guitar. He hit the strings harder, playing louder in order to drown out the voice that sang, rising in his skull. The sinking sun warmed through his eyelids.

"Yo," said a voice.

Moses kept playing.

"Yo."

Moses didn't stop, but he squinted at the speaker. Nothing but a shadow with the sun at his back.

"Where the girl?"

Moses plucked a last note, rested his palm on the strings so that nothing lingered.

"Where yo' girl at, the one who sings?"

Moses stared at the haloed man for a moment, then sipped his beer.

"Speak English, bruh?"

Moses shrugged and started to play again. The shadow marched away, toward the overpass. Moses stopped after another bar. He sat for a breath. He rose and went inside, screen clacking behind him. Rodrigo sat on the futon, watching the news in a language he couldn't understand.

Gripping the guitar by the neck, Moses swung it like an ax into the wall. The body splintered. The strings groaned, whipping out of whack. He swung it again, smashing the guitar to pieces. Wreckage fell and scattered.

Divots in the drywall. Moses's heart rattled. He glanced at Rodrigo, and his friend's eyes swiveled back to the television.

THE IRON BARS OF THE FENCE OUTSIDE THE HOME IMPROVEMENT center's parking lot pressed through Moses's wet shirt where he sat against them. Next to him, Rodrigo snoozed in the heat, cap over his eyes. Moses watched a stray dog panting in the shade of a palm out on the neutral ground between lanes. He feared that it might run into traffic. Push the thought away. No room for it here in the heat, the unimpeded sun. The day wore on. No work. Men spoke into prepaid cell phones or drew in the dirt with sticks or sat in silence, praying, perhaps. A righteous Honduran paced and shouted to them in Spanish as he read from the Bible.

Moses had lived all over northeastern Mexico—Nuevo Laredo, Reynosa, and Matamoros, for a little while. He met his wife, Esperanza, at a dance in Piedras Negras, and after they were married he took her home to Las Monarcas and they moved into his mother's house. By the time he left for El Norte it had become necessary, and he did it with a full heart because it was for Esperanza and it was for their young daughter. Moses argued with his personal torment—I loved them. I loved you, Esperanza, I know I did.

He closed his eyes and faced the sun. Too much time. The border between their hearts had turned his to stone, and all these years later he had trouble recalling Esperanza's face. Luz looked like her, though, and reminded him, but now Luz was gone.

He couldn't remember the feeling of right and well-intentioned purpose with which he had first left Mexico. Acknowledging this failure— this shortcoming that he had foreseen and taken futile measures to avoid—made him feel weak. The only solace to be found, if one could call it such, came in pushing forward, numbing his mind, working. Yet the truth built inside him all the while. You can rebuild a place, but that does not mean it becomes your home.

He had lived in Arizona and in Texas. For a month he had lived in Oklahoma, but nobody knew of that save himself because he had done some things there—after Esperanza died—that he would never be proud of. He went back to Texas then, and eventually came to Louisiana with Luz. But more than by location, he saw his past categorized into periods:

with his family, without his family; with people he knew, without. And dreaming back through his life, he saw that his existence had merely been those different periods smashed up against one another. And so who was he, this anchorless being? He couldn't even say he knew himself.

THEY WERE UPTOWN, CLEANING OUT AN OVERGROWN BACKYARD. It took all day. They ripped vines from trellises, sprayed against wasps. They uprooted hackberry saplings and trimmed dead palm fronds. It felt like the height of summer, though the calendar still read April, and in the afternoon the lady who owned the house brought them glasses of iced tea. It was an unusual occurrence. Rodrigo told Moses to thank her in English, tell her how he appreciated it, and Moses did. At the end of the day the lady paid them better than Moses had expected, and so even though this had been their only job of the week they ducked into a po'boy shop a block down the street to spend their few extra dollars.

The place wasn't cool, but the respite from the sun was nice. They sat at the bar and ordered draft beers and perused the paper menus. A small television hanging in the murk over the bar flashed an aerial image of an oil rig engulfed in flame. The vantage rotated, revealing other craft tossing ineffective streams of water into the fire. Moses had watched this on the news every night for the past week. The rig had already sunk, but the news continued to show this image.

Rodrigo trailed a finger over the menu. "Where are the fried oysters?"

Moses reached and tapped the oyster po'boy. On both of their menus, the oyster price had been crossed out by hand and rewritten as ten dollars more expensive.

The bartender, a young woman with red hair and freckles, noticed where they were looking. "People are worried about the oyster beds with the oil, ya know?"

Moses frowned. Rodrigo whispered for an explanation after she had moved on. They both ultimately ordered fried catfish. The bartender set to wiping the bar top, and they sipped their beers and watched the television.

Rodrigo began: "Has she—"

Moses cut him off. "She hasn't called. My mother has not heard from her, either."

The screen flashed another aerial shot, a nacreous slick on the Gulf's surface. Moses knew what the coming weeks would bring: he remembered beaches drowned in tar, asphyxiated dolphins washed ashore, docked fishing boats, a crippled seafood industry. He had been a young man when the Ixtoc I well blew. Thirty-one years ago. He'd been seventeen or eighteen. A few years before he'd begin making trips to El Norte, and long before he'd see Esperanza dancing in Piedras Negras. After the oil spill, he had traveled to the state of Tamaulipas with his own father, worked on crews, slogged through fuming sweeps of sludge. His nose going stuffy like it was plugged with oil. A feeling that wouldn't wash from his skin for days. He remembered all of it.

Next to him, Rodrigo shook his head, frowned at the television.

"If the oil comes ashore," Moses said, "there will be work."

Rodrigo already knew it.

"Do you want that?" It was the young bartender. She asked it in poor Spanish. She dropped the rag on the bar and crossed her arms. Moses was momentarily taken aback. "I study Spanish in school," she said in English. "You want oil to wash up in our wetlands? Is that right?"

Moses replied in Spanish, a flinty edge to his voice. "It will happen with or without my blessing. I have seen it before and I see it again now. But if my wishes truly matter to you, then let me say I hope for work only. It is just a shame that when there is work, it often means something terrible has happened. I never forget that, if it matters."

She stared at him. He had gone too fast, and she didn't comprehend. Rodrigo glanced around the room, as if somebody else in the restaurant might have understood.

Moses spoke again to the young bartender. This time in English. "I am sorry," he said, attempting a smile. "No. I do not hope for oil to come ashore."

THEY SIGNED ON WITH A CONTRACTOR AND BUSED DOWN THE river delta. They received reflective vests and suffocating jumpsuits. The corporation had them sit through a safety seminar, some executive lecturing from projected slides under a white tent on the beach. Afterward, Rodrigo asked him what it had all been about, so Moses translated the basic message: "The company wants you to drink plenty of water."

They went out on boats and laid arms of floating orange boom meant to cradle oil. Word came through—the slick was fifteen miles off-shore. The next morning it washed in, great brown waves of it. It reeked and clung to them as they moved down the beach with shovels and thick contractors' bags, scooping up the uncooperative sludge. His skin burned from the fumes while he sweat. Front-end loaders crawled along behind them, unleashing buckets of bright white sand. They will be digging up oil on this beach for years, Moses thought.

A week later they were in Mobile Bay, floating boom, waiting for the onslaught. But by the next dawn the currents had shifted and the oil hammered Pensacola instead. They loaded onto the bus and set out.

The bus took them to the water and turned onto the finger of island beach that separated the bay from the Gulf. A procession of big yellow machines stretched along the sand for miles, back to the waterfront hotels and condos. Men wearing the same reflective vests crowded the shade beneath a large pole tent.

The bus drove until the road ended at a parking lot full of news vans, a milling crowd. Out on the point of the island sprawled a stone fort, squared in by its battlement. He heard one of the men say that Geronimo had been locked up there, a long time ago.

"What is it?" Rodrigo asked.

"An old prison," Moses answered.

Beneath the tent, the corporation issued new crinkly metallic suits and provided another safety seminar. The beach looked as bad as Moses remembered the Tamaulipas beach looking three decades before. Vast puddles of the stuff. Primordial muck. He could see the tar rolling in the heart of the waves. The beach was brown-black as far as he could see. Clumps of crude rolled ashore like footballs, melted down in the heat.

They shoveled, scooped, moved along. Moses set his gear down, ran away from the water, and vomited. Then he went back to work. They covered a lot of ground. The loaders crawled through and shat white sand. The beach looked new. An hour later a fresh tide of oil came in. They were at it all day.

When dark fell, the foreman asked for volunteers to clean through the night. He explained that They—whoever They were—needed the beaches to look good for the television crews when the sun came up. Moses volunteered himself and Rodrigo.

They received hard hats fitted with infrared headlamps. The foreman explained: It was sea turtle hatching season, and this bit of protected beach was nesting ground. The infrared would allow the baby turtles to find the water; a normal flashlight was the same wavelength as moonlight and would disorient the hatchlings. The red lights filled the dark, turning the beach into another planet. It became difficult to distinguish oil from sand. Moses neared the water and a small crest broke around his boots, coating them with crude. He realized he wasn't seeing sand at all, and he wondered what in fact they were saving the sea turtles from, guiding them back into this mess.

The foreman found Moses in the middle of the night and called him over. The foreman pointed to Rodrigo. "He's with you, right?"

"Yes."

"I hate this," the foreman said, "believe me." He removed his helmet and scratched his head and put the helmet back on. The otherworldly glow made him look angry even if he wasn't. "My boss just passed through and ordered me to check you and your pal's IDs."

"ID? Why?"

"Fort Pickens." He gestured to the old prison looming in the dark. "There's some law says illegals can't work on federal ground. I didn't know. Now I need to see some paperwork on you both."

Moses stared at the man. "But we are working."

"I know," the foreman said, massaging the bridge of his nose. "My hands are tied."

Moses dropped his shovel and didn't answer. He removed his gloves, rubbed his eyes. Rodrigo approached, asked in Spanish what was happening.

"Look," the foreman said. "I'm not even supposed to do this, but here's your pay for today." He proffered two one-hundred-dollar bills.

"One for each of you. Take it and go. Anyone asks, I don't know nothing, all right?"

Moses looked at the money and looked at Rodrigo. Rodrigo, language aside, understood. Moses walked to the water and looked out over the Gulf, where new slicks were surely rolling toward him. There was something more, too. Something else, out past everything he could see. It pulled at him, but he couldn't reach it. Rodrigo was silent on the beach. The foreman followed him to the water, begged him to take the money. Moses couldn't answer. He was dreaming about the turtles.

ACKNOWLEDGMENTS

Without the energy, conviction, and skill of literary agent Elizabeth Copps, it is likely this book would still remain on my hard drive. I can't thank you enough, E.

Laura Brown, my editor, works incredibly hard. Thank you for lending your inimitable talents to this book. It is an absolute joy to be one of your authors.

Thank you, as well, to Maria Carvainis and the MCA crew: Martha Guzman, Bryce Gold, and Samantha Brody. Thank you to everybody at HarperCollins, particularly Jonathan Burnham, Amy Baker, Cal Morgan, Kathryn Ratcliffe-Lee, Keith Hollaman, and Joanne O'Neil. Julie Hersh, as well, thank you.

Huge thanks to my dear friends and early readers: David Parker, Michael Pitre, Chrys Darkwater, Andrew Ervin, Kelcy Wilburn, Riley Sise, and Julian Zabalbeascoa. Each of you offered invaluable insight and your own, unique brands of encouragement. I love you all.

Joseph Boyden and Amanda Boyden: as far as I'm concerned, I lucked into your workshop many years ago, and everything else has followed. This novel benefited beyond measure because I've known you as teachers, mentors, and friends. Much love to you both.

Danny Goodman: model reader, writer, friend. Without you, buddy, none of this goes.

Ryan Rogers, how often did we talk about this book? Thanks for everything, my man.

I'm also grateful to Scott Collins, Charles Broome, and Jeffrey Marx for enthusiastic reads and indispensable advice.

Nicole Martin, Kate Stastny, David Pomerleau, Marc Paradis, Andre Bohren, Erin Walker, Jamie Amos, Spider Stacy, Louise Stacy, and Casey Lefante: y'all are the best.

Ronald Avila, Roy Kesey, Javi Sanchez, Michelle Sanchez, and Jessica Viada: thank you for your expertise and your generosity.

Special thanks to Adam Sargent, Skip Horack, Colin Walsh, Brian Sullivan, Tim Sise, and Ellen Barker.

I also counted on Tom Crane's boundless encouragement. Thanks, Uncle T.

To everybody in the Creative Writing Workshop at the University of New Orleans, especially Rick Barton, Randy Bates, and Joanna Leake: thank you, for so many things.

I'm sorry if I've forgotten to mention anybody. Many wonderful people helped, in one way or another, over the years.

Mom and Dad, you made sure I dreamed. A long time ago, when I told you I wanted to write, you did nothing but love and support me, as always. Alex, Sami, and Tommy, I'm grateful for you guys every single day. I've learned so much from you. And all my family, thank you.

Kate, the inspiration you provide never ceases. I can't imagine this book existing without you being my partner first. I write for you.

Jonathan, little guy, I'm so glad you are here.

© Bradny Vicknair

ABOUT THE AUTHOR

NICHOLAS MAINIERI's short fiction has appeared in the *Southern Review, Southern Humanities Review,* and *Salamander,* among other literary magazines. He lives in New Orleans with his wife and son. *The Infinite* is his first novel.